JOY STEPHENS

Siridean

Legend of the Faerie Cross

ISBN: 0615768636
ISBN-13: 9780615768632
Library of Congress Control Number: 2013905365
Joy Stephens, Martin, TN

To my lovable husband, Brian.

Thank you for inspiring this story

and for twenty-plus wonderful, adventurous years.

I'm looking forward to at least sixty more.

Acknowledgements

Thanks to my editors—Tiffany, Ben, and Elise—who kept me on the straight and narrow path to grammar and punctuation heaven. I tried to aim somewhere between one's love and one's hate of commas. And, heartfelt gratitude to the rest of the wonderful team at Amazon CreateSpace.

To all my beta readers, you will never comprehend the depths of my appreciation for all your comments and suggestions to make *Siridean* stronger. To Brian Stephens, Janine Lock, Keith Holloway, Katie O'Malley, Jamie Bennett, Tiffany Emerson, Leigh-Ann Davis, Natalie Medling, Lauren Lowry, Nicole Gunter, Hannah Quarles, and Scott Huff—THANK YOU!!

My husband, Brian, who dabbles in all things creative, took my vision for the book cover and made it an unforgettable, visual reality; you're the best! To an equally talented art aficionado, Marcie Hicks: thank you for studio time and the beautiful shots of Beth Ann. To my model, Beth Ann Ogg, you captured the essence of the Siridean perfectly, from your blowing, branch-enhanced hair to your captivating beauty.

For those involved in the filming and production of the awesome book trailer for *Siridean*, I give two bandages up. Actually, there was only one person on the crew who needed a stunt double and they know who they are. ☺ Couldn't resist. Josh, your vision in filming and editing is astounding. Everyone should know the person and the name—Josh Bennett—of Josh Bennett Photography. I can't brag on him enough; go to http://josh-bennett. com to check out his work. Jordan Stokes, you can relax your intense face now; thank you brother for your willingness to join me in this project. You were truly what I had envisioned for the brooding Rafe. To my Aishling—or Sam Milam—I couldn't have asked for a more perfect princess/faerie slayer. Special thanks to Chuckie Milam, Janine Lock, and Brian Stephens for hauling equipment, props, and doing a lot of grunt work in the July heat; you guys rock!

Thanks Dad and Mom, for putting everyone up in the Holloway House during the video shoot and for the still-bragged-about gourmet meals. You two have supported me through all of life's junk and joys. God blessed me with the best parents on the planet. I love you, and I'm so proud that you are mine.

To the winner of my book dedication—my husband, Brian—I won the day you made me your bride. Thanks for believing in me and allowing me the time I needed to bring this book series into the light. I love you!

Contents

1. Legend of the Faerie Cross 1
2. Faerie Slayer 9
3. Warrior Persona 17
4. The Branch 27
5. Shadows Beyond the Veil 37
6. River fane 45
7. Rumors 55
8. Scandal 63
9. Fire Tetrahedron 73
10. Hogueras 79
11. The Follow-Through 87
12. *Plaza de Toros* 97
13. Fire Jumpers 105
14. Penitent Angel 113
15. Alone In A Crowd 123
16. Ash And Burn 129
17. A Moment with an Angel 137
18. Live Your Life 145
19. Dream Song 151
20. Dream Wander 159
21. Fragmented 171
22. Stolen 177
23. Paradoxical Freedom 185
24. Adjusting 191
25. The Blood Avenger 199
26. The Great "What If?" 205
27. The Searcher 215

28.	Soul Tempest	225
29.	*Amor De Mi Corazón*	233
30.	Kaillech And The Angels	241
31.	Féth Fíada	247
32.	An Angel Whisper	253
33.	Adrenaline Junkie	259
34.	Hide And Seek	267
35.	Flags And Flames	277
36.	Short Circuit	285
37.	Mortal Angel	293
38.	Forbidden Wish	297
39.	Saint Status	303
40.	Ina And The Butterflies	313
41.	Fate Sealed With A Kiss	321
42.	Crosscurrent Drifting	333
43.	Quantum Entanglement	345
44.	Comrades In Comayaguela	353
45.	Moonlight And Madness	359
46.	The Uffern Ultimatum	369
47.	*Derecho*	377
48.	Beyond the Reaches of Time	383
49.	Bad Blood	391
50.	Love And A Lie	395
51.	Atmospheric Disturbances	399
52.	Storm Front	407
53.	Lost Searcher	415
54.	Uninvited	423
55.	Blood Book	431
56.	The Soul's Lantern	437
57.	Rise of the ten Colds Moon	445
58.	Spun By The Fates	453
59.	Diabolical Masquerade	459
60.	Demons And Dragonflies	465
61.	No Mercy	475
62.	Fighting Fate	481
63.	Mirage	489

There are those who say that angels walk among us.

Love...

Of Heaven 'tis the brightest amazement,
the blackest abasement of Hell,
'Tis a race with Heaven's lightning and thunder,
It is savagery in the blood, and pain in the bone,
and greed and despair in the mind.
It is to be thirsty in the night and unsated in the day.
It is to carry a memory like a thorn in the heart.
It is to drip one's blood as one walks.

Early Irish—Anonymous

Series Prologue

Lifting his crude marine chronometer, the demon tyrant calculated the time. They were late. A gale-force squall had thrown the ship off course, but now the rogues of the underworld sailed hellbent on the choppy sea toward the pyramidal island, backlit by the silvery moon. The rugged rock mass, nine miles off the coast of Ireland, had an eerie glow made even more ominous by its imposing size.

Satariel stood near the mast with the sea breeze unaffecting his slicked-back hair. They drew nearer to the island and he sniffed the air. "The evil here tastes so peculiar, and I can smell the stink of archaic faeries in the mist," he grimaced. "That stench I certainly don't care for, but I guess it can't be helped in this instance. Cast out the anchor!" he yelled above the din.

This was to be a diabolical masquerade of the darkest kind: a gathering of generally opposing forces to plot the end of an innocent.

The ship came to rest against a sloping stone platform jutting out at the waterline, and the demon leader sought out the light of the lanterns hanging on four posts at the bow of the vessel. A wicked grin replaced his natural smirk. Gazing at the parchment once more while the men secured the ship, he recalled the purpose for this alliance.

> The Gaelic seer's prophecy has been fulfilled.
> The Siridean is born.
> Meet at the Isle of Skellig in the needle's eye
> the eve of Samhain in the year AD 2020
> the hour of Ótta.

It was the darkest, latest portion of night—somewhere between midnight and dawn—a demon's favorite time. Satariel looked into the black water, able to see the hammerheads several fathoms below. Craning his neck he looked up toward the rock wall disappearing into the heavens. The moonglow turned the gathering mist into a dark halo that crowned the bluff.

"Well, let's get on with it!" he shouted to the creatures. He moved toward the gangplank, rolled up the twenty-year-old summons, and tucked it into the inside pocket of his newly acquired leather jerkin. He gained a great deal of smug satisfaction by wearing the attire of an Irish war hero. That was the plan at least.

The quickest way was to scale the bluff hanging over the sea, which was an easy chore for hellions with the extreme heat stored in their body-like shells. But a convenient demon gift was the ability to project a portion of that inward fire outside of themselves. Placing his hands on the mountain, Satariel forced the heat out, melting the rock enough to get a good handhold; then he and the demon army blazed a trail up the cliff. Lava sludge dripped into the water below from their pillage.

It took five minutes from base to brink, and when the demons reached the top, Satariel clasped his charred hands behind his back and took a moment to survey his kingdom.

His second-in-command hissed, "The faeries have preposterous limitations. This had better be worth it, since we had to meet on their turf."

The demon leader scowled, musing over the race he felt was beneath his own. "The thin places aren't navigable until tomorrow night on Samhain." He turned to see his followers forming a tight-knit circle around them. "Sometimes Tarlach cheats, though. Tonight he chose the pyramid, the gateway to the Celtic Otherworld, because he can't be seen here. He also can't wander from here. The force field in this place is incredible, almost numbing."

Satariel opened his mouth to let the magnetism sizzle with his inner fire. "Come!" he commanded. He strolled toward the precipice, and the demons obeyed.

They moved through the needle's eye, and Satariel could taste the tranquilizing breath of the bonfire. Obviously it didn't faze him, but he turned to see a dozen of his servants topple to the ground, lulled by the sedative. He rolled his eyes and kept walking. This was not their kind of fire. They had joined forces a couple of times in the past with the savage faeries, the Alorcán, but still they possessed skills they each held in strict confidence.

Slithering through the crevice, Satariel and his remaining horde entered a cave-like area enclosed by large boulders. The mystic fire was uncomfortable but not unmanageable. He would certainly not give the fiend the satisfaction of seeing him flinch.

Taking in the scene, Satariel eyed ten creatures lounging on the floor around the Alorcán leader. They looked like saber-tooth tigers, except for their ebony hair and albino-white eyes. The remaining six faeries took on the appearance of their master: astounding Minotaur-like beasts with grayish, spiky, crocodile skin and broad, bladed talons for hands.

The look on the faces of the ghastly faeries was priceless to him when they saw his apparel. "You like it?" he jested with the two guarding the entrance as he smoothed an imaginary wrinkle from the sleeve. Their sneers told him he had accomplished his purpose. Smirking, he moved on and took his place beside the faerie leader on a makeshift stone chair by the fire.

"Tarlach, my old friend," he said with an air of mischief, sticking his hands into the flames to further prove he was unaffected. "Didn't know we were having a costume party. I'd have come as something more grandiose than a boring, old human."

"Satariel," the faerie leader responded. His eyes narrowed and a low growl rumbled while he attempted to harness the rage he felt at the demon's lack of propriety. Getting immediately to the matter at hand, Tarlach asked, "So, where's the Siridean now? I know yer group was keepin' a much closer eye on her while she was off in Costa Rica. I visited her only once when I went to retrieve the music box she so adamantly denied stealin' from me." The Alorcán leader snarled.

"Just returned to Ireland. She's not going anywhere for a while. My scouts are keeping watch—with no help from your kind I might add. It would be helpful if you could keep your underbreds in control. They've almost given away our location on three separate occasions. All brute, no brains."

Four of Tarlach's Gaelic pets converged on the demon tyrant, teeth bared and hissing, while both leaders stared at each other with the appearance of apathy. The other demons didn't move from behind Satariel as he had already issued a command of passivity from his mind to theirs.

"Ye and yer brood are welcome to return to hell anytime," Tarlach fired, looking down at his nails. "But then ye'd miss all the fun...and yer revenge on that dark angel, Raphael. Not to mention pow'r o'er half the realms. A fifty-fifty split."

The guards backed down but remained close to their master as the talks continued.

"Half you say? I thought you'd be more greedy," Satariel said. "And I do want that deserter back in chains." The dark ruler's eyes flamed. "I'm in. What's the plan?"

Producing a worn-leather book from inside his cloak, Tarlach replied, "I hold the only existin' copy of the Book of the Sluagh Sídhe. It was me brother's. I took it right before I killed him for the second time," he stated matter-of-factly. "There's a revelation in there, a whole chapter just for her. It tells what the girl will become. She doesn't e'en know, nor does her High King grandfather who rules the Otherworld. Aishling knows about her paternal ancestry and the fact that she's descended from the great Maolán war faerie, Morrighan, who's a half-breed. But what none of 'em realize is that the Siridean's mother was also a half-breed, part human and part abomination. The mixture was too overwhelmin' for Mrs. Delaney's bloodstream, and she died of a supposed blood disorder right around the age she should've begun her transformation. But for Aishling, well, 'twas the perfect combination makin' her a potent full-blood."

He leaned back and let Satariel soak in all the information.

"A full-blooded what? What will the Siridean become exactly?" Satariel retorted.

Tarlach ignored the demon's tone and opened the book to a drawing. "This." He pointed to a picture—yellowed and frayed at the edges—and watched Satariel gawk at it. He closed the volume, placed it back inside his cloak, and then leaned forward, with his elbows resting on his knees. "Once she begins the transformation, it'll be more difficult to stop what's comin'."

"So we take her out now. I'd be happy to expedite her demise," Satariel replied. In his mind, he plotted what he would do to her first.

"Nay," Tarlach said, shaking his head. "The angels are helpin' her. She has more than a legion of guardians. She *is* currently human after all—well, slightly human. The angels are as unfamiliar with the ways of the faeries as they are familiar with demon lore. They need the Siridean to navigate the realms where they can't go."

"Hmm." The demon leader grimaced, thinking. "Our numbers are growing as well. What do you propose?"

"Well, there is a way," Tarlach replied with a smug sneer.

"I'm listening."

The leader of the vile faeries rose to pace by the fire as he continued. "The book tells of the curse that was placed on the Delaney clan by Arawn, the most pow'rful Alorcán sorcerer noted in the Annals of Uffern. The writings reveal that the Siridean is to marry the prince of the next most pow'rful clan by the time she reaches full physical and mental adulthood, or a terrible curse will befall the whole of the Delaney tribe, and the balance with the Otherworld will be thrown into chaos. If the prophecy doesn't come to pass, the Siridean will not have the pow'r to deal with our clan, and we would rush in and wipe out the Delaneys. The Challenger, along wit' the Maolán, would be o'ertaken in the Otherworld, and we'd then rule Paradise and the lower realms. They, of course, have remained untouched thus far because of the angels. But a day is comin' when that won't be the case."

"So the girl is twenty now. Has she shown any signs yet of the metamorphosis?" Satariel inquired.

"That's hard to say. What works in our favor is that she wavers between the Kavanaugh clan leader's son and yer enemy, Raphael. They're both wrong for her—she'll soon see—if my plan works."

"Forgive me. I haven't spent as much time in Ireland as other places. It's already so deliciously evil. But aren't the Kavanaughs equal in power to the Delaneys?" Satariel asked.

The faerie leader turned around and smiled; his face changed back and forth between his normal form and the double-headed dragon within. The demons behind Satariel fought to remain composed.

As he calmed down, Tarlach grunted, "Me pets get all riled up wit' so much talk o' the clans." He closed his eyes for a moment to gain control. Then he moved back to his seat. "This is where the story gets so grippin'." He placed his palms together and clicked his claw-like nails against each other in a staccato beat that echoed in the enclosed space. "It may come to an all-out war, but we've got allies topside who are workin' to push the sworn enemies of the Delaney's into pow'r. Kavanaugh will have to scramble to hold his position."

Satariel stared into the fire, taking in all the information.

Tarlach resumed his plot, "The Siridean's loyalties will be tested to the breaking point. It's a shame, really—the princess's weakness for the broken angel. She would've been a worthy adversary." The Alorcán commander snickered and shook his head. "Ah, the Irishman who tries to win the hand of the esteemed princess—he'll certainly have his work cut out for him. She could choose not to go wit' any o' the princes. The girl would still have exceptional pow'rs, and she'd be immortal o' course, but the Irish are a stubborn lot. I'm bettin' on her feelings for Raphael to keep her in the earth realm—especially if we keep manipulatin' the situation."

"Well, let's hope true love wins," Satariel mocked.

"Indeed," replied his fair-weather ally.

Charged silence reigned in the needle's eye. With such combined villainy in one locale, there would never be calm.

"Any word on that rogue faerie?" Satariel asked. "Why don't we just send him in to stir up the war?"

Tarlach howled with ominous laughter. "As resourceful and untamed as that creature is, e'en the Dullahan can't slay this curse. Our scouts returned recently wit' no word on its whereabouts. The beast was last seen at the ruins of Mellifont Abbey a fortnight ago. None of the pansies will get close enough to him to give us any accurate information. They say he's too volatile," he scoffed.

"Of course he's unruly. You and I made him," Satariel boasted, and the two roared with laughter. The entourage filling the room soon joined in the revelry. As the ruckus died down, the demon speculated, "He could very well interfere with our plans. Do you think the mongrel knows who she is?"

"Maybe not. And that would be our good fortune, wouldn't it? Maybe he'll destroy her before he finds out, and we won't e'en have to lift a finger."

1
Legend of the Faerie Cross

(Aishling)

Blackrock, Ireland

Black snowflakes crept down from the sky, their advance deliberate, methodic. All the money in the world, which my father seemed to have, couldn't keep the demons from chasing me: Aishling Morrighan Delaney, aka "the princess of Clan Delaney."

Everything was messed up. I was wearing the "Happy Birthday" sash across my chest that my best friend Claire always insisted I wear for my special day, but this was not that day. My twentieth birthday was more than a month ago, on October 31—the night of Samhain, the Celtic New Year's Eve.

This was December 7, and the Ten Colds Moon was rising. My fate stalked me. Didn't look like I was going to make it to my belated birthday party.

I leaned into my horse, Kheelan, as he tore across the bracken and bramble of the moor and beyond through the amethyst fields of devil's bit, outrunning the faerie's freak show. The spiky shrubs of the moor pricked my legs as we attempted to outrun the Fates and the black snow that blew in like a gathering sandstorm, trailing us. This princess thing in Ireland can get a girl killed fast, or maybe it's just me.

I am the faerie slayer of the seventh order and the twenty-eighth generation, the prophesied Gael Siridean, the Searcher. As such my head is crowned with a supernatural bounty, and the price is high.

In search mode power surged through me, lending me strength for the battle. My cobalt-blue eyes burned through the black veil of the parallel realm, allowing me supernatural vision into the dark places of the Otherworld. My long, wavy raven hair rose and floated around me of its own electric will. Stupid, blatherin' curse!

The thread of my life frayed in rapid succession, as did the hem of the black-velvet, medieval-style dress I borrowed from Claire. She was throwing me a themed party this year. If I made it out alive tonight, she was going to kill me for ruining her dress and making her worry. Maybe she'd grant me mercy when she saw my drenched, haggard appearance with thistle strewn throughout my hair and dark eyeliner no doubt having left claw marks down my cheeks. I couldn't tell her what really happened here tonight. I couldn't tell anyone.

The storm shook its angry fist in my face. Death pursued me now; yet I was not ready to go. I pushed Kheelan harder through the thundersnow. Lightning spread like giant tentacles, stretching and whipping the furious sky. It illuminated the wispy fairy flax that gave the illusion that we were riding the waves of a furious ocean. The static-charged snow soaked me through, crackling and sparking as it shocked me continually on its journey to the earth. The wind chill was more than I could bear, and being wet and icy was not helping. I could feel the frostbite nibble at my feet and hands. Although it was just four thirty in the afternoon, the massive horde of dark ice crystals captured the essence of midnight.

There was only one being with the power to bring the dagger-like snow with him, and the beast bore down on me, stalking closer and closer.

The six-pointed faerie cross stone that hung around my neck sent out rays of eerie sapphire light—the High King of Ireland from the Otherworld reminding me that I was not completely alone. Without it I'd be lost in the near-blackout conditions. My centuries-old grandmother, Morrighan, who is the leader of the Maolán—the noble, warring faeries who protect humanity—gave the stone to me on my twelfth birthday. She warned me never to remove it, and I never had.

Many people would consider my journey to be filled with intrigue and mystery, but to me, dancing with the supernatural has been my life's constant rhythm. My Gaelic ancestors' world was filled with superstition. They believed that within every natural object lived spirits with whom our clan could commune and connect in different ways. I had never really believed in such notions; I assumed them to be only folk tales that were exaggerated with the passing of time. That was until the day I was given such an object. This was different. It reminded me of what I once read in the ancient script that my deliverer gave me. When I held the stone, I felt safe in the refuge of my master, Diaga. I had never seen him, yet I knew he was always there guiding me. Others collect delicate trinkets the way I began on that fateful day to amass weapons and stones, but not just any old stones. These were the stones from which the legends of my people had been built.

I was five years old when I first heard the legend of the faerie cross. Uncle Brádach, who lived just across the River Fane, always had bonfire parties to celebrate each of the four Gaelic festivals. This particular one was the festival of Lughnasadh on July 31. I remembered it was this festival and not another because the lightning bugs were out in abundance that night, and I kept imagining they were the evil Alorcán faeries advancing to get me.

"Meet 'round the fire, young lads and lasses, for the tale of the faerie cross is at hand," Uncle Brádach had said with his usual flair. I leaned forward with my hands folded under my chin and my eyes wide with fearful expectation. Then he began.

Four times a year the faeries draw nigh
O'er moor and thistle when the full moon is high
Gather ye cross rocks to fend off the storm
The Alorcán rages in turbulent swarm
Faerie dust ascend
To my weary soul fly
Maolán descend
Else in the bog tomb I lie.

"Wee sprogs, beware! Tonight the faeries roam just like they do on Samhain, Imbolc, and Beltaine. Ya see there are realms beyond this'n—the one most famous to our people bein' the Otherworld. And between that world and this'n, there are thin places. On the nights of the four festivals, those places open up, and faeries, both evil and good, cross o'er between the two realms. If ye e'er come by the thin places, ya can hear 'em callin' to ya, and yer drawn to 'em like nothin' ye've e'er experienced. Stay away from the thin places on the nights of the festivals, or ye may be sucked in, ne'er to return!" he further warned.

When he had finished saying this, I sat up straighter. I nodded my head as if to agree that I would never—under any circumstance—ever visit a thin place.

"It's also said that hell's demons can creep through the thin places, passin' from their realm into ours anywhere there's a fire. We could have one tryin' to slither through right now," he revealed. The way we scampered from the fire, you would have thought we were being invaded at that very moment.

"Come back, lads 'n' lasses." Uncle Brádach chuckled. "I have something that'll help ya." I warily moved back to my seat while I kept a watchful eye on the fire, and he pulled out a rock like none I'd ever seen before. I was so fascinated that I allowed my eyes to divide their time between the fire and the rock. Protruding from the stone were two shiny onyx pieces in the shape of an old Roman cross.

The stone was passed around from one small hand to the next, and Uncle Brádach continued, "Aye, young Aishling. The shiny pieces are indeed crystals e'en though they're not clear. Legend says the magical stones are the tears of the good faeries. They weep o'er the comin' battles, and when their tears hit the earth these stones are formed. River Fane is full o' them. Mind ye, don't go near the river 'til the thin places are closed up. But I'd well advise each of ya to find some faerie cross stones and keep 'em near ya. There's pow'r in the rocks—the pow'r of Diaga."

"There are Searchers out there who weigh the souls of the demons and have authority to deal out justice. But the Searchers also come to the aid of children as they search to and fro on the earth and in the realms beyond. Ye must believe in the pow'r of the rocks. Ya must have a faerie cross stone on ya at all times. And when in trouble, draw the symbol of the cross rock in the earth. The Searchers will come to rescue ya."

Fifteen years later and I was now one of those Searchers my uncle talked about. The stone had shown me many times its power, but tonight—the night of my belated birthday party—the light from the stone fizzled, and I wondered how long the spirit cast on me by Diaga could defy the gods of the black abyss. I shivered as the snow seeped through to my skin. My frosted breath hungered for warm shelter from the frigid night. A low hum rioted with the wind. As it grew louder, I turned to see a flock of what appeared to be Herculean dragonflies chasing me. Fear pulsed through me. I flicked the reins harder, pushing Kheelan to win this mystic derby. Flying in a spiraling helix formation with glowing-blue eyes and their wings fluttering so fast I could only see a blur, they advanced.

This was not Samhain, yet the faeries had invaded our realm. My actual birthday had always made for interesting gossip among the clans, for bizarre events usually happened—incidents I had to leave unexplained. I went into the marshes on the nights of the four Gaelic festivals every year to protect the same people who called me "mad" for doing so. After all, everyone knew to stay away from the thin places. One rumor was that I got sucked into the Otherworld and came back different, and I guess there was some truth to that.

Turning west I headed in the opposite direction of the wicked storm front, up into the mountains where the black clouds hovered and waited. The snow retreated for a time, and I could see ahead into the forgotten forest. Kheelan had never run with such fury; it was as if he knew that my life depended on his speed now. His breath churned like steam while he crashed through the woods, dodging trees and trampling fallen limbs. His thundering hooves, sweeping me away from danger, lulled me into a false sense of calm. I leaned into his neck to keep the branches from scraping me, and the earthy, leathery smell of his hair was heaven in that moment of torment. The climb became steeper the farther we went. I wrapped my arms around the sides of his neck and held on.

It was hard to believe that earlier that afternoon, I had brushed Kheelan's midnight hair until it glared under the stable lights. Now it was matted and knotted with briars. We were no match for the violence that sought us now. Wrapping myself into his comforting mane, I prepared for the onslaught. With precision, the tempest hunted us down and engulfed us in its paranormal blizzard.

I pulled the hood of my cloak up farther to protect my face as much as possible, and I looked behind me into the daunting massacre laid out in the storm's wake. The forest was pillaged. Trees were being uprooted and pitched like matchsticks thrown from a box. In the midst of the turmoil, as if he was stirring the chaos as he rode, the Dullahan advanced toward me with his bulky head in his sidesaddle. The most fearsome faerie of our legends, a creation of the demons and their devilish counterparts, the Alorcán faeries, wanted me dead. I must have been getting close to the cave—the one the creature didn't want me to find. The headless faerie with its severed bones jutting up from its open neck drew closer and closer to me. Bile rose in my throat, but I pushed it down. I needed the Maolán faeries to aid me in this battle, but they had all they could handle at the moment with attempting to hold back the gates of hell.

I readied my taggert—a fancy word for a specially-made, otherworldly blowgun that shoots faerie cross darts. It was one of the few weapons that would kill the Alorcán faeries. I aimed and shot, but some sort of force field knocked the dart off course. Drawing my claymore from its sheath, I prepared for the showdown.

Trying to escape my doom, I pushed Kheelan harder. The image of a dark angel with a scar running the length of his cheekbone flashed in my heart, which gave me enough bittersweet pleasure during the time of impending tragedy to keep me fighting. Pretending I could cut a deal with my relentless pursuer, I begged him in my mind, *Just please, before you deliver my death sentence, please let me say goodbye to the man I love.*

2

Faerie Slayer

(Aishling)

Seven years earlier

As we rode in the limo through the sunny Irish countryside, I snapped out of the vision of the Dullahan's pursuit, and five very worried faces, belonging to my twin best friends, Patrick and Claire Kavanaugh, as well as three Delaney guards, invaded my personal space. The vision, seven years in my future, had been so dark that I now squinted against the brilliant sunlight. I looked down to see Patrick's fishing pole on the floorboard, and I felt a bit calmer knowing we would go to the river after school. My dad often called me a river rat. Apparently proper girls and princesses didn't get muddy. But that was my normal pastime—what kept me sane—or being in the Kavanaugh Stables with Uncle Brádach and Kheelan. Uncle Brádach was Patrick and Claire's uncle, but I claimed him as my own. He ran the Kavanaugh Farm's Connemara Pony Breeding and Stables.

"What happened? Did you faint?" Claire shrieked while Patrick held my hand. For the past few years I had been having visions of a disturbing future, but never before had they seized me when my friends were around. With my free hand, I clutched my chest while an ache ripped through me. For a moment I couldn't speak. The vision had troubled me more than I could truly explain. The man's face that had soared across my mind had been in shadows, but I had seen enough to know that it hadn't been Patrick's, and Patrick was supposed to be my destiny; the Fates had written it into my life game. The man in the vision had been human, but not quite, and I had loved him so much that tears sprang to my eyes, which doesn't happen often. Although I had never seen the man before, I felt his presence even now.

"Asher, what's wrong?" Patrick pleaded. When I just shook my head, speechless, he addressed the driver, "Mr. O'Fallon, please take us to the hospital. Asher needs medical attention."

His words woke me up enough to speak, and I pulled the tears back. "No, I don't. Please take us to school, Mr. O'Fallon. I had a bit of a headache, but it has passed."

"Very well, miss," he replied, and he pulled through the gates of the school. Hoping they would drop the subject, I flashed a ready smile at my friends.

It was my freshman year at Dundalk Academy, and I was excited to finally be in high school with my friends. They were sophomores, so they were ready to show me the ropes. We pulled into the courtyard of the private school on the first day of the opening quarter. Patrick, Claire, and I were three of a dozen PKs (Parliament kids) at the academy, so the school was used to paparazzi and armed guards. It looked like this day was going to be full of both.

The limo parked and our guards fanned out; the news crews rushed in, hoping to chronicle the life of Parliament's children. The adventures of the elusive Irish Parliament and their families always made for good news when a reporter was actually able to catch a break and get a family member to open up.

They usually started with the same question: "So what's your life's story?" In a joking tone I would respond, "You wouldn't believe me if I told you." My life's story? Well, the truth was that most people didn't want to know about the other dimensions that surrounded them. They prefer to remain in earth's bubble, conscious or subconscious. So with loyalty to my clan and protection of all mortals as my calling, I had always given the public the abbreviated version of my life.

"Miss Delaney?" asked a young woman approaching me with a microphone in hand. The guards always allowed a few minutes of questioning. It was good for my father's career and reminded his constituents that he was a solid family man, although I was always coached incessantly before any interview. Most topics were off-limits.

"Yes," I acknowledged her. The bumbling cameraman attempted to tame the springy electric cord on his outdated camera while I tried to tame my electric hair.

The news anchor glared at him, and then she turned to me with a smile. "Sources say your father is reorganizing the Provisional Irish Republican Army in an attempt to reunite Ireland. Have you heard him say anything about it?"

"No," I answered truthfully. I felt several pairs of the guards' eyes cutting toward me, accompanied by nods.

"A number of prisoners from former paramilitary groups have been released in compliance with the Belfast Agreement. I believe that two of your cousins, Powell and Sean Delaney, were released with this group. Can you confirm?"

"No," I said, again, leery of the questions and of my father.

"Okay, on to lighter topics," she said with a gleam in her eye. "What's it like being a clan princess?"

Blowing my long bangs out of my eyes in frustration, I gave my autopilot answer: "It's amazing! I love being part of a family that serves the people, a family that's able to influence government in the best way to bring about change for the good of the people." I topped that one off with my rehearsed smile. I glanced over to where Patrick and Claire were being questioned by their own reporters, and Patrick shook his head at me, laughing, as he had heard my most recent answer. The reporter looked down at her list of questions, and I stuck my tongue out at my goofy friend.

Patrick and I belonged to each other—privately, of course. From the time that we were old enough to run and play, we had been inseparable. The old stone bridge across the river that linked the Delaney and Kavanaugh lands near our homes was like a lifeline drawing us to each other. From the window in my room, I could see across the river to the Kavanaugh Stables and beyond that to the great Kavanaugh castle imposing on the hill—a reminder of the mighty warriors who had built it so many years ago.

Patrick was a passionate, stubborn boy who had been born with an excess dose of charisma; he was destined to be a politician just like his father. He knew I was his biggest fan and often used this knowledge to his advantage. Claire was a spunky, tell-it-like-it-is, fashion-savvy, boy-crazy girl. She was my confidante, and I loved her like she was my own sister.

After the newswoman had the cameras shift to take advantage of better lighting, I turned back with a serious face as she asked, "When is your next violin recital?"

"I believe the maestro has set the date for the fourth of October," I replied, still distracted by Patrick.

"We know you are the lead violinist in the region, but do you have any other hidden talents? Any secrets you care to divulge? Just one."

Pausing, I looked away, thinking of the certain facts I could never disclose to this reporter or anyone. A year ago on my twelfth birthday, the Phantom Queen, Morrighan, had visited me. She'd told me that soon she would send a guardian to me who would explain my purpose. Then she gave me three items. The first one was the faerie cross stone that hung around my neck at all times. The second one was my dagger, encrusted with faerie cross stones. The third was my taggert. It had regular darts with it, but it also had darts made from the dust of faeries to be used when threatened by beasts that were not of my world.

Power ran through my veins. I didn't know what that meant, but I was sure that soon I would find out—if this visitor from the Otherworld my grandmother had spoken of ever made his grand entrance.

Instead I turned to the reporter and answered, "I can decipher *ogham*." I remembered to smile again.

"Well, that's a first," the reporter said. "I've never heard of anyone studying the archaic Irish script before."

My mouth swung like a pendulum to the right in what could be considered a half smile but plummeted back to the middle as I considered my odd life. The greatest portion of my existence could not be discussed with the outside world. Not only was my life different from the general population because I was a clan princess, but my guarded physical world was inhabited by spirits from other dimensions, some of which I could not be guarded against. The visions had been clear in that regard.

While my thoughts went elsewhere, the reporter tried again to break through my barrier of secrecy. "Do you have a sweetheart?" she asked, hoping for some juicy gossip.

"Next question," I said, laughing, trying to rush her along. Frustrated, she flipped through pages of questions I'd left unanswered, and my mind started to drift again to the answer to the question she had just asked.

It was one of my family's most well-kept secrets: the fact that I was unofficially betrothed to Patrick. The Delaney and Kavanaugh clans had been at peace for more than two centuries, each clan controlling their respective side of the River Fane. As with most Irish clans, however, there was a very thin line between friendship and war. My life was to be exchanged for continual peace between the clans. Okay, so maybe it wasn't that drastic; Patrick was my closest friend.

At my birth Anlon Kavanaugh, Patrick's father, had made a pact with my father, Tiarnan Delaney. Patrick had been born a year earlier and was the heir to the Kavanaugh clan's lands. I was an only child as well as the great-granddaughter of the Challenger—the ancient High King of Ireland—and therefore I was the sole heir to inherit Delaney Castle and control the clan's lands. A marriage alliance had been formed on that day, linking the two clans in peace through the future marriage of myself to Patrick.

I know what you're thinking: marriages like that just aren't done in the twenty-first century. Well, they were in my world, and this was my reality.

To make matters even more interesting—or terrifying—when I was eleven, my father sat me down for a very serious discussion regarding the Delaney-Kavanaugh merger. Recalling his words, I replayed the memory.

"Aishling, what I'm about to tell ya can ne'er leave this room? Do ya understand?" he asked, pacing in front of me as I sat below him on the couch. "T'would mean the end of our clan if ye e'er spoke of it."

Nodding, I trembled. "Yes, sir."

He glared at me for several seconds, relaying the serious-ness of his claims. I sank into the seat cushions, trying to make myself smaller, for I had never felt a greater fear—at least, not since mom's spirit had soared to the Otherworld and left my own spirit in chaos.

"There's a guarded prophecy within Clan Delaney that's been handed down among our leaders for ages—a prophecy about ye, Aishling."

"Me, Father?" I remembered feeling so confused.

"Aye," he said, grabbing the back of his neck while he paced. "A Gaelic seer predicted your birth centuries ago." He stopped and turned to face me. "Ye are the Gael Siridean. 'Tis a great honor, Aishling."

"What does it mean?" I scooted forward on the couch.

"Some things ye'll figure out as ya go along in life. The most important thing is that ye have the pow'r to stop the curse."

"Curse?" I said, a ghostly cold overtaking me. I rubbed my arms. "You're scaring me, Father."

"And rightfully so. Ye should be afraid."

"How can I stop it?"

He sat down on the footstool in front of me. "Ye are to marry the prince of the next most pow'rful clan—that bein' Patrick Kavanaugh, o' course—by the time ye're fully grown or the curse

14

will strike the whole Delaney tribe, and the balance wit' the Otherworld will be thrown into chaos. The Alorcán'll wipe out the Delaneys and then rule the realms."

How hard would it be to wed my best friend? "Okay, when the time comes, I'll marry Patrick," I said with conviction.

He stood and strolled to the door, but turned back. "Remember what I said, ye mustn't tell anyone, especially the Kavanaughs, about the prophecies and the curse. If ya do, they'll dissolve the alliance out of fear that the curse might come down on them too."

The secrets I'd been bound to uphold infiltrated my psyche, but my unwelcomed guest—the reporter—sidetracked me. She asked a question I felt was safe to answer because the Irish people could identify with my response, and I would never reveal the deeper meaning: "If you could describe your life in one word, what would it be?"

I didn't even have to think about it. "War."

The next obvious question overflowed from the curious asker: "Why?"

"Well, life is war, love is war, and peace is not far from war," I said from experience, even at my age. "Every day is a struggle of one sort or another. Sometimes it is up to us to pick our battles, but sometimes they are chosen for us. A power greater than us has a hand in it, but ultimately it is our conflict to engage. It is our choice to resist and hide or to run at full force into the battle."

3
Warrior Persona

(Aishling)

My first day of high school was relatively uneventful, with exception to the daymare I relived at inopportune moments throughout the school hours. I made it to all my classes on time, ate lunch with Patrick and Claire, and headed to meet my bodyguards at the limo at three o'clock. They had been standing in the shadows all day, trying to be unobtrusive. Yet, it was hard for everyone—including me—not to notice them.

The vision I had starred in that morning made me feel terror-stricken as I rushed from class to class, like I was walking the gladiator's trail to the coliseum and was about to face ten seasoned warriors by myself. It seemed as if a movie screen was flashing its scenes on the locker-clad walls. My costar, the handsome stranger, would not release me. And the creepy beast that had hunted me—well, I caught myself looking behind me more than once and scouting out evacuation routes from the building. It appeared I had a few years until the story of my life landed at the box office, and for that I was more than relieved.

When I jogged down the front steps of the school, somehow I could feel excitement sizzling in the air. Call it intuition or some great skill I'd inherited, but I knew something was about to change.

Patrick and Claire waited for me in the yard. Since it was the first day, Patrick didn't have hurling practice after school, so we headed to the waiting limo. Laughter filled the yard as teens escaped the grind for a few hours.

Weaving in and out of the crowd, I said, "'Persona' is the word of the week in literature."

"Okay. That was random. Per…sona," Claire drew out the word. "Per…sona," she purred.

Patrick chimed in, "Persona—Person A, the first person in a scientific experiment." He turned to me, "Say, weren't you Person A in some mental experiment that went wrong?"

I swatted him on the arm, laughing, "Actually one's persona is the way he or she appears to the world or wishes to appear to the world."

"Persona!" Claire said again.

"So, take Claire for example," Patrick said. "Everybody knows she's into herself, but she wants people to think she cares about them." He mocked her, saying, "Per…sona."

"I care, you dork," she snapped. With an exaggerated huff, she pranced toward the limo, nose in the air.

Patrick and I watched her go. We turned to each other, trying to hold in our laughter but failing.

We loaded up for the drive back to the castles. Claire slid across the seat followed by me and then Patrick. Stoic guards sat facing us as the vehicle pulled out of the schoolyard.

"Ready to hit the water, ladies?" Patrick asked as he slung his arm around my shoulders.

Claire squiggled her nose in disgust and filed her perfect nails. "You two go ahead."

"So today your Barbie persona is set on hyper-drive," he said, switching to his imitation of Claire. "Oh, no, my hair might get wet!"

She leaned across me to punch him in the stomach, and he uncurled from around me to grab her arms as they wrestled over my lap. This scenario was so common; I just sat there for a moment with my arms crossed, rolling my eyes.

"Halt!" I raised my voice. "Or I'm going to go all ninja persona on the both of you and kick you out of my car!"

They broke away laughing. Claire went back to filing her nails while Patrick turned to look out the window. Then he put his arm around my shoulders again and leaned down to kiss the top of my head.

"I'd fancy a look at that ninja persona later. I could use a good laugh, Asher," he bantered, which earned him an elbow to the gut.

"Ow!" he bellowed. "Remind me not to tease you. You've gotten stronger over the summer."

For a moment all I could hear was the whir of the wheels jetting us down the pavement, as I worried over hurting Patrick.

But the silence inside the car was short-lived. My best friends were in constant competition with each other. I guess that stemmed from sharing a womb for nine months.

Claire couldn't let Patrick win. She wanted the last jab. "This morning Patrick's doomsday persona took over. 'Oh, Asher's dying. Oh, Asher, Asher!'" She rubbed her eyes like she was crying while she made sobbing sounds.

"All right, theatrical Barbie! Shut it!" he bossed and shoved her shoulder with the hand that was around my back.

My head dropped backward to rest on the seat, where I had a nice view of the sky through the moonroof. "Where did I leave my patience persona?"

Patrick and Claire burst into laughter and tickled me without mercy. Soon we were all on the floor and rolling at the feet of our guards, who remained still and watchful.

"Time-out!" I squealed, trying to catch my breath. By that time we were flat on our backs, and I could feel the bump of the old cobblestones on the bridge to my home.

When my butler, Sullie, opened the door, he found us still on the floor. I knew Sullie considered me a bit eccentric, but he loved me. He just smiled and motioned toward the castle door, bowing, and announced, "Lady Aishling. Lord Kavanaugh. Lady Kavanaugh."

"Afternoon, Sullie," Patrick saluted. He snatched his fishing pole from a guard, popped out of the vehicle, and sprinted toward the stone cabin down by the river, around the bend from the castle.

"See you guys later. I'm going home," Claire called out while I emerged from the car.

"Bye, Claire," I yelled before running after Patrick. I reached the cabin a few steps behind him and jumped up onto the porch. We both grabbed our waders from the hooks where they hung waiting for adventure, yanked them on, and fastened the suspenders. I plucked my fishing pole and tackle rucksack from the wall.

"Good first day?" he asked. I followed him down the steps while slinging the rucksack onto my back and pulling my arms through the straps.

"Yeah, I guess so. Not much different from middle school, where people treat the resident PKs either like royalty or like scum, depending on whom they're loyal to politically. I just ignore the jerks and hang with the *real* people," I said, shrugging.

"That's my girl."

I couldn't resist: "I noticed today that your status is elevated even higher at Dundalk Academy than at our old school. I guess being a PK plus a jock scores you extra points with the girls." I smirked, trying to make him sweat. To his great honor, he didn't shed a drop.

"But I only have eyes for one girl," he said, turning his emerald eyes my way and winking. I blushed. Stupid Irish-fair skin—I never quite managed to hide behind it.

We reached the rolling water and stepped off the bank. As these were the last days of summer, the air was still humid, so the cold spray felt good through the waders. It took about twenty minutes of slipping and sliding downstream, but I caught the first fish. Patrick and Claire weren't the only ones who competed against each other.

While I unhooked the sea trout and threaded its mouth through the stringer, I repeated our fishing mantra: "You owe me a faerie cross."

As Patrick cast his line, he said, "Remember that beast I fought last time? Today, he's mine. Then you'll owe me a cross rock."

The Kavanaugh and Delaney security details swept by on both sides of the river on horseback, heading in opposite directions. I wondered if this aspect of my life would always be the same.

Patrick and I trudged on through the waist-high waters and rounded the next bend—my favorite part of the river, where the shallow water poured over a bed of jutting rocks as far as the eye could see. I loved those rapids. It was so peaceful with the tamarack and pine trees rising up all the way to the next curve, making it appear like a secret cove. Drops of sunray billowed down through the green canopy to spotlight the springy ferns covering the forest floor. I plopped down to rest on a low rock, and Patrick lay on a boulder above me, his legs dangling over the side.

"I may just take a nap," he groaned.

"You'll never get the twenty-pounder with that attitude. I guess I win," I said.

"We never pay up 'til we get back to the cabin. I've still got time."

While Patrick talked, I watched a string of glittery substance floating on the air in front of his face. With a euphoric expression, he inhaled and then fell asleep with a smile on his face.

Alarmed, I jumped up, splashed over, and climbed the boulder to get to him. "Patrick," I said, frantic, slapping his face back and forth, trying to get him to wake up.

"See, this is what we need to avoid in the future, Lady Aishling," a hulking figure said, bounding down the hill toward me. His thick, medieval-Gaelic brogue was so raw; I squinted in concentration to match the words with their meanings. "I hope to remedy your defenselessness and reaction time."

I jumped to my feet atop the rock, looking through the trees, but there were no guards in sight, and I had nothing with which to defend us. I leapt from the stone onto the opposite side from the approaching stranger, where I was a little more shielded in case of an attack.

"What do you mean? How do you know my name?" I addressed the being that now pushed through the final pine boughs to face me. When I saw the large, faerie cross medallion hanging at the middle of his chest I relaxed, although marginally. It was the torque encircling his neck that made me emerge from my hiding spot and kneel before him. It was a gold collar with the Delaney crest in a cross rock on the front, worn only by six powerful faeries: the Gaelic Council of Seacht.

"Forgive me, master."

"The name's Cearnaigh—not master—and you can stand up, child. We won't have any of that formal dippin' and swayin' nonsense when I come 'round."

I stood and smiled at him, taking an instant liking to the faerie, who obviously had been sent to me from the Otherworld.

"As I was sayin', I am Cearnaigh O'Brallaghan, Irish faerie of liberation and justice, guardian of the realm gateways, servant to the Gaelic Council of Seacht, and blood bearer for the crown. And it's me honor to meet ya, my lady," he said, bowing to me.

"That's quite an introduction, Cearnaigh. I'm Aishling Delaney. That's all."

"Don't e'en get me started on yer numerous titles, young lady," he said, shaking his head.

I motioned to my sleeping friend. "Is Patrick okay?"

"Ah, 'tis only a wee bit o' Diaga dust. I'll wake 'im when we're done."

Cearnaigh sat down on the riverbank, patting the spot next to him, and I lowered myself beside him. I stole glances at the massive warrior as he puffed out his chest and took in the view of the river. His red hair was shoulder-length, wavy, and spiked on top. His sharp nose was made less intense by his fierce, lime-colored eyes held up by battle wrinkles and a line of blue paint underneath each. Bushy, red eyebrows and a full beard tried to disguise multiple blade scars, but they didn't quite fulfill their purpose. He wore a tunic of green tartan cinched at the waist with a broad belt, and he had on brown trousers. His boots were remnants of fur and leather, held together with leather straps wrapped up the leg. The sheathed claymore hanging from his belt had a decorated hilt with a dozen faerie crosses with glowing, sapphire crystals. I followed his gaze to the river.

"Are ye quite done with yer perusal of me, Lady Aishling?"

In spite of myself, I couldn't hold in the very unladylike gale of laughter that erupted from within me. When I had calmed down, I replied, "Quite done, yes."

With a toothy grin that revealed a missing front chomper, he looked back to the flowing water. "We don't have a lot o' time today, my dear, but I'll return tomorrow. Just a few things for ye to think on before I go. As ya well know, the Alorcán threaten the clans and our way o' life. They'd like nothin' better than to dethrone yer ancestor, the great Challenger, and have their leader, Tarlach, take over as High King o' Ireland."

"Not a blatherin' chance!" I injected, fearful of what it would mean for all of Ireland. My gaze shot to Patrick, still lying on the rock asleep. What would become of us if this change occurred? We'd be annihilated.

"That's the spirit!" Cearnaigh said, beating his chest with his right fist. "Thought ya might feel that way, lass. Good blood in ya. Delaney's good stock, I say."

He reached into his leather pouch to retrieve an old, rolled-up piece of parchment and handed it to me. "There are many prophecies surroundin' ya. This is just one."

I unrolled the paper and read:

Prophecy of the Gael Siridean

Alas, the carrier's purpose fulfilled
By the birth of the millennial Blood Moon

On distant phantom isle awaits
Cheating an unjust doom

The Searcher rides through gathering storm
To find the Lost Cave of Malachent
Where the faerie cross blade doth not weaken or waver
But cuts to breach the faulty vent

If by the stroke of the Ten Colds Moon
The Siridean slays the indomitable beast
The Bearer will be unshackled
And all will be restored to peace

I read the prophecy through twice, and it still did not produce much clarity. "Well, I can guess at part of it since I had a whoppin' vision this morning that showed me some of the things here," I said, still locked in on the puzzle.

"What'd ya see?"

"I saw myself a bit older, maybe twentyish. There was black snow not so much falling as creeping down from the sky." I shuddered. "Kheelan was carrying me away from the beast. We were trying to outrun the Dullahan. It was so cold. I was searching for something, and my faerie cross was lighting into the adjacent realm. It seems the fiend didn't want me to find whatever it was. He was tearing up the countryside trying to stop me. Then these foot-wide, bat-like dragonflies showed up." I left out the part about being in love with someone besides Patrick. "And they were chasing me too—or maybe they were trying to help. Don't know." I rubbed my forehead.

"Wicked demon faerie! The Dullahan's unstoppable, and we've tried," Cearnaigh mumbled to himself.

"If it's unstoppable then how am I supposed to slay it?"

There was silence. Cearnaigh looked as though he wished he could retract his statement. His jaw snapped shut, but then he spoke with authority.

"Ye are the Gael Siridean. Yer battle has already been set, Lady Aishling. What ya have to decide right now is if yer goin' to show up. If ya choose it, I vow to make ya more ready to slay the beast than any Gael in history. We have recorded the mongrel's whereabouts throughout the history o' the realms whenever it's sighted. We know many things that will not defeat it, unfortunately, through trial and error. Many brave soldiers have given their lives to this quest. Their descendants look to ye, Siridean, to finish this."

"Why me? I'm probably the least qualified Delaney. The Challenger must be desperate." I stood and paced by the stream. "Father does not cease to remind me of what he calls my 'less refined qualities': erratic, stormy temper, impulsive, mind off in faraway places—just to name a few."

"Flutherin' blimey! And I had ye pegged for a smart lass," Cearnaigh ranted. "Did ya really look at the girl in the vision? Did she look like anything held her back?"

"No," I mumbled.

"Did she cower in fear under the foot o' the great beast?"

"Well, no, she didn't. She rode—I mean I rode like lightning with no fear of death. I just knew I had to find a way to protect my clan."

"Are ya tellin' me ye are two people? That you and this *warrior you* from the future couldn't possibly be the same person?"

Covering my mouth with my hand as a giggle escalated, I said, "I get your point, okay?"

"All right then." Cearnaigh stood and stretched. I stood too, looking back at Patrick.

"Yer family sent me from the Otherworld to teach ya the art of combat, Delaney-style. As they have taught me, I will teach you if ya accept yer callin'."

I took a moment to consider as I looked upward to the puffy clouds. Somehow I'd always known there was something out there for me—something risky I'd have to do alone. Now that I had some knowledge of what that was, I couldn't hide from it. Cearnaigh was there to train me, but it was my fate to slay the beast, not his.

"The calling has given me no choice but to accept, Cearnaigh. Even someone as young as I am can realize that." I nodded in compliance.

"Very wise indeed." He grinned.

"Better find my warrior persona," I mumbled to myself.

"Huh?"

"Oh…nothing."

4

The Branch

(Aishling)

"**N**ow to yer training. I'm sure ye watch yer father at times when he engages in Bataireacht—stick fighting," Cearnaigh boomed.

He handed me a blackthorn shillelagh, a knotty stick about four feet in length with a rounded knob on one end. "Early thirteenth birthday present from Morrighan. Hold it wit' both hands, parallel to the ground." He helped position me. "Yes, that's it." He held his stick the same way and moved forward. I blocked him by turning mine to the sky. Then his stick was a blur as he took one hand off it to pop it toward me twice. I fell to the ground.

"It's okay," he said, reaching out to drag me to my feet. "Delaney-style." He wriggled his eyebrows. "Ye'll get it. The art of the fight runs in yer blood. Took me a while to get the hang of it too when I came to work wit' the Delaneys."

Cearnaigh postured. "Again," he barked.

This time when he started forward, I ducked and popped the stick out twice to batter his knees. It caught him off guard, but on my upswing he grabbed my arm and placed my back to his chest while he thrust the stick up against my throat and bore down. My stick was still in my hands. I swung it up to knock him on the left shoulder and stepped back to the right. I ducked out from under his arm and struck him on the back. As he turned around, I jumped back a few feet, placing my stick in both hands, ready to defend.

"Told ya it ran in yer veins," he marveled, rubbing his shoulder. Hoof beats pounded through the moor, heading in our direction. "Guess that's me cue to go." He pulled out a pinch of what looked like dried red clay. "Same time, same place tomorrow, Lady Aishling." He blew the strange powder in Patrick's direction.

Patrick sat up, rubbing his eyes, and Cearnaigh disappeared.

The next day Patrick insisted on fishing, and the dust of Diaga knocked him out again—this time on the grassy banks with a goofy smile on his face. Cearnaigh appeared by the riverside, drew out two Gaelic claymores from underneath his red-tartan cloak, and handed one to me. "Another gift from Morrighan," he said, presenting the sword carefully, as if he was in awe of it.

We began fencing practice—the Celtic art of the sword—with Cearnaigh teaching me proper stance and hand positions. He told me to close my eyes and visualize myself in the flight of the faeries. He said that my movements while in flight would help me to master the art of fencing as well as martial arts.

I closed my eyes and I was transported back to that one night each year when I joined the ranks of the earthly faerie battalion. At the end of the harvest season the Irish held the festival of Samhain to bring in the Celtic New Year. I had studied violin from a very young age and had learned, as any true Irishwoman should, how to transform the mighty violin into a lively fiddle.

At the festival, I would join the dance called the Flight of the Faeries. This was an almost magical event, and people came from far away just to witness it. The timpani drums would build in intensity, and everyone would gather around the large, open-air pavilion in Blackrock Park. The structure had a long, wide ramp built years ago just for this particular event. The faeries and I—around twenty of us—would run at full speed down the ramp, pixie dresses billowing around our ankles, and fiddles held to our chins as we soared into the night. The captivated audience would collectively gasp as they watched us leap through the air around the fire, twisting, leaping, all playing in unison. It was a mystical sight to behold.

Although I wondered how that could possibly correspond to sword training. When I opened my eyes I found out, as Cearnaigh was standing en garde, and my training began.

Over the next six months, in the forest of the Cooley Mountains, I became a swordswoman. Often in the beginning, Cearnaigh would throw my sword as we fought. But in a short amount of time, I was able to parry and block his attacks, leaping and twisting as if in flight. His visualization exercises had worked well.

Those were more peaceful, safe years in Ireland, before heightened security became a necessity. My father was rarely at home, and our servants assumed that once I went to my wing of the castle I stayed there. Security patrolled the outside, but I knew their schedule, and I escaped through the tunnels below the castle, through the gardens, and up into the mountains behind the house. During the second week of school, my private tutoring sessions started for an hour as soon as I arrived home, with a different subject each day. All my lessons took me away from Patrick and I missed him.

When I finished with my tutors each day, I would rush to the hills, brandishing my sword, and Cearnaigh would appear, charging at me from the depths of the dark-jade forest. He had me jumping logs as he pursued. Cearnaigh sliced at many trees I was using as shields. He chased me up boulders and taught me how to jump from such heights with my sword in hand. It was a tricky skill to learn without killing myself with my own weapon or breaking my own limbs from the fall; I was bruised and sore for weeks. The forest was silent other than the clashing of our swords and the thundering of my heart, for the animals had long since fled from our intrusion.

The day I knocked Cearnaigh to the ground with the point of my sword angled over his chest, he looked up smiling. "Okay, Aishling. Well, I think ye've got the basics of the sword. Did ya bring yer taggert?"

He pushed himself off the ground while I gathered the two black, tube-like structures from my fiddle case along with my dart belt. I told him what Morrighan had said about the darts.

"Aye, take heed to 'er words. The weapons made from the faerie cross stones are to be respected, lass."

I watched as Cearnaigh fastened the two pieces of the taggert together and demonstrated the correct procedure for installing the dart, aiming, and releasing. He placed the weapon in my hands and had me visualize the target, which was a red kerchief he had taken from his pocket and attached to a tree about three hundred meters in the distance. Then he had me stand with my feet shoulder width apart.

Looking through the scope, I lined up the dart gun with the target and blew through the mouthpiece. I followed his advice, or I thought I had, but my first attempt at shooting the gun left me minus one practice dart, lost deep in the forest somewhere. It took longer to master the taggert than the sword, but we continued to practice with both weapons each day until I was comfortable with them.

One afternoon we were resting from a grueling duel when he produced a bottle and a tiny brush from inside his bag. "Come," he said, and I moved to sit at my teacher's feet. "The ampelos will infuse strength into you."

"Ampelos? I'm still learning the ancient language, Cearnaigh. You're gonna have to help me out." I laughed.

"In the ancient script, my child, it's the branch."

He dipped the brush into the bottle and then lifted it to stroke the bristles across my right cheek, up my temple to my forehead, and across the crest of my right eyebrow. The paint was midnight blue, and it was interspersed with flecks of the dust of Diaga, which glittered like diamonds. I felt like a painter's canvas, soaking in the artist's passion and inspiration; so tedious were his brush strokes, so masterful his details, I could feel every fine line he produced on my skin.

The sun was setting through the yew trees when he brought out a small mirror and held it up for me to see my reflection. There were no words I could have uttered that would have conveyed to him the beauty of his craftsmanship. I was amazed by his work but also alarmed, for I didn't know what it all meant. A hawthorn tree sprawled and rambled over half of my face, all the way to the tip of my hairline. In the dim light, the diamond dust glimmered, lighting the whole tree. Amid the branches were hidden weapons that he had distorted, making them appear as one with the tree. I saw my shillelagh, the taggert, the double-edged claymore, a faerie cross dagger, and a leather pouch on a long strap. There were also a shield, a six-pointed faerie cross rock, a chainmail suit of armor, and a cloak with delicate scrollwork. On the tree he also placed the ogham symbol *Huath*, which looked like half of a capital H.

"As ya know, the hawthorn is rich in symbolism to our people. The heart o' the hawthorn bleeds contradiction. A dual nature wars within. Its strikin' blossoms hide its lethal, spiky thorns. Many of its properties cannot be explained, so the tree is seen as a source of magic wit' vast pow'r. Ye are one of the branches, Aishling. Beautiful yet deadly. And the magic roils in ya."

"What about the pouch and the other objects on the tree, Cearnaigh?"

"All in due time, ye shall receive," he said, smiling. "Ye'll love those, 'specially the cloak. Ya won't be able to use the other things on the tree until Morrighan gives them to ya on yer birthdays. The cross rock is on the tree for ya to contact me anytime ya need me. If I can come, I will. Pull it down from the tree and press it into the one hangin' around yer neck. The rocks together will communicate with mine."

With that said, he stood and spread his arms wide, his cloak sweeping out like broad wings. "Come, child," he said. "There's one more challenge ye must accept so ya can draw your strength from the Branch whene'er ya need it."

Moving to stand in front of Cearnaigh, I was a tad curious and a bit edgy about what lay ahead. "I'm ready."

With a sparkle in his eyes, he motioned for me to move in so he could hug me, or so it seemed. He grasped me in a Cearnaigh-sized hug and laughed. "Cloak Handlin' 101—when travelin' wit' someone else, always hang on tight." There was a swishing motion, like the sound of fabric whipping in the wind. For about thirty seconds, I had the impression of what it might feel like to float in space: weightless, dark, terrifying.

When Cearnaigh pulled the cloak back, we stood on the boulder-strewn banks of a small river, about ten feet below us. The roar of the churning water was deafening; it curved and smashed into the rocks with brutal force. Looking up, I could see we were in a tight canyon with sunlight barely able to penetrate between the stone cliffs rising up on either side. Dropping my gaze to the water, my spirit sank. I had a bad feeling about this.

"Where are we?" I asked, hugging my arms as a swift breeze stole through the canyon.

He moved to stand beside me. "Fuíl River. And these are the Rapids of Rua."

At first I was afraid to know the answer to my next question, but I trusted Cearnaigh. Setting my resolve, I faced him. "What am I to do?"

He turned to me and the look on his face was one I'd seen on Uncle Brádach's face many times: it was an expression that showed he'd pledge to go through whatever it was for me if he could. But I knew he couldn't.

"Ye must go deep. 'Tis the only way to battle the thin place into the next realm and reach the source. Ye must drink of it seven times, and seven times ye must draw air."

My gaze shifted from his torn look to the impossible waters. My soul shuddered, but the warrior in me held her stance, held in the quake so Cearnaigh would not see my fear. "What is the source? How will I know when I find it?" My jaw clenched.

"Ye'll know," he nodded. "Ye'll know."

He slunk away, his shoulders bent. Then I stepped to the edge; my thoughts were in turmoil. Becoming a faerie slayer was a dangerous occupation. "Okay," I told myself, "Just take a long breath and go deep. Look for an obvious source to drink from. This is the way you transform; of course it's gonna be hard." I blew my bangs out of my eyes. Then I unrolled the hairband from my wrist and twisted my hair into a ponytail. "But the payoff's worth it. I'll be helping my people." Without another thought, I jumped in.

My head pounded in the torrent. The angry current carried me downstream. I went under and fought my way back to the top, gasping for air. Sucking water into my windpipe, I choked and coughed. Darkness surrounded me as my body slammed into rocks in an underground cave in the bend of the river. The hostile water lifted me and rammed me into jagged boulders. I had to get out of this hole.

This madness reached beyond my control. It felt as if my legs were being pulled from below. With all my strength, I forced my head above the rapids and coughed up more water. My body submerged again and I struggled to resurface. My chest bowed out as I grasped the boulder and pushed myself up enough to inhale sharply. Something like an ocean riptide dragged me under and this time there was no escaping it. The light grew dimmer and dimmer, and the noise became more peaceful the farther down I went. My lungs screamed for release. The faerie cross hanging on my chest emitted a comforting light.

Soon I neared the river floor where grass-like vegetation tickled my arms. In full frantic mode, I searched for the source, but I didn't know what I was looking for. Somehow I felt I needed to go back upstream to the rapids, but I had to get a breath first. I surfaced a few seconds later, gasping for air and bobbing in the waves as they crashed over my head. Diving back under, I swam down to calmer waters and fought my way upstream.

On both sides of the underwater world, vast tree roots extended up the mud walls as far as I could see upriver. It was eerie but strangely beautiful. Many of the roots were thicker than baseball bats, and they were all shiny, smooth crimson in color. In order to continue on my journey, I rushed to the surface again to draw in air. I was closer to the rapids now, so I had to turn my back to the downstream flood so I could breathe. When I had drawn in as much air as I could, I darted back underneath the flow.

I followed the intricate root system toward the Rapids of Rua. The river curved to the left and the water went from murky to clear in an instant. A shining white light glistened ahead and I swam faster to reach it. This had to be the source, and I had to take a breath—soon. The light was like a thin root that unraveled and wafted toward me, spirit-like, as I approached it. When I grasped the root, an energizing charge jolted through my system. The root wound around my arm, locking on to me, and the tip of it moved toward my mouth. I grabbed it with my free hand and shoved the root between my lips, taking a greedy pull of the thick, bitter drink. The root unwound from my arm, and I burst upward. Breaking the surface, I inhaled deeply and dove back down. By the seventh and final time, I felt powerful, altered— transformed.

Climbing the rocks, I sat down by the river and looked at my glowing, reddish skin. I wrapped my arms around my body and tried to hold in any heat I had stored.

"It'll die down in a few hours…the redness." I heard Cearnaigh say, as he came up behind me, placing his warm cloak around my shoulders. I pivoted and sprang to my feet, dipping my head as a sign of respect to my teacher. "I knew you could do it." He looked so relieved.

"I feel strong," I said, staring at my arms.

"Aye. Pow'r from the source'll help ya fight all life's battles."

Looking around, I noticed there were no trees to be seen in the narrow canyon. I wondered where the roots led. This truly was a special place.

Turning back to him, I saw Cearnaigh watching me. As if he could read my mind, he answered my unspoken question, "The roots from the rapids are completed in ye, Aishling—the hawthorn. They nourish ya. They're yer lifeblood. When the branches twist and tangle onto your cheek, know that the pow'r Diaga pumps through ya is thick and strong like the roots, piercing and savage like the thorns, unyielding and bold like the trunk, and entangled within ya like the branches."

His words were forceful and chilling. Yet, through the process of transformation I felt new—whole. I knelt down and opened my satchel to grab my mirror so I could admire his artwork again, but the hawthorn was gone from my cheek. "What happened?"

"The marking will appear when ye go into battle to intimidate yer pursuers. The weapons on the tree will be yers simply by touchin' the tree in yer mind. Then ye've gotta think a weapon into existence in yer hand, and repeat the phrase '*ta me i gcruachais*' [tah may ih grew-kuss]."

"I need your help?"

"That's right. Hawthorn. Power. You and the tree together. The roots'll sustain ya. Ne'er forget the pow'r ye wield from the Branch."

Following a year of stick fighting, sword fighting, target practicing with the taggert, and getting close to mastering the Gaelic martial art form known as *ealaíona comhraic*, Cearnaigh prepared to return to the Otherworld on my fourteenth birthday.

My mentor had become a great friend, and I was heartbroken to see him go. "Will you come back from time to time to visit?"

I asked him. We were sitting on the bank of the river where we had met a year earlier.

"I promise," he assured. "Ya never know when I'm goin' to show up to test yer abilities."

"I'll be ready for ya." I laughed, and he shoved my shoulder until I almost fell over.

His robust laughter bounced off the rocks so heartily, even the lazy coots and mute swans took flight.

Too soon his smile faded. "Aishling, ye have a great responsibility placed on yer shoulders. The Challenger and the whole of yer clan are countin' on ya to be ready. Take care of yerself, lass, and keep practicin'."

"I will," I promised. We both stood, and he grabbed me in a breath-stealing hug, which I returned with equal strength. Then he turned and journeyed into the forest. In our day-to-day battles, he had also taught me to conceal emotion, and it physically hurt me to drag the blurring teardrops back down from my eyelids, but I accomplished it with great effort. My vision cleared and I positioned myself in battle stance with my sword. I kept watch until he blended with the shadows.

5

Shadows Beyond the Veil

(Rafe)

hy am I so drawn to this particular fire? I wondered, as I pushed through the final barrier of the Otherworld and endured the fiery torture of the tall flames before landing on the ground beside a woodpile. Usually a demon chose his fiery portals based on a certain energy surrounding the blaze, like a party atmosphere—the rowdier the better. Yet, there was no such energy in this place. However, there was a lingering aura of sunshine that drew me into its joy and warmth.

Even after so many years as a demon, I was still not completely immune to all my old feelings of angelic euphoria, erratic though they were. I couldn't recall the last time I had felt anything but torment—until now. My name is Raphael Delacruz, aka former commander of the ethereal armies/former angel of healing.

While my body completed its transformation to the shell of a man, I writhed in agony under the full moon. Even though the pain was excruciating, it was well worth it to come up from below for a little while. During this process I was concealed from human eyes in a parallel dimension, and I could show myself to them whenever I desired.

There was no one around the bonfire. The partygoers had only recently vacated; I could tell that from the strength and height of the blaze, along with the drifting scent of a cauldron of nettle soup. So I remained invisible for a short while and lay staring at the twinkling lights in the heavens, trying to remember what it was about them that I should know. Images tried to surface, but the five evil spirits living inside me blocked and crowded them out.

Those demons were compelling me to stand. Someone was coming. I reared up and stomped toward them like the prowling demon I was, hiding behind the veil between worlds. Then I heard laughter of a boy about fifteen who was chasing a girl of about the same age around the fire. I stopped short and zoomed in on the scene. The boy's heart was the perfect candidate for demon invasion—a bit too much ego for one so young, not much of a challenge for me. I left him alone for the time being.

But her heart? It was shielded by angel's wings. I had never seen such peculiarity in my time with the beasts. When I observed the black-haired beauty, her allure brought me to my knees, and her inherent kindness swept over me. A bit of spunk in her made me—a demon—smile in a happy, non-sinister way. She stood right in front of me almost like she could see into the adjoining realm that should have kept me invisible to her.

The girl's laughter abruptly ceased, and she crept to within inches of my upturned face, reaching into the darkness toward me. I could have snatched her then and taken her back with me through the fire. The girl was superhuman; I could sense she was different. Satariel would reward me if I took her to him. Tilting my head, I studied her again. A memory snaked upward in my mind, but the coil looped in on itself, refusing to manifest. Feeling shame for the first time in a long time, I shook my head. I knew I could never take her there, for the others would surely abuse one so pure.

The demon side of me wanted to possess her, but it was not in the way one might think. In her undefiled state, the girl needed a friend on the other side. She was so young and small. I decided I would try to remember this portal and come to her during the seasons of the thin places, to make sure she remained safe from the other demons. Something about her made me want to be good.

My head tilted during my study of her. The girl grabbed the odd pendant hanging from the chain about her neck and held it away from her chest. Her face scrunched as if she'd felt a brief stab of pain. Light from the rock shone on me and nausea set in, weakening my stance. My claws extended and I snarled as I stepped toward her, my eyes locked on the venomous pendant. Then she looked me straight in the eyes as she backed away.

"Come on. Let's go," she said to her friend, her voice unwavering. She was a brave one. I wasn't sure how she had sensed me, but it was apparent that she had.

I followed the girl from afar, not wanting to frighten her further. She waved good night to her companion and then ran across a rustic stone bridge and into the castle on the opposite side of the river. After a while I made my way around the side of the structure. Even through the thick, stone walls, I could hear the soothing sounds of music coming from deep within the heart of the fortress.

When I pushed through the thin place into the realm that held her, I was in a dark, damp underground tunnel. I felt uneasy. This was too much like the prison I had to call home, without the fire of course. The music echoed through the hollow chamber, and I crept toward it hoping to find the girl. About twenty feet down the corridor, I saw a dim light coming through a partially opened door. I was close. She could have seen me if she had stepped into the hallway.

I stood before the door, watching her through the crack as she knelt on the earthen floor, facing the opposite wall. A flashlight resting beside her cast her faint silhouette onto the archaic stonework of the dungeon's wall. In her hands she cradled a music box. The melody I heard gave me the same feeling I'd had when I'd first encountered her. I felt different. My mind revolved at a high rate of speed. The noise in my head intensified, and I grabbed my ears to stop the ringing.

I moved away from the door, bracing myself against the wall as an onslaught of images and emotions from long ago assaulted me. Some were pleasant; some were troubling. Others gave me hope. I remembered parts of what I once had been. All the torture of hell had made me forget that I was once an angel of the first order. Or it could have been that the pain of my loss and the guilt of my sin had made me want to forget. Whichever cause was truer, I wasn't certain. What I did acknowledge, however, was the fact that I had once had a great life, and I had discarded it as I would have a ripped cloak. I absorbed the music, and I remembered the triumphs of my former existence as well as the sorrows that had ended it.

While the roaring of my thoughts subsided, I drifted away on a thundering mass of clouds; riding the wind was a perk of being an angel. Another flash came, and I saw myself healing people all over the world. Yes! I was the healer, Raphael. I had once been very good. Another flash—war. I was the commander of legions of angels. And the last flash—I saw myself bent over a broken, dying child, a face mangled beyond recognition. A soul departed to the heavens, and eternity's hand charged across the great divide to embrace it. I saw my face upturned to the sky, waiting for the order to heal.

About a decade ago, my angel unit was sent to stop a clan war in Ireland. The Delaneys and the MacEgans had been fighting again in the open countryside among their homes, but now were fleeing. The *Gardaí* [Irish police] sent to control the situation advanced through a minefield, and several had already been massacred by the time we had arrived. Unseen by the humans, we war angels guided the remaining *Gardaí* unharmed from the horrors of the battleground.

We were about to leave when the nightmare decided to haunt one more soul. A young mother ran through the group of men; she was screaming that her daughter was missing. Surely the girl had an angel or more with her, I assured myself as I ran in fast forward back to the battlefield.

During my warp-speed sprint to the place of the recent blood bath, my gaze was drawn to the sky where another battle was taking place—fortunately in a parallel realm not meant for human eyes. There were maybe a dozen angels fighting valiantly; but they were greatly outnumbered by a horde of demons. That many guardians were protecting one human girl? Such a thing was unheard of, even with these—the Malakim—who were like the CIA of angels. I puzzled over the enigma while I searched through the thick, morning fog.

When I reached the edge of the battleground, I prayed that the child had not wandered into the minefield. As my vision pierced the misty cover, I saw movement in the distance straight ahead. With my supernatural hearing, I strained to hear the sound being carried along the wind. Floating on the breeze were the notes of a tinkling music box delivering a mournful ballad. It was very fitting, I thought, for what had just transpired in this place.

Then an alley in the fog opened up like a zipper folding the layers back on either side, and I saw her: a heartbreakingly beautiful little girl, about six years of age, dancing in the minefield. She was oblivious to all the blood staining the ground below the blanket of fog and was unaware of the danger in which the dark souls had placed her innocent life. She twirled with her eyes closed, cradling the music box in her hands.

To my right, another movement drew my eye. Shrouded by the fog, he sought cover, but a break in the mist exposed his face just long enough for me to recognize him. Zakai, wearing the forehead medallion of the Amonati (decidedly malevolent angels in the process of turning dark), was making a quick getaway. Zakai falling? I couldn't believe what I had just seen. The Amonati's presence here, along with the child's guardians being distracted, could only mean one thing—the girl was in mortal danger.

Why her? What could the Amonati gain from destroying an innocent child? I ran toward her, up the path that had been carved out for me through the fog. But I was too late. In terror I watched as the little girl skipped and danced into the path of the landmine that took her young life.

I remembered now. That was the day I lost my soul. The day I saved her. Now that the memories had been resurrected, I couldn't let them die again, but it would take a focused effort to allow them to remain alive. I tried to preserve them in a tiny corner of my mind that I had fought to keep free from the great, dark presence.

When the music stopped, my mind was once again invaded by the revolting hellions that had been repulsed by the offensive melody. I watched as the girl hid the box away, and I heard her peaceful sigh as she stood.

I revealed myself to her for a few brief moments. She didn't even flinch as we stood staring at one another, and I could sense her heart rate elevating only a small degree. How strange, I thought, my curiosity boiling over. Her merciful eyes wrapped me in their warmth and understanding. Maybe she was studying my face to try to conclude whether I was friend or foe. I couldn't be sure, of course. I only read hearts, not minds.

It was time for me to go. The demons inside were forcing me back to the fire. I could do nothing but obey. The thin place would be solidifying soon, and I was not one to be trusted to stay on earth, for Satariel was well aware that I had not given him my allegiance. While I was pushing backward against the unseen veil, the thin place that would shift me to the next dimension, she took one step toward me.

"Wait!" she implored.

My brow lowered in confusion. She had not fainted at the sight of me, which I had rather hoped she would do so I could touch her cheek to wake her, and she was not insisting that I leave. Most extraordinary! The thought of taking her with me was almost irresistible. Almost.

My voice was raw and gruff as I answered her. "Stay back. Don't come any closer," I warned for her safety. If she moved any farther in my direction, she would be sucked into the realm of darkness, and I was still conflicted over my wicked thoughts of abducting this strange, sweet creature. My voice must have pierced her, for she bent over, grasping her ears.

Before she was able to recover, a sparking of the veil warned me of its impending closure. Waves of electricity ricocheted off the stone walls of the underground room. I reached to touch her arm to make her forget this incident. But I fear I didn't get a good enough grasp on her before I was pulled into the vacuum and transported back through the fire.

6

River fane

(Aishling)

Beltaine, an ancient Gaelic festival celebrated each year on May 1, was a time when the Otherworld was close at hand and beings were able to cross to and from the Land of the Dead. Demons and their somewhat companionable rivals, a faction of Irish faeries, were particularly fond of this night. There was nothing they enjoyed more than entering the earth realm and wreaking havoc.

It was tradition for Uncle Brádach to host his annual bonfire party to celebrate Beltaine, and it was a greater tradition still for him to scare all the youngsters with his colorful stories about the faeries. I remember many sleepless nights following such celebrations, but at the mature age of almost fifteen I was well past being shocked by his tales. It helped knowing that Uncle Brádach was telling the truth—that his stories weren't fiction. It helped to be prepared, and on this particular night I was thankful that Cearnaigh had trained me well.

Patrick and I had made plans earlier to sneak away from the party when the full moon was high. Having entertained the crowd with a fiddle duel with Uncle Brádach, I made small talk for a few minutes with Claire before ducking into the shadows. I jogged into the stable, found my fiddle case near Torin's stall, and put the instrument away. My taggert was tucked in the long side pocket of the case, ready for any trouble we might encounter. I propped my foot up on a feeding trough to refasten my leg sheath and inserted my dagger, which was decorated with more faerie cross rocks. It had been my gift from Morrighan for my fourteenth birthday last fall.

"Patrick, where are you?" I whispered, anxious to be gone on our hunting expedition. Being the impetuous—or foolish—teenagers we were, our plan was to track down faerie cross stones...and faeries. With the unique moonlight of Beltaine, the crystals on the stones glowed like pockets of blue flames flaring from the river floor.

"How long ya been waitin', my *bogadán crua?*" Patrick asked as he neared the stall. He had been calling me his "tender-hearted toughie" since childhood as I was known to champion the cause of the less tough kids at school and had been in my fair share of scrapes whenever I saw someone being bullied. As I'd grown up, I'd learned a bit of self-control and found more psychological ways of dealing with injustices. I'd never backed down from a verbal battle with a bully, and in a short time they'd always left with confused glares, a little less sure of themselves and I hope, a little wiser.

"What took you so long? I thought I was going to have to come back and drag you away," I grumbled. He opened the stall door and led Torin out.

"Patience, dear Asher. Are you that eager for a tangle with the creatures?" he asked, mounting his horse.

"No, it's just that my security detail will be looking for me soon, and I don't want to go home. Not for a while anyway. I left them a note that you and I were going riding. That should keep them off our backs for a while."

"Well, why are ya just standin' around?" Patrick griped with a grin. He offered me his hand as I swatted his leg. I swung up into the saddle behind him and wrapped my arms around his waist, and before long we were flying into the night.

While riding I thought about this boy I was holding. Patrick seemed more like a twenty-five-year-old man trapped in a sixteen-year-old's body than a teenage boy. He'd had so much responsibility placed on his shoulders already, being the Kavanaugh prince and heir to all the Kavanaugh clan lands. Patrick had also been trained for war from a young age. Anlon Kavanaugh would accept nothing less than the best from his son; thus, Patrick was the top swordsman in his fencing class at the academy.

He was also well built and handsome. My prince. His father made him keep his strawberry-blond hair in a formal, short style, and his sandy-colored face was clean-shaven. When I looked into his emerald eyes, I felt the comfort and familiarity of the forests surrounding my home, the strength of the evergreens, but also the tumult of the waves crashing into the Emerald Isle. Already he was a force to be reckoned with.

Being on the high school hurling team, he worked out a lot after school, and his shoulders had thickened and widened in the past year. He was already six feet tall and was still growing. I was proud to be by his side as he walked me to my classes at school each day. In August he and Claire would be going off to college, and I was already feeling lonely. Just thinking about it made me hug him tighter as I laid my head midway up his back.

Patrick raced Torin beside the river, chasing the shadows of the moon, both rider and horse knowing the lay of the land intimately. Summer was drawing nearer, and the scent of fresh-cut grass and hawthorn rode the night air.

"Do you smell that?" I asked him, smiling. As he took in a deep breath, I repeated the phrase Uncle Brádach had taught us many years ago: "*Ne'er cast a cloot til Mey's oot.*" In other words, don't shed your winter clothes until the May flowers are in full bloom.

"I'd say we dressed in accordance with the rule of the hawthorn then. It's the perfect night for a ride and a tromp in the river," Patrick said.

On the river floor, the faerie stones shimmered like vibrant sapphires, and above the stream hung a mystical blue glow. The River Fane shone like this four times a year during each of the Gaelic festivals, but the certainty of it never detracted from its magic.

Patrick didn't slow down until we were only a couple of miles from the property line separating the Kavanaugh's land from the MacEgan's. He neared the bend in the river by the forests and slowed Torin to a canter before stopping at the river's edge. Jumping to the ground, he reached up to pull me down.

We both put on our waders for this sport, and Patrick stepped down off the bank and reached for me, helping me keep my balance on the wet stones among the river rapids.

Plunging my arm into the icy flow, I realized that even though spring was drawing to a close, the snow from the Cooley Mountains still fed the river, and a shiver ran up my arm and through my body.

I lifted a glowing rock to inspect it; the cool mist from the rapids stung my face. "Wow, look at this one!" I said, turning toward Patrick to show off my find. He and I had gone rock hunting for several years on Beltaine, so I should have grown accustomed to this familiar sight, but somehow this year was different. As I looked up at him standing so close to me, the moonlight played across his features and accented the ice-blue, glitter-like sparkles across his face and hands caused by the spray of the river on this rare night.

"Asher, I...umm" he said, stumbling over his words. He pulled me to him.

"Yes, Patrick?" We had never kissed, but I had been wondering what it would feel like to kiss my best friend who just happened to be my boyfriend and future fiancé.

"You're radiant...so beautiful. When I look at you standing there, glowing like the rock you wear, I get a feeling that you can never be mine. It seems like there are things you haven't told me. If you are to be Lady Kavanaugh one day, I need you to tell me things, like what's behind the stone and where you always run off to after school. We can't have secrets from each other, Asher."

His breath hitched as he waited and held on to my arms. I looked across the stream to the moors beyond the north bank.

Tipping my chin up to force my gaze, he tried a more subtle approach. Bending down, he kissed my cheek. Then he leaned his forehead to mine.

"Patrick, I can't," was all I got out before he took me in his arms and silenced me with a gentle kiss. Wrapping his arms around me, he stood just holding me in the middle of the river, his lips soft and warm against mine. *So this is what love feels like*, I thought as my heart pounded in time with the water over the rocks. After a moment in his arms, the roar of the river fell silent, and my legs began to float away in the current.

Reaching to catch me, Patrick was caught off balance too, and we both fell into the frigid pool. My waders filled before I had a chance to right myself, and I came up sputtering water and laughing like I hadn't laughed in years. Patrick swam over and slapped water in my face, and a liquid battle ensued.

Trying to escape I climbed the bank and almost made it to Torin before I looked back and noticed that Patrick had gone still in the water and was facing downriver toward the forests. At the same time, Torin whinnied, instinctively moving closer to me. My first thought was that the fun was over; castle security had found us and it was time to go back home. Except for the fact that Patrick was facing the wrong direction.

Looking beyond Torin I saw what appeared to be a man standing in the shadows by a tree.

"Who are you and why are you trespassing on Kavanaugh land?" Patrick shouted with an air of boldness and authority, which forced the man to look at him instead of me.

I assembled my taggert and readied it with a cross dart. After all this was the night for faeries, and we had never seen any person this far out in the wild moors. Patrick had watched me practice a couple of times with the weapon and I knew he was stalling so I could prepare. I had to be calm. Even though I'd never used the taggert for defense, I felt that I would be prepared if only I could get my nerves to cooperate. While I was trying to calm myself down, a power came over me, a feeling of raw strength and courage, and the faerie cross hanging around my neck sparked. I held up the rock and pointed it toward the man. Its strong beam cut through the darkness and illuminated the mark of the Alorcán—two intertwined, surly dragons inside the stranger trying to break free. Dropping the rock back to my chest, I steadied myself behind Torin and prepared to fight.

"Well, if ye must know, my name is Aodh. And as for the matter of trespassin'? Well, since I've inhabited this land for o'er six centuries, I'd say it's you two who're intrudin'. Now, hand o'er the lass, and we'll be on our way!" the man shouted back.

"We?" Patrick asked, looking to the trees.

As if on cue, about a dozen beautiful maidens stepped from behind the trees, shimmering, almost translucent. Much like fireflies they blinked, one after the other, and moved closer to us. Their beauty was spellbinding, and I wrenched my eyes away in order to seek to save Patrick. I was tugging on my dart belt, assuring I had enough ammunition to free us from this onslaught, when I heard a hideous roar. Peering around Torin I watched as the maidens transformed into gruesome-looking beings. Wild-eyed and burly, they converged on us.

"Faeries!" Patrick smirked with a look of intense hatred on his face. The man who'd been addressing him changed form in front of us and turned into a larger version of the other advancing creatures.

"Don't risk yer neck for one mere girl, ye foolish lad. Just get on yer horse, ride away, and we'll let ye live," the beady-eyed monster yelled at Patrick.

"You see, that's where we have a problem, you and me," Patrick said, trying to stall the advancing army until I was ready. "She's not just any old girl!" Patrick spat at him. "She'll one day be the Lady Kavanaugh. So back off!"

Charging from behind Torin, I tossed Patrick's sword toward him so he could catch it by the hilt, and I trained my taggert toward the coming horde.

"Well, well, what do we have here?" the being said, pausing for only a moment. "Now ye've both hung nooses around yer necks. Bring them to me!" he yelled. The sound was like the boom of a low-flying jet, and the nearby trees recoiled.

Standing just the way I'd practiced, I blew into the mouthpiece of the taggert, and a force greater than my own sent the cross dart flying with incredible speed. It struck the nearest monster, and he fell and disintegrated. Having never seen one of the darts fulfill its intended purpose, I was mesmerized by the result. The faerie screamed and writhed; I couldn't take my eyes off it.

"Asher, they're coming!" Patrick said, trying to wake me up. Pulled out of my daze, I reloaded. Patrick was standing ready with sword drawn like a mighty Celtic warrior.

"Asher, you have some explaining to do," Patrick whispered, after I'd dropped another creature. "Besides that I want you to know that I love you."

"I love you too, Patrick."

"Do you think you can use that thing as we ride away?"

"I think so."

"When I say 'now,' I want you to jump on Torin facing backward. I'll be right behind you."

The faeries were now about thirty yards away.

"Now!" he shouted.

A burst of adrenaline hammered through my body, and I leapt onto the horse in an inhuman amount of time. Patrick jumped behind me, and I leaned across his thigh to aim behind us and take out the next closest faerie.

While we rode away, a strange, yet familiar sight played out in front of me. About fifty of the largest, most spectacular, blue-glowing dragonflies whirred by me, heading straight for the monsters. They had to be the same ones from my vision, only I could see them clearer this time. When they reached the tree line, they seemed just to disappear. The faeries were no longer advancing toward us. Several were retreating to the forest while the few remaining ones looked as if they were fighting the air. They were screeching in agony at some unseen force.

As the steed tore across the plains toward home, I hid my face in Patrick's chest, and he wrapped his free arm around me to help control my shaking.

"D-did you see that, Patrick?"

"Yeah, we just slayed those faeries," he said, punching the air.

"No, Patrick. The dragonflies. Did you see all those dragonflies?"

He peered down into my eyes as Torin trekked upriver. "What dragonflies, Asher?"

And then I was floating.

When I opened my eyes, I was lying in my room at Kavanaugh Castle, surrounded by all the Kavanaughs, the heads of security, and my doctor.

"What happened?" I tried to sit up. "Why do I feel so…d-dizzy?" I stammered, holding my head. "Oh…oh!" I babbled as realization hit.

"You thought you saw the Dullahan riding across the moors, and you passed out. Remember?" Patrick said to cover what he thought I might say. Several in the crowd whispered.

"Well, Beltaine makes everyone a li'l skittish," Uncle Brádach chimed in. "Why don't we all let the girl have some space now? She's fine. They don't make 'em any sturdier than my Aishling." He came to sit on the edge of the bed and effectively shooed the onlookers out of the room.

After closing the door for privacy, Patrick moved around to the other side of the bed and sat down.

"So what really happened out there tonight?" Uncle Brádach asked. I could tell he was not going to back down until he had some answers. We could never keep anything from him.

The silence roared in the room. Patrick and I glanced at each other.

"Okay, who's gonna start? Ordinarily I'd say there's no use boilin' your cabbage twice, but I'm willin' to make an exception in this case. Spill it, son," he said to Patrick.

After Uncle Brádach was filled in on the events of the evening, he looked at me with pain in his expression. "Why would they want to take ya? How'd they even know about ya?" His face and neck turned crimson, which I knew meant his blood pressure was rising.

"Calm down. I don't know why it happened, but Patrick and I will be more careful. Won't we, Patrick?" He nodded in agreement.

"Where'd ya get the darts, Aishling?" I was so afraid that he and Patrick would want me to have a psych evaluation once I told them.

After a long moment of uncomfortable silence during which I twisted the bedsheet into a wad across my stomach, I finally relented. "From Morrighan."

"The wife of The Challenger from your family's history books?" Uncle Brádach questioned. He thrust his hand through his hair, while Patrick turned white. I nodded, wondering if they believed me, but then Uncle Brádach validated me.

"Aishling, ye've been visited by the war faerie, the great Morrighan?" He was awestruck.

"Yes."

"When? How?" Patrick interrogated.

"For several years now. She comes to me on my birthday, on the night of Samhain, when she can cross over from the Otherworld."

"Why'd ya never say anythin'?" Patrick asked, hurt that I would keep something this big from him.

"To protect you," I said, looking at Patrick. "And you," I said, turning to Uncle Brádach. Grabbing both of their hands, I pleaded with them. "No one can ever know of this. Promise me!" I begged.

Looking like mirror images of each other, the two men ran their hands through their hair as if in torture before they vowed their silence.

Uncle Brádach was known as an expert in Irish folklore. It made me nervous the way he was looking at me—like he was seeing me as a whole different person, like he was in my head picking out the secret curse…like he was about to lose me to the legends of our homeland. I was so tempted to tell him everything, but I knew I couldn't.

1

RUMOIS

(Aishling)

Summer passed much like a river rapid, and then Patrick was packing for his first year of college. The day before he left we cantered through the Cooley Mountains on Kheelan and Torin. We battled the wind to Foxes Rock and dismounted at the peak. I stepped close to the edge and leaned into the blowing gusts with my arms out to the side. The strength of the air stream kept me upright. Patrick tugged the hood of my jacket and I fell backward into his arms. I laughed as he wrapped his arms around me from behind, and I leaned back into his chest.

"Alright, daredevil," he teased. "Who's going to work on taming you while I'm gone?"

"I'll never be housebroken, Patrick. Why bother?"

He turned me around and held onto my arms. His face turned all serious and broody. "Aishling…try. Please, try while I'm gone to harness your adventurous side," he urged. "I know the whole housewife ideal is a stretch for you, but a senate leader can't have a wife who spends all her time in the moors. There'll be expectations—responsibilities," he unloaded.

Turning back to the view of the valley below, I took in my home, the land of my people I was willing to bleed for. I feared I would never be the woman Patrick needed me to be. "I understand, Patrick. I know what's at stake," I yielded.

The curse seemed to blow in with the wind and bind us together—squeezing the life out of what should have been a carefree young love. I did want to please Patrick, and contrary to his belief, responsibility was a concept I could never escape.

He wrapped an arm around my stomach and kissed my temple. "I'll miss you," he sulked.

"You'll be too busy to miss me."

"Never," he laughed.

Patrick was going to Columbia University in New York to study political science. Little did I know at the time that the boy I loved, my best friend, would lose a noticeable part of himself when he went to America. His early flood of calls and letters tapered to an annoying trickle—a drop of news here and there—but nothing substantial. Our relationship was changing, and I felt powerless to stop it.

My senior year of high school was hollow without Patrick and Claire. It was difficult for me to make friends, so I deepened my relationship with Kheelan and the wild—less drama that way. Classmates often saw the PKs as royalty, so they avoided us. Having guards follow me around all day didn't help matters either. However, the biggest barrier to friendship came in the form of my after-school activities; weapons training took up all my extra time. And my role as faerie slayer put a damper on any hope I had of appearing like a normal teen. The rumors about me started after my fifteenth birthday that October.

Patrick couldn't come home for my special day, but Claire was able to make it since she was in college in Dublin, not far away. At dinner I was surrounded by Kavanaughs at the bonfire party. After I blew out the candles, cut the cake, and opened presents, I gave everyone a goodbye hug and made my way toward home.

Samhain was much warmer than usual this year. I snuck into the stable and stacked my gifts on the hay in Kheelan's stall for safekeeping. Then I saddled Kheelan, leapt on his back, and steered him out the door farthest from prying eyes. Uncle Brádach would not be happy with me if he strolled in and saw Kheelan gone, but I had to go. Tonight the faeries roamed, and it was my duty to destroy them.

There was enough moonlight bouncing off the ground for me to be able to see my way to the cabin. I bounded out of the saddle, ran in to grab my gear, and slung the armed taggert across my shoulder. Vaulting back into the saddle, I nudged Kheelan into a trot. Soon we galloped with the flow of the river. Clouds stole the moon and a gentle rain fell. I lifted my face to the sky to drink in the delightful freedom, and I laughed just because.

Kheelan's hoof beats were hypnotic, and I leaned my head on his neck to gaze into the fast-moving stream. A neon-blue fog hovered above the river. *There must be thousands of faerie cross rocks this time. Patrick should be here.* I pouted.

At the bend of the river, I turned Kheelan to the open moors and we chased the night, with the faerie stone lighting the way. Up mountains and through valleys we wandered. The rain eventually faded to a drizzle and I reached up to twist my hair, squeezing water from my tangled locks.

Morrighan appeared in the marshes at midnight. Not wanting to risk an injury to Kheelan in the deep marshy pits, I dismounted and trudged among the tall weeds and puddles, trying to avoid the deeper ones. I was glad I had worn my knee-high, waterproof boots. She waited for me to come to her, so I had no choice but to wade through the gooey mud. In the middle of no-man's-land, I bowed before the Maolán queen.

Without delay or celebration, she handed me a shield and a leather pouch. "The pouch is filled with the dust of Diaga. Use it sparingly. At this point, just know that it will incinerate the Alorcán."

"Thank you, *Maimeó* [grandmother]."

"Goodbye, Aishling," she said and disappeared.

In the early morning hours Kheelan and I crossed onto MacE-gan property. With our extreme distance from civilization and the time of day, there would be no one about to object to our trespass, I rationalized. I led Kheelan down a steep grade and we followed a tight ravine for a while. Rock cliffs rose up sharply on both sides. Kheelan tromped through the shallow water that rippled down the path. The ravine opened into an evergreen forest and we moved between the cedars. Pine needles crunched on the woodland floor.

My head whipped to the right at the sound of a child's giggle. The melodious notes of overflowing happiness lured me in that direction. I followed, even though the faerie stone pulsed and sent out rays as if scouring for danger. A thin place had to be near; an irresistible pull beckoned. The Otherworld called to me. It was strange that I felt a kinship with this place, like I'd been here often; yet, I had no memories to back up my suspicions. I pushed Kheelan onward. Innocent laughter now surrounded me, and I panned the area from left to right. What appeared to be shooting stars blasted through the trees. The lights chased each other around the forest and zipped through an unseen veil up ahead, darkness once again invading.

Kicking Kheelan into full speed, I raced head first into the unknown. Entering the Otherworld was like a rocket blastoff that lasted about ten seconds. When everything stilled, Kheelan whinnied and stamped the ground. I rubbed his neck, trying to calm him.

"I know, boy," I crooned. "The weird feeling will wear off soon." At least, I hoped it would.

We were still in the forest, but everything felt different. The air was musty, as if the tree canopy needed to open its windows and air out, and the laughter had turned to weeping. The pitch of the wailing changed to a shrieking screech, and I pivoted in the saddle to see what was coming.

Out of the fog, a young woman with a feline face drifted just above the ground. Her bushy, flame-red hair framed her body as a lion's mane. The black dress she wore hung provocatively around her chest, and the skirt was tattered and shredded to her waist. The second most feared of the Irish creatures from legend drew nearer to me, and I needed to move. *Banshee!* My mind blared in warning. She was about twenty feet from me. As she stalked forward, her mouth widened to the height of a lion's when it's preparing to roar. Her teeth were thick white needles, and the shriek she released had me burying one ear into Kheelan's mane as he stormed away, while my arm protected the other ear.

Kheelan dodged trees and soon broke free of the forest. At full gallop, he tore across the moor. I finally lifted my head once the pounding had stopped and peered behind us. It seemed we were alone now. We continued through the glen until we came to a cluster of grassy mounds that swelled up from the earth. Smoke billowed on the breeze—the remains of a doused campfire. I pulled on the reins to dampen the clip clop of the hooves, but my timing was not good. Before I could bring Kheelan to a full stop, we were surrounded by nearly a dozen faeries with taggerts pointed at us. The men wore golden headbands with emblems, the origin of which danced on the periphery of my mind, but I couldn't quite recall the symbol's significance.

"I mean you no harm," I asserted.

Another male faerie moved in the shadows toward the circle of taggert-toting faeries. He carried a torch and an air of authority.

"Weapons down," he commanded them. They lowered their taggerts in unison and slung the straps over their shoulders.

When he entered the ring, I noticed there was a kind face on the massive faerie, but one that scarcely hid the power brimming the levy beneath. This was not a being to trifle with. He looked at me with such a protective, intense gaze that I wanted to reach out and soothingly touch his troubled brow. He was a good six-and-a-half feet in height and had the body of a trained, sculpted soldier. His shoulder-length, raven hair was tied in the back with a strip of old scrap cloth, and long strands had escaped and blown around his face as if he'd been running or fighting. The faerie looked like he was around nineteen or twenty years of age.

He wore a black-wool Irish *léine*, or tunic, from the sixteenth century that fell to his upper thigh and was cinched at the waist with a rough, wide, brown-leather belt, with brown pants underneath. His knee-high boots were made from rabbit skins and were tied about his legs with strips of leather. The clothing was definitely late medieval.

Diagonally across his chest was another broad, leather strap that held his taggert and dart pouch on his back. His belt grasped a battle-ax on one side, and a Gaelic claymore very similar to my own on the other side.

The leader of the men stepped up beside me and bowed. Then he gazed up at me with a smile of familiarity. "Hello, Aishling." He reached up to touch my hand, and the last thing I remember was falling from the horse.

I woke sometime later to the sound of men talking in the next room. I tried not to stir. Maybe I could overhear some valuable information, like what I needed to do to get out of there.

The first voice was scratchy, older. "We can't keep her. She's not ready."

"I need to tell her. I want to tell her," my rescuer brooded. I could hear him pacing.

The older man sighed, "Ye'll have to wait. The time has been determined."

"But she found me. How do ya explain that?" The handsome faerie's frustration built along with the stomp of his stride. "She didn't just wander in. Don't ya get it? She remembers. Her overachievin' brain must have—in a sense—rewired itself and retrieved some of the memories we had converted into dreams."

"It's extraordinary—yes. But still the timing is off," the older man stressed. "We must let the girl go."

A fist ramming into wood rattled the window by my bed. "I'm tellin' ya...she remembers her visits here as a child. How else would she have come to us, to this exact location?"

60

"Kaél, my boy, our clans have waited centuries for the Siri-dean. That's bound to have strained yer patience. A few more years—ye have to give 'em to her. I'm sorry," the old man's final answer resounded. The door clicked shut.

"Fine!" the younger faerie growled. "But ya didn't say I had to return her this instant."

"Ta me i gcruachais," I spoke in my mind.

I felt the tree etch onto my skin, and the feel of it took my breath away. The hawthorn was so vivid in my mind's eye—the gnarling branches, the long spiky thorns, and my weapons hanging from its limbs. Stretching on my tiptoes, I grabbed my sword and opened my eyes.

Before the faerie opened the door, I leapt to my feet, sword in hand. "Let me go and I won't hurt you," I negotiated.

He moved to the right and I shifted to compensate for his steps. A smile burst across his face. "Ye're amazing."

"You're delusional if you think I'm staying here."

He moved one step closer. My eyes formed tiny slits, and I gripped the sword harder. "Careful. Wouldn't want you to lose that handsome face."

"Ah, so she thinks me handsome, eh?"

Unruffled, I met his gaze. "Step away from the door."

"Yer mark makes ya even lovelier than I e'er imagined."

"How do you know me?" I pointed the sword toward his chest.

He turned away from me to put his fists on the wall as he growled. "I'm bound by oath to hold my tongue." When he twisted back around, his face held torment. "Aishling, please put down the sword. I would never hurt ya. This oath I vow to ya."

In his stance and his words, I found truth. "So you'll return me to the border, where the thin place portal crosses worlds?"

"Aye," he bowed, never taking his eyes from mine.

"And you'll do this without delay?"

"Aye...for one small favor."

Head tilted to the side, I scowled at him. His face was serious and his eyes were gentle. I knew—without doubt—he truly would never harm me. How this knowledge seemed embedded in me was a mystery.

"And what is it that you require?" I challenged.

"May I study the contours of yer soul, my lady?"

My brows scrunched as I propped the point of my sword into the dirt floor and leaned on the hilt. "May you study *what?*"

"I'd very much like to study the path of yer eyes."

"You can't just go around lookin' in peoples' souls!" I shook my head. "How would you even go about that?" He took a step forward and I put a hand out to stop him. "*Not* that I'm agreeing," I objected to his boldness. "Not yet, anyway."

He eyed my weapon. "Do we really need that?"

I narrowed my eyes while I contemplated. Laying the sword in my right hand, I closed my eyes and sent the weapon back to the hawthorn. I had not heard him move, but when my eyelashes fluttered open, he was there, towering over me. When I looked up at the faerie, a peculiar sense of rightness accompanied his impish grin.

"May I?" he asked.

With a curt nod, I tilted my head upward to meet his gaze. His pupils radiated a blue light as he glared into my soul. I felt invaded—vulnerable. It was only a brief second or two before he tore his sapphire eyes away from my own, but I felt weak.

"You—" So many emotions coursed through my system, I didn't know which one to focus on. I bent over to catch my breath. "What did you do to me?"

He moved backward and looked at the ceiling as he locked his hands behind his neck. There were no more words; I was stunned into silence.

"When ya leave here, Aishling, ya won't remember our encounter. I'll take ye back now." He stepped through the door, and when I could get my legs to move, I followed.

8

Scandal

(Aishling)

I woke to shouting.

"What is the meanin' of this intrusion, MacEgan?" my father shouted.

Groggy, my eyes labored to open, and through tiny slits I could make out the entryway of Delaney castle. Strong arms cradled me.

"How 'bout ye explain to me why yer daughter was caught trespassin' on me land, Delaney?" Zhawn MacEgan demanded. My eyes shot open.

"What's wrong with her? Did ya drug her or somethin'? I'll have yer head!" My father rushed forward and slammed Zhawn to the wall.

"I could've taken her to jail, ya know. She *was* on me property. But I thought I'd try the neighborly thing and bring her back home. And this is how ya repay me? Ye ne'er change, Delaney—as hotheaded and ornery as ever, I see."

My father let go of him and stepped backward. "I'm sure the girl didn't realize she was on yer land. It'll ne'er happen again, I assure ye."

"See that it doesn't. The girl is quite mad, out ridin' the moors on Samhain, and so late at night. She was spoutin' all manner of gibberish when my sons found her. Ya ask me—I think she fell into the Otherworld. Mess with yer brain, that will." Zhawn MacEgan glared at me.

"Let's go," the MacEgan barked. The man holding me settled me on my feet, and I propped against the wall, unsure if I was stable enough to stand yet. The door slammed and my eyes settled on my father's livid face.

Our butler stood in the background, watching the interchange. "Sullie!" my father growled.

"Yes, Lord Delaney," Sullie replied. He stepped forward.

My father's eyes locked me in their predatory rage while he spoke to the servant. "Bring me my strap."

The butler attempted to intervene on my behalf. "But, Sir, I'm sure Lady Aishling is sorrowful for her actions."

My father turned on him and yelled, "Never question how I raise my daughter! Do as ye're told or leave!"

"Yes, Master Delaney." Sullie hurried away.

My father paced in front of me. "Ye'll ne'er be caught on MacEgan land again. Understood?"

"Yes, Father," I mumbled.

"Ye are the princess of Clan Delaney! Act like it! No more foolish ridin' in the moors at night. What if the Kavanaughs find out about this stunt?"

Sullie returned with my father's leather whipping strap. The look the butler threw my way was filled with grief and a longing to help, but there was nothing he could do. He handed my father the strap and fled from the room.

The pain of the wounds on my torn back hardened my heart toward my father as I lay on my stomach on the couch in my bedroom after my beating. I struggled to breathe; each inhale made the gashes stretch and ache. At least I had not given him the satisfaction of seeing any tears. I had drawn upon all my training from Cearnaigh to block the emotional pain, which was far worse than the physical pain.

The MacEgans spared no time in telling of my escapade. At school, three days later, I was greeted with whispers and stares.

Many students appeared scared of me, and I heard the word "mad" more than once during the day as I passed clusters of students. What hurt so much about the whole situation was that I rode into the moors on the nights of the festivals to protect the same people who called me "mad" for doing so. Ah…the heavy price of such a secret.

And…the rumors continued. On February 1, the night of Imbolc, my father was out of the country on business—fortunate for me. Dressed in my parka, thick clothes, and snow boots, I was prepared for the winter weather advisory the forecasters had given. Kheelan had his horseshoes pulled a month ago to prepare him for the hard winter ground, and I had fastened a waterproof, heavy turnout blanket around his midsection to help insulate him against the cold.

As I wondered which direction to head, I closed my eyes and visualized the double-headed dragons, lurking within the Alorcán faeries. My Siridean senses were growing, and I perceived faerie activity opposite from Delaney territory. Kheelan and I took to the moors, deep into Kavanaugh country.

At the border between Clan Kavanaugh and Clan Ó Raogáin lands, which was not so far from the outskirts of Blackrock, a skirmish unfolded—four Alorcán faeries against one Maolán. The lone Maolán soldier was battered and wouldn't hold out much longer. I kicked Kheelan into high gear, and he galloped toward the fray. When we neared the fighters, I brought up my taggert and shot an Alorcán in the neck. The creature fell to the ground, out of commission. I tried for another one with the blowgun, but the dart was dodged by a hulking faerie and traveled off course. The three faeries now faced me, one of them holding the injured Maolán faerie by the throat.

Kheelan roared with a wrangling snort and pawed the ground before he reared up on his hind legs, kicking out toward our enemies. While Kheelan come down on all four legs, I cautioned the three, "Let the faerie go." I pointed my taggert toward the Alorcán on the far left. "Do it, now!" I yelled.

The Maolán was shoved to the ground, and a dagger hurdled through the air toward my chest. "Shield," I called out to the hawthorn while the marking wove onto my face. Instead of an actual shield appearing in my hand, the dagger seemed to hit a wall a foot in front of Kheelan, and the weapon dropped to the ground. "Huh!" I said, shocked and relieved. "Good to know," I said to myself, impressed with my new armor.

The three Alorcán troops sped away. I pushed Kheelan forward and brought up my taggert, shooting one of the retreating scoundrels in the back. The Maolán faerie behind me called out for help. I scowled at the two running away. Maybe I'd catch up with them later. Wheeling Kheelan around, I rushed back to the troop and dismounted. At the hawthorn tree, I drew down my pouch and opened my eyes. "Hold still," I told the young man. "This ought to fix you up." I lifted his shirt and rubbed Diaga dust into his wounds. He arched and moaned as the wounds closed. Then he sat up and shivered.

"*Go raibh maith agat* [Thank you], Siridean," he exclaimed.

"You're welcome. Now come on, let's get you out of here." I offered him a hand to help him up. "Which direction is the thin place?"

He pointed west. I helped him up into the saddle. Then I vaulted up behind him and we set off. "What's your name, soldier?"

"Curran Delaney."

"Nice to meet you, cousin. I'm Aishling Delaney."

"I know. The Siridean," he smiled and shook his head.

"That's what they tell me," I smiled back.

"None of 'em will believe I met ya. Ye're like a *duine cailiuil* [celebrity] in Mag Mell."

"Just tell Cearnaigh that Aishling said she was ready for Cloak Handling 102."

He turned and smiled again.

I could feel the lure of the Otherworld and I reined Kheelan in. "This is as far as we go, Curran. Glad to have met you."

"Likewise, Siridean." He jumped down and turned to bow to me. Then Kheelan and I turned back the way we had come.

A little later, the snow descended in a frenzy of wind and pelting ice crystals. I pulled on my fleece facemask and goggles. As I readied to push Kheelan toward home, three more Alorcán, in addition to the two escapees from earlier, attacked us. Dipping my hand in the pouch, I grabbed a handful of dust and slung it in the faces of two of the closest faeries. They went down.

The other three moved in on me. I called my dagger from the tree and leaned down to plunge it into the faerie clawing at my leg. The remaining two pulled me to the ground with my back pressed up against Kheelan's side. One caught me in the cheek with a right hook while the other creature rammed his fist into my stomach. I struggled for breath.

In my mind, I grabbed my sword. It appeared in my hand, and I slashed into the arm of the faerie on my right; the other faerie belted me so hard in the stomach again, I landed flat on my back in the snow. My sword flew into the icy drifts. I called it back just as the faerie started to jump on me, and I brought the sword up to thrust through the beast. Settling on my hands and knees, I coughed up blood.

I needed to finish off the wounded faerie on the other side of Kheelan. Staggering to my feet, I stood over the beast and thrust the sword down into its chest. Then I fell to my knees again as the snow whirled around me. Falling face forward into the snow, I let the cold numb the aches. I knew if I didn't get up soon, I'd die there. But I couldn't move.

Kheelan saved my life. He kept nudging and nudging me with his head until I stirred. Then he lowered himself to the ground so I could crawl onto his back.

When I woke up, I was in a hospital bed hooked up to beeping machines. Uncle Brádach was holding my hand, but he had nodded off to sleep. The face of a hulking angel floated through my mind. Maybe I'd dreamed it; I shook my head. But then I recalled a brief time on the edge of Blackrock where I had opened my eyes and seen the angel, leading Kheelan toward the city center.

I tried to sit up but I yelped in pain and fell backward onto the pillow. Uncle Brádach jerked awake.

"Aishling, what happened?"

Panicked, I looked around the room. "Father doesn't know I'm here, does he?"

"No, child. Stop yer frettin'." He grasped my hand with both of his. "Someone from the hospital called yer home, but Sullie answered. He contacted me. Said it was best to leave yer father out o' this if we could. I told him I'd come tend to ya."

"Thank you," I grimaced as I shifted in the bed. "How did I get here?"

"Kheelan came prancin' through the middle of Blackrock with you unconscious, barely clinging to his back. Night cop called in the cavalry and brought you in. Kheelan's tied up at the fire station."

I stared at the ceiling. *What a mess!* "When can I get out of here?"

"Not for a few days, I'm sure," he estimated. "Let's see. Your list of injuries would be: hypothermia, broken ribs, internal bleeding, concussion, a gash in the leg that required thirty stitches and a blood transfusion. Shall I go on? There's more."

"Eh," I babbled. "I get the point." I blew my bangs out of my eyes. I was unsure how to use the dust of Diaga on these types of injuries; I'd have to ask Cearnaigh.

A nurse walked in to check the I.V. bags. *Great...just great!* I scooted down in the bed, like I could hide. *As if I'm not already the biggest freak in school!* I recognized the nurse as one of the cheerleader moms from Dundalk Academy. I wondered over her assessment of this incident—me in full winter gear with goggles still resting on my forehead a couple of hours before dawn, clothes bloody, face black and blue. And if she had heard about the horse...?

I didn't look at her directly. Soon she left.

"Yer father's gone for the week, but he'll be back, Aishling. Ya know he'll be hearin' 'bout this debacle from someone."

Terror scratched at my face and hysteria boiled inside me. "He can't find out," I squeaked. Tears fell.

"Calm down, lass. Maybe we can keep it from him." Taking off his tweed walking hat, he swiped his hand across the top of his head. "But, Aishling, why were ya out in the moors again, especially on a night like this? Ya could've been killed. Do ya know how crazy worried that makes me?"

"I'm sorry. I'm so sorry, Uncle Brádach, but I have no other choice."

He huffed out a breath and locked his eyes with mine. "Morrighan call ya out there for some reason?" his voice cracked.

I looked away from his torment. I hated what this was doing to him. Shifting in the bed, I winced and whimpered.

"You need more pain medicine," he insisted.

I inhaled a shallow breath and flinched. "No."

"Alright, stubborn lass. Get some rest. We'll finish this conversation when ye're well."

When that monumental year ended, and Patrick returned to Ireland, my black and white turned to a million shades of gray. My normal carefree summer turned dark in the shadow of Patrick's confession—sowing un-Patrick-like oats as if he'd left his values behind when he went to the states. It deluged both our lives with the kinds of stains that don't ever quite fade from one's spirit.

"The clans expect an honorable marriage between us, Patrick," I spat at him, turning to stomp down to the River Fane. Not to mention the fact that I loved him—and I thought he loved me. How could he do this? He dragged his way to the water. I could hear the pebbles crunching behind me as he stopped.

"Asher, I'm sorry. I don't know what else to say," he mumbled, reaching out to touch my shoulder.

With the unwanted contact, I wheeled on him. "How dare you touch me!" My volatile temper leapt outward, and I shoved Patrick back several feet. Tears sprang to his eyes, revealing emotions I'd never seen him display. I stared at him, not believing what I was seeing. He was broken. My Patrick was broken, and I didn't know what to do. I was the betrayed one here.

With my eyes and body firing, I shoved down my compassion and looked back at him. "I waited for you for a year. A year! Keeping the marriage alliance strong because that was what I wanted. I wanted you!" Pacing by the river, I continued my tirade. "Sure, we were betrothed from a young age, but you've always been my friend, Patrick, and I love you. Friend love turned into more-than-friend love over the years—for me at least. I mean nothing to you!" The core of my heart met the disillusionment of what I had always assumed to be my balance—my center. Crossing my arms over my chest, I stared up into the gathering night, too angry to let the scorching tears flow. "Does this American tramp even know you have a fiancé?"

He took several steps toward me before my gaze lowered, pinning him in place about four feet away. "I was so stupid," he babbled, running his hands through his hair. In obvious pain he continued, "It was as if my body and mind were possessed by demons this past year. I would never intentionally hurt you, yet I did in the worst way. I don't know what to do."

"What are you going to say to your family? What will you tell my father?" I stewed.

"I don't know," he groaned. "Help me, Asher."

"Help you? Oh no! This one's all on you." This time I got up in his face. "Help you? Help me, Patrick. Help me explain to our people that their future High King has lived with a woman for the past year—a woman who is not Irish and not his betrothed.

Help me explain to them that this king's firstborn is not of full Irish lineage and, again, not by his betrothed! You disgust me!" With that, I turned and ran into the castle.

Over the next few months, after his confession, Patrick had scoured the borders of our broken relationship to try to reclaim the shards of trust he had shattered so carelessly. Ultimately this was his quest, and I'd resigned myself to the fact that I couldn't join him there. I didn't have the strength to pick up these pieces for him, knowing that many of the fragments would forever remain buried. Whether or not light would ever shine again through our now stained-glass love story was yet to be seen.

He was never the same after that year. Guilt will do that to a person—take the heart captive and trample the soul.

9

Fire Tetrahedron

(Rafe)

Idied that night—the night I found her—the man I used to be buried beneath the blanket of snow we were standing in. Displaced in the moment, her eyes embraced me, and I realized I would never be the man I once was.

This is the story about the night I began to inhabit a new time, a new place. This was the night I found harmony in a world that was destroying itself, the night my soul was rescued from the very pits of hell. When I met my first human angel. For an angel is simply a messenger, and she had delivered a very vital message to me that fateful night: hope. Everything that could fuel a fire converged, igniting a chain reaction so forceful that my existence was permanently altered.

Where there is fire, there are demons. And Almeria, Spain, had plenty of fires this particular night—hundreds upon hundreds of bonfires. You're probably asking yourself, "Why would anyone choose chaos over peace?" I'll get to that part of my story later. Right now I want to tell you how I began my crawl out of the fire.

It was December 21 and the celebration of Hogueras. The city was animated, full of energy. This festival marked the beginning of winter, and it was the shortest day of the year.

Standing in the city square, I was in a perfect position to witness the colorful panorama in all directions, but I was having trouble focusing. I was disoriented and my mind was twisted: the result of too much time spent with the filth of the underworld.

Brilliant fireworks lit the night sky while gigantic, wooden holiday statues, constructed just for this festival, were set ablaze. Small bonfires were also set throughout the city for the fire jumpers. According to the custom, fire jumping was done as a symbolic shield against anything evil, including demonic possession or illness. If the festivalgoers knew how many demons had crawled out of the fires and were lurking all throughout the city, they would have run in terror.

Moving through the square, I tried to see the colors of the scene, but I saw only varying shades of black and gray. The laughter of the children surrounding me was nonexistent, as if I were deaf to happy sounds. How much longer would I be able to survive this black abyss in my soul? Satariel, the dark one, had sent me—told me to have a little fun, get into some mischief. The devil can always hope, right? I was disappointing him greatly with the amount of trouble I was not inciting or engaging in. But my heart had not been completely incinerated in the flames; I knew to whom it belonged.

Thousands of people had turned out for the festival despite the inclement weather. There had to be six inches of snow already on the ground. Lifting my face to the sky, I watched the huge flakes continuing their freefall to earth. White, pure. My gaze sagged to the ground. I knew I would never be that being again. I was sin's blackest stain.

The crowd pressed in, and I made my way through the square, rambling among the mini heaps of fire. I stopped in front of a massive pyre that was shooting flames and smoke high into the air toward the heavens. Staring at the statues of Christmas angels, I thought about how ironic it was, for I was that being: a burning angel. For a long time, I stood and watched the inferno. Then I moved closer and closer to the flames; the statue now was melted beyond recognition, eaten by the blaze.

Having smelled the burning flesh of the scorching demons inside the fire, I stepped forward to rejoin them in the flames. After all, that was where I belonged, and I deserved to serve out my eternal sentence. The fire was reflecting in my eyes. I could feel the flames licking my skin, drawing me in. Yet, before I could step any farther, two men moved in to restrain me. After they pushed me to the ground and rolled me, smothering my fiery clothing, I surged to my feet and sprinted from the scene.

Pushing through the crowds, I made my escape down a dark alley and paused there to refocus. There was an echo of clinking bells, and I turned toward the sound. Time seemed to slow down and speed up in sporadic bursts. Moving toward the festive lights at the end of the passageway, I followed the call of the resonating music. I made my way over to a choir standing near the great fountain and listened as they sang the carol "I Heard the Bells on Christmas Day." I felt the first stirrings of hope within my soul, as the words of the song pierced me:

And in despair I bowed my head:
"There is no peace on earth," I said,
For hate is strong and mocks the song
Of peace on earth, good will to men.

Then pealed the bells more loud and deep:
He is not dead, nor doth He sleep;
The wrong shall fail, the right prevail,
With peace on earth, good will to men.

The lyrics moved me, and I desperately searched hearts. Hope had eluded me for so long that I had to find out: Was there any good left in the world? Satariel wanted us demons to use the knowledge we acquired from heart searching to his advantage, and I was weary of his schemes.

While probing souls I pushed through the crowds. I ran toward the majestic cathedral, and I could see the light pouring through the vivid stained glass reflecting off the snow, which turned the white powder into a pirate's treasure of rubies, emeralds, sapphires, and amethysts. An orchestra was getting ready to play beside the nativity scene. I turned in a maddening circle, still searching hearts. I knew I shouldn't have been this close to a place of virtue. I knew I was standing on sacred ground, but....

It was then that the piano plinked the first soft notes of "O Holy Night." It was as if a powerful light was pulling me toward the music; my ears became opened, and I could hear the sweet melody of a tune I had once sung myself in the heavenly chorus. While the beacon reached out to me and I grabbed hold, I saw her step in front of the piano, lift her bow in the air, and glide it gracefully across the fiddle held tightly to her chin.

Delving into the deep chambers of her fascinating heart while she played, I found hope, compassion, love, and beauty. The girl was maybe sixteen or seventeen, and she was the most exquisite creature I'd ever seen.

Her eyelashes drifted to her cheeks as the music built. At the crescendo toward the end of the piece, her eyes opened and were transfixed on mine, as if she knew the power I held. As if she knew I was invading her personal space even though I was standing a good fifty feet beyond the crowd and was partially shielded behind a giant fir tree. When the last note finished, echoing against the walls of the small courtyard, thunderous applause broke out for her, and she bowed with her eyes cast low to the awestruck crowd.

When the next song began, I ducked between the tree and the stone wall and tried to fight back these unfamiliar emotions, but that was just one more lost battle I'd tried to win on my own. While my tears overflowed, I determined to fight my way out of the fire where Satariel endlessly scorched my body and soul. I'd have to accelerate my search for the new captain of the angel army and plead with him to take my case to the archangel before the deceiver found me and put me back into my smoldering cage. He had lengthened my chain a bit since those first years, but I was still being watched, although not as closely anymore.

I didn't understand how she found me there amid all the noise and the darkness of my current refuge. Lying facedown in the snow and gasping for air to quiet my audible grief, I felt a light touch on my shoulder. In swift motion my back clung to the wall like the cornered animal I was, and I stared into the most angelic face I had seen—well, in too long.

From my crouched position, I watched as she dropped to the ground in front of me. Her onyx hair billowed around her like the waves of the ocean on a moonless night. In the dim light of my shelter, her cobalt eyes seemed to illuminate the shadows, and I was mesmerized, spellbound. I had never seen it before outside of rocks and caverns, but this angel's eyes were in the shape of the Star of Ceylon, a feature that would have been undetected by mortals. A twelve-rayed star fanned out from the center of her eyes just like in the star sapphire. The eyes suggested she was otherworldly, and I sensed a difference in her molecular structure from the humans surrounding us.

"You are in despair," she said, with a melodic cadence and an empathetic brow. She reached out to hold my hand, and I felt warmth. Not the flaming-fires-of-hell-kind of heat that I had been living in for over a decade, but the warmth of compassion, of human contact. "You seem lost. What can I do to help you?" she tried again, her tone soothing.

This seraph was sincerely concerned about me, the spawn of hell.

"Are you cold? Can I offer you some food, maybe get you shelter for the night?"

As I got to my feet, she stood with me—still connected, still reaching out to me to try to ease my burden. The snow was blowing harder now. The crowds had moved on back to the city square for the lighting of the monumental Christmas tree. The only sounds now were the sleet bouncing off the windows and the echo of my own heart locking into place, like the sound a safe makes when the code is cracked and it is opened. Somehow I knew I would be forever linked with this magnificent mortal.

We emerged from the shadows, and I couldn't hold back my strengthening smile. Her return smile was so radiant, I felt as if the warmth of daybreak had cascaded across my long-too-cold heart.

"Thank you for the offer, but you've already given me everything I need and more. I'll never forget your kindness."

With humility and grace, she nodded, and I watched her stroll away—an angel walking among us.

The snow soon captured her in its dizzying whirl. "Aishling," I whispered as I watched her disappear around the side of the imposing fortress. An image slammed into my mind, and I pitched forward onto my knees in the wet snow. A young girl. Soulful, blue eyes. A tunnel. The music box. As the tune I once heard played in my mind, the demons roared, competing with the wistful strain. I grabbed my head to take the edge off the mind-racking assault and turned onto my back to lie in the frozen powder. Staring up into the tumbling snow had a calming effect on me, and the cold seemed to silence the predators within. As my body temperature dropped and my mind was able to rest, I drifted with the snow into a peculiar dreamworld where devils and demons didn't roam free, hell was only a myth, and an angel with streaming, black hair guided me toward the light of a new dawn.

10

Hogueras

(Aishling)

On my sixteenth birthday, I was away at Trinity College in Dublin for my first year of college. I had gone to an advanced private school, and with the help of tutors, I had been able to graduate from high school a year early, as had Patrick and Claire. She and I were roommates, and I was thankful she was not a light sleeper. Otherwise my leaving at midnight would have prompted a lot of awkward questions.

I went for a stroll in the shadows on the edge of campus, and Morrighan met me there. She told me she had given me a chainmail suit of armor for my birthday, so I could now access it from the hawthorn.

Ever grateful for my eccentric gifts, I bowed before the war faerie, but she remained as aloof as ever, disappearing into the shadows without a backward glance. I headed back to my dorm and smiled on the way, remembering the text message I had received from Patrick a few days earlier. He had asked if he could fly in and go with me to meet Morrighan. I had promptly returned his message with a capital "NO," explaining that she would not allow it. He was disappointed, but who was I to challenge a faerie's command?

November and December were hectic as I tried to juggle college classwork with orchestra practice. The Trinity College Orchestra had been chosen to perform at the Hogueras Festival in Almeria, Spain, on December 21. Being a college freshman at the prestigious Trinity College at the age of sixteen was an accomplishment, but being chosen as the lead violinist for the festival was probably the highest honor of my life.

We landed in Almeria in the late evening on December 20. As I exited the terminal, I wrapped my thigh-length, navy-blue admiral coat around me to fend off the arctic wind, and I tugged my matching newsboy hat down over my ears. I had hoped to have the mild, summerlike weather that was typical for this area of Spain even in December, but as luck would have it, we left snow in Ireland only to find the potential for it the next day in this place a thousand miles away.

A local bus transported us to the Hotel Vincci Mediterraneo. On the way I caught glimpses of the ocean at twilight as we sped through the city. I was so excited! We were going to tour Almeria the next day, followed by the performance of my life that night.

I felt awkward leaving my orchestra friends behind once we entered the hotel, but by then they were accustomed to my being surrounded by guards. My bodyguard, Brógán, and I were headed to the suite on the top floor; it had a private elevator that could be locked down once we were in the room. Of course in case of fire, there was also an emergency door in the room that led to a stairwell. I had overheard the manager telling Brógán in the lobby earlier that the door was as thick as a bank vault's.

Once we arrived at the sixth floor, Brógán drew his gun, locked me in the elevator, and completed his security sweep before allowing me into the room. To the left of the elevator, there was a kitchen with a massive wall of glass that overlooked the ocean. There was a large living room with crimson couches and a mega television that took up a major portion of the wall between the two bedrooms. Despite the fact that there was an extra room, he chose the couch nearest my room and dropped his things there, carried my bags to my closet, and then locked the elevator.

I was comfortable with Brógán; he had been my personal guard for three years. He was like a big, militant brother ready for combat, especially when it came to boys who showed interest in me and were not named Patrick Kavanaugh. He had orders from my father.

Weariness and a chill I couldn't escape overtook me; all I could think about was getting into a hot shower. Once I had chased away the cold under the steamy spray, I pulled on my fleece pajamas and stepped out of my room to explore a little bit and see if there might be some hot cocoa in the kitchen. A quick search through the cabinets revealed only coffee. Disappointed, I decided I'd just have to curl up in bed to get warm. Brógán was laying his weapons on the coffee table as I finished my survey of our suite.

"This place is something else!" I skipped across the living room. "You have a king-sized bed in there. It's a shame to let it go to waste," I said, urging him to get a more comfortable night's rest.

"And miss savin' yer hide if some *diabhalóir* [devil] comes barrelin' through that window?" he said, pointing his revolver toward the glass wall in the kitchen. "Not on yer life," he said, raising his gun toward the ceiling and cocking it.

"I can take care of myself, you know." As soon as the last word left my mouth, his laughter ricocheted off the walls. He really had no idea. I let him believe I was defenseless; it helped him feel more macho, I guessed.

"Good one, Aish." His knife made a grating noise as he ran it up and down a sharpener.

"Believe what you want, Brógán. It may just be *me* saving *your* hide someday," I said smugly and proceeded to my room. "Have a pleasant night on the couch then." Closing the door, I could still hear him laughing. I did a double back somersault and landed in the center of the bed. Smoothing back the covers, I had the last laugh as I snuggled into the warmth.

I was drifting off to sleep when my phone buzzed. The incoming text was from Patrick. "Have you arrived yet?"

"Yes. Very tired, though," I replied.

"Well, happy dreams then. *Ádhraím thú, mo bogadán crua!*" [I adore you, my tender-hearted toughie!]

"Love you, Patrick."

"Love you too."

I placed the phone back on the stand and smiled, but only halfheartedly.

It was said that Hogueras was the night the devil came out to play. Well, I had not seen the evil creature with the pitchfork surface yet, and I didn't think the devil himself could ruin this night. My nerves were a tiny bit frazzled as I helped the other orchestra members set up for the concert. I could hardly think of anything else. The notes and the melodies I would be performing during my solos soared through my mind in an unrelenting, repetitive loop.

It was cold out in front of the Alcazaba Fortress and cathedral, where we would be performing. From that height on the hill, I could look out and see the whole whitewashed city of Almeria, skirted by the Mediterranean Sea beyond. This was just my second trip outside of Ireland. It was one of the greatest adventures of my life except for the fact that Brógán had to accompany me everywhere. He was all right, I guessed, as far as bodyguards went. He was in his midthirties and not entirely out of touch with what made teenagers tick.

Following the setup our group spent the remainder of the morning visiting the sites of Almeria. We explored the winding streets and admired the unique architecture in route to the art museum. After spending an hour there, it seemed we wandered into every shop along the main thoroughfare. I bought Uncle Brádach an authentic-looking bullfight poster with his name listed as the matador. He'd get a kick out of that, I was sure. And I bought Claire a locally-made red flamenco dress with black polka dots that she was going to flip over. After loading up on souvenirs and eating at a quaint café near the promenade, we wandered down to the beach.

It was uncharacteristically cold for that area of Spain, or so the tour guide had told us earlier, and the snow clouds were thickening over the city. I was thankful that our conductor had recommended we bring coats with us. City workers were setting up stacks of wood all along the beach in preparation for the week's activities. I had never heard of such a strange custom, but fire jumping was a popular facet of the Hogueras Festival, and I was curious to watch.

By evening, the snow had frosted the cityscape with hues of white and ice blue. Our orchestra group, with Brógán tagging along close behind me, had just finished watching the parade and the burning of some of the giant holiday statues, and we were making our way to the cathedral for the Christmas performance. We passed so many bonfires on our way and watched as individuals sped toward them, hurdling the flames. I wondered if Brógán would allow me to do some fire jumping after the concert. But as quickly as the thought came, I knew the answer. He would insist on returning to the hotel. He was way too protective, but as he had informed me on numerous occasions, he was just doing his job. I knew deep down, though, that it was more than just an obligation to him. Since the day we had met three years earlier, he had treated me like a little sister, shielding me from even the tiniest hints of danger.

Hundreds of people awaiting the concert had filled the pavilion in the courtyard of the cathedral. Cheery fires danced in the fireplaces down each wall, providing heat for the guests. The snow was tapering to a slow pace, and my heart started thumping in double time. I'd never played before such a large crowd. Our high school concerts had not been well attended by the community back home in Blackrock.

By the time the concert was in full swing that night, my nerves were still cooperating. When it came time for my main solo, I strolled to the front of the piano and lifted my bow. Tuning out the crowd, I closed my eyes and let my heart play the music I had stored in my head from a young age.

"O, holy night, the stars are brightly shining…"

A strange sensation pricked me as the last note faded, and I could hear the music of my childhood coming from somewhere. It sounded like the song of my music box that I had buried in the tunnels underneath the castle not many years after my mom had died; but instead of instrumental music, it was as if the tune were being hummed in a familiar bass voice. I'd not heard those sad notes in years, and it made no sense that I was hearing them here and now.

When I opened my eyes I saw him, and the music became louder, stronger. He looked as if he heard and felt the music too. The young man, who looked to be around nineteen, towered over everyone in the vicinity—his combative stance like that of a fighter with nothing to lose. Most puzzling were his fire-ravaged clothes and his kind, remorseful eyes—intensely focused on me. As I returned his stare, he ducked behind one of the snow-covered pine trees near the edge of the cathedral. My solo had been a peaceful tune. So what had caused such a forceful reaction? I wondered.

As soon as my concert was finished, I rushed to the area where I'd seen him, hoping he'd still be there. I had the feeling that I knew him somehow, or that I should have known him. The vague picture danced around the edges of my memory, refusing to come into the light. I called Brógán off, and he stood at a distance where he could see me in case I needed assistance, but he was far enough away to give me some privacy.

When I approached the tree, I heard heart-wrenching weeping, and I reached out to touch the man. He seemed surprised that I had come to him. A shifting stirred inside me, and I ached to ease his despair. When I asked him if there were anything I could do to help him, he just smiled but kept crying even though the smile was soon overpowering the tears. He was so ruggedly handsome, I couldn't help but stare. Soon his smile turned to laughter, which for a moment seemed awkward, but I figured he was laughing at my involuntary gawking.

We both stood at the same time, and he reached out to hold my hand. The snow was starting to fall harder again, forming a crystalline veil between us, making the memory I had of him even fuzzier. I couldn't hold on to it—that tiny fragment of familiarity—the fact that I should have known this man. About that time his hand sparked in mine, and I pulled away, lost for a moment in his gaze. He thanked me for checking on him, and I nodded and dragged myself away. I even thought I heard him whisper my name. My mind must have been playing tricks on me.

Turning the corner in front of the fortress, I had a strong urge within me to turn around and go back to him. I stopped to consider, even looking over my shoulder as I wrestled within myself, but after a brief moment I continued on my way. Shaking my head I thought about how inappropriate it would be, not to mention that something about him frightened me. When he and I had first seen each other, I was not so sure it was love at first sight as much as it was a stirring within me that he and I were connected in some cosmic way that was still to be unearthed. It was a knowledge that we'd somehow been involved, maybe in a parallel realm or another time period. There was a big part of me that was rooted to him in ways that didn't yet make sense— and a big part of me that loved him beyond reason without even knowing his name.

11

The Follow-Through

(Aishling)

The following morning our bundled-up group took a stroll under the palm trees at Nicolás Salmerón Park, which ran along the seashore. The waves were angry, announcing their displeasure to the lingering snow clouds. I was not quite myself either—the waves and the sky mirrored my mood. The memory of the intriguing stranger from the cathedral had not released me throughout the long night. I felt a growing sadness that I'd probably never know who he was or recall the memory that had evaded me when I had first seen him.

Most of the group rushed to the beach, but I hung back, choosing to sit on a bench on the promenade above the sea. Brógán was a comfortable distance away, always watching, making sure I was safe.

Amazingly, as if I had summoned him from my intense thoughts, I saw the stranger approaching me from the beach, his eyes searching mine. My gaze only left his long enough to call off my bodyguard. When I turned back, I watched as the wind lifted and a snow devil whirled around him, but he was a stronger force and moved toward me unfazed. My lips parted in a sigh, and the cold air slammed into my lungs, leaving me breathless.

I noticed that my mystery man had found some new clothes somewhere. In place of a fire-tattered rogue was the most attractive specimen of mankind ever created: sculpture-perfect handsome, wearing a long, charcoal-gray peacoat, jeans, and black biker boots. His shoulder-length, wavy hair, the color of coffee beans, was charmingly tousled by the wind. His naturally tanned face revealed devil-may-care dimples that, accompanied by his rebellious smile, said to me, "Yes, I'm potentially break-your-heart dangerous."

But the way he now stood in front of me almost defenseless, and the way his copper-brown eyes spoke to me almost seemed to say, "I would never harm you. I'd fight the devil himself first." The eyes tell a lot about a person, and his burned into mine, willing me to put my trust in him but also luring me to fling caution into the turbulent waves. His eyes gave the illusion of a lion's pride stalking through the tall, brown grass at sunset. They told a tale of innocence as well as temptation in a single glance. The pull was too strong. I had to look away.

Blocking the worst of the wind from my face, he asked, "May I sit down?"

The closer he drew to me, the greater the physical force compelled me, and I had to look up. His smile was charming as he looked to the ground before returning my gaze.

"Sure," I replied, feeling the first stirrings of hope that I might get answers to my questions but also that this strikingly attractive man just might find me attractive too.

As he sat beside me, he looked over his shoulder and nodded toward Brógán as if acknowledging and accepting his authority over me. He then turned to face me, charming me with such a rich smile that I couldn't help but reciprocate. My smile was so instantaneous that it took me off guard. We both nervously laughed and looked toward the sea, needing a moment to recover.

"I'm sorry you had to see me that way at the cathedral last night," he said, looking sheepish. "I've had a bit of emotional turbulence lately. I didn't mean to disrupt your moving performance."

"You didn't interfere," I spouted, trying to put him at ease. "I was worried about you, that's all. You seemed so lost."

"Let's just say that now I'm found," he said, smiling as he edged a little closer to me.

"Do you want to talk with someone about what was bothering you? I'm a good listener. I could try to help."

He shook his head, looking toward my boots. "I had a decision to make. The follow-through with an important choice always brings clarity of mind and heart. I'll be fine now, I promise," he said, turning one of those potent smiles on me once again. I could have literally fainted at one mere glance from him.

"I feel…" I started, almost admitting the feelings I'd had as I'd left the cathedral the night before, but thankfully I caught myself. "I don't even know your name," I said instead.

"Raphael," he said, reaching out to lift my hand and brush his lips across my knuckles. "It's a pleasure to meet you, Aishling Delaney." His eyes captivated me. Neither of us said a word as he held me under some kind of spell.

When I was able to breathe the words, I whispered with both unease and thrill warring within me, "How do you know my name?"

"I have friends in really low places," he said in a teasing tone. When the look of shock did not leave my face, he said, "You were the star last night, remember? They were handing out programs to the show. Your name was an easy find."

"Oh," I said, crinkling my brow.

"And what are you feeling? You started to say something earlier but stopped yourself. I'd like to know," he said, inching even closer to me as the wind kicked up.

I felt the heat of embarrassment spread through my body, and I knew that my face was giving me away in the most vulnerable moment of my life. "Never mind," I said, hoping he would drop it.

"All right then. I'll tell you what I'm feeling, but I need you to look at me while I say it."

My gaze ascended to his gorgeous face, as he revealed more words that stunned me.

"When I saw you last night, there was some kind of force drawing me to you that I couldn't explain. I thought about it all night, but the feelings didn't produce any truth on the matter. You are the most exquisite creation I have ever witnessed, but that doesn't explain the feeling that pulled me to you at first. Do you understand any of this?"

A screaming blush raged across my face, and his admission bolstered my confidence enough for me to make my own confession. "I had a similar feeling, and it kept me awake last night too. There's something there," I said. Fear took hold of my heart, shaking my joy in this bizarre yet unbelievably blissful moment.

Right in the middle of one of the most life-altering discussions of my existence, I was forced to leave him. The orchestra members ran toward the promenade, shivering, obviously ready to be out of the cold.

"It appears that I have to go, Raphael," I said reluctantly.

He let go of my hand, and we stood, meandering to the place where my group was now assembled by the dancing fountain.

"I'll catch up with you later, Aishling," he said, smiling that roguish grin of his that made my heart dance.

"Oh yeah? And how do you plan on accomplishing this feat?" I challenged him, backing toward my group as he made his way to the beach.

"A group as large as yours sticks out like—"

"Like what, Raphael?" I smiled, enjoying our banter.

Shrugging his shoulders he said, "Like a faerie on Beltaine, Miss Delaney." I was speechless at his reference to my other life. Did he know about *me*? How could he? As I paused he lifted his fingers to his temple, and then with a mock salute he turned and jogged toward the sea.

When my group stopped to eat lunch at the Bistro La Plaza, I looked for him. Through the frosted window, I searched the passersby on the sidewalk, hoping to catch a glimpse of the one who was dominating my thoughts. No such luck. During my afternoon nap, I dreamed of him.

For supper the orchestra dined at the famous Bello Rincón restaurant. The scenery from our window seat was breathtaking.

To my left a massive stone mountain swallowed up the view, and the sea crashed mercilessly into the base of it, sending shoots of water high into the sky. Even with the gray skies threatening more snow, the seagulls were soaring high above the waves. I turned away to search the faces of nearby diners. Still no Raphael. Every time the door opened, I looked. It was turning out to be an extremely long day with no sign of him to ease my mind.

We returned to the Hogueras Festival on the promenade for the second night of festivities. A popular Spanish alternative rock band was jamming by the dancing fountains. Two of my orchestra friends, Aela and Lasair, hung out with me in the standing crowd. A new song rumbled into gear and the driving beat had them jumping along with the rest of the masses while I stood motionless with my mind elsewhere.

Aela grabbed my arms, laughing. "What a rush! Aishling, come on—you're off P.K. duty right now. Feel the vibe." I watched as Lasair got caught up in the next song, her hands clapping to the inane beat and her long, red hair swinging over the top of her head back and forth.

"I'm trained not to feel the vibe," I said, ready to get away from the noise. "Hazard of being a parliament kid." As I started to turn, Aela looked over my shoulder and let out a slow whistle.

"*Ta tu guh halainn! Rábaire!* [He's beautiful! A strong, vigorous man!] Sexy hunk on the beach checking out our Aishling!" Aela purred as if she were on the prowl, ready to strike if I didn't. She yanked on my arm until I turned. Looking down at the sandy shoreline, I saw Raphael staring at me with that two-sided grin again, one side cocky and one side unsure of himself. I sighed and moved toward him in spite of myself. The very steady, sane side of my brain was saying "no" to me, but my more dormant side, the part I continually denied pleasure, said, "Oh yes!"

"Wait up!" yelled Aela, and Lasair followed her. "Yeah, we saw you with him this morning. He looked really into you." They turned toward each other, about to burst with excitement. "We just want a close-up view. You don't mind if we tag along, do you?"

"No problem," I said. We had wandered down the stairs when Brógán caught up to us, following about ten feet behind. I could see Raphael to my left, watching me. I looked his way and smiled before heading toward a small group of teens gathered around one of the bonfires. As the girls and I got lost in the crowd, Raphael moved in to stand next to me, touching his fingertips to the ends of mine. I closed my eyes as a sensation rocked me. I was so aware of him. I shuddered while he slipped his hand into mine. It felt like the most natural thing in the world.

"Good evening, Aishling," he leaned down to whisper in my ear. I closed my eyes, trying to calm myself. The crowd of teens gathered around us at the bonfire seemed to fade into the background, leaving just him and me.

After a moment I looked up at him and he winked. I bit my bottom lip as I smiled and forced my gaze away from him, back to the fire. "Hey, Raphael," I said, trying to go for nonchalant. But I was afraid he had already seen how much he affected me.

Bonfires were lit again all down the beach, lighting up the waves. Smoke and the scent of *suspiros de monja*, the Spanish equivalent of funnel cakes, lingered in the air.

"What's everybody doing with the papers?" I asked him.

"That's just one of the many legends of Hogueras. The Spanish believe that on this night, if you write down your heart's desires and toss the sheet into the fire, your dreams will all come true."

"Well, let's get to it," I said, smiling. "Got a sheet of paper?" Not moving his eyes from mine, he pulled a small notepad from his coat pocket, along with a pen. I looked down at his hands and looked back up to see his awesome grin. Sitting on the ground, he knelt beside me, handing me paper and pen. I wrote a few lines but had to stop when he started peeking over my shoulder. "If you look they won't come true!" I said, scolding him with mock Irish ire.

"Sorry! I'll make my own list," he said, flinching playfully.

About five minutes later, when we both were finished, we ceremoniously tossed the papers into the flames. Neither of us spoke as we watched the letters filled with our dreams fade to ash. We were sitting close together by the fire, toasting our hands.

I was still watching the flames when Raphael broke into my thoughts. "Why the bodyguard, Aishling? I feel as if he's shooting darts at me with his eyes."

My gaze roved to where Brógán was standing, ever watchful. "It's no big deal, really," I said, trying to downplay my bodyguard's role in my life. "My father's just overprotective." Instantly I felt guilty for telling a half-truth.

Raphael had become so quiet; I chanced a peek at him only to find him staring. I thought he must have known I wasn't being completely truthful with him, but then he said the oddest thing in phrasing that sounded more like I was having a conversation with Morrighan than someone who was only a few years older than I was.

"You intrigue me, Aishling Delaney. I must know you—every enchanting morsel, even the tiniest bits of information you may find tedious." I guess my blank look tipped him off. "Oh, that was too intense, wasn't it? I'm sorry. I have little practice when it comes to this sort of thing."

"That's surprising," I said. "You seem to be one of the most self-assured guys I've ever encountered. Yet at the same time, there is something so innocent about you, like you've just begun your journey on earth. And that combination fascinates me."

I felt tension pouring off him in choppy waves, so I attempted to redirect it into a ripple. "I *love* Butler's chocolate flake truffles." I smiled, trying to get him to relax. He looked up, confused. "You said not to spare even the most tedious morsels. Well, when you said morsels, I couldn't get truffles off my brain. I've only just discovered Butler's. It's unlucky for my jeans that it's within walking distance of my campus in Dublin. I've already gained a couple of pounds. Now, you see, that was probably TMI."

"TMI?" he prompted.

"Too much information," I offered. My eyebrow lifted in speculation.

"Oh no, not at all. That's exactly the kind of details I need. And by the way, your jeans look great on you."

"Uh…thanks!" I muttered, turning three shades of flustered.

"You're welcome. What else? Anything!"

"Well, let's see," I said, my finger on my lips as I thought. "I can sit down and read a book for twelve hours without moving from that exact spot except for maybe a short bathroom break. I know that's rather dull, but when I get wrapped up in a good book, I feel as if I'm transported somewhere else. I get to be someone else."

"Hmm. That makes me sad," he said, reaching out to play with my fingers.

"Why would that make you sad?"

"Not the reading part, but your last statement. Why would you want to be someone else? You seem perfect to me."

Dropping my head I played with the tiny rocks at my feet, tossing them one by one into the fire. "Most of the time I find reality too challenging," I finally replied. "I like to escape if only for a little while."

"Okay. I guess I can understand that."

I looked up to see my bodyguard approaching on the other side of the fire. He gave me the nod. It was time to go. Raphael and I stood together, brushing the snow and sand off our coats.

"Will I see you tomorrow?" I asked.

"I believe that is a certainty," he countered, smiling that slow, heated smile I loved. He reached out to brush my cheek with his fingertips, and I sighed as I turned to leave him.

When I was midway between him and Brógán, he called out, "Aishling?"

"Yeah?" I said, pivoting back to him.

"I forgot to tell you that the memories are coming back. I almost have you in my mind. I'm so close. I feel it."

Smiling, I nodded and then turned to march in the direction of my steaming guardian.

"All right, Aish, we're goin' to have a serious talk about this behavior," Brógán ranted as we hiked back to the hotel.

"Okay, we will talk about it, but not tonight, please! I'm tired, and I just need to be alone with my thoughts right now," I pleaded.

"Yer killin' me, lass," he rebuked. "All right, tomorrow then."

"Thanks, Brógán." We walked the rest of the way in silence.

That night, even with the cooler temperatures seeping into my room, I was sweating like it was summer. Maybe I had a fever, I thought as I tossed from side to side, trying to find a comfortable position. All at once there was fire in the room and blazes were crawling up the walls; the room was awash in bright reds, yellows, and oranges. The heat was overwhelming.

As I panicked, I saw Raphael charging toward me from a far-away place. He looked like a great medieval warrior, but he also had wings. Okay, now I was hallucinating for sure, but what a happy delusion it was! He gathered my sleeping body from the bed and covered me with some kind of cloak as he charged back with me in his arms the way he had come. I felt more protected and alive than I ever had in my existence. After a short while, I didn't feel the heat anymore. When we were out of harm's way, he pulled the cloak back and cradled me.

Something was really wrong in this scene. Raphael was the same age he had been when we'd met a few days earlier, but I was about six years old. I bolted upright in bed, darted into the restroom, and flipped on the light switch. As I heaved in air and looked at myself in the mirror, I was back to normal. There was no fire. I was sixteen, and I was in Spain for the festival, I reminded myself. While my breathing normalized, I tried to make sense of this. It seemed so much like a vision—so real—

but I had never had a vision before while I was asleep. No, this was a dream—pure and simple—a product of my overactive imagination and my growing infatuation with the tall, handsome stranger. My reflection smiled with me as I remembered how it had felt to be near him. I flicked off the light switch and crawled back into bed.

As if angels were caressing my brow, I fell into a deep slumber and dreamed of nothing but soaring through the clouds for the rest of the night.

12

Plaza de Toros

(Aishling)

The next morning I put on my jeans, sweater, and boots. Then I threw on my short black coat with the belted waist and brown faux-fur lining in the hood and completed my look with my favorite brown knitted hat. Smiling confidently and waiting for Raphael to surprise me sometime that day, I strolled with Brógán to the hotel restaurant for the complimentary breakfast.

A short time later, our group boarded the bus. We were heading to the Sierra Nevada mountains for some snow skiing. It was a fifty-minute ride up into the hills, and I was able to put off any serious discussions with Brógán by way of my iPod earbuds. As we pulled into the Alpine-style village of Pradollano and stopped near the entrance to the ski resort, I looked toward the newspaper kiosk on my side of the bus. Sitting on a bench, enjoying the morning paper, and smiling at me over the top of it was none other than Raphael. *How does he do that?* I wondered, shaking my head.

Aela inched up behind me in the aisle and whispered, "You have got to be the luckiest girl alive. I'm so jealous. See if he has any brothers or even a distant cousin."

"Okay," I said, smiling.

By the time I stepped off the bus, Brógán was already having a discussion with Raphael.

"I assure you I mean her no harm," Raphael was saying once I caught up to them. "If it would put your mind at ease, you can frisk me. I have no weapons."

"Well, I just might do that!" Brógán warned, balling his hands into fists at his sides.

"Cut it out!" I snapped at my guard. "Good morning," I said to Raphael.

"Good morning, Aishling," he reciprocated.

Turning to address Brógán, Raphael said, "I was hoping to accompany Aishling to the slopes, if it wouldn't be an imposition."

Brógán grudgingly relented. "All right," he barked, "but I'm watchin' ya." He moved with boldness into Raphael's personal space.

"Yes, sir. I understand," Raphael answered. "Shall we?" he asked me, pointing the way with his outstretched hand.

It was easy to ignore the fact that Brógán was with us at every turn when I was having such a perfect afternoon with Raphael. The one place we weren't followed was on the chairlifts. During those breathtaking rides up the mountain, Raphael would hold my hand and look me in the eyes as if trying to memorize my face for the coming months when we would be separated. We didn't speak of parting the next day. It was a subject filled with too much disenchantment.

When we met the group in front of the resort at the appointed time that afternoon, we were the last to arrive, much to Brógán's chagrin. We rounded the corner laughing and we spotted the orchestra conductor giving instructions to the group.

"Are you by chance going to the bullfight tonight at the Plaza de Toros?" Raphael inquired. The way he asked made it seem as if he were as anxious as I was for more time together.

"That just happens to be on our schedule for this evening," I said, smiling up at him.

"Most tourists will be there tonight, so I was hoping you'd be among them," he whispered as we neared the group, not wanting to interrupt the conductor. "I'll find you there." He touched my hand, and a spark ignited as he jogged toward the busy street.

I floated through the rest of the afternoon.

Following supper we left the restaurant and boarded the bus. I had a hard time hiding my enthusiasm from Brógán. We were sitting in our seats before he started in on one of his famous lectures to me about the intricacies of security—the speech I knew I had coming.

"Aish, ya know I could get fired for lettin' ya spend time with that fella, right?"

"Don't worry about job security so much, my friend. If my father ever fired you, the Kavanaughs would snatch you up. Your obsession with my safety is well documented and known throughout County Louth and beyond. Trust me on this."

"So ya don't like havin' me as yer bodyguard? Is that it?"

"Brógán! You know that's not true. You're my bodyguard *and* my friend. I don't mean to put you in uncomfortable positions. It's just that I feel so restrained all the time. I need to live a little. Don't you see?"

"I understand, Aish. It just makes guardin' ya that much harder when I can't be right wit' ya, like last night at the beach or today at the ski resort."

"Well, since we're having this open, adult conversation, I will tell you that Raphael is going to be at the bullfight, and there is no need to worry. He's a good guy."

"Ahh!" he groaned. The conversations occurring in the seats around us halted at his thunderous intrusion.

"Sorry," he said, grinning wolfishly at my peers with his clenched jaw straining.

As the chatter resumed, I looped my arm through his.

"Yer goin' to put me in an early grave, *óg cailín* [young lady]," he said, shaking his head.

"Thanks for understanding, Brógán." I squeezed his arm.

We pulled up in front of the Plaza de Toros. The stadium was in the heart of Almeria. Bullfighting seemed to be the pulse that electrified the city, so it was only natural that it would be at the center. Our group gathered around the large bull statue at the main entrance for a photo op before rushing to the gate.

An usher seated us in the lower balcony. The place was energy personified—multiplied times ten. Looking for Raphael was proving to be an impossible chore as the seats filled up and people stood to wander to the concessions or restrooms. I had saved him a seat on my right at the end of the aisle. Brógán occupied the seat behind where Raphael would be sitting.

While I looked for him, I took in my surroundings. It was a sensory overindulgence. Festive shawls in a garish array of colors and patterns were draped across the upper and lower balcony railings, encircling the entire oval. Someone was corralling a bull into a gate across the way. There were several horses galloping around on the dirt below, kicking up dust. The smell of fresh earth mingling with untamed animal rose from the floor.

Practicing in the oval there were at least a dozen matadors, wearing flamboyant costumes made up of the traditional embroidered short jackets worn with high-waisted pants and hats that looked like black-felt circles with stubby wings. The garments were tailored in elaborate scrollwork and patterns. Several stood out to me: one of royal blue and gold embroidery with cardinal accents and one of blood red with sunglow highlights. We had been waiting for fifteen minutes when the toreros who had been practicing exited the ring.

Not long afterward, the noise in the arena pitched to a deafening volume as the bullfighting entourage entered the arena to great fanfare. Three matadors, two lancers on horseback, and three banderilleros rushed in, their hands in the air, working the crowd. The banderilleros, according to the pamphlet I read, were bullfighters who placed barb-pointed, colorful flags on the top of the bull's shoulder. They were judged on their bravery as they attempted to run as close to the bull as possible without being gored or trampled. It all seemed so barbaric to me.

Amid the smiles and cheers of the crowd, the entourage focused their attentions on the ring while a mighty bull was released from a corner gate. The beast charged violently toward the matador in red. I was so involved in witnessing this new experience and biting my nails in fear for the men down below that I didn't notice that Raphael had slipped into the empty space to my right until he touched my arm. I jumped.

As I looked at him, the noise of the crowd grew dim, and the colors swirling all around us inflamed. I'm not sure how long we were caught up in the moment, but I know when it ended. Brógán leaned forward and cleared his throat right in my ear. I turned to scowl at him, and then I settled in my seat with Raphael very close beside me.

With the raucous blare of the masses, Raphael had to cup his hand around my ear so I could hear him. "I've missed you these past few hours," he breathed. A shiver worked its way down the length of my spine.

I shouldn't have been so thrilled to see him, but I couldn't stop the feelings parading through my heart. Patrick's betrayal still lay heavily on my mind. I wanted to bury the past in the past, but the skeletons kept resurrecting themselves. Every time I tried to picture myself married to him, I saw him with her: a faceless, nameless girl who had muddied my marital future and placed the Delaney clan in jeopardy.

Leaning over I whispered back, "I missed you too," and he reached to link his fingers with mine.

The bullfight was no match for the excitement building in me at Raphael's touch and his attentive manner. I turned my face away from his view, as if I were looking for someone in the crowd, so I could bite my lip to keep a happy sigh from escaping.

"Are you hungry?" he asked, drawing my attention back to him. "I passed a vender on the way in, selling fresh churros with lots of sugar."

"No. Thank you," I responded, not wanting to waste one second of our time together. "Do you live here in Almeria?" I asked.

"No. Just passin' through on my way back home."

"And where is home?"

"Home is more a feeling than a place, wouldn't you agree?" he stated, avoiding my question.

"Well, yes, but—"

"Oh look!" He pointed to the ring below, where a banderillero was placing a lemon-colored flag across a bucking bull's shoulder. I just knew that man was about to be trampled.

Covering my eyes I said, "I can't watch. I will pray for that man. Please don't tell me if it ends badly. Okay, Raphael?"

"Okay." He snickered.

As my lips moved in silent prayer, the roar of the crowd strengthened.

"You can open your eyes now," he said.

Looking at Raphael sideways, I opened one eye. "Are you sure? The bull didn't gore him or anything, did it?"

"See for yourself." He pointed toward the ring and smiled.

When I looked I saw the man in vivid tangerine clothing—who I'd been sure had just died—riding atop the massive beast as if it were a tamed horse. "Huh!" I exclaimed. "Well, would you look at that?"

We made small talk until a shout went up from the stands, and our attention was turned back to the events unfolding below. "*Estocada*! [death blow]" they yelled in unison. With their encouragement the matador thrust his sword into the bull, and the creature that had come out a short time ago with both fists flying now fell over dead.

"Ooh. Uhh," I said, covering my mouth with both hands.

"Gross enough for you?" He laughed.

"Poor bull," I said, my face scrunched up.

As the next bull was loosed into the pit, it went on the attack, dodging the banderilleros on its way to a matador who was dressed in aqua green and white, holding a bright flag of chili-pepper red. My eyes were focused on the fight when Raphael leaned over and whispered into my ear again, "Come fire jumping with me tonight."

He rested back against his seat while he awaited my answer, rubbing his thumb across the top of my hand. I couldn't think of any way that I could slip past Brógán. My mind raced, desperately searching for some loophole, some excuse, some miracle that would allow me to be alone with Raphael on my last night in this dreamworld.

I cupped my hand around his ear. I didn't want *you know who* to hear any part of this conversation. "I don't know how I'll be able to slip past my bodyguard," I told him with my face drawn in regret.

"No problem." His dimples flashed. "Just be ready around eleven thirty. I *will* come for you, Aishling," he said, almost like a threat. My better senses warned me that I shouldn't go off with him alone, but the need to see him one last time before I got on the plane the next day won out over reason. I nodded, and he exited the stands in such a rush, I barely saw him go.

13

Fire Jumpers

(Aishling)

Brógán and I made it back to our hotel room at 10:15 p.m. I prayed that he would be tired and go to sleep soon. But, as my not-so-good fortune would have it, he plopped down on the couch, flicked on the television, and browsed channels with the remote.

"Good night," I said as a colossal hint.

"*Oiche mhaith, codladh samh* [good night, sleep well], Aish," he said, sounding as if he still had plenty of energy.

Wondering just how Raphael planned to pull off this stunt he suggested, I entered my room and locked the door. I had a little over an hour to kill before I was supposedly going to be sprung from detention. I was about to sail on the prohibited waters of freedom, and I could already feel the wind in my face.

Rummaging through my suitcase, I pulled out my favorite pair of distressed jeans and my thick, baby-blue sweater and put them on. My black, furry snow boots that Claire had given me for my birthday completed the ensemble. In the bathroom I ran the brush through my long, unruly hair and added some gloss to my lips. Pleased with my reflection, I turned out all the lights and stood in front of the window, watching the fireworks and looking down on the illuminated city.

Sometime around 11:30, I heard a faint noise coming from the front room. I tiptoed to the door and listened. Maybe my luck was changing. I could hear Brógán snoring.

The room's phone startled me, and I rushed to grab the receiver, holding it up to stop the noise. I listened for a second before answering, waiting to hear the snores coming through the thin walls. As the sounds of deep sleep resumed, I whispered, "Hello."

"Aishling?"

"Yes?"

"It's me—Raphael."

"How'd you get my number?" I asked, puzzled again at his resourceful ways. "Never mind," I said, realizing I didn't care. I was just excited that he had called.

"I'm here. Come to the emergency door."

"You got the emergency door open without setting off the alarm? How did you—? Never mind again. What about Brógán? He's such a light sleeper. I'm shocked he didn't hear you open the door."

"He's deep in sleep. Trust me," he said with an impish tone to his otherwise angelic voice.

"I'm going to leave him a note so he won't worry in case he wakes up. I'll be just a minute."

"You do that." He snickered. "I'll be waiting. Hurry!"

I hung up the phone and hastily scribbled a note, explaining that I would be down at the beach. Then I grabbed my coat and tiptoed through the room that stood between freedom and me. I was shocked that Brógán never woke up, but then again this was my night, and nothing was going to spoil it.

Raphael pulled the door back as I approached. To my amazement I could see that it was indeed two feet thick. This man baffled me.

Without a sound he shut the door and grabbed my hand, and then he raced with me down ten flights of stairs and burst through the final door out into the snow. With the adrenaline that was rushing through my body, I could have run five miles without slowing my pace.

"These people know how to throw a party, don't they?" I said as we crossed the street in front of the hotel.

"Yeah, it's great, isn't it? This way," he said, tugging me toward the boardwalk. Even this close to midnight, the promenade and the beach were filled with hundreds of people looking to join in every part of the festive holiday, not wanting the magical night to end. I knew exactly how they felt.

Trudging toward the bonfires was a slow process as we churned up not only sand but also snow. "They have a lot of smaller fires going down there," he pointed down the beach, "better for us first-timers, you know," he said, looking down at me and not glancing away. My heart was responding so erratically to this man.

We stopped beside a smaller fire, and Raphael let go of my hand to bend down and stoke the embers. Then he added some more wood, and the flames grew higher. Smoke from the bonfire rose around us and burned my eyes. The wind blew my hair across my face, and I grabbed the loose strands, wrapping them behind my ears as I watched the firelight cast shadows across his dangerous features. Shivering more from the feelings he stirred in me than from the cold, I turned toward the fire, rubbing my hands together above the warm flames.

"Well, it has died down enough now so we can jump. Are you ready?" he asked, challenging me.

"Oh no! You first. It was your idea," I said, laughing.

"Okay, but I must inform you that the first one of a group of friends to jump is the one whose wish comes true." He backed up a good piece in order to build up some speed, but I ran for the fire and leapt across before he had a chance. My fencing skills aided me in my tumble and fall. Then I rolled to a standing position on the other side and baited him with my victorious smile.

Jumping over the fire, he ran straight for me. "Why, you little scoundrel!" he joked, tickling me.

"I can't breathe," I said between tickles and laughter. He lifted me off the ground and held me sideways, pinning my arms securely across my body with one arm as he used the other as a playful means of torture.

A stranger jogging by saved me. "Hey, you guys, it's midnight. Come on!" He motioned toward the sea.

Raphael set me on my feet, giving me that black-sheep smile again as he grabbed my hand, and we ran toward the water with every ounce of speed in us.

"Why are we running into the ocean at midnight in the freezing cold?" I asked. I thought that was a reasonable question that required a timely answer, before I became a large ice cube floating in the sea.

"An old Spanish legend says if you jump seven waves at midnight, you'll have good luck for the whole year," he claimed, shrugging his shoulders like it made absolute sense to him.

"Well, by all means, let's fire jump *and* wave jump. Everybody needs extra luck. I am Irish, you know. We take luck hunting very seriously." I looked over at him and smiled, and he returned the favor with an almost Irish smile—the kind that touched the eyes.

When we reached the water, I gasped as the first cold wave slammed into my thighs. Before I had a chance to run back to the warmth of the fire, he picked me up and whirled me around.

The frigid breeze snaked down my spine. He stopped spinning, and his face came closer and closer. Fireworks lit up the ocean and the night sky, and I could see his face in indigo and lime sparkles. I felt like he was going to kiss me, and the feelings of my betrayal came back to preoccupy my mind. About the time I looked up to the sky, he tossed me into the next wave, and I came up sputtering.

"Who's the scoundrel now?" I playfully shoved him, but my push had no effect. He stood strong and steady in the pounding waves. Soon my body was shaking, and my teeth were chattering.

"Sorry, I really couldn't help it," he said, attempting a look of remorse. "Let's get our seven wave jumps in so we can get you back to the fire."

I couldn't get to the fire fast enough once I'd completed my seven jumps. Raphael borrowed a blanket from someone down the beach and hurried to sit with me. He wrapped it around us both and rubbed my arms.

We sat so close together, his arms around me under the blanket, that I felt nice and toasty even though my clothes were still soaked. Rather than making me feel uneasy, his touch felt a lot like coming home. He smelled of salty sea, charred forests, and cinnamon spice—as bewildering and attractive a combination as the man himself.

He hummed a tune that was unfamiliar to me, and I chanced a tiny look up at him as he stared out toward the sea. The man beside me was so different from the one I'd met forty-eight hours earlier. Now he didn't seem to have a care in the world.

Before I could look away, he caught me staring. With a wide grin he leaned over to touch his lips to the top of my head. I didn't know how to react to that, so I looked back to the fire as I twisted the edge of the blanket in my hands.

As the shivers subsided and the warmth from the fire spread, I was able to form a question without my teeth banging together.

"Will I ever see you again, Raphael?"

He had a serious expression on his face as he answered. "I'm going to try to come to you, Aishling. Please know that wherever I am, my thoughts will always be with you."

I nodded solemnly and wrapped my arms around my knees.

"What time is your group heading back to Ireland?" he brooded.

"Tomorrow morning at 8 a.m."

"Mind if I come and see you off?" He stared into the fire.

"Not at all. We're meeting out in front of the hotel."

"I'll be there!"

The fire hissed and crackled while the ocean played its own tune. I could have stayed there forever.

"Wait here. I'll be right back." He jumped up and wrapped the whole blanket around me, and I watched him run down the beach toward some huge boulders jutting up out of the sand.

Raphael was full of excitement and intrigue, and I was drawn to him despite my inner warnings. The faerie cross hanging on a chain under my sweater grew hotter, and I wondered, "Why now?" I had to pull it away from my body, holding it in a wad with my sweater, to keep it from scorching my skin.

He came back toward the fire, playing a guitar he must have hidden among the rocks earlier in the day. In my music appreciation class, we had just been studying Spanish music in preparation for our trip this week. The tune he played was Spanish in origin, probably flamenco—the kind of music that tells a story. The melody was very soothing, and he circled the fire while he serenaded me. As frozen as I was, I still looked up at him in appreciation, realizing this was the best night of my life.

He was such an enigma. If I were to meet him in an alley, I would truly fear for my life. There was an edge to him that frightened me, yet at the same time there was an innocence that left him appearing vulnerable and me feeling secure.

He came back to sit by me amid the sand and the snow; he strummed another tune—one that was unlike anything I'd ever heard before.

"What's it called?" I asked him.

"Oh, it's just a tune I've had rolling through my head for the past few months, trying to drown out the demons." He played while I tried to decode his cryptic answers and behaviors.

"I'm still curious about your tears from the night at the cathedral. You were weeping almost as if someone had died," I said.

"Someone did die, but I'd rather not talk about that—not yet anyway. Can you let it go and remember me as I am now? You make me different."

As I looked at him with compassion, I didn't know what kind of trouble he was facing. But what I did know was that he stirred my heart in a very forceful yet tender way, and I could sense his harmlessness. Call it intuition or whatever you please, but I knew that this man above all others would never hurt me—despite the scorching stone against my chest signaling danger.

"Okay. Well then, tell me more about yourself—something I might not think to ask, something mysterious," I teased. My dark eyebrows lifted into my unruly bangs as I smiled at him.

Flustered, he countered, "I can be persuasive when I want something." With a weak smile, he put his guitar pick in his mouth and chewed on it as he looked out toward the rolling sea. I'd never seen anyone else do that.

"How so?" I inquired.

His head dropped as if he were afraid to answer me. "I knew you were going to be on the promenade at the precise time you were there yesterday," he said, looking at me shyly. As I gazed at him, I did a double take; I just knew his pupils blazed for the briefest moment, but when I looked back at them they were smooth copper.

With my pulse racing, I looked away. "In this day and time, we would call that stalker-esque behavior," I said, half kidding, half serious.

"Aishling, I'm afraid my social skills are a bit rusty. I don't mean to frighten you. I just needed to see you and explain about my behavior at the cathedral. If you want no contact from me, all you have to do is say the word. I will honor your decision."

"I like you, Raphael," I admitted. "I'm not sure what the future holds, but I'd like for us to keep in touch." Actually my feelings were so much stronger than "like," but these emotions were all so utterly confusing and eerie that I tried to banish it from my mind. However, my mind refused to obey.

With a magnificent smile, he reached out to touch my cheek briefly, and the touch warmed me to my toes.

Catching me off guard, he took the pick from his mouth and asked the most unusual question: "If you had the chance to spend the day with one of God's angels, what would you want to do?"

I took a moment to reflect on what I'd want most. "I guess I'd want the power to heal for a day. Maybe the angel and I could visit places like Africa and cure people, or bring them water and food. Give them at least one day of peace. What would you do?"

He returned the pick to his mouth, moving it around between his teeth, making a rhythmic clicking sound. After a few seconds the clicking stopped; he took the pick out and moved it between each of his fingers with only the movement of his hand. "I'd want to see my father and beg his forgiveness." As he said it, his eyes misted, and I was distraught, wondering what his secrets were and how I could help.

"Raphael?" I said, reaching out to touch his arm. I didn't know what else to say.

"You're so good, Aishling. Really good. That's why I...."

"Why you what?"

"Never mind."

"What?" I demanded.

"Why I had to seek you out," he said. There was a degree of pain and indecision on his face. "It's not just the goodness I see in you. You may think I'm crazy, Aishling, but I feel as if I've known you before somehow, some place in a faraway dream."

"I know what you mean," I answered anxiously.

"You do?" he asked, surprised by my answer.

"Yes, but I still can't put my finger on it. It's almost as if there's a crucial chapter of history in my memory dedicated to you, but the harder I try to extract it the deeper the memory burrows down into the darkness. It's almost as if something outside of me is blocking it on purpose."

Shifting in front of me, he grabbed my arms. His eyes bore into mine, as if he were trying to make the memories come. Something distracted him, and he looked away, frightened. My world went black.

14

Penitent Angel

(Rafe)

Daylight was fading and the shadows of evening grew long as I remained in the dungeon, longing for a chance to bare my soul. Regret cloaked me as I waited in the Land of the Dead, even though one could say I was still very much alive. From where I sat, I could see the first stars of evening through a small window about twenty feet skyward.

"Aishling," I whispered to myself in agony over and over as I thought back to those stolen moments from the Hogueras Festival, and further back to a little girl strolling through a minefield. Why hadn't I seen it before? My mind must have still been so warped and seared from my time with the demons that I hadn't immediately sensed her. The cadence of a heart has a unique rhythm. I had sensed a peculiar pattern in the girl and now in the young woman. Humans develop two hearts in the early stages of life and they join to become one. But a supernatural being keeps the two hearts separately. Together they produce a hum like a song, and her song was as rare as she was.

The little girl who had moved me more than a decade earlier was now a stunning young woman with a heart to rival the angels' themselves. The girl who kept changing my life—and whose path I in turn kept altering—didn't even know what I'd done. She didn't know what I was or that my life now hung in the balance because of the decision I had made many years ago in regard to her. Having read her heart at the festival, I would have traded my life again for hers even now, regardless of my fate.

It seemed as though I'd been in the dungeon for months, although I had been shackled only five days since that fateful weekend. Aishling and I had been sitting on the beach when I'd sensed the demons coming for me. I couldn't let them find me with her. It was too dangerous. If anything ever happened to her, I'd take myself back to the fires of hell and have Satariel turn up the heat for eternity. I did the only thing I could do in that moment: I touched her with my demonic ability to do so, and she blacked out in my arms. I hoped she would never remember the pain or the stress that shock had placed on her fragile body. Gathering her in my arms, I had raced back to her hotel, zigzagging through the city alleys to throw off my pursuers.

When I'd reached the hotel, I'd raced up the stairs to her room. I had opened the door wide, and light from the hallway had spilled onto the couch where her bodyguard lay, still incapacitated from the same jolt I'd used on him earlier. After all I couldn't allow him to find her missing and interrupt the pivotal night of my life. I hated to leave Aishling, but knew I had to go. Placing her on the chair beside the bed, I reached out to touch her still damp hair.

"Goodbye, Aishling," I whispered and I leaned down to kiss her forehead. I touched her again, and she stirred. Before she had a chance to open her eyes, I was gone.

I hadn't been there to see her off the next morning, and I worried what she thought of me. Was she concerned when I didn't show up? Was she angry? No, not Aishling. Disappointed maybe. Would she miss me as much as I was missing her? How could she possibly? These thoughts assaulted me while I waited for a decision about my fate.

After leaving Aishling that night, I had tried to outrun the demons, but they had all the alleys blocked, and they eventually cornered me on the edge of the city. Satariel had skulked into the midst of the group and spat ash in my face.

"So you thought you could run from me?" he had said. "The great Raphael, commander of the ethereal armies indeed! Or should I say *former* commander?" He mocked me while the others laughed raucously. "Get him back in the chains," he ordered his soldiers. I promised myself I wouldn't go back with them to hell. Fighting with every bit of strength I had left, I took down the first two that were coming at me. Cursing, Satariel threw thick, web-like metal chains, effectively pinning me to the ground. As he started toward me, I heard the sound of angels' wings, and I was terrified and relieved in the same instant. Even the Dark One cowered as the war angels circled and landed around me in a protective arc.

"He's no longer your concern," the new commander stated in a controlled manner. "Remove the chains!"

The order was obeyed, and Satariel slinked away with his proverbial tail between his legs. He had to get in one parting shot, though. Sneering, he looked back over his shoulder, and yelled, "You won't last with them!" If I hadn't been so happy at that moment, I might have gotten up and jeered at the sight of his retreating back.

Overcome with gratefulness and fear, I lay face down on the ground among the angels in a gesture of submission. The archangel must have received my plea for him to send a legion of angels to my rescue. I was in awe of the sight of them and felt the longing within my soul.

They had brought me to the Paradise realm of Hades to await a kind of interim judgment. These types of hearings were rare. I should know, having escorted only two beings to this very place in order to stand trial when I had been the leader of the army.

I've been around for thousands of years, but these last few have been the most desolate. For ten lonely years I'd lived the existence of a demon, and for ten years I'd prayed for this day, for the chance to be redeemed. As I heard the guards coming for me, I said another quick prayer.

Two guards led me up the circular stone staircase and down the long hallway to the grand hall where sentencing was carried out. Having his orders from the Master, the archangel sat on a throne of judgment. We had once been friends, Artemis and me. But I had betrayed him also on that fateful day, and now he looked at me with a mixture of anger and loss. His face twisted in pain at shared happy memories before he put on his mask of authority.

"Raphael, what say ye in your defense?" Artemis the archangel questioned me before I was even seated in the chair facing him.

I was so regretful of where I'd been and what I'd been made to do while with the demons that I could only hang my head in shame. Tears from deep within sprang to my eyes, and I waited until I had them controlled before looking up to answer. After all I didn't want him to think I was playing on his sympathies. That was not the case at all. I deserved to be disciplined more, even after ten years of grueling punishment.

Aishling's face flashed through my mind at that exact moment, and I was able to face Artemis with a little more dignity, knowing that part of what I'd done had been for the greater good. The world had improved on the day she was born, and the world had been, in a sense, saved on the day she was reborn.

"I have no defense, sir, but one request. Make me your servant. Allow me to fill my days with Diaga's business instead of demons' chores. Anything that you ask of me will be done. Do with me as you will," I said, broken.

Artemis looked away in deliberation. "Well, that changes things. The great Raphael has nothing to say for himself—no defense."

"No, sir. I deserve the punishment I was given."

"Well, now, that puts me in a bit of a dilemma. I was told to deliver a sentence that I deemed fair after hearing your defense. But I've heard none, not even the tiniest bit of groveling."

"Is that your wish, Artemis, to see me beg?" I asked, maybe with a little more heat than I had intended.

Seething, he glared at me until he realized I was serious. Then he seemed to soften, dropping his head and wringing his hands. "Raphael, no, I do not want to see you beg. It pains me to see you here like this. I questioned why I had to be the one to determine this outcome. But now I know. The Master knew I'd be the most merciful even to a traitor."

"I'm sorry I hurt you, Artemis. I'm sorry I hurt all of you," I said as I looked around the room at the five council members flanking him. "I know I allowed my pride to rule at that moment, and I'll always regret it. But I'll never regret saving her. Even through these ten years of torture, I couldn't bring myself to regret that. I know I can never reclaim my position, and that's okay. Menial tasks are fine. I'll do what you say. Make me your prisoner."

While I watched the council confer in whispers, I wondered what would become of me. Then I realized it didn't matter as long as they didn't send me back to hell.

After an agonizing few moments, a hush fell across the room. Artemis said, "Raphael, please rise for your judgment." I did as I was told. "I'm sure you are already aware that this has happened, but just to be clear I will repeat the decree. Raphael, former angel, you have been stripped of your titles and former position."

As I nodded in acknowledgment, he continued. "Now, as to the matter of your plea for mercy. We do not wish for you to return to the lower realms. Your gifts of healing are far too valuable and needed in the earth realm. Since pride lead to your fall, you will become a servant. You will take up the cause of the poor, the orphans, and the widows. We feel that the best way for you to fulfill your duty is through medicine. Therefore you will attend medical school and become a doctor. With all of your experience as the angel of healing, this will merely be a formality on earth. You must have a piece of paper saying you've been trained, so you will complete your training at an institution that will be designated for you."

"Anything else?" I asked, my excitement growing.

"Beginning today you will become mortal until such time as the council has determined the fate of your immortality. Since your body will be changed, you will have some significant wounds and scarring from the burns you have sustained. While those are being tended to, you will not be expected to carry on coursework. But as soon as you are able, you will enter college. There will be angels assigned to you who will watch and report on your behavior. I trust that you are sincere in your desire to be back among us, so I don't expect any further trouble from you. Do I make myself clear?"

"Yes sir, and thank you for this opportunity."

As I turned to go, Artemis spoke in a tone reserved for old friends. "Raphael?"

Turning back, I waited for him to finish. "It's good to see you, my friend. You can't imagine how I've longed for this day."

Smiling, I said, "Me too. Me too."

When I awakened I had no way of knowing how much time had lapsed. Pain coursed through my entire body as I shifted in bed. Lifting my head I looked at my surroundings to find out where I was being held. A nurse rushed in and pushed me back down.

"You're going to reopen those stitches. Now be still. You hear?" She fluffed my pillows and checked my IV bags, fussing loud enough for anyone to hear. "I tell him to lie still, but no, he's got to go jumpin' around, breakin' open stitches. Man ain't never goin' to heal if he keeps bustin' open stitches!"

She then turned to check my bandages. "What have you been dreamin' about, Mr. Delacruz? You've been fighting all the nurses and doctors in your sleep. Nobody can get you calmed down. We have to give you sedatives, and they've been lasting half the time they do for most patients. Must be some kind of nightmares for sure. A man doesn't fight like that unless he's chasin' demons or bein' chased, I tell you. So which is it, Mister?"

The demons were still in my head, but how could she know that? "Where am I?" I asked instead.

"You, sir, are in the great city of Lubbock, Texas, at the University Medical Center's Timothy J. Harnar Burn Center. You're a lucky man, Raphael, a very lucky man."

"How'd I get here? How long have I been here?" I closed my eyes and Aishling's face lit up the dark places. Was I still living in her time period?

My eyes popped open as the nurse spoke. "Ambulance brought you in two days ago. The driver saw you lyin' in a ditch. Uh-huh, you must have angels watchin' over you. That's for sure." A smile of relief spread across my face.

The nurse moved to the table, picked up a large, manila envelope, and brought it to my bedside so I could see the contents. She pulled out a wallet and showed me my driver's license, cash, keys, and credit cards.

"Can I call you Rafe?" the sassy nurse said with a smile. "Raphael sure is a mouthful."

I nodded in consent.

"I don't know what trouble you're in, Rafe. But lookin' at that amount of cash in your wallet, not to mention the credit cards, I know for sure this wasn't a mugging. Somebody wanted you dead. You'd better watch your back when you get out of here. The police are here to take your statement."

After numerous questions in response to which I explained to the cops again that I didn't remember how I had gotten there or who had done this to me, my nurse came back in to redress my wounds. If I'd said "demons," they'd definitely have me locked away in the nuthouse.

"Now, let's take a look at these skin grafts." She pulled back one of the dressings, and I cringed as part of my skin stuck to the bandage. *So this is what physical pain feels like? That's different.* "Sorry, Rafe. Those cops stayed too long, and the grafts got dry. Hold still while I get some ointment on them."

After a painful hour of her peeling away the dressings and applying the salve, I was exhausted and ready for a nap.

Sleep was created for humans, to allow the body and mind to rest. But Satariel had other plans for my unconsciousness that afternoon. "Hello, traitor!" he yelled in my mind. I could see his image as clearly as if he were standing in that very hospital room. "So, you think you can just leave my ranks without consequences, do you? I told you this wasn't over! You *will* return to hell! You hear me?"

A fiery whip struck my chest, and I awakened screaming. Lifting the covers to investigate the burning sensation, I observed no new burn marks, although the area where he had hit me felt like someone had just laid a scorching iron there.

There was a flurry of activity in my room while I was restrained and given an injection. Soon I was able to escape the mental torment. As Aishling's face soothed my aches, I entered the most calming dreamworld. I wandered through the fields and moors with her for hours. There was no laughter as sweet as hers, no look as innocent, no bond as strong between two people.

But when I awakened in the early morning hours, she wasn't there.

Throughout my weeks of treatment, thoughts of Aishling kept me company. I didn't even know the girl—not really—yet I still felt an overpowering need to protect her after so many years. And our recent reunion in Spain had generated a mind full of future scenes of us together. I wondered where she was or if I'd ever have the chance to be near her again. After all I was human now! I marveled, looking down at my hands and wiggling my toes. And humans had relationships, right? I could go to Ireland and look for her, I thought with a sudden joy that seemed to blur the last decade into a sea of smoke and fire until the last ember died out, leaving a clean slate, a new beginning.

I knew from my time with her in Spain that she was already in college. I had seen in her heart her compassion for the poor. I wondered what major she would choose. Probably social work. *I wonder if she's dated anyone since we met,* I thought with a surge of jealousy as I broke through another set of restraints the medical personnel had used to bind me. This time it took much greater effort than the previous times, and with each passing day I felt my supernatural strength diminishing. The angels did leave me with one gift: heart reading. But what good was it when the one heart I wanted to see most was lost to me?

"Aishling!" I yelled, and the nurses came running once more with drugs to dull the pain.

15

Alone In A Crowd

(Aishling)

ireworks boomed outside the window, and I jumped in my confused slumber, knocking the phone off the nightstand. "Where am I?" I said out loud to the dark room. My head felt like I'd had tiny, electric pins stuck all over it and the breaker had tripped and reset again. Shivering, I felt my way along the wall until I found the light switch. Once the room was illuminated, I remembered where I was, but the details of just how I had gotten there were foggy.

Moving into the bathroom, I stripped off my clammy apparel and rushed under the hot spray of the shower. As the heat restored my thought processes, his face rushed into my mind in a hurry, and I gasped, almost choking on the water running over my head. Raphael! Turning the water off and wrapping the towel around me, I wondered where he was, why he had just disappeared, and how I had gotten back to my room. I had no recollection of being brought there. My time with him couldn't have been a dream, for I had been fully clothed, soaked, and chilled to the bone when I had awakened.

The hotel had provided a thick, white terrycloth robe, and I wrapped it around me as I moved toward the window. Opening the curtains I stared out at the red and yellow ocean as a giant fireworks display erupted over the choppy waters. One moment the water was brilliant and the next black, just like this night had been for me. Raphael had been the very best part of it, and now he was gone. He had promised to see me off in the morning, and I held on to that hope.

After drying my hair and putting on my pajamas, I snuggled under the bulky comforter, the Hogueras Festival now a cherished memory. Falling into a troubled sleep, my body volleyed back and forth like a metronome. In my dream I saw myself as a young girl, about six or seven years old, and I was dancing out in the field north of the castle. I began to fly to the heavens. A man—no, an angel—was running toward me as my feet left the earth behind. While I twirled in the white sky, the angel grabbed my feet and pulled me back to earth. I looked down, but before I could see his face the metronome ground to a halt, and I sat up in bed, wiping tears from my cheeks.

I awoke the next morning with a renewed spirit. Raphael would be there in front of the hotel to see me off. I just knew it. There was a dynamic chemistry between us that was undeniable. Even though all we could attain was a special friendship, I wanted him at the top of that list. I skipped breakfast in the hotel dining room and hurried to the sidewalk out front, hoping he'd get there early. Brógán ran alongside me with his coffee sloshing out of its cup and a bagel sticking out of his mouth.

"What's the rush?" he groaned.

I became a human statue with the stream of people rerouted, flowing around me like a city roundabout.

"Meeting someone?" He tried again for an answer from me, but I was busy straining my neck to see over the crowd. "Is it the cathedral guy again?"

"Brógán! It's a harmless friendship thing." Scrunching my face, I debated with myself on the particles of truth in that statement while I searched the crowd.

He never showed.

Winter was especially brutal near the Cooley Mountains that year. Being so cold natured, I was glad that winter was a bit less harsh in Dublin. January and February passed with no word from Raphael. Patrick and I swapped almost daily text messages or chatted online. I had not seen him since before Christmas, when I had left for the Hogueras Festival in Spain, and I was missing my best friend. I was also very busy, and he didn't understand the restraints on my time. As I sat at my desk in front of my dorm room window, I smiled and then scowled at his most recent outrageous message:

"What up, Asher? *Conas ata tu?* [How are you?] R u avoiding me for any particular reason? Should I send more roses? WHY R U NOT RETURNING MY TEXTS?"

"I texted u day b4 yesterday, u crazy *muirneach* [lovable person]! I'm REALLY busy right now w/midterms coming up. Please—no more roses. No room left in the room. LOL!"

"OK! U try to do somethin' nice for somebody & they don't appreciate it. ;)"

"I think good idea = Patrick should stop trying to make Asher feel guilty. :P"

"I think good idea = Road trip to New York to see one's best friend. How 'bout? Or in your case, airway trip. Big period @ the end for seriousness."

"That would be great! If I had a weekend free between now and Beltaine, that is. :(Back-to-back orchestra practices and shows. Price of being famous. LOL! How's school? U still goofin' off?"

"I'll have u know, I got my Admin. Law & Public Policy paper done in 1 day!! Felt pretty good 'bout myself!! Then I remembered I have to write my World Lit paper b4 tomorrow & have my Legislation case study done by Thurs."

"Well, at least I know the case study will be a stroll by the river 4 u. You've grown up w/legislation case studies debated in your home."

"Yeah, yeah. Hey, change of subject. You know those pranks you & I were plottin' last week? Well, Jed & I took yours & Satan's inspiration & put vegetable oil in our suite-mate's half-used shampoo bottle. Dude didn't have time to wash it all out b4 class. Can you say 'grease head'?"

"And this from a future politician! LOL! Why didn't he just use your shampoo?"

"Now THAT is the question of the day. And college can't be all about textbooks. U know me. I'd go insane."

"Yeah, I know u, all right! Well, gotta run. Try being good 4 a change. Love u!"

"Being good is overrated. :) Love u too! *Slán* [goodbye]."

In early March there was a break in the blustery weather, and we experienced a taste of springtime. Shorts and flip-flops broke out on campus and students trying to soak up the elusive sunshine were sprawled on blankets across the lawns.

I was checking my campus mailbox. Uncle Brádach sent me something at least once a week, and I was due for my letter. He knew how much I counted on him, and he had never let me down. The letter I pulled from my box, however, was not from him. It was from Patrick. Opening the envelope, I realized it was empty.

"Very imaginative prank, Patrick," I said out loud, rolling my eyes. As I was about to throw the envelope in the trash, something fell out. I leaned down and picked up the seven-leaf clover. Smiling to myself I pressed the petals in my Spanish textbook and strolled out into the warmth of the day.

The next week Patrick came to visit me at college on his spring break. We went to the St. Patrick's Day parade, watched several hurling matches at Croke Park, and hung out.

As happy as I was to see my best friend, our reunion was tainted by the guilt I felt. Thoughts of Rafe had consumed me since Christmas. Wherever I roamed on campus, I looked for him. It was silly, I know, but I couldn't stop myself. Patrick didn't seem to notice my preoccupation, though, and for that I was grateful. But guilt is a complex emotion. Whenever it rushed in like a barometer for the soul, gauging my faults against Patrick's, I always came out sunny to his stormy.

He and his girlfriend had broken up after that first year of college because of his betrothal to me, but the flashback had been etched in my mind, and as much as both of us wanted to forget the past, neither of us could shake it. After all, this had been *my* faerie tale, and I deserved to be the only princess in the eyes of my prince. When he was back at school in America, he dodged questions about his time there. I had no way of knowing for sure if he remained faithful to me.

Patrick had an Irish life—one where we were platonic friends again and he was happier, one where he could forget for a little while the realities that always awaited him in America. In that life he was responsible for a child, a son named Connor, whom he had kept secret from his family. Also in that one there was another woman, his child's mother. I felt deep down that they still had feelings for one another. The woman was definitely not a gold digger, or she could have already ruined Patrick. He had still been successful in keeping his son out of the spotlight, which made me wonder how close he was with Connor's mother.

16

Ash And Burn

(Rafe)

Since I had bleeding around some of the grafts and a prolonged infection at one of the donor sites on my thigh, I remained in the burn center for seven agonizing weeks. On the day of my release, the sassy nurse who had been my main caregiver wheeled me out to the front of the hospital where my cab waited.

"Now listen here, Rafe! You best be stayin' out of trouble. No more fires, you got it?"

"Yes, ma'am!" Laughing at her, I stood up from the wheelchair and allowed her to help me into the taxi. As she started to close the door, I saw a tear slip down her cheek, as if she was going to miss me. Maybe I wasn't so bad after all.

"Go find this Aishling girl and make sure she knows what a lucky woman she is." My mouth flew open as the door was shut and the driver sped away. I must have done a lot of sleep talking, I thought, as the city flew by.

Fifteen minutes later the driver pulled up to the apartment listed on my driver's license. Carrying my meager belongings to the door, I used the key from the manila envelope and let myself in.

When I closed the door and flicked the light switch on, an old friend startled me. "It's about time you got here."

"Vitale, my brother!" I rushed to embrace one of heaven's finest, cringing from the impact, as I was still sore. "What brings you here?"

"Oh, just making sure you found your way home. You look rough, Captain."

"Yeah, well, I've been to an actual place called hell and back, you know?"

"Why'd you do it, Raphael? Why?" He looked so distressed.

Taking a seat on the couch, I ran my fingers through my hair, which had gotten way too long during my hospital stay. "Can't I have five minutes to rest before you launch your interrogation? I can't talk about it. Even after ten years, the wounds are still too raw."

Peeling off my shirt, I applied salve to other raw wounds. Vitale gasped at the sight of my chest. "What did they do to you?"

"Nothing a little time won't mend."

"Right." Looking awkward, Vitale took a seat across from me. "So I guess I should get to the details of my visit."

"Might as well," I responded. I winced as I peeled off a dry dressing from a wound on my abdomen.

"I guess you've figured out why I'm here, so I'll be stating the obvious. Artemis sent me to help you get settled."

"And?"

"To keep an eye on you. Make sure you're not—"

"Acting like a demon?" I interrupted.

"Come on, man. Cut me some slack."

"I'm sorry, Vitale. I'm just having a bit of an identity crisis here, you know? I realize you're just trying to help."

"Well then, let's discuss what you'll be doing. Here are your admission papers into the internal medicine program at Texas Tech here in Lubbock. Since this is the end of February and midsemester, you won't be able to start until May. I've left a stack of textbooks on the table in the kitchen so you can begin your unofficial studies. With your experience and knowledge, you should be way ahead of everyone in your classes, but you must learn modern techniques and use of technology in medicine. Do you feel up to a driving lesson?"

"And who do you propose is going to give me a driving lesson?"

"Me, of course." Vitale looked insulted, but his smile gave him away.

"What do you know about driving?"

"In preparation for your entrance into the earth realm, I've been researching things that will help you be human. I'll have you know I've sat in many cars over the past several weeks, learning which buttons do what and how to work those pedal things. I even had a fluke chance to drive a devil-red Lamborghini Diablo; tell me that's not ironic." He held up a hand in a matter-of-fact pose. "And I've learned I'm an excellent driver."

"Aren't angels supposed to be humble?" I laughed.

"Just stating the facts, my friend. You wouldn't want to be taught by a novice, now would you?"

"I guess not." My thoughts drifted to Aishling as Vitale rambled on about grocery shopping, clothes shopping, and the church just down the street. It had been more than two months since I'd gone to Spain through the fires of Hogueras. My skin grafts were healing, and I had to find her.

"Of course, you should have enough clothing until summer. I picked out everything in your closet," he was saying as I tuned back in.

I hurried into the bedroom and rummaged through his selections. Pulling out a black turtleneck sweater, I knew this would be in my luggage to Ireland.

"Yeah, this one will cover up my burns," I said to myself as Vitale looked on.

"That's why I got the same sweater in five different colors. No need to thank me."

I clapped him on the shoulder. "Thanks! Now how about that driving lesson?" The sooner the better, as far as I was concerned. The ability to drive might come in handy once I got to Ireland. I didn't know how long I'd be staying there.

Vitale stayed with me for a full week, initiating me into what he believed it meant to be human: proper conduct and social behaviors, hygiene, cooking and eating food, cleaning the apartment and doing laundry, cell phone usage, and familiarizing me with my surroundings. We also visited a homeless shelter and a YMCA, where I'd be volunteering once I'd healed.

At the end of the week, we were saying our good-byes. "Raphael, I guess you've noticed they didn't strip you of all your power."

"I know I can still examine and interpret heart language. Why did they allow that?"

"Who knows? I think the Master has a soft spot for you."

"And I for Him."

"From what I understand, some of your other abilities may return to you gradually. Just thought you should know so you can harness them."

"Yeah, thanks for the heads-up."

Vitale clasped the back of his neck with his hand and rubbed, looking down at the ground. "One last thing, Raphael."

"Yeah?"

His sad eyes met mine. "A word of caution. It's also possible your demonic bent could resurface."

Pivoting to the window, I brushed a hand through my scratchy beard stubble while I watched children playing chase on the playground. "Thanks for the warning, friend."

"Well, it's time for me to hit the air current. If I leave in thirty seconds, I can step right into the jet stream and take a free ride before I have to return home."

Smiling, I hugged him.

"Call for me anytime, and I'll be back to help. I'm sure they'll send me here from time to time to check on your progress."

"I'll be fine," I reassured him, hoping he wouldn't be checking on me anytime really soon. He might not approve of my plans to visit the Emerald Isle.

Vitale saluted me as a sign of respect for my former position, and I returned the salute with gratitude for this new life I was being given. I hoped I wasn't about to blow my chance before it even began. As soon as he left, I contacted the airport and purchased a ticket on the next flight to Dublin, Ireland. Luck was on my side, and I was booked on a flight leaving early the next morning.

On the plane I reviewed various scenarios I might encounter in my search for Aishling. Her security guards would be an issue. Would she be angry with me since my disappearance? Would I be able to explain without explaining everything? What excuse could I possibly offer her?

"Keep it simple," I told myself. I would never lie to her, so I would give her as much detail as possible.

The plane made its descent along with the lowering of the sun on the horizon. I had brought one carry-on bag, so I wouldn't have to waste time at baggage claim. Before the seatbelt safety light dimmed, I was on my feet, bag in hand, heading toward the nose of the plane. My quest for her was almost a reality. I hoped she would be as happy to see me when I surprised her on this day, a week before the great Irish celebration of St. Patrick's Day.

"Trinity College," I called to the taxi driver as I slid into the backseat. The rearview mirror reflected my scar back at me, and I wondered if Aishling would find me repulsive now. The swollen red line slashed my left cheekbone, a constant reminder of my last run-in with the demons.

Twenty minutes later, after a lot of Gaelic swearing at the other cars, the driver dropped me at the front entrance of Trinity College. Ambling through the arched stone gate, I wandered down the cobblestone path toward the imposing campanile, which housed the bell that was now chiming out the eight o'clock hour. I decided to try the library first. Aishling was a very responsible person; she might be studying. A scholarly looking gentleman walked by, and after a short conversation he pointed me in the right direction.

After entering the library, I craned my neck to take in the barrel-shaped ceiling that ran through the building like a long wooden train. On either side there were two tall floors filled with fiction and facts. Stepping through one of the archways to my left, I wandered down the rows of books and searched hearts. I felt that she was near, for there was a sweetness filtering through the musty air of the ancient place of learning.

I saw her security detail before I saw her. There were five of them surrounding her, trying to keep up as she ran for the door. I heard her laughter, and my heart beat faster. Seeing her again, if only for this moment, was enough to alleviate the ache I'd suffered in her absence. But one glimpse would never be enough, and I didn't know what I'd do if she were to send me away.

Following at a distance, I found a door leading out the side of the building. I made my way outside and turned in the direction she was heading toward the front. It appeared she was going toward the campanile where I had just been a half hour earlier. The stars were twinkling through the limbs of the trees that were concealing me. As a shadow chaser, I raced among the tall bushes, locking on to a cluster of six human shadows moving toward the great fountain in the courtyard behind the bell tower.

Her guards fanned out and were joined a few moments later by an additional seven guards coming from the west side of the library. There was a man striding in their midst who looked to be in his late teens, maybe early twenties.

"Patrick!" I heard her cry out as she jumped into the young man's arms. "You came to surprise me on your spring break!" she said.

"Of course I did, love," he said, lifting her long bangs away from her face and kissing her cheek.

Beside the massive oak trunk, I fell to my knees. She loved him. I saw it in her heart, and I couldn't bear it. Without realizing what I was doing in my distressed state of mind, I erupted with a feral roar, and three of the guards sprinted toward my location. Pushing my face down on the ground, they held me there while Aishling and this Patrick fellow looked on, trying to peer into the shadows but they were unable to see me. I turned my face sideways and watched as she was taken from me.

How I came to be at the campus security office didn't register with me, and I didn't think of the trouble I might have found myself in. I only saw her. Her beauty was astonishing—anyone could see that. But nobody could see her the way I saw her—from the inside out. This Patrick didn't deserve her. His heart was good overall, I sensed. But there were some tarnishes that were pretty pronounced, and I didn't like him just on principle.

It took a while for me to explain to campus police why a university student from Texas was wandering around the grounds of a college in Ireland. They had nothing to hold me on. After all I had no weapons with me and no police record. Later that night, they let me go. By then Aishling was long gone—and so was my passion for life on earth.

17

A Moment with an Angel

(Aishling)

My first year of college ended, and Claire and I packed up and headed to Blackrock for the summer. On the night of Uncle Brádach's Beltaine party, Patrick and I snuck away again to search for faerie cross rocks. The stars were sparse and the blue sparkles from the cross rocks were dull. The night was drab—no faeries. It was as painfully uneventful as my life had been since Raphael had soared in, given me wings, and then forgotten to explain to me how to use them. The magic was left in a holding pattern as I refused to give up on it. "Someday," my heart whispered to me. Someday, he and I would meet again.

I had hoped for faeries on this night. I needed something to awaken my drifting spirit—something to make me feel alive. Such feelings of loss and confusion had pummeled my soul without mercy over the past several years that I was almost ready to go in search of some of the more notorious thin places, just to add some adventure to my monotonous life.

Patrick and I worked in the stables all summer, fished down at the river, rode horses in the moors and mountains, hung out with Claire and our friends in Iniskeen Village, and appeared to be a normal and happy couple when my father was around.

One fine Tuesday before we were to separate and head back to our respective colleges, he and I were out by the lake behind the castle. I had packed us a picnic lunch, and it seemed like old times. After eating we were lying side by side in the rowboat, letting the wind carry us across the lake. We were doing my favorite thing—cloud watching. I sprang up and stared down at him.

"What is it, Asher?"

Thinking back to that night on the beach with Raphael, I wondered how Patrick would answer the question that had been posed to me. Not understanding the full extent why, his answer had become important to me. "If you had the chance to spend the day with one of God's angels, what would you want to do?" I asked him.

"Hmm, good question. Can this be anything?"

"Yes."

"It doesn't have to be something otherworldly?"

"No."

"Could I have a special power?" he asked.

"I guess so."

"Will it cost me?"

"You sound like a lawyer. Stop skewing the question. It's supposed to be simple, Patrick."

"Okay! We're testy today I see."

"I just want to know is all."

"Let me think. If I could have anything...." He tilted his head back to watch the clouds as he pondered.

"No, this isn't like a genie wish. You misinterpreted the question."

"Well, please repeat it then."

"Never mind," I said as I started rowing back toward the dock.

"Wait a minute," he said, grabbing the oars from me. "I'm thinking."

While I waited on him, I watched Kheelan and Torin grazing in the nearby pasture.

"Okay, I've got it," he said, looking to the mountains beyond. I watched and waited.

He shifted toward me, with a look of defeat, revealing his grievous soul. Looking into his shamrock-green eyes now misted with tears, I waited for him to speak. His earlier teasing had been replaced with a somber tone. "You're my angel, Asher. If I possessed any power in this world, I'd want to undo the past so you'd see me the way you used to see me, even if only for a day."

Speechless, I embraced him, wishing with all my might that his dream could come true. I hated to see Patrick hurting, even if he had done this to himself. I didn't know what to say. There was nothing I could say, so I let the silence linger while I held him.

Thinking back on that day at the lake made me sad as we hugged good-bye a week later. He was headed back to school in New York, and I was headed to Dublin. Claire hurried me to the limo that would carry us to school, me to my sophomore year, and her to her junior year. Punching her brother on the arm as she passed was her way of saying "I love you" to him. I'd grown up with them both, and I knew they had their own special way of expressing their feelings.

As I peered out the window at the passing countryside, I wondered even how to define what I was feeling. My heart was divided. Patrick had been very attentive during the summer months and there was comfort in familiarity; but we were still fractured. I barely knew Rafe, but I kept thinking about him. Maybe I had just built him up in my mind. With him there was adventure and the thrill of the unknown—this indescribable, exhilarating dream bound up in a stranger.

In October, on my seventeenth birthday, Patrick sent me a huge bouquet of Irish wildflowers—my favorite, Gentiana verna. For years he had been reluctant to pick them even though he knew of my obsession. Silly, superstitious soul! He often chased after me, yelling, "Stop!" as I plucked them from the craggy floor of the moors. It was said that death followed the recipient of the Gentian. If that were true, I'd have died a hundred times before now; I was not a believer. Tucked in the tiny envelope that came with the flowers was a single seven-leaf clover. What was I going to do with him?

That evening Claire threw me an elaborate party. She rented a private dining room at Shanahan's on the Green in the heart of Dublin. More than one hundred people were invited, and there had to be at least that many in the spacious room. She had hired a grunge band, and we were still listening to the music late into the night. I lost track of time.

At a quarter past midnight, the stone around my neck grew hotter as the band jammed on.

"Oops," I said to myself.

After explaining to Claire that I had to get back and do some homework, I waved goodbye to those sitting near me and made my way outside, followed by Brógán. Morrighan's light, like magical, swirling stardust for my eyes only, led me into the nearby park. At that time of night, there was no one around.

"What's the hurry, Aish?" Brógán never had any recollection of the time I spent with Morrighan on my birthdays; she always put him to sleep with Diaga's dust. The light vanished at a bench on the path, and soon he was groggy. I helped him sit down and then hurried to keep up with the light burst. The rose-colored lanterns illuminating the path toward the fountain gave the illusion of security and peace. Still, I assembled my weapon just in case.

At times I had to run to keep up with Morrighan. Finally she stopped on the other side of the fountain in an unspoken gesture, meaning I should stay where I was. She disappeared. I wondered, "Okay, is she punishing me for being late to our usual midnight birthday appointment?" I had on my winter coat, but the chilly fall air made me shiver, which turned icy as I saw someone approaching me from the canopy of trees near the fountain. I leveled my taggert toward the moving target. Then the physical shiver turned to an emotional tremor within me as I saw a familiar figure step into the light. It was as if the onyx night had become a crystal-clear sea on a brilliant day. The gun fell from my shocked hands.

"Mom!" I shouted. I took one impetuous step toward her, but then she stopped me with a nonverbal cue of her hands. "Mom?" I said again, trying to understand her reluctance to be near me. As we stared at each other across the distance, I couldn't help but think of all the time we'd lost. All the hurt I'd felt for so many years came rushing out. "Why haven't you come to see me before now?" I cried.

"I've wanted to, Aishling. Believe me, I've wanted to be with you every day, every moment."

"Then why? Why has Morrighan come, and Cearnaigh, but not you? All these years, every birthday I hoped it would be you who came to me, and every year I've been disappointed." My passion overflowed in tears.

"Oh, Aishling, I'm so sorry. It's so difficult to explain. I'm not sure I can even try to explain it to you, and I don't have much time. But I promise you will understand soon. My baby, how you have grown! You are stunning!" she said, holding out her hands toward me as if she wanted to gather me in her arms. "I've missed you unbearably. Oh, how I wish I could hold you again, but I'll have to settle for holding you in my heart."

"But Mom, I'm right here. You can touch me and I you."

"No, I'm sorry, my dear, but you cannot touch me. I wish it could be so, for I would rush to you in an instant and hold you to myself until the world stopped spinning, but it can't be."

As my mother stood ten feet from me, my tears became sobs. She had come so far to see me, yet there was still a barrier between us, and I was not allowed to reach into her new world.

"Aishling, don't weep for me, for we'll see each other again someday. I have faith that you will find a way."

The air around her crackled as she stepped closer to me. She crossed her arms in front of her face as a shield.

"Mom!" I shouted, running toward her.

"Stop, Aishling!" she said in a frightened tone. I obeyed and stopped in my tracks. The electricity calmed as we both stood still. But it was getting late, and I knew the thin places would be closing soon.

"I'm lost, Aishling. I'm in a realm parallel to the Otherworld and this world."

"Lost? But Morrighan brought me to you," I said, confused.

"It was blind luck that brought me near enough to the thin place where Morrighan enters here on your birthday. I followed her in the adjoining realm, and she led me to you. Since my death I've been in the Otherworld with my people on the Isle of Tír na mBeo. One night recently I thought I saw you on the island. I ran after you, but something happened. I don't remember. When I woke up, somehow I was no longer on the island but was lying in the marshes of an unfamiliar moor. I saw the Dullahan in the distance. Morrighan told me you are the Searcher. She said you're the one who can help me and that you have powers the Maolán don't understand."

"The Dullahan is there? What am I to search for, Mom? What can I do? I'll do anything!"

"Your Uncle Brádach may be able to help. He knows all the old legends. It would be a good place to start at least."

"Okay," I said, troubled. "Are you safe, Mom?"

"Don't concern yourself with my safety, *a pheata* [Mama's little darling]." She looked above her as the air crackled once more and her light dimmed. Time was running out.

My hand grasped the air in front of me, and Mom lifted her hand in a similar gesture, both of us fighting to remain in the dimensions that held us yet longing to cross over. For a moment we stood that way, connected even with the space between us. I knew that everything was going to be okay because she still existed, and I was going to fight my way to her.

"I love you, Mom!" I shouted amid falling tears.

The unseen veil that held her hostage revealed itself, turning electric green when she stepped closer to threaten it. She bellowed as if in pain as she thrust her sword into the lurking shield, but it retaliated. She looked tortured as she reached out for me.

Her hands began to gnarl and twist as she shoved them through the charged barrier. Her attempted escape had her falling to the ground. She lay sideways, held her injured arms to her chest, and tried to appear unafraid and strong.

I bolted forward; my war cry drowned out the better judgment that sought to make me halt this madness. If I died, I died. Mom needed me. Maybe the thin places *had* made me unstable after all these years. I lifted the taggert as I ran, shooting faerie darts into the morphing force field. Patches opened, but they sealed right after penetration. I jumped through the air toward one of the holes, but a hooded figure caught me midjump and carried me back to my prior location, away from the thin place, and settled me on the ground. Shaking my head, I tried to make sense of what just happened. The beast, whatever it was, was nowhere in sight. Mom was on her knees, trying to get my attention. I jumped back to my feet.

"Be alert, Aishling, and know that I love you...always."

Her burnt hand was raised to me as if she were stroking my face. She faded in the yellow light.

"I love you!" she whispered again before she was pulled away.

I sunk to my knees in pain from my loss and whispered, "I love you more" to the aloneness of the night.

18

Live Your Life

(Aishling)

Anger overwhelmed me and more tears threatened, but Cearn-aigh had taught me to overcome emotion, and I called on my warrior strength now. I bit back curses on the Fates and swallowed the bitter taste of uninvited, traitorous tears. With restored composure, I stood to leave, and a figure emerged from the trees.

"Cearnaigh?" I questioned, remaining where I was but in my mind moving near the hawthorn, ready for whatever was coming next. He stepped into the light then, and I saw the tunic of green tartan and the familiar screaming-red hair of my mentor.

"Come here," he said, opening his arms, and I moved into his embrace, accepting his comfort.

After a moment I stepped back in realization. "It was you who stopped me?"

"Aye. Ye'd have been hurt, lass—or killed. Promise ye'll ne'er try that again," he pleaded and placed his strong hands on my shoulders. Lifting his bushy eyebrows, he waited for my reply.

I nodded. That was all I had in me at the time.

"Okay then," he acknowledged my compliance and moved to sit on a nearby bench.

I had just sat down beside him when the air sparked behind us. He and I swiveled off the bench, and I reached out to the hawthorn to retrieve my sword while the marking appeared, tingling onto my face. We watched the pavilion as Morrighan flowed down the stairs, every bit a queen, even though up close

145

I could see the scars from her many years as the fearsome war faerie of clan Delaney. I was sure most queens never saw battle. I was proud to be from this lineage. A Delaney never shirked from his or her duty no matter the gender.

She wore a voluminous blue gown that matched our sapphire eyes, and her hair was as long and black as mine. She stopped in front of us and stared at my face. "Cearnaigh did an exquisite job with your mark."

He bowed to her. "Thank you, my queen."

"So you already know my mom is missing, *Maimeó*. Has anything been done to try to rescue her from that horrible realm? She's in trouble!"

Not one to sugarcoat the facts, Morrighan said, "Your mom is trapped on the phantom island Uí Bracile, the favored realm of the Dullahan."

I dropped to the bench. It was true; my mom was in danger of being chased by the monster in that awful place. I had to do something.

"Nobody crosses that border," Cearnaigh chimed in. "Most don't have the pow'r to. The rest wouldn't dare try."

"The Council doesn't understand what he would want with her," Morrighan replied. "Your mom's not blood kin to the Delaney's and she's not a warring faerie, so when she died she didn't cross to our realm, Mag Mell. If the demons and Alorcán want someone to hold for ransom, the logical choice would be you, Aishling, not your mom."

My head was spinning.

"Legend says that ya can't find a thin place in that realm— ever. It's as solid as stone," Cearnaigh fumed. "The faerie had to have taken your mom there. She didn't just wander into its lair."

Morrighan moved to stand in front of me. "What if the Dullahan was watching the entire episode with you and your mom a while ago? Maybe the creature's trying to gather more information about you, Siridean. I'm sure the beast knows of the prophecy. I think it wants to find your weaknesses. It knows you have power, too, and it wanted to see just how much. Either that or the beast knows you'll come after her. Then the Alorcán will spring a trap."

This was not happening. My mom was dead, and the Dullahan was disturbing her in the afterlife? That was vile, revolting.

"My mom said I have powers the High King doesn't recognize. How?"

"Do ya not feel it, Aishling?" Cearnaigh spoke, his voice ragged, concern forming a thick unibrow above his eyes.

They were both staring at me. It was all too much to handle. I jumped up, turning away from them. The River Liffey flowed nearby. I couldn't see it, but I closed my eyes, listening to the soothing flow of the water.

"Sometimes I feel a surge of strength that's not human," I said, turning around. "I just assumed it had something to do with the marking."

"No, Aishling," Morrighan said. "The marking is a tool of Diaga—a little magic that helps you when we can't be there."

"So why do I sometimes feel like I could turn into a tornado and barrel through a mountain?"

Cearnaigh shifted on his feet while Morrighan's eyes expanded. "That is due in part to your Delaney blood mixed with my Maolán blood," she said. "There's some ancient power flowing through you. Everyone reacts differently to the genetic coding. Although with you being the prophesied one, I could imagine yours is stronger than most."

"And why can I swim underwater for an hour without surfacing for air?" Two pairs of stunned eyes regarded me in lengthened silence. "Yeah, I just learned that recently." They looked at each other. I pointed to my feet. "No big, long tail here. Not a mermaid," I said in full snarky mode. "Ever since the episode at the Rapids of Rua I...well, a lot of things are different. I feel different."

Morrighan paced while Cearnaigh gazed at the frosty ground.

"I'm drawn to fire, and I don't know why," I finished, leaning my back onto a nearby tree trunk and staring up at the stars.

"Aishling, why have ya been keepin' all this from us?" Cearn-aigh came closer.

"I didn't want to face it. I've been trying to ignore the stir-rings within me."

He looked at me and said, "This is not a working of Mag Mell. This is not yer fate as we know it."

Bowing before the phantom queen, he said, "I must be on my way to the Moerae, my lady."

"You can go to the Fates?" I interrupted. I had always thought they were just mythological beings.

"Yes, Aishling. Someone has altered yer course, and we need to know who. The Moerae may not be willin' to share. I'll have to take gifts. Yes," he said, and I could see him making a mental list.

He rambled to the bench to sit and think. "It can't be. Well, I guess...."

"What are you going on about?" Morrighan squawked.

He turned to me with his mouth agape. "The prophecy, Aish-ling. Do ya remember what it says?"

"Of course I remember. I've read it so often, I have it memo-rized." Then I quoted:

Alas, the carrier's purpose fulfilled
By the birth of the millennial Blood Moon
On distant phantom isle awaits
Cheating an unjust doom

The Searcher rides through gathering storm
To find the Lost Cave of Malachent
Where the faerie cross blade doth not weaken or waver
But cuts to breach the faulty vent

> If by the stroke of the Ten Colds Moon
> The Siridean slays the indomitable beast
> The Bearer will be unshackled
> And all will be restored to peace

"It makes more sense now," Cearnaigh mumbled. His face was white. "Aishling, I think the carrier is your mother, and her purpose was fulfilled by yer birth on the millennial Blood Moon."

"So that's why she's trapped on Uí Bracile. She's still alive! The prophecy says she's cheating death," I said with hope filling my soul.

Cearnaigh chimed in, "And this lost cave must be where ye'll have to go to find the entrance to that realm. This must be where the beast enters the earth. There's got to be a crack in the dimension shield there."

"Right, and I need to know when the Ten Colds Moon will occur."

"I'll try to get this information from the Moerae, Aishling," he pledged.

My gaze shot to the ground. I was considering the next part of the prophecy just like I had done when I was thirteen, and I was sure this was where Cearnaigh's thoughts had gone as well.

"And how am I to slay it?" I asked, looking to both of them.

"I've trained ye well. Ya have the ancient power in yer bloodstream. I have no doubt ye'll be prepared." Cearnaigh smiled, trying to reassure me. "Ye are, after all, *the* Gael Siridean. There is no other."

"Lucky me." A slight smile crossed his face. My smart mouth used to make him guffaw, but this had been a rough night. "Do you really think I can rescue mom from the Dullahan?" I asked my mentor.

He grasped my hands. "I have no doubts, my lady." He winked. "On that note I must be off, but I'll return to ya as soon as possible."

I reached up to kiss him on the cheek. "Thank you, Cearnaigh."

"You're welcome."

He disappeared, but Morrighan stayed. She handed me the cloak I had seen on my marking but had not yet received. "Happy birthday," she added, almost businesslike. "Cearnaigh can help you practice using the cloak some other time. I know you've used some of the Diaga's dust and you are familiar with its general purposes. Follow me and I'll show you how I used it to put your guard to sleep. You must get the dosage just right. You don't want him to have long-term damage."

I paid very careful attention to her instructions, for I didn't want to give my bodyguard brain damage. She had me practice a few times.

"On humans the dust merely puts them into a temporary fog much like sleep," she continued, "but you throw a pinch of this onto an Alorcán faerie and it burns them up like acid. Probably your best weapon."

"Yeah, I've seen it," I shuddered.

"Remember, just a pinch. That concoction's hard to come by."

Her appearance shifted and shimmered. I could tell she needed to return to the Otherworld. "What can I do in the meantime, Maimeó? While I wait on Cearnaigh, how can I help my mom?" Defeat cascaded down my face.

The response she gave was almost a human one coated with the smallest particle of maternal instinct. "Aishling, you must live your life, my dear. You need to trust us to do for your mom what you can't do right now. Your time will come."

"What can you do?"

"We can distract the beast, for one. There are ways. We'll figure this out. The Dullahan hasn't harmed her yet, so I don't think that's his purpose here."

"Have you ever fought the creature?" I asked.

She spun around and glided toward the pavilion, her velvet gown floating inches above the ground. As she blended with the shadows, I heard her whisper, "Yes."

19

Dream Song

(Rafe)

It was early December, nine months since I had last seen Aishling—when I had gone to visit her at college and found she was in love with someone else. Wishing for her happiness while suppressing my own was proving to be a futile occupation. My studies in the medical program helped me to lay aside thoughts of her for short periods of time, but Aishling was always there, rushing back to me during those quiet times of respite I allowed myself in between school and volunteer work. I needed to see her again. An idea formed in my mind of its own accord.

Three days later I travelled through the gates of Trinity College Dublin. I would not make her aware of my presence. I just needed to be near her once more—to say good-bye in my own way. As I walked across campus, I glanced upward to the fierce celestial dome—the winter sky splashed orange-red and blue flame. Too soon the scene gave way to nautical twilight, and I zipped my leather jacket, jamming my hands into the front pockets.

With purpose I strode toward her heart. I would not allow this closure to bring sorrow or regret. It would serve to lessen my anguish and help me move on. Lantern light spilled onto the cobblestone walkway as I joined a crowd in Parliament Square by the chapel in the center of the college. It appeared some function had just concluded inside one of the buildings, and the masses were dispersing.

I stopped under a tree and waited, watching for her to emerge. I knew she would—her heart was drawing nearer to mine. Then she stepped through the door, and when I saw her I wasn't prepared for my physical response. I had this overwhelming hunger for air, but my human body had lost its sense of irrepressible breath. Breath. An angel's breath is invigorating, capable of doing miraculous things. But this human breath was painful as I fought against the normally involuntary function. I felt dizzy, immobile, and I staggered sideways to take hold of the tree to steady myself, gasping to sate the hunger.

She was with a girl, one whom I sensed she loved like a sister. They were laughing as they sauntered down the steps, heading in the direction of the dorms. I was hidden in the shadows a good distance from her. On the wings of the breeze, I sent a message wafting to tickle her ear: "I love you and you alone, my angel." She wrenched to a stop and turned, looking all around. Groups of people conversed while her guards formed a protective circle ten feet in diameter around her.

"What's the matter?" the bodyguard directly behind her asked. She glared at him with her hands on her hips.

"Nothing," she replied and turned back around.

"Did you hear that?" she asked her friend.

"Hear what?" the girl replied.

"I guess I'm imagining things," she said before pivoting back and continuing in the direction she had been going.

The chamber of her heart where I resided flamed, and I felt the most soothing sunshine communicating with me across the otherwise cold darkness. My eyes closed on a pure sigh of delight. I followed from afar and watched her until she disappeared into the dorm. Dashing around the outside of the structure, I stopped when I felt her stop. There were some tall bushes below the window, and I sank down behind them with my back to the wall, comforted by the fact that I was able to be so near to her. The air was chilly, and I blew into my hands to heat them. For a long time, she stood at a window about twelve feet above me, and I was so warmed by her presence I forgot all about the frigid night. I wondered if somehow she could sense me too.

Since the time we had met last December, I had grown so attuned to her heart dialect I could feel when she moved and when her breathing slowed. As she drifted to sleep, I sang the ancient song of angels into her dreams, ensuring she would feel only joy—at least until the realities of a new day. Throughout the night I held vigil, varying the dream song in places, composing for her a new song. Her heart swelled and ebbed in soft waves with the music; I was captivated, consoled.

Dawn approached, her first light dancing through the trees. I pushed myself up from the wall and smiled because I was able to do this one small thing for Aishling. I left for the time being, needing some rest myself. At the entrance to the school, I turned left and found a hotel nearby, and fell asleep as soon as my head touched the pillow.

In early afternoon I awoke, showered, and put on some warm clothing. I was anxious knowing I would have to make the most of this day, for I would be leaving the next morning. After grabbing my long wool coat, I found my way down to the hotel restaurant, where I ate a hurried lunch. Then I stopped in a flower shop to buy a tiny bouquet of blue cyclamen, its color identical to Aishling's eyes. The meaning behind the flower—a farewell wish of love for the object of one's devotion. The florist took a dozen of the flowers and wrapped a lace ribbon all the way along the length of the stems. When she had finished, she placed the bouquet in a white box for me so I could hide it in my backpack.

The sun was still high and vibrant as I roamed underneath the campanile and stopped there to scan the area. Despite the cold many students lingered in standing clusters throughout the yard or lounged on concrete benches. The ground was a swirl of color with some leftover autumn leaves still drifting and settling on the earthen floor. I stood behind one of the pillars of the pavilion and spotted Aishling.

She was alone except for her bodyguards and was reaching down to capture a leaf of vivid crimson that kept blowing just out of her reach. I had to take advantage of the moment. The second that she secured her prize, I used my renewed angelic ability of breath to stir the wind, and the leaves funneled around her in a peaceful whirlwind. I heard her laughter; nothing brought me greater joy than that sound. When I silenced the wind, she was still holding that single leaf, intense determination lighting her features as she held it up to the sun. I laughed heartily, hidden a good distance away in the shelter of the bell tower.

She tucked the keepsake in a textbook in her leather satchel, which was lying on the ground at the feet of a very intense-looking guard holding a fully automatic weapon. He didn't even look down as she knelt; his eyes were scouring the yard. Unexpectedly she stood and took off running, leaping into the air in what appeared to be some fancy ballet move. Following a rather hazardous vault, where she leapt high, twisting her body in a full revolution, she landed gracefully at the feet of another guard and curtseyed grandly. A huge smile split her face as the guard smirked slightly, trying not to be distracted. She was uninhibited—a little mad perhaps—but engagingly so. I lifted my camera to capture the triumph in her charming expression.

After gathering her satchel and violin case, she and her brigade started down the path, and I followed, being cautious not to draw undue attention to myself. I wondered what her life must have been like—always surrounded, wondering each day if today would be the day that her family's enemies decided to seek revenge. There was only one guard with her in Spain; it was obvious that the enemies were closer to home or there was current unrest in Ireland.

I had not moved far from the campanile when shouts rang out behind me, and I turned to the disturbance. A ruckus brewed near the bell tower. I stepped off the sidewalk, concealing myself between two groups of students loitering on the grass outside the administration building. I watched Aishling—ready to aid if she were in danger. But her bodyguards had already set up a defensive formation around her. A camera crew jogged toward her, hurling questions.

"Miss Delaney, our sources tell us that your father is responsible for the ongoing paramilitary activity. They say his plan is to unite Ireland even if by force. What do you know of this?"

Her guards held the reporters back, but Aishling stepped closer. She looked uncertain of how to answer, and I wondered how much she knew about her father's dealings.

"I know nothing of my father's involvement. Excuse me," she said politely before turning away.

Undeterred, a young reporter blurted, "Your father was recently elected the new president of Sinn Féin, and there are validated rumors that the political party is linked to the Provisional Irish Republican Army [PIRA]."

Aishling turned back to him with a look that indicated she was unfamiliar with this information. "Just what are you trying to say, Mr...?"

"Quinlivan. The name's Quill Quinlivan," he said, handing a business card to one of her guards. "If it's true that there are links to the PIRA, then your father could be creating a new civil war. Under the Belfast Agreement, the paramilitary groups were to decommission their weapons by May 2000. Is it true, Sinn Féin is noncompliant with the provisions of the agreement?"

I came close to blowing my cover just then so I could punch the badgering reporter in the face. Before that happened, however, she turned away. I followed in the grass along with a group of students who were now crowding in and trying to find out what the interrogation was all about.

"No comment," I heard her say as she sashayed away, head held high.

The news crew barreled after her, and the reporter got in one more comment before being slammed to the ground by a bulky soldier. "Miss Delaney, the Northern Bank of Ireland was robbed today. The thieves got away with $26.5 million euros. The PIRA is being blamed. Our source says the robbery was strategically planned to occur while the Sinn Féin was in talks with the Irish and British governments about a peace settlement. If the two groups are linked, well—"

Half a dozen of her guards rushed her away from the crowd while the other ones forced the news crew in the other direction.

Several minutes passed before Aishling and her entourage came near to the Samuel Beckett Theatre. I hid around the corner out of sight. Before she disappeared into the building, I heard her conversing with the guard who had been with her in Spain.

"Aish, I don't think ya should go to practice today. Why don't ya let the other guards and me take ya away for a few days, just 'til this latest fiasco of yer father's dies down?"

"Brógán, I'm *going* to practice," she said, stiffening her spine. "I can't control any of my father's behavior, but I can surely control my own, and I'm not going to let him ruin my life. I'm considering moving out of the castle for good and renouncing my claim to anything with his name on it. But I'm concerned with what will happen to the innocent members of my clan. They deserve better. And there are other reasons I can't discuss."

Holding his hands up in a gesture of defeat, he said, "Fine! We'll do it yer way, ya stubborn lass!"

"Such talk could be considered insubordination," she challenged, smiling as she sprang up the steps and opened the door.

"I'll show ya insubordination," he played back, as he rushed up the steps and nuzzled her head with his knuckles. She ducked away, laughing.

She was a strong, classy lady to appear so unruffled by such accusations against her family. My admiration of her quadrupled.

A sign near the entrance indicated that today was the dress rehearsal for the *Nutcracker* ballet. I waited outside for about five minutes and entered with a crowd of students who were coming to watch the performance. I sat toward the back, wondering what role Aishling had in the production.

The ballet began; I heard the melody drift up from the orchestra pit, but I couldn't see her. The stage lights lowered to an icy blue. Girls dressed as faeries in white dresses danced in procession onto the scene of snow-bowed evergreens. As they lifted their arms to fly across the stage, they scattered snowflakes into the air. While the music crescendoed, I saw Aishling floating across the floor, weaving in and out of the other dancers. When she spun in the air, strumming the violin, the stage lights caught her just right and she sparkled from head to toe. It had been a long time since I'd seen anything so magical.

I was so caught up in her beauty and the technical difficulty of her performance, I didn't realize what was happening until it was too late: Aishling had stopped dancing. She launched straight through the crowd of startled ballerinas so fast it seemed impossible. In her wake, she left several toppled dancers who had crashed into each other during her dash to the front of the stage.

"I'm sorry. I'm so sorry," she said to them, wincing. She was shielding her eyes against the bright stage lights and was looking in the general direction of my seat.

20

Dream Wander

(Rafe)

The shadows assisted me as I escaped behind a wall in the back of the auditorium that led to a side exit door. I ran away, not once looking back to see if I was being followed. On the edge of campus, I found a small garden and stopped there to catch my breath. The day was drawing to a close and the soft glow of the sidewalk lanterns illuminated the paths. While I stood before the cascading fountain, my sensitive hearing picked up delicate footfalls advancing toward the garden. I parted the limbs of the balsam tree and saw her coming my way. With barely any time to think, I took the flowers from my pack and laid them on a wrought-iron bench tucked between some bushes, along with the letter I had written to her before I'd left my hotel room earlier in the day. Of course I hadn't signed the letter. The words could have been from any suitor or secret admirer wishing to secure her hand. But I hoped that when she read them, she would think of me.

The balsams formed a thick natural fence around the outdoor sanctuary with another gate near the main street, a few feet from where I was standing. I just had time to exit and hide on the other side before she came rushing through the other opening. I parted the limbs above the lawn seat and watched her.

She looked around warily, circling the garden and searching the dark places. Then she discovered the flowers and the note. When her guards caught up to her, she stopped them near the entrance to wait for her. I watched as she moved to sit on the edge of the bench, laying her fiddle beside her. She lifted the blossoms to inhale the sweet scent and gently ran her fingers through the lace. Then she lowered the flowers to the bench and reached for the note. Glancing around once more as if she feared that she might be intruding on someone else's moment, she took a second to consider before slipping the sheet of paper from the envelope and unfolding it. Using the light from her cell phone, she was able to do to me what I had been doing to her since the day we had met: she read my heart.

My love,

'Tis with sweetest torment I find myself penning this letter. Confusion awaits my every step, and I am left dangling over this everlasting inferno—the ache of masked passion. Reviving your embrace, my happiest memory, brings both exultation and defeat. To speak my heart would make the coming years without you more endurable, knowing I had laid bare the recesses of my spirit and given you the choice to run away with me to another realm, a faraway universe. But I fear I cannot declare my devotion to you, for it has been forcibly withheld.

Instead I've traversed the fires and leapt through the flames in search of your heart, only to be barred within sight of my hope and the revelation to you of my deepest desires. If only I lived in your world. To attain your love in return, would unleash refreshing rivers, invading this dry desert of my soul, soaking in to soothe my unspeakable agony. Then I could offer you a renewed man, thirst quenched in rapturous joy. Then I could give you an eternal kiss. Then you would forever be...my angel.

X

No expressions of emotion betrayed her feelings as she stared into the fountain that reflected wavy light onto her face. I watched for a sign, anything. Surely she knew the letter was meant for her. No sob escaped the private princess as her eyes remained locked on the fountain, but then I witnessed a silent downpour of tears, a torrent tumbling to her arms. Yet, she remained still, her gaze fixed on the pool in front of her. A moment that will forever haunt me—solitary, restrained grief.

A bird swooped to drink from the fountain, breaking her trance. She wiped beneath her eyes, and then she folded the letter and placed it in the violin case slung across her back. Resigned, she picked up the flowers and went with her guards back toward campus. There was doubt, but I saw the possibility, the rekindling of the fire attached to my face in her heart. I'm not sure why that thrilled me so, knowing that this was good-bye. But somehow I knew I would eventually be okay, with the knowledge that wherever she was or whatever she did with her life I'd be there in the depths of her mind, and she would know she was treasured even if from afar.

Sleep was out of the question. The campus was in the shape of a thick cross, and I trudged the entire perimeter—twice. By that time most of the room lights had blackened, so I wandered to her dorm and sat beneath the window once more. I knew going back there was a mistake. The garden was supposed to be the end. With my back to the stone wall, I slid to the ground, feeling her heart aching inside my own; it was squeezing and erratic, and I pulled at my hair.

When I lifted my head, there was a visitor at my side.

"Vitale? What are you doing here?" I protested.

"I sensed you were in trouble, my friend. The real question is what are *you* doing here? This is not your purpose."

Passion welled within me as I tilted my head upward to the light streaming from her window. If this were not my purpose, then why did I feel this intensity, this fire? "Why not, Vitale? Why can't I be this as long as I fulfill my other duties?"

"You don't belong here."

"That's not good enough!" I said, straining to look upward again. The light had gone out. My duty was to sing to her, and the angel was getting in my way. "You've got to give me a better reason than that, Vitale."

"I had hoped you would get over this obsession with the girl, but I must inform you that your orders are to stay away from her in particular."

"Why?"

"You know why."

Frustrated, I stood to roam to the sidewalk and back, thinking, pacing, plotting. Stopping in front of him, I asked, "Will you allow me to say good-bye? You know—with my old powers?"

"She cannot know that you've been here. It's not wise to make her aware."

"I thought of a way. Trust me. Please, friend."

Vitale groaned and rubbed his hands up and down his face—clearly agitated. Relenting, he handed over his cloak. "This is against my better judgment," he debated, "but I'll allow it this one time."

"Thank you," I answered and shoved my arms in the angel's cloak.

I gave him the name of my hotel and the room number, and asked him to wait for me there. As soon as he left, I turned to the old, stone building. After pulling the hood over my head, I whisked the cloak around and thought of her—only her. In less than a millisecond, I was standing in the shadows of her room, removing the hood so she wouldn't be as frightened.

Aishling was alone and restless, tossing, struggling with the sleep faerie. Angry tears lashed my eyes, and I wondered what darkness had invaded her dreams. I couldn't bear it. With urgency I began to hum the dream song—the one I'd created—from my mind to hers. She moaned, but then a stillness came over her, serenity replacing the storm. I hated to disturb her just yet; her mind needed to rest. So I sat in a chair and sang to her for a little over an hour.

She was immersed in unconscious reverie, but still I had to give her a choice whether or not to join me in dream wanderings. If she refused I would have to respect her wishes, for an angel can't impose his will on another. Angels are able to call mortals away, sort of like an out-of-body experience in a dream state. When angels are guarding humans, they help to protect them from emotional trauma. So the dream wanderings commence in the form of play, helping the humans to solve their own problems through fun and games in the mind.

Holding my hands palms up, I produced a light that gave off a soft glow, illuminating the room. "Aishling," I whispered into her dream. In her mind I watched as she turned to look at me. As realization struck her, she swung her legs off the bed, moving to a sitting position.

"Raphael?" she asked groggily, rubbing her eyes. "Is it you?"

"Yes, it's me, angel," I responded.

She stood but did not approach me. I watched her brows ruffle. Her fingers laced together in front of her and she tilted up on her tiptoes. "I've missed you," she said with childlike honesty.

"You have no idea how I've longed for you, Aishling. Please come!" I begged as I opened my arms to receive her. She jumped into my waiting embrace, and I held her close. Rubbing her hair, I was intoxicated by her familiar scent—warm citrus sunshine.

After a brief time, she straightened to look at my face so close to her own, since I was still holding her off the floor. "You brought me flowers," she said.

"Yes," I replied, smiling.

"But the letter confused me."

"Yes, I suppose it did," I said, unwilling to clarify. Changing the subject, I asked, "Will you come with me, Aishling, to explore with me the possibilities for your life, for your future?"

"Of course."

With her permission, I whisked the cloak around to seal us in. "Where do you want to go?"

She thought for a moment, as I held her to me and we floated through the clouds. "I want to run with you on the Cliffs of Sliabh Liag," she said, laughing.

"To the cliffs!" I said, charging toward them in my mind, and we laughed together. In a moment I touched her bare feet down on the fertile grass atop the hillside. In the dream it was a perfect, sunny day. The waves crashed below as she ran at full speed, teetering on the edge to peer into the battling surf.

"Come on, Raphael!" She motioned to me with her hand. I was beside her in an instant, watching the sunlight give a glimmering sheen to her onyx locks. Then she reached out to hold my hand, and we stood looking out to sea, content in the moment.

Glancing sideways at me, she winked. Then she leaned forward, pulling me with her over the edge of the cliff. This was a dream after all—one that she was creating. We flew down toward the water and landed on a massive sea stack jutting up out of the ocean a good ways from shore.

"I've always wanted to come out here to this mass," she said, holding on to the side of the boulder.

"Then I'm glad you made it happen."

Without warning play swords appeared, one in her hand and one in mine. Her rage-filled eyes flashed, surprising me out of the previous playfulness. She lunged at me as we hung on to the side of the rock, and she yelled in thick Gaelic, "I'll slay all ye bottom dwellers! The Alorcán will be no more!" Fencing in a complete revolution around the sea boulder, our play swords crashed as we hung above the waves that licked at our feet. "Die, you scum of the Otherworld!" she shouted, her technique with the sword so skilled that more questions filled my mind, begging to be answered. For one second I looked down, and she jabbed me in the ribs with her plastic weapon.

"I win!" she exclaimed, the sound echoing off the water, her smile jubilant. Our swords disappeared, and she looked thoughtful.

"What next?" I asked.

"As with my future, I just want things to be simple right now, bordering on the outskirts of ordinary," she responded, grabbing my hand once more and flying back to the cliffs. We fell from about four feet above the earth, landing in a jumble of limbs, twisted up in each other's arms. When we settled, her back was to the ground and I was leaning over her, still cradling her head. "I want you in my future, Raphael."

I heard her say the words, but I couldn't believe them. What about the guy I had seen her with just months earlier?

She reached up and pulled my head down to brush her lips with mine. I didn't hesitate. I was enjoying her dream far more than I should have. With the warmth of the sun and the feel of her body so close, I could have remained in this simple moment for all of eternity and been satisfied. Her hand was on my cheek, and she looked soulfully into my eyes, trying to get into my head, pick out my secrets. I looked away. She and I were already connected far more than we should have been.

"So you want a lullaby," I said, gazing between her lips and her eyes, "but all I hear is a symphony." Desire burned within me, and I gathered her up in my arms, cradled her in my lap, and pressed my lips to hers, coaxing her own to part. I held her head to mine, not giving her the choice to back away from me. The demons within me took hold of her dream wander, making it their own, and I joined them, stumbling in my purpose. I fought them back and broke the connection, settled her on the ground, and stood up to take hold of my emotions.

After a brief time she stood, tilting her face to the sun, a look of delirious joy on her pale face. "You kissed me back," she said, biting her bottom lip as she smiled. "I like this dream very much."

I couldn't help but be confused by her casual tone given what had just transpired. I figured that by now she would have banished me from her dream. "Why me, Aishling? Why do you want me in your future?" I wrangled with a gruff voice, the demons still not in check.

She shrugged her right shoulder and bent to lift a wildflower from the patch of grass at her feet. "It's so hard to explain," she mused, twirling the maroon clover between her fingers. "When I saw you at the cathedral in Spain, I knew you. I don't even know how that's possible, but I did." Stopping in front of me now, she touched my arm. With passion she said, "You're my fire, Raphael. That's why I need you in my life. You warm me. You've changed me. You give my life color." Her cheeks flamed, and I knew I could not ignore her plea, but still I couldn't answer her.

This particular dream wander was becoming too real. I had never participated in one so emotionally charged; probably because I was so involved with this dreamer.

"Let's live here in this dream," she pleaded, burying her face in my chest. "That's my wish," she whispered. "I'd leave everything behind right now to come away with you."

Wrapping my arms around her, I let the silence linger. I knew I should have changed the direction of her wandering some time ago, but I couldn't stop the flow or her words. I wanted her. I wanted to steal the cloak and not take her back to the earth realm. I would keep her. But that was complete insanity, and I knew it.

For a brief time, I allowed myself my own dream. "Okay," I said. "This is our place. This is where we'll live." She tilted her face skyward, and I leaned down to plant a kiss on her tear-stained lips, raining kisses from there to her cheek to her forehead. We stood just like that, holding each other; the sea waves crested and fell in beat with our combined breath, until I realized the time. She would need to wake up soon. I couldn't keep her from her real life any longer. Before she could protest and I had further time to talk myself out of it, I whisked the cloak around, returning to her dorm room without another word.

It was possible that in the future she would remember the next moment, but more likely she would just connect it to the dream. "Aishling, the dream wander is over. Look at me!" I begged, and she sat up in bed. With a dazed expression, she lifted her gaze. When she saw me, instant tears formed in her glowing sapphire eyes, which were so luminous I fell to my knees in front of her. A deep pain tore at my heart. I reached up and cradled her face in my hands.

"Raphael," she pleaded. "Don't go away."

167

I brushed her tears with my thumbs and my head drooped. My breath caught and my throat pinched. Closing my eyes, I welcomed the soul-escaping tears. My eyes met hers once more and I pulled her to me. Our lips joined. I wrapped my arms around her and we both shook as the kiss deepened and our grief combined. I couldn't leave her. I didn't have the will.

A command invaded my thoughts: a demand issued by Vitale that I leave Aishling immediately. I pulled away from her and growled. My eyes flamed. I couldn't stop them. Aishling gasped and covered her mouth with her hand. Shaking my head, I tried to calm down. When I looked at her there was no fear, only concern in her eyes. She let me take her hand in mine. I lifted it and brushed her knuckles with my lips.

"You're mine...always," I proclaimed.

With that, I disappeared from her life.

Rambling through the heart of Dublin in the predawn hours, I allowed the sorrow to pour from me in unending tears. I wandered for miles beside the River Liffey, searching its black depths for any form of shallow peace. At daybreak, with no inner truce forthcoming, I tromped back to the hotel room, threw the cloak at Vitale, and left him reeling. Then I stormed away, forcing myself to freeze that soul chamber that was so attuned to hers, cutting off that emotional communication that had become too painful to bear. The cold outside was nothing compared to my now frigid heart. Mortals call it "selective mutism" when one of them cannot communicate with another even though they may have the desire. Due to some trauma, their bodies and minds refuse spoken interaction with a certain person. Even though I knew I would still think of her in the coming years, I was no longer connected to the language of her heart that had been my companion over oceans and rivers of time.

For the next two years, I went through the motions of life and academia. Pouring myself into my studies and research, I accelerated myself through the General Internal Medicine program. In July I would be starting my residency in a small town in the mountains of Costa Rica. That would be quite a change of pace for me, going from the Texas flatlands and commercialism to a place where hills dotted the landscape and the clock ticked slower.

Maybe Costa Rica would be an escape for me. I could hardly imagine any Irish people living there in the jungle, reminding me daily of what could have been. Maybe I'd stop longing for the girl with ink-black hair and an aura of gold. I had tried to forget her, believe me. But the harder I tried, the sharper my memories became of her. My frozen heart was in the pre-melting phase, but I was still trapped underneath the glacier I had constructed. All I could conceive in my mind was the abysmal pain I would endure if I ever truly surfaced.

21

Fragmented

(Aishling)

The next October, a few weeks before my eighteenth birthday, I met with my college advisor to finalize plans for my senior year. Toward the end of April, six months from then, I would be moving to Costa Rica for a year to complete the requirements for my Spanish major. In order to graduate, I needed a year of language and culture immersion in a Spanish-speaking country.

I'd been fascinated by various languages since my early years. I'd chosen Spanish as my major to appease my father even though I would have preferred to continue my studies in the Semitic languages I'd begun learning in high school. Father had been okay with my choice of majors; he'd seen it as necessary that I be able to converse with the Spanish-speaking servants at Kavanaugh Castle once Patrick and I were married.

We had a housekeeper at the castle who spoke Spanish with just a few common English phrases—just enough to get her by and not test my father's patience. She had taught me the basics of the language, and she'd always spoken in her native tongue around me to help me practice Spanish.

In college my short-term goal took form while my long-term plans remained at odds with my heart. Short-term, I wanted to live in an underdeveloped, Spanish-speaking country and either teach English or work as a translator. Long-term I was playing with the idea of escaping Ireland and everything that weighed me down there. Of course this was one thought I kept from my father. He never would have allowed me to work toward the goal of completing my Spanish degree if he had known what was on my mind.

Initially, when my advisor had mentioned different countries where former students had gone to finish their programs, somehow I had felt a peculiar pull to Costa Rica. He found the perfect place for me: a small town named Tilarán located in the mountains. I would be living and working at an orphanage there that needed an English teacher but couldn't afford to pay one.

During the third weekend in October, I went home for my birthday. It was a week early, but I had a huge paper due at the end of the next week, so I knew I wouldn't be able to go home for my actual birthday. When I got there, Father was in his office with the door closed, and I was never supposed to disturb him there, so I wandered out to the gardens, drifting among the wildflowers and the water features.

I was lying on my stomach on the grassy floor surrounded by pink rhododendrons and blue clematis; I had just plucked a large bloom and was inhaling the perfumed aroma when a vision transformed the scene around me. Enveloped on every side by a group of giant angels who were dressed like warriors, I was riding on horseback toward something at nighttime. Dressed like a warrior too, I looked fearsome and uncharacteristically angry. I lurched upward, dropping the bloom, and the vision dissipated. The morning sun shining down on me now was comforting in contrast to the darkness of the vision I'd just experienced.

Running my fingers through my hair to pull at the tangles, I pondered the puzzle piece I'd just been handed through the vision. I hopped up, brushed off my pants, and proceeded toward the side door of the castle. Drawing closer to the open, wrought-iron gate between the gardens and the castle grounds, I could see my father standing with his back to me underneath the portico of the side entryway where I was heading. It was very unusual to see my father out in this area unless he was conducting business on the back patio.

Through the gate I watched him. He was standing there looking down, but I couldn't see what he was staring at from that angle. I moved through the gate and ducked behind the wide trunk of a sprawling tulip tree. I climbed up into the cover of the tree, for I knew he wouldn't notice me there amid the thick, green canopy. Positioning myself on one of the upper limbs, I looked down in surprise at first, but then I understood what he was staring at and why.

My mother had been the best gardener at the castles. Even the hired gardeners had looked to her for advice. Through the years she had worked in the gardens for pleasure, and she'd always entered and exited through this side door; she kicked off her dirty gardening shoes right there under the portico. Since her death twelve years ago, her gardening shoes had never been moved.

It was a good five minutes that I watched my father staring at those tattered shoes as if he were reminiscing about Mom. It was apparent that he was grieving, for today was the anniversary of her death, but I'd never seen him show any emotion one way or the other after that first year. This was confusing, yet refreshing, to watch. He cared. He still loved her, I thought, which softened me toward him in a way I'd not been able to do for years.

I watched as he buried his face in his hands and wept. My compassionate nature told me to run to him and wrap him in my arms, to help heal and share the pain that I felt too, but I knew he would brush me off. He would be furious with me that I'd caught him immersed in his private pain, so I only watched as he gazed at those old, muddy shoes. I cried with him, yet separate from him. After a few minutes, he opened the door and disappeared inside.

Straddling the tree limb and leaning my back onto the trunk, I gave in to my own grief and let the sorrow flood me. What was almost sadder than my mother's death was the fact that my father was still in my life yet nowhere to be seen. It had been a year since I'd seen Mom in the park. And it had been a year of futile research, scouring through Uncle Brádach's mind and legend books, trying to find the answer to my dilemma. Of course he didn't know the precise reason for my inquiry. It would have brought up too many questions, and I had been sworn to secrecy. I often wondered where she was, and I feared for her as she roamed alone. I was so angry with myself. This Siridean job didn't come with a manual; I was just supposed to figure things out. A hero got answers. They sure didn't sit around moping. Feeling fragmented, I jumped down from the tree and went into the castle to wash my face.

My father had nothing special planned in the way of a birthday celebration. He did take a break from work long enough to eat supper with me, but even that was cut short by the arrival of a small unit of soldiers in the front foyer. Trying to make small talk, I moved with him from the dining room toward the entryway of the castle.

Then I broached a topic that I had forgotten to mention earlier, but one that I felt he would find agreeable. "I spoke with my advisor about the country for my language and culture immersion, and I've decided to move to Costa Rica for my senior year."

For the whole length of the hallway he was silent. From time to time I glanced up at him, but his face gave nothing away. "No," he finally replied.

My tennis shoes squeaked on the polished floor as I came to an abrupt stop. I stared at the back of his head, dumbfounded. A few feet ahead of me, he curved in my direction with cold eyes, daring me to question him. I'd given up trying to understand his moods a long time ago. I sure didn't understand this one. He knew I had to move somewhere for my Spanish immersion year to complete my degree. Why would it matter to him which Spanish-speaking country I moved to as long as I would be relatively safe?

"But, Father, the arrangements have already been made. I've even spoken with the headmaster of the orphanage where I'll be working. She's expecting me to be there to teach English at the end of April. I thought you'd be happy that I chose Costa Rica. It's safer there than it is here. What's wrong with it?" I asked, trying to understand his hostile disposition.

With his hands in his pockets, he seemed to study the portrait of Mom hanging on the wall in front of him. Then he shoved his hand through his hair and through gritted teeth replied, "Do whatever you want."

He turned and strolled around the bend in the corridor, and I let out the breath I'd been holding as I stared after him. Shaking my head in frustration, I followed him and headed to my room. I passed by the dozen or so soldiers, all wearing black berets with small badges bearing the symbol of the Easter Uprising of 1916. These weren't my father's usual guards protecting him because of his political position. They were wearing the sign of the PIRA. Had the reporter been right about my father? I no longer doubted what he was capable of. I missed Mom so much. She would know how to stop him.

Some birthday, I thought, as I lay across my bed, listening to music and looking through a magazine Claire had given me. After turning the pages for all of two minutes, I flicked it off the bed and lay back, staring at the ceiling. Closing my eyes, I thought of Patrick. He had broken my trust, and for the past few years he himself had been broken, almost unrecognizable. He begged me to forgive him and, of course, I had. But actions have consequences, and to me the marriage alliance was annulled. However, I still loved him fiercely. Most of my memories were tied up in him.

Patrick secretly bankrolled his own bodyguards to watch over his son. So whenever he came home for summer vacation or holiday breaks, his son was protected back in the states. I often wondered what he would do after graduation this May. If he planned on pushing for our marriage, it only seemed logical that his son—the next Kavanaugh heir—would move to Ireland to take his place with his clan. I would hate to be in Patrick's shoes during that conversation with his parents.

Time was running out; I was moving into my adult years, and the curse beckoned. Yet I evaded and steered clear of any talk of our enforced marriage. I knew Patrick feared for what my father might do to me for something that was his fault. Needless to say, I was ready to get out of Ireland. I was in desperate need of some new memories.

A fire-blazed reflection ignited all my senses, one that refused to diminish in its intensity. *Raphael.* I turned my head sideways on my pillow to see the small bouquet, long dried out, nestled on my nightstand. I lifted it to inhale the memory of that night in the garden as I ran my fingers through the lace. *He had to have been there.* Sitting up on the bed, I unfolded the note he had left for me on the bench that night, and I read it for the hundredth time. I recalled the dream that had been so real. He had been in my room. He'd said I belonged to him, and then he'd left me.

It was time for me to move on.

22

Stolen

(Aishling)

At the Kavanaughs' annual Celtic New Year celebration that evening, they had a birthday cake for me as usual. Mrs. Kavanaugh always made sure of it. They moved the party back a week this year just for me, and I was so grateful they'd made me a part of their family. Uncle Brádach, Patrick, and Claire showered me with gifts. They knew better than that, but they never could seem to resist, knowing that my father never made my day very special. I guess he just always assumed that with the $100,000 his accountant kept in my checking account at all times, I would go and buy whatever I wanted, which was not the case.

Patrick and Claire never had understood why I didn't want to take any of my father's money, but I had always suspected that he had come by most of it dishonestly, and I didn't want to be a part of that. I knew that he made a good living in Parliament and that he had made some wise investments, but that didn't explain his tremendous wealth. Just to be on the safe side, I had started working in the stables for Uncle Brádach when I was fourteen and had saved most of the money I'd earned working after school, on the weekends, and during summer breaks. Also, since I would be turning eighteen, I would be inheriting my mother's money, which she had inherited from her parents when they had died. So I was going to be okay financially on my own; that was important to me.

Before the fireworks display, I was sitting on a hay bale and absently watching the bonfire, when a blanket was set on my shoulders. Patrick appeared beside me.

"So, Costa Rica, huh?" he said, bumping my shoulder with his.

"Sí, señor," I said, pushing back at him.

"Things aren't going to be the same around here without you."

"I'm not leaving yet. You and Claire act like I'm packing up and flying out tomorrow. I still have a whole semester of school left. I'll be home most weekends until then."

"I know. I just have a hard time thinking of you going halfway around the world, no matter when it is."

"I'll be back before you know it. Okay, no more gloom." As if in answer to my statement, the sky lit up with brilliant colors. The sparkles rained down from the sky, and Patrick looked at me with the gaze I'd always recognized as mine—the one he had reserved just for me. I knew that no matter what the future held, in time pain could be patched, and this boy would always be my best friend.

A week later, on my actual birthday, Morrighan didn't come. I guessed she had given me all the weapons I could possibly carry.

The holidays and then the spring semester passed by fast, like Kheelan when he was racing against Torin; the anticipation of something new and adventurous around the next curve drove me on, a challenge issued and accepted. Before I had much time to contemplate the extreme changes that were about to take place in my life, it was April, and I was packing for my long-awaited internship in Costa Rica. Over the weekend it seemed that Patrick, Claire, and I spent every waking hour together. Patrick had flown in to see me before I left, and Claire had come home from Dublin for a few days. She was so proud of me for taking this journey, but Patrick was much less than thrilled. Still he tried not to put a damper on my excitement.

That Sunday afternoon, we saw Patrick off, and then Claire and I gallivanted to the old bridge, where secrets had often been dispensed and time lazed away. We perched on the thick stone parapet facing the river, and Claire became her melodramatic self. "I suppose I'll just have to deal with texting you each day that you're gone," she said with a theatrical pout.

"That will be kind of hard since I'm not taking my cell phone."

She sat up straight, looking indignant. "Not taking your cell phone! What will I do if I need you and you're not right there?"

Laughing at her, I replied, "If there's an emergency, you can reach me on the phone at the orphanage. But there was a wonderful mode of communication created a long time ago. Oh, something called a letter."

"You can't be serious—me write a letter? I barely have time to do my nails," she said with a princess-like air. "Actually, I broke a nail last week while texting," she sulked while examining her right hand.

"See! Texting's a hazard. It's the universe telling you to pick up a pen."

Claire became quiet as she looked downstream. "I'm sure going to miss you, Ash."

"I'll miss you too," I said, hugging my stand-in sister.

A few nights before I left, I was in Delaney Castle by myself—besides security personnel and servants, of course. Spring was in full force, and I could smell the fresh-cut grass from my bedroom window. Dusk had not yet captured all the day's warmth. I needed to get out of the house; it was just necessary to get outside and breathe.

Feeling nervous and anxious, I needed an extreme dose of Mom. Moving through the damp corridors under my room, I used a flashlight to locate the place where I'd stored her music box so many years earlier. I'd taken great care in wrapping it in a thick cloth when I was ten years old and left it hidden, except for on very special occasions with Patrick and Claire. My father had become bolder in his search for it, and I didn't want to take any chances of him finding it. Holding it in my hands again felt like home—love—Mom. I knew I would be packing it in my luggage for my trip. For tonight, though, I needed a memory infusion. Since my father was in England for some important political meeting, I felt safe taking it topside.

Cradling the box, I grabbed my jacket and headed through the kitchen to the back patio that faced the black forest. I sat back in one of the lounge chairs, cranked the aged knob on the music box, and closed my eyes. A light wind blew over me, and I pulled my jacket over my upper body like a blanket.

The music produced such a soothing calm that I soon drifted and dreamed, although this was more reality than dream. It was my fifth birthday. My mom and I waited in the castle for dad to get home. Uncle Brádach, Patrick, and Claire were with us as well. I smiled in my sleep, happy that I was still able to recall happy times with mom. These memories were more vivid when I dreamed.

When dad's car pulled in front of the house, I skipped across the front lawn into his waiting arms. "*A Thaisce* [Ah-Hash-ka means 'My Treasure']! *Breithlá shona duit* [Happy Birthday]! He grinned as he kissed the tip of my nose and carried me into the house. Back then he made me feel like his treasure, as his pet name for me suggested. It was so hard to see him as he was now, when I could still feel his embrace, still hear his festive whistling, still see the love he had for me in his eyes then. Now, there was a darkness in him that was disturbing.

After I blew out the candles, my dad did the honor of turning me upside down and gently bumping my head on the floor five times, and then an extra bump just for good luck. *Crazy Irish traditions!* I smiled. In my dream I saw my mom lean behind the antique piano and pull out the old music box.

A constant, building source of tension between my father and me over the years, revolved around that ancient, weathered music box that my mom had given me on that day. It didn't help matters any that I was rarely parted from it. There were too many good memories tied to it that were associated with mom, and I couldn't let it go. It seemed that all he saw in the music box was her, as well; but unlike me, he didn't want the reminder.

The music box was not remarkable. There were no marks on it that indicated its origin. It was made from a silver metal that was now tarnished with age, and it was shaped like a medium-sized book. There was a handle on it that made it easy for me to hang onto as I ran through the fields or rode on my horse.

That night, when mom had tucked me in, I learned why she had given me such an unusual gift.

"Music is well said to be the speech of angels," mom quoted. "That Thomas Carlyle is a very wise man, for certain."

"Mama, was this your music box when you were my age?"

"Aye, and now it belongs to you, *A Pheata* [Mama's little darling]," she crooned, as she touched my cheek.

"The music is pretty."

"Yes, I know. It used to comfort me in my sleep when I was about your age. The song in the box is about a young human girl who befriended a faerie named Kían, one of the Maolán. Every night the faerie guarded her while she slept. One night the Alorcán came for her. At first the faerie was outnumbered. He turned to the sleeping girl with terror in his eyes for what awaited her. But then a magical thing happened."

"What was it, Mama?" I asked, with wide eyes.

"A host of angels swept into the room, encircling the girl, and protecting the faerie. The Alorcán had no choice but to retreat."

"Then why does the song seem so sad?"

"Och!" she parried. "That's another story for another time, dear. Maybe when you're a bit older." She tickled me. "Right now, my little princess needs her sleep." I giggled while she stood and pulled the covers up around me.

"Mama, I've been having nightmares. You're too far away on the other side of the castle. When I cry, you don't hear me, and I'm too scared to walk down the dark hallways by myself."

"Oh, sweetie, I'm so sorry." She brushed the hair from my brow. "But that's why I gave you the music box. I know what you're dreaming about. I had the same dreams. We're connected, you and me."

"How's a box supposed to help me?" My nose wiggled and my face scrunched.

"You may not understand all the reasons until you're older, but for now I can tell you that this box will drive away the Alorcán. You mark my words; there'll be no evil faeries interrupting your dreams, *a ghrá* [my love]. There's magic in this music," she said, patting the old treasure. Her words settled in the depths of my mind. "Even when you think the music has stopped, the tune plays on. Legend also says that the music in this box can even help a demon recover some of its humanity, or its angelic nature if that is the case. Now, that's power. You have nothin' to fear."

"But, Mama, I'm afraid of them."

"The Alorcán?"

"Yes," I fretted.

"Shhh. You need not worry 'bout them. You have angels watchin' over you, *a ghrá*. You have more power in this room right now than all the Alorcán have combined. Good will always win over evil. Never forget that," she whispered, as she leaned down to kiss my cheek.

She flicked the lamp off and walked to the door. "May the angels sing through your dreams," she purred.

I shifted on the patio chair. Why was it so hot all of a sudden? In my lethargy I shrugged off my jacket and tried to sit up, but the heat was weighing me down, smothering me. The music from the box was still playing, even though by my watch I could tell I'd been asleep for a while. This made no sense. The music box had to be cranked every few minutes. I leapt from the chair with the heightened sense that someone was there watching me. Power spiraled and surged through my limbs. My gaze shot to the woods and back to the castle. I realized that the music was gone—and so was the music box.

23

Paradoxical Freedom

(Aishling)

The night before my flight out to Costa Rica, I stood in my room, practicing what I was going to say to my father. Scared to death he would reject my proposal, I took deep breaths as I wandered down the hall to his private parlor. He sat on the couch watching a rugby game—which was most unusual.

"Hello, Aishling," he said as I sat on the couch near him, "Are ya packed, then?"

I looked down at the navy rug and then up into his unyielding expression. "Yes," I answered. I chewed on my lip for a moment while I told myself, *Just blurt it out. Go on. Get it over with.*

"What is it?" he asked, perturbed.

My mouth rushed forward before I lost my nerve. "Dad, I really don't think I need any guards in Costa Rica. I mean…who would be looking for me anyway five thousand miles away, living in a hut in the jungle and working with orphans?" Out of air, I looked up at him as I breathed deeply, trying to analyze what I could see in his eyes.

He turned back to the television. "The guards will not be goin'."

I stared into the stone fireplace for a moment, speechless. This news was unbelievable. Trinity College was under strict obligation to keep the destination for my senior year classified, as this would have made a great news story but one my family needed to avoid. But no guards? With suspicion, I cut my eyes back to him. "What? Really? Why not?"

Without moving his gaze from the screen, he replied, "As ye said, who'll be lookin' for ya so far away? The guards aren't necessary."

There was more going on here. I could feel it. But I was not going to argue. "Thank you, Father." I stood to go.

"Oh, Aishling?" he said, stopping me.

I pivoted toward him. "Yes?"

"There'll be no consortin' wit' the men folk while ye're away. Am I understood?"

"Yes, Father."

He nodded. "Go then and finish yer schoolin'. In a year, ye'll take yer place with the Kavanaughs."

The following morning I flew to Costa Rica in the Delaneys' private jet—an added security measure. For the first time in my life, I felt somewhat free even though it was paradoxical, for I would never have the luxury of being truly free. After a ten-hour flight, the plane landed at the Liberia International Airport, and I exited right onto the tarmac. As I walked down the stairs and my feet hit the runway pavement, the Costa Rican heat seemed to melt my sandals.

The assistant to my father's personal assistant carried my trunk to a waiting car, and I followed him, rolling my suitcases behind me. After Dónal and I said our good-byes, I had the driver take me to a nearby car dealership, where I purchased a very used Volkswagen bug. The owner promised me that with regular tune-ups, the car would run for another eighty thousand miles. After paying him 827 Euros ($1,115 U.S. dollars), and getting his help to point me in the direction of Tilarán, I set off toward the place that would be my home for the next year.

April is the hottest month for Costa Ricans, and my car and I both experienced heat exhaustion as we made our way down the two-lane, pothole-weary road. My newly purchased old car, of course, had no air conditioning. Reaching behind me to my suitcase in the backseat while navigating the narrow, curvy road was a bit tricky. But soon I had it unzipped and pulled a T-shirt up front with me to wipe the sweat from my face. This was a big climate change from Ireland in more ways than just the heat. But I loved the adventure.

The unusual scenery was so distracting I almost rear-ended an old, bluish truck with two goats in the back. A couple of miles after that blunder, I decided to pull over to a roadside café to buy some cold water. On the surface the hut was very inviting. It was surrounded by lush foliage and vibrant native flowers in all colors. As I made my way to the entrance, a man wearing knee-length rubber boots met me carrying a very serious-looking machete.

"Hola," he greeted me. My eyes moved from his friendly posture to the machete and back again. "Oh, sorry about that. Been chopping weeds all day." He placed the gargantuan knife on a table to his left. "Can I help you?"

"Do you have some cold bottled water?" I asked.

"Sure do. Come on back." Laughter and music drifted from the hut about thirty feet back through the foliage, so I felt a little more at ease. I followed him through a maze of greenery beside a small pond with a water wheel, and then we passed a turtle that had its head tucked in its shell.

We entered the cool shade of the hut, and he called out to the young woman who was about my age behind the counter, "Hey, Alexa, get this young lady some water, will you?" I could only see her profile as I sat down at the semicircular bar.

"Coming right up."

"So what brings you to Costa Rica?" she asked, once she had set the water in front of me. Condensation dripped from the bottle before I had time to unscrew the cap.

"I'm going to Tilarán to teach English for a year."

She looked up and our eyes met. A force like a hurricane came over me, and I clamped my hands down on the bar to hold myself in place. In the vision it was nighttime, and this woman was very frightened. She and I were in the jungle. I could hear a volcano crackling and spewing lava, but it didn't feel like that was what we were running from. It was some other dark presence. She took off running, and I chased her. She opened the door to what I assumed was my room at the orphanage. She handed me something....

"Miss. Miss! Are you okay?" she was saying to me as I came back to the present.

Shaking my head to dispel the lurking demons, I answered her. "I'm fine. Just too much heat I guess." I studied her face, trying to figure out her connection to me. Her deep tan, long brown hair, and wide hazel eyes showed off her native Costa Rican heritage. After a moment of observation, I knew we had never met. I was sure about that.

"That's quite an Irish accent you've got there," she said, looking almost as if she were sizing me up too.

"Yeah, I just can't seem to do anything about that," I said, smiling, and she smiled back.

"Why Tilarán?"

"There's an orphanage there, and they need a teacher," I said, shrugging my shoulders.

"Vista del Mar," she commented.

"Yes. How did you know?"

"It's the lone orphanage within a hundred miles of here."

"Hmm," I said. "Well, my name is Aishling Delaney, by the way." I held out my hand for her to shake.

At the mention of my name, she looked at me as though I were about to jump across the bar and strangle her. Nobody had ever had this reaction to me saying my name before. There was noticeable fear in her eyes. Now it was my turn to ask, "Are you okay?"

With a guarded posture, she raised her hand to grasp mine. "I know what you mean about that heat, Miss Delaney. It's a pleasure to meet you. I'm Alexa Consuelos." In the course of our short conversation, she had built a wall. What was she hiding? And why was she looking at me as though I were evil?

"How much do I owe you?" I asked as I stood to leave.

"It's on the house."

"Well, thank you. Costa Rica has such warm people."

"We try."

"Good-bye," I said.

When I was almost to the entrance, the young woman said, "Oh, Aishling, I hope those pesky Irish faeries of yours didn't follow you here—we have enough to contend with."

Taken aback, I pivoted toward her, my face scrunched in concentration, trying to make sense of this encounter. So she knew Irish legend.

"I'll keep that in mind, Alexa. *Buenos días* [Good day]."

Unease built in my stomach as I made my way to the car. This Alexa had seemed safe enough—innocent even—but I had seen her in my vision, and I knew, as sure as the Delaneys ruled the Otherworld, that I'd see her again someday.

24.

Adjusting

(Aishling)

About thirty minutes and many pineapple fields later, I read the sign "Tilarán 10 km." I could see the towering windmills looming in the distance. As I rounded a curve, my heart threatened to bludgeon through my chest. I slammed on the brakes. Coming straight for my tiny, metal cage with wheels was a whole herd of cattle that stood taller than my car. They would soon overtake it and me if I didn't come up with a plan. They were running at a slow pace but nonetheless running.

When the herd was almost to my car, I ducked and covered my head, as if that would protect me. I counted backward from ten for some strange reason. By the time I'd reached zero, I ventured a peek, and the cattle were being herded into a pasture, curving in a perfect arc. A Costa Rican cowboy came riding by on his horse and tipped his hat to me as the last of the cows moved off the road. *I did say that I wanted adventures*, I thought, smiling to myself as I drove on.

I made my way through the town, noting the shops and places I'd need to visit when I had some time off. A few minutes later, I was coming around a lake, and soon I saw the rusty sign for the Vista del Mar Orphanage. Pulling up to the building, I felt a strange sense of home yet at the same time an almost paralyzing trickle of fear. This was going to be my first attempt at independence. As if my life were being steered by the supernatural, I knew I was supposed to come here at this point in time. I couldn't explain it, but for months I'd had a feeling, an intuition that this place held an important key to my future.

Heading into the main building, I entered the office and saw a middle-aged woman behind a desk, bent over some paperwork. The metal loops on my bag clinked together when I placed it on the sofa, and she looked up.

"You must be Aishling," she said as she came around her desk to kiss me on both cheeks. Unaccustomed to such greetings, I froze at first but soon recovered with an answering smile. Already I liked this woman, and we'd only just met.

Still holding my arms, she said, "I'm Señora Martinez. We spoke on the phone."

"Yes. It's nice to meet you, Señora, and it's great to be here. I've looked forward to this for so long."

"Well, we have too. The children have been so curious about your coming. We didn't tell them until a few days ago. We knew they'd drive us crazy. Little Ina has asked me several times a day, 'Now, when is Miss Delaney coming?'"

We laughed as she led me down the hall toward the cafeteria, where the children were eating lunch. When I entered I felt like a rock star. Several of the children ran to hug me around the waist, and Señora Martinez had to clap her hands and send the children back to their seats before I was mobbed. We stepped up to a tiny stage about eight feet square and a foot off the ground.

"Settle down, children!" she scolded, and the room fell silent except for a few crying babies. I'd never seen children obey so quickly. That would be a pleasant added bonus, I thought—children who listened and showed respect to those in authority. Turning to me she said, "Miss Delaney is finally here. She'll be teaching your English class for the next year and helping with the daily chores. I expect all of you to make her feel at home here and to obey her when she tells you to do something—or *not* to do something, Oscar Menendez." Everybody looked toward a boy of about fifteen years of age who clearly was not embarrassed by being singled out for obvious past mischief.

She introduced me to all the staff and gave me a complete tour of the facilities. When we visited the students' dorms, a young girl rushed forward to hug me; her deep-mahogany hair swung toward her chin in a cute bob. Looking straight up at me from where her arms held me captive, she claimed, "Señorita De-waney...*grandes amigas* [great friends]." Then she pointed from my heart to hers. I lifted her into my arms and conversed with her in Spanish.

"Is that so?" I said, smiling.

"*Sí.*"

This child had already won my heart. I smiled in wonder. "You must be Ina." Her tiny tan face brightened, revealing two missing front teeth.

"How do you know my name?" she asked, surprised.

"Lucky guess. How old are you, Ina?" I inquired.

"Six years, but the señora says I seem much older." She smiled.

The señora cut into our conversation then. "Well, Ina, Miss Delaney and I need to finish our tour, and she needs to get settled into her room. Say good-bye for now."

"*Mucho gusto* [Nice to meet you], Señorita," she said as she leaned over to kiss my cheek right before I settled her feet back on the floor.

"*Hasta luego* [See you later], Ina," I said as I waved at her before heading back down the hallway.

While exiting to the front of the orphanage where my car was parked, Señora Martinez called for some of the older boys to help with my luggage. The hut where I would be staying was about a ten-minute hike from the main building through the edge of the jungle, near the cliffs overlooking Lake Arenal. The path was wide and its borders were strewn with vibrant green foliage and tropical plants. My favorites were the heliconias, with their fiery, red-orange, waxy fronds tipped with fluorescent yellow and lime green, hanging in pairs down a zigzag stem. As we strolled down the path and rounded a curve, the trees gave way to the fearsome Volcán Arenal churning smoke in the distance. I was anxious to see what it looked like at night.

At the tiny hut, Señora Martinez placed the key in the knob and unlocked the door to my oasis. When I stepped through the entry, the image of the young lady I'd met at the roadside hut coursed through my mind. I could almost see her standing right in front of me. This was the place from the vision. The room was nothing special by most standards, but it was perfect for me. I turned in a slow circle, noting the simplicity of the hut.

The room I was standing in was the extent of the place besides a small room in the right back corner that I assumed was the bathroom. To the right of the door, there was a small kitchen table with two scarred wooden chairs, and behind them were a refrigerator, a sink, and a stove. There was very little cabinet space. To the left of the door, there was a worn, red sofa and a coffee table. A built-in chest of drawers protruded from the middle left wall. And in the back left corner was a full-sized bed with a round table beside it that held a time-worn lamp. Two boys followed me in carrying my suitcases, and another two brought in my trunk.

"Well, Miss Delaney, we'll leave you to get settled in. You may want to wander down the path to the cliffs sometime this afternoon once you've put your things away. Dinner is around five o'clock. Rest up today. It may be the last moments of sanity you get, I'm afraid," the señora said as she moved to the door.

"Thanks for the warning, and thank you so much for everything, Señora. This place is great!"

"You're welcome," she said to me, then turned to the students. "Come on, guys. Let's give Miss Delaney some privacy."

As I lay in the dark later in my new home, I thought about my mom, fearing for her in that realm she was in with the Dullahan. A shudder volted through me. I had to get her back. Everyone kept telling me there was nothing I could do for her until the Ten Colds Moon. Wiping angry tears away, I sent a curse to that vile beast; I knew the creature couldn't feel my ire, but it made me feel better nonetheless.

I wondered what my mother would think of my decision to come here, and if she was watching over me right now. I missed my music box. It was my tangible connection to her. When I listened to the tune, I felt like she was right there with me. Every night she had come into my room to tuck me in. Before she left, she would wind the knob on the box and sing the song that went with the tune. Now even that connection had been taken from me.

It seemed that mom and I were being ripped apart at every turn. On the night when I'd fallen asleep outside the castle and had awakened with the music box gone, I'd been frantic. Every cushion on the patio had come under suspicion and, therefore, had been tossed off their metal frames. I had the castle staff fan out and search, but none of them admitted they had moved the box, and none of them had noticed anyone coming onto the property. Why steal a music box? It made no sense, and it still made me sad and angry.

"I miss you, Mom. I know you're there. Well, good night. I love you," I said to the darkened room. I could almost hear her playing our little goodnight game when I would say "I love you," and she would say, "I love you more." With contentment, I smiled as I closed my eyes on my first day in this foreign land.

After one month at the orphanage, I felt like I belonged there. Apart from my weekly calls from Uncle Brádach and Patrick, there were few reminders of home. Most of my weapons training had been completed, so Cearnaigh wasn't engaging me in war games, catching me off guard at inopportune moments to test my abilities. There were no servants down the hall trying to cater to my every whim, which I'd never wanted them to do in the first place. I could choose what I wanted to eat and where I wanted to go. Most importantly, my father wasn't standing over my shoulder and placing impossible demands on me.

Adjusting to daily life at the orphanage was somewhat difficult for me since I was accustomed to a stricter routine. Breakfast was "around" eight thirty. Around nine to eleven o'clock each morning, I taught English in the pavilion in the yard. And lunch was around noon. In other words I was taught not to pay too much attention to the clock.

During the early afternoon hours, I became well acquainted with a novel idea called "*siesta*," where I either took a nap at the hut or played in the courtyard with some of the children. Following siesta I helped milk the cows, do the laundry, and whatever else needed to be done. Supper was around five o'clock, and sometimes I helped prepare that meal in the afternoons if all the laundry was caught up, which was a very rare occurrence. I helped feed the babies during lunch and supper unless all of our volunteers showed up for the day.

After supper at the orphanage, I was free to do whatever I pleased. Sometimes I would go to the cliffs to practice my fiddle, or I'd take my taggert into the woods, set up targets, and practice my shooting.

Near the hut, I had found a red-eyed tree frog habitat and I often wandered there after dark. Their swollen-neck clucking sounds always greeted me. The faerie cross light would pass over their neon-green bodies, and hundreds of crimson eyes would follow me. The frogs would leap from tree to tree, forming a canopy-in-motion overhead. Some usually landed on my shoulders or my head, but I didn't mind; I was kind of fond of the wee critters.

Before bedtime, I'd always work on lesson plans for the next day. Many of the children had asked about my faerie cross necklace. Since I wore it every day, their natural curiosity had been stoked. There were forty-six children in my class, so I went to my trunk and gathered some of the faerie cross stones I had brought from home. Using my tools, I bent the bell caps (metal prongs to hold each stone) to the proper width around each rock and secured each with epoxy cement. Then I ran a leather cord through the loop on each one and tied each in a secure knot.

The day I brought the necklaces to class, I told the students part of the legend behind the stones. "There are many theories as to how these stones came to be in our world. One of those stories is that the faerie cross stones (staurolites) fell to earth as pieces of a great meteorite that exploded into tiny pieces as it entered earth's atmosphere. Another theory says that they were pushed up from the core of the earth through thousands of years of the earth's plates shifting. However, the story in Ireland is that the stones are the tears of faeries that fell to earth and crystallized into the rocks you see before you now, and they protect children from anything harmful."

As I handed the children their faerie cross necklaces, they uttered "ooh's" and "aah's" like they'd just been handed priceless treasures. "The last story I told you about the faeries is just a legend. It doesn't mean that you can go out and do foolish, dangerous things and live, Oscar Menendez," I said, smiling at the teenager, fully aware of his stunts by then.

"But if you were to find yourself in trouble, there are Searchers out there who roam the earth and help the children who call to them. You must believe in Diaga's power and carry the cross stone at all times. And when in trouble, ye must draw the symbol of the cross rock in the earth. The Searchers will come to rescue ya."

"What I'd like for you to do now is to get in your small groups and come up with a story of your own about the rocks. It can include part of the stories I just told you. Work together to write down the story in English. We'll work on these tomorrow too, and then each group will read their story aloud on Friday."

At the end of the week, the children read their stories to the class, and I was so proud of their progress with English and their creativity. One of the groups came up with a story that had the hairs on my arms standing on end. The story painted a picture of an evil faerie who'd acquired a faerie stone and used it to terrorize a small, unsuspecting village. The attention to detail that they gave the character made it seem as if they'd lifted him straight out of my nightmares—and my visions.

25

The Blood Avenger

(Aishling)

One evening at dusk, I was down on the cliffs playing my fiddle. As the music built, I closed my eyes, reveling in the sheer power of the melody. A strange calm had come over me—that calm-before-the-faerie-attack feeling. Then a vision overtook me.

I was sitting on this very spot on the cliffs, but it was darker—nightfall. I was looking down toward the beach on the opposite side of Lake Arenal. It was then that I saw him—the faerie who terrified every Irishman: the Dullahan, Avenger of Blood. He was the character from Irish folklore that had given many a child—and more often adults—nightmares that stuck with them.

A chilling cadence drummed in my chest in time to the hoof beats of the frightening horse the creature sat atop. As I watched, the horse rode through the surf of the water below. The Dullahan was holding his own head up in his arms, turning it from side to side, searching for something—or someone.

My pulse spiked, the vision dissipated, and the deep lavender of dusk soothed me once more. A shiver crept down my spine while I tried to steady my breathing. Did the vision mean that this sinister creature had followed me here—that the Dullahan was coming for me? Spooked, I decided to call it an evening and head back to the hut.

As I ran I recalled the first time I'd ever heard the legend of the Dullahan. I was at Uncle Brádach's house for another one of his famous bonfire parties. I was around six years of age and was sitting on my mother's lap in front of the fire.

Uncle Brádach was the best storyteller; I don't believe there has ever been a *racaire* [storyteller] in all of Ireland who was his equal. He had often scared the wits out of Patrick, Claire, and me with his fine use of Irish folklore and his storytelling fervor. He could make his listeners believe they were actual characters in whatever tale he was spinning.

"Aye, the Dullahan is said to be a myth, a legend, somethin' the old bogtrotter Donndubhan Delaney came up wit' one night when he got flutherin' drunk and wandered the hillside," Uncle Brádach had said. "But don't ya be fooled wit' the idea that this Irish faerie is a mere legend, for he still roams the moors and the hillsides in Ireland and elsewhere, lookin' for those on whom he will pronounce *death*!" he squawked. His eyes got bigger and his excitement grew.

"Ya see, the Avenger of Blood was once a normal lad just like you and you," he said, pointing to Patrick and another boy in the crowd. "This boy had a formidable father, old Riaghán MacClancy, who used to beat the livin' daylights out of him just 'cause he could. The father also had a newborn son and three daughters, but none of 'em incurred the wrath of the father. Just him.

"One day MacClancy went too far in his beatin', and the lad died. Life moved on for the father at a normal pace—'til about seven years later. The father was gatherin' the harvest out in the fields late one evenin' when he heard hoof beats. He couldn't see anythin' 'cause he was surrounded by corn—it had grown so high that year it was e'en a foot taller than he, and he was a very tall man. Thinkin' it must be a neighbor come to pay him a visit, the man ran toward the sound comin' from the end of the rows of corn. When he got to the end, he saw nothin' there. He stared around, frightened, for he could still hear the hoof beats as they grew louder and louder, comin' right at him. The man ran back into the corn rows, hopin' to escape from whate'er or whoe'er was hauntin' him. The noise was deafenin'. But the hoof beats kept comin' like a horse was ridin' right beside him, parallel through the never-endin' rows as he ran. He held his ears with both hands. 'Make it stop!' he shouted.

"About that time he had reached the other end of the row and stumbled, fallin' to the ground. He looked up into the distance t'ward the nearby forest and he could see a light. As the light drew nearer, he could tell it was fire. As the fire came closer, he could see it was comin' from the nostrils of a great horse. As the horse rode on, chargin' in his direction, he could see the form of a man clingin' to the horse. When the being yelled in a demonic voice, he could tell that the voice wasn't comin' from a mouth, for the form was headless.

"When the horse and rider were almost right on top of him, he could see then that the man did have a head, but it was strapped to his side. As he examined the head, he saw the eyes and features of his son—eyes that had once looked away in fear of him were now starin' at him in defiance. 'Please, don't hurt me,' the man pleaded. The form hissed at him, and the horse blew out a stream of *fire* t'ward the ground where the man lay a-tremblin'."

When Uncle Brádach got to the part about the fire, he leapt forward and clapped his hands in the air. I burrowed back into my mother's chest. Patrick, who had been sitting on a log beside our blanket, moved to sit beside my mother. He looked around and then grabbed my hand.

"With an unspoken warning, the Dullahan turned the horse around and galloped back the way he'd come. The man breathed a sigh of relief as he got to his feet. His son had spared his life—or so he thought. But the Blood Avenger thought that death was too good for this vile man who had the nerve to call himself a father.

"For the next year, the Dullahan haunted the man. Just when he'd feel at ease again, the creature would return to steal his comfort. The father began to see the Dullahan's mangled face in the features of his other son. He'd hear that gruesome hiss in the laughter of his daughters. He saw day as night and night as unfathomable blackness with no hope of the moon to break it up. Everywhere was darkness that mirrored his rotten soul.

"Eight years after the son's death, the Dullahan appeared again much the same way he'd come the first time. It was nightfall and the father was headin' back home after a hard day workin' in the fields. The Blood Avenger appeared right in front of him, blockin' his path to security. The father gauged the distance to his front door, thinkin' if he could just make it there he'd be safe. His children and wife would be waitin' for him just on the other side of that door. He could smell the meal his wife had worked so hard to prepare. He could imagine his favorite young daughter jumpin' onto his lap as soon as he sat in his chair and took off his mud-caked boots. But the life he'd built for himself was to be taken from him that night.

"I know what yer thinkin'," Uncle Brádach had said. "Ya think that the Dullahan killed his father, but nay, he did not. He wanted his father to suffer in pain and misery as much as he had all those years, before his death and beyond death.

"Ya see the lad had been in the Paradise realm of the Otherworld, for he was just an innocent child when his father killed him, and his soul was sent there for comfort. But the longer he inhabited that place, the less comfort he found. The more time he had to sit around and think, the more he thought about his brother and sisters and the thought that their father might be hurtin' them now that he was gone. His hatred for his father grew daily, steamin' within him, risin' like a boil, changin' him. The bitterness that festered in his heart drove him into the great abyss. He chose to go there, knowin' the darkness that awaited him and realizin' that he might ne'er find his way back to the Paradise realm or even be allowed to go back there.

"The great gulf that spans the middle of the Otherworld is a dangerous and ghastly place for the soul to inhabit. It's not as horrible as the lower realms of Sheol, where there is such darkness ye can't e'en see the fires that torture ya, but it was still dangerous and dark. Small fires were kept burnin' here and yon in the deep canyon, whose walls ye could not scale. As the boy wandered for years in the abyss, he learned the tricks of survival there. He became such a leader, takin' others under his wings when they'd find themselves in the gulf, that he formed a gang. The group watched each other's backs and took care of each other.

"Unknown to him, a horde of demons and Alorcán faeries happened to cross o'er into his dimension during one of the Gaelic festivals, when the supernatural veil between worlds is thin. His gang had weapons, but they were no match for such evil. The demons singled him out as the leader and threw their thick, heavy chains around his legs, draggin' him across the ground, away from those who'd come to depend on him. They had read his hard heart, and they began capitalizin' on his hatred for his father.

"Whippin' him with their chains every day, the demons hardened him more. The Alorcán played mind games with him. Leanin' their heads to his, he could see pictures of his family. They had fabricated scenes of his father beatin' his siblings, all the while drivin' him mad, deceivin' him, strengthenin' him, turnin' him into the worst monster since the devil himself. The demons and Alorcán faeries had no clue as to the extent of what they were creatin' or what it was capable of. For the monster had characteristics of both units, makin' him virtually indestructible, givin' him free reign o'er the realms.

"When he had entered the great gulf, his body had been changed to somethin' between a mortal and an immortal life form, so he had the look of a human. At the point of his darkest state, when his soul was its blackest, the demons and faeries decapitated him, condemnin' him to an existence of servitude—deliverin' death sentences. It was there that he became THE DULLAHAN." When he got to that last part, Uncle Brádach threw his arms out like an explosion, and we all jumped at his words. As we settled back down, he finished his story.

"So on the anniversary of his own death, eight years later, the Dullahan would deliver the final blow to his father. He would force him to live in exile away from everythin' and everyone he loved. His father cringed before him, and the Blood Avenger lifted his finger, pointin' first at his father and then t'ward the forest. The creature didn't have to speak a word for the father to understand his meanin'. He knew he was bein' sent away. Legend says his father lived out the remainder of his days wanderin' the earth, beggin' for food, homeless, attacked by wild animals, and always wonderin' if the Blood Avenger had destroyed his family."

Uncle Brádach went on to state, "Legend says that when an individual has been wronged more than the Dullahan was in his human life, a new Avenger of Blood emerges to take the place of the prior one. The old Dullahan's spirit is then able to go on to the Paradise realm of the Otherworld and be at peace, knowin' that justice will ultimately come."

26

The Great "What If?"

(Aishling)

t was a Friday night and my friend Maria, a worker at the orphanage, had invited me to her house for dinner. I always loved spending time with her big, noisy family. She lived by the river, and they had a pavilion by the water where they ate together. They picked all of their fruits and vegetables from the land around the house for their meals. I had never tasted an avocado that was so rich in texture and flavor. After dinner we swam in the river until dark. It was getting late, but I didn't want to leave.

Everything was quiet at the orphanage as I parked out front. The path to the hut was dark as usual, but for some reason my faerie cross was lighting the way. Since this was not normal, I strained to distinguish the sounds of the night and was careful to guard my steps. Close to the hut a monkey swung down and caught a nearby limb. In the confusion, I stepped on a twig, snapping it in two. I froze.

An arm came up around my neck, and an attacker squeezed my windpipe. Remembering my training, I closed my eyes and called my sword to me. Then I stepped back and ducked to get out of the chokehold, swinging my sword up in front of me as I swiveled to face him.

"Cearnaigh! What the devil!" I spat, heaving in air.

"Ye were ready. 'Tis good," he said without apology. He tromped through the door of the hut and flipped on the light switch. I followed him in and shut the door.

"I've wondered when you'd be back from the Moerae."

He sat on the couch, and I plopped down in the chair facing him.

"It's a very complicated journey, and I will say it wasn't entirely fruitful," he said, wiping his brow.

"So I take it you've brought news."

"Aye. The Moerae accepted my gifts."

His entire face scrunched in pain as if he were working on purging the sure-to-be-dreadful news from his core.

"What is it, Cearnaigh?" I grabbed hold of his right arm.

"They revealed that yer destiny is comin' full circle quicker than we'd anticipated. The Ten Colds Moon will rise on December seventh."

"This year?"

"Aye."

"But that's not the night of one of the Gaelic festivals. I know the Dullahan can come any night, but the Alorcán can't."

"He won't be comin' to ye, Aishling. Ye'll have to find the Lost Cave of Malachent, and ye'll have to go to him."

"But what about Mom? How will I get her back to her people once I rescue her?"

"The Moerae revealed that when the Ten Colds Moon rises, there'll be what they call a geomagnetic excursion, meaning there'll be a slight decrease in the earth's magnetic field, and the thin places will open. Ye'll be able to bring yer mom safely through."

"Yeah, safe until the Alorcán trap us outside the cave, you mean."

"Faith, Aishling. Remember that the open thin places assure we'll be there too."

"What didn't they tell you?"

"Where the blatherin' cave is."

"Well, how am I supposed to find this lost cave if you and the rest of the Otherworld don't even know where it is?

"We're tryin', Aishling. Maybe the location will be revealed to ya in one of yer visions. We can't lose hope."

So I would face my doom in just a few months. In a moment like this, most people would say, "My life flashed before my eyes." Not me. I was focused on what the future would hold.

"What are ya thinkin' about so hard, Aishling?"

"You know, I'm not afraid to die because I know I'll live on—in the afterlife I mean."

"What is it then, child?"

"As I grew up, there was always one main task on my mind, one thing I had to accomplish: the marriage alliance. I need to marry Patrick to stop the curse and save my clan. I've always accepted it as my duty. Then when I found out that Mom was captured by the Dullahan, nothing mattered more than getting her back."

"Do ya fear the beast? Is that was this is all about?"

"I've thought about the devilish faerie so much over the years that I've gotten numb to the situation. Since you gave me the prophecy when I was young, I've had time to accept our show-down. You may think this is strange, Cearnaigh, but what I fear most is not accomplishing my tasks before I die. What if the Dullahan kills me before I save my mom? What if she has to spend eternity running from that headless freak in that forsaken realm? What if the beast takes me down before Patrick and I marry, and the curse hunts my people? I have to finish what I start."

I stood and paced, making mental plans. Lost in thought, I must have spoken some of them aloud.

"What did you just say?" He barked so loud that I stopped and faced him.

"I said, 'maybe I can convince Patrick to elope.'"

"Aishling, stop! Yer goin' to win. My girl, my warrior, will not be defeated!" He stood and advanced toward me. "Yer pow'rs are equal to or even greater than that coward's."

"I would hardly call the most ferocious faerie in history a coward," I said, smiling, enjoying his antics.

"Sure, he's a coward. Do ye hide in yer house because ye're afraid the beast might show up on yer doorstep one day?"

"No."

"Are ye afraid of rovin' in the dark 'cause he might slip up on ya? O' course not. That coulda been the beast out there tonight. Ye were ready to do battle with me, and ye woulda been ready to battle the dark faerie. But what does the monster do? He hides. He waits. Only a coward does that."

"Well, when you put it that way...."

"That's the spirit! If I didn't think ye were ready, I wouldn't send ya to face him. I don't care what the Fates say. But the fact is, there is no one—*no one*—more qualified than ye are, not e'en Morrighan. Ye're gonna be just fine."

He moved to open the door. "Now on to a fun lesson. No more fearin' and frettin' tonight. Grab yer cloak from the hawthorn."

"*Ta me i gcruachais*," I implored, touching the tree, and I felt the comfort of the marking winding its thorny, flower-covered branches onto my face. When I looked down, the cloak was already on me. I lifted my arm to study the bold scrollwork on the sky blue material. I touched the fabric and it felt electric.

"Whatever ya do, don't put the hood on yet," Cearnaigh cautioned.

"Aye, aye, boss. How is this garment a weapon?"

"Come, and I'll show ya." He opened the door for me with a look of excitement I'd never seen on him before.

"Well, let's get this shawl on the road, then, shall we?" He snorted at his corny joke and slapped his knee. "Did ya get it? Shawl—cloak?"

At first I stared at him like he was goofy, but then I couldn't hold it any longer, and my smile burst. "Yes, I got your joke. Ha!"

I moved into the dark night and waited for him to shut the door. I felt the strength in my veins, almost electric, as it engaged the fabric. The cloak flowed around me of its own accord, fighting to contain its power.

"Whoa!" I said as if speaking to a horse. I tried to pat down the cloak, but it encircled me, almost fastening itself in the front.

Cearnaigh reared back and guffawed. The monkeys—the ones I called my pets, which hung around the hut all the time—ceased their chatter. When Cearnaigh's yapper shut, the rustle and swish of tree limbs resumed.

We stood in the darkness of the jungle with a faint breeze stirring the vegetation. The world smelled of jasmine that was trying to compete with the sulfurous fumes of the volcano but was coming out the loser.

When Cearnaigh settled down, he was all business. "Now," he said, "let's start with something easy, somewhere close by. Once ya pull the hood up, it'll surround yer face, and the cloak will lock. Then ye picture a specific place in yer mind, and the cloak takes ye there. There's pow'r in the garment. I'm sure ye remember how it felt when ya traveled wit' me to the Rapids of Rua. It'll feel like yer floatin' in space, but ye'll be travelin' at the speed of light. Now pull the hood up and get a vivid picture of the cliffs in yer mind, and I'll meet ye there. If for some reason ye get off course, just keep thinking of the hut."

I did as he suggested, and the sensation mimicked his description. When I pulled the hood up, the cloak enclosed me like a bubble. There was no light coming in, only a blanket of blackness, and I was a bit unnerved and just a little claustrophobic. But I had no sooner pulled the hood up and thought about the cliffs than I felt the force stop within me, and the cloak floated at my ankles again. I pulled the cloth away from my face, and the lake winds assaulted me as I listened to the freshwater waves below. When Cearnaigh landed beside me and pulled back his hood, I could see his brawny features lit by the half moon.

"That was incredible." I laughed, pulling on his arm with both hands. "Can other people fly with me in here?"

"Aye. If part of the cloak is touchin' them, they'll end up wit' ya—even yer horse. O' course he won't like it. I can assure ya of that. The animals get a wee bit fidgety jumpin' into the unknown."

"I'll remember that," I said, thinking of Kheelan, missing him. "Let's go somewhere farther away."

"Like where?"

"Ireland? I miss Kheelan."

Chuckling, he said, "Ah, not tonight, lass. Ye'd surely get caught. Ireland is six hours ahead of us on the clock. The stable hands would catch ya. And, as a side note, ye should only use the cloak to transport ya to places off the beaten path where ya won't be seen. Yer magic needs to remain hidden. Ya don't want harm comin' to those ye love."

"True. I'll remember, Cearnaigh."

"Where to then?"

"I don't know." I thought for a moment. "How about one of Costa Rica's beaches?"

"If ya don't have a specific picture in mind, some kind of landmark, then ye'll land at a random one near here."

"Well, let's go."

"Give me yer hand," he said. "I'll have to let ya navigate this time. Don't want us to end up on separate beaches."

When I grabbed his hand, our cloaks seemed to bind together, running up our arms. Draping the fabric over my head, I thought of swaying palm trees and a nice, calm ocean. When I pulled back the cloak, my feet were buried in soft, white sand. I took off the cloak and handed it to Cearnaigh while I kicked off my flip-flops.

"I'll be back." I grinned. Then I ran for the ocean and dived into the waves. Diving without scuba equipment was awesome! The faerie cross lit the way as I explored and swam with the schools of tropical fish. It was about ten minutes before I went up for air. When I broke the surface, Cearnaigh was sitting on the beach, staring out to sea. I plopped down beside him and smoothed my wet hair back from my face.

"You should jump in. The water's amazing, Cearnaigh."

"I'll take yer word for it. Never was much of a swimmer meself."

I snickered at the big, bad warrior being afraid of the water. He pushed out with his right arm, shoving me sideways. Rolling in the sand, I laughed until my laugher wore out. I felt gritty, having sand cling to my wet body.

"One more dive and then we can go." I jumped up and ran for the water before he could protest.

When I washed back up on the shore, I toed on my flip-flops, and Cearnaigh wrapped my cloak around my shoulders. As it was late, the beachgoers had deserted the sand and sea. The only sound was the relentless push and pull of the waves on the shore.

"How is this cloak my most dangerous weapon, Cearnaigh?"

"As ya can see, it'll be great for helpin' ya disappear when ya get into a jam."

"Yeah, I can see the value in that, but what else does it do?"

An evil grin captured his face. "Don't take yer eyes off me cloak."

I watched as he took off his own massive coat. Then he twirled it around in front of him like a matador teasing a bull. By the white of the moon, I could see the fabric become electric as if it were using the static in the air. Hypnotizing charges sparked in front of me. I dropped to my knees, and then the lights went out.

"Aishling…. Aishling," I heard someone say in a laidback manner. Opening my eyes, I focused on a long, scruffy red beard above me.

"Cearnaigh? What did you do to me?"

"Just a little sleep spell." He shrugged his shoulders while I sat up, brushing the sand from my arms.

"That will be seriously useful," I said, eager to learn more. "What else?"

"There might be a few more tricks up my sleeve."

"Let's see 'em."

He turned the loose fabric of the sleeve inside out and folded it upward, revealing an arsenal.

My mouth opened wide. "Oh, you meant literally." He was demonstrating some of the finer points when a swarm of dragonflies whistled around me. Stumbling backward in the sand, I fell on my bottom, and the strange creatures soared around me in a fixed pattern. From time to time, their wings would tickle my arms and legs. Their immense size was freaking me out, besides the fact that dragonflies were kind of creepy anyway. I closed my eyes, hoping that once I opened them again the buzz-like hum would have ceased and the dragonflies would have flown on their merry way.

"Shoo, ya snake feeders!" I heard Cearnaigh gripe as he tromped toward me. I could feel the wind off his hand as he swatted the air around me.

The buzzing increased, and the face of a man appeared in my mind—a very handsome man. He was trying to communicate with me.

"Crap!" Jumping up, I opened my eyes and put my arm out behind me. It looked like I was throwing a softball underhanded, but when I released my hand in front of me, the creatures scattered, soaring in a frenzy about twelve feet above.

How did I know to do that? It appeared that they had moved at my command.

"Those hawkers seem to like ya," Cearnaigh teased, looking up at the whirling mass.

They were the same ones from my vision a long time ago, the same ones that shot past Patrick and me the night we were attacked by faeries. They flew in that orderly helix pattern, like an acrobatic strand of DNA.

"Okay. How 'bout we get out of here?" My eyes were locked on the sky. I didn't know who or what was trying to intrude on my mind, but I didn't like it.

We whipped our cloaks around at the same time, the intelligent hoods connecting on the fly. I didn't even have to pull mine up myself this time. The cloak must have sensed that we were in possible danger here, so it helped us out. I so loved this piece of fabric. The sounds of the ocean receded and were replaced by the "ooh ooh" of my hut monkeys. Cearnaigh and I lowered our hoods together.

"On that note I'll say good night, Lady Aishling." He bowed.

"It was fun. Thanks for guiding me tonight."

He merely nodded.

"Do you think I can get Mom back, Cearnaigh? Do you really think I can win?"

"I have no doubts, *a leanbh* [my child]."

27

The Searcher

(Aishling)

Entering the girls' dorm, I was heading to gather some of the wash when one of the girls rushed up and gave me a hug. "Telephone for you, Señorita Delaney," she said and then ran away. After rushing to the front room of the orphanage, I flipped on the light switch, and lifted the phone's receiver in my hand.

"Hello," I said.

"Hello, gorgeous!" A male voice laughed into the phone.

"Patrick! It's so good to hear from you."

"Sorry I couldn't call last week. We're working on a very important piece of legislation. I've had little sleep over the past few days."

"How's the Senate treating you?" I asked, anxious to hear news from home. Patrick had graduated from Columbia University last May and had been appointed by the *Taoiseach*, the prime minister of Ireland, to a seat in the *Seanad Éireann*, the Irish Senate. His father and mine had a lot of pull with the Taoiseach, and this was an expected position for Patrick right out of college. His goal was to work in the Senate for five years and then transition into the *Dáil Éireann*, or House of Representatives. The Dáil had much more power to promote change in government than the Senate, but he was thankful to be in this position as he worked his way up the ladder, and I was so proud of him.

"Fair," he answered. "How's Costa Rica treating you? Are the orphans all dirty and malnourished?"

215

"No! They are neither. How could you say such a thing, Patrick?"

"Whoa there, *a ghrá* [my love]. Sorry, didn't mean to get you all riled up. I shouldn't pay so much attention to stereotypes. I just worry about you. I can't be there to protect you from yourself. You care too much, Asher."

"Somebody's got to care." Softening, I said, "Oh Patrick, you should spend some time with them. The children are so bright and happy. They're so giving, even with so little to give."

I could tell he was shaking his head as he said, "Always having to save someone. Aishling Delaney—rescuer of vagrants and lost souls."

"You're making me sad, Patrick. You mock me."

"Sorry, Asher. I'll try to be more understanding of your mission there even though I wish you were here with me. There are orphans in Ireland too, ya know."

"All right, I'm hanging up now," I said.

"Wait. Change of subject, I promise."

"I'm listening," I said, still miffed.

"So Claire's been dating one of our own."

"What? Who?"

"You'll never guess. It caught us all by surprise."

The suspense was killing me. Between his negative talk about the orphans and this, I wished I had special powers that allowed me to reach through the phone and throttle him.

"I'm not even going to try to guess. There are too many possibilities. Just tell me!"

He laughed so hard; I had to hold the phone away from my ear. For several seconds he was unable to answer. Settling down he said, "Brógán's little brother, Niul, has his sights set on Claire, or maybe I should say that Claire has her sights set on Niul."

"My Brógán? Niul who works as a stable hand for Uncle Brádach, Niul?"

"Yes to all questions."

"Way to go, Claire! I've always liked Niul."

"Are you trying to make me jealous? If you were, I would have to admit that it's working. I've heard how all the women think he's 'the man.' I don't get it."

Now it was my turn to laugh. "Thank you for not getting it. What do your parents think about our Claire dating below her station?"

"Dad says it's just harmless flirting. He had a long talk with her a few nights ago about her betrothal to Áed Ó Lochlainn."

"Poor Claire. She'll never get along with Áed. Didn't she tell your father that?"

"Oh she told him, all right. You know Claire. She's not about to hold back her feelings on any matter. That doesn't change the fact, though, that she is promised to Ó Lochlainn."

Hearing his emphatic tone in regard to Claire made me wonder how Patrick viewed our betrothal. Was I to become his property? Or would our lifelong friendship make a big difference? Since he had begun his work in the Senate, I'd noticed slight but steady changes in him. He was becoming more like his father: very businesslike, serious, less fun-loving. And then I thought about my upcoming duel with the beast and wondered whether Patrick and I would even make it to the altar.

"Asher?"

"Yeah, I'm here."

"I asked you a question."

"You did?" In my worry over things I couldn't change, I'd missed whatever he'd said.

"Seen any faeries in Costa Rica?" he repeated.

"Not yet. I guess I left them all with you."

He chuckled, and there was another brief silence.

"How's Connor?" I asked.

He was silent long enough for two children at different intervals to come in and hug me. "He's getting along fine, growing like wild buckwheat." I could hear the hesitation in his voice. "I jabbered with him on Skype just last night as a matter of fact."

Might as well throw out the untouchable pot-of-gold question. "So...how do you plan to break the news to your parents? Connor's what...three years old now?"

Another brief lull weighed down the phone line. "Asher, I'm sorry we even have to discuss this. I really am."

"I know, Patrick. Will Connor and his mother be coming to live in Ireland? I mean, he is your heir."

"Haven't got it all figured out yet. Getting used to my job is taking a while. I hired American guards to watch over Connor, and his mom has cooperated so far."

It was obvious that this was still a sensitive subject between us. He didn't offer further details, and I didn't press him for any.

"Well, I'd better run," he said. "It's going to be another late night."

"Patrick?"

"Yeah?"

"Don't change for them, okay? Don't become like my father or yours. Be Patrick. I need to know that this one thing is not going to change while I'm gone. I need you to be you. You're my best friend, and I want the security that no matter what we go through in the future, this bond will remain intact."

"I'm yours, Asher. You know that."

After an awkward moment of silence, I said, "Well, good night then. Love you."

"Love you, too."

As I tread down the path toward home, I had no idea how completely my life was going to change in the course of one evening.

When I reached the hut, I decided to grab my fiddle and head to the cliffs. It was dusk and the full moon was rising, so I knew there'd be no trouble following the path back home later. Finding my usual spot, I sat down cross-legged, with my back straight, my chin tilted to the fiddle, and I played my favorite tune, "*Mo Ghile Mear*," to usher in nightfall.

I had felt lonely a lot in my life, but tonight there was a strange overwhelming sense of aloneness that I couldn't quite put my finger on. Uncle Brádach used to tell me one of his old Irish proverbs when I would come to him in one of these moods. He'd say, "Long loneliness is better than bad company, child." I could hear his voice like he was sitting right beside me.

My music kept me entertained for an hour or so while I tried to shrug off the blues. Tonight I was feeling extra homesick. I made a mental note to call Uncle Brádach the next day so he could give me some of his famous words of wisdom.

Time evaporated when I played the fiddle. It was bedtime before I realized it, the moon bright in the sky, and I decided I'd better call it a night. I'd just placed my fiddle in the case when I heard a noise coming from the encroaching jungle. Something was advancing toward me so fast, I almost had no time to arm my taggert.

When a person emerged from the jungle, I was standing ready in a defensive position, the faerie dart aimed at her chest. My heartbeat was flying, and my lungs were filled, as I ached to send the dart flying. The young woman, just a few years older than me, fell to her knees. She appeared to be a native of Costa Rica with tan skin and dark brown hair. As I shifted to the left, the moon lit her face, and I froze. It was Alexa, the one I'd met at the roadside stand on my first day in Costa Rica—the one I'd seen in the vision—which had now become reality. She kept looking toward me and then back at the ground, trembling in fear. Since I was distracted by her odd behavior, it took me a few seconds to realize she was holding something in her arms. Lowering the blowgun I stepped toward her. With the light shining in her face, I could see she kept looking beyond me, never in my eyes, but there was nothing there. I couldn't understand her behavior.

"Alexa?" I asked, already knowing the answer. "You are Alexa, aren't you? If not, then you have a twin sister."

Ignoring my question, she said, "You are the Searcher! I knew it!"

"What do you mean? How do you know? Why did you just call me that?" I asked, amazed that she knew the prophecy.

She shielded her eyes with her free arm and looked above my head again, then to my right and to my left, like something more brilliant than the moon was in the space all around me. I didn't know what to make of her behavior. Jumping to her feet, she wobbled due to the weight she held in her arms, and I reached out to steady her.

"You're the one I've been looking for. When I first met you at the café, I wasn't sure, but now I am. You need to come with me. Please, Aishling!" she begged. At this request—or order, I wasn't sure which—she took off running up the path toward the hut.

"Why are you running?" I called out to her, but she didn't turn around. I had seen a lot of strange phenomena in my young life, so I wasn't afraid at first, but I kept my blowgun ready as I slung my fiddle case strap over my shoulder and went after her.

As I ran I heard blaring hoof beats, as if a horse were riding through the jungle following the young woman. I stopped my pursuit of her, angled my taggert toward the direction of the hoof beats, and prepared for whatever was coming. Seconds passed, sweat and fear trickled down my neck, and the hoof beats grew louder.

When I felt that the horse had to be right on top of me because of the intense noise, the reverberating sound stopped, and the darkness was still. *I must be going crazy,* I thought. I turned in a circle, expecting to be caught off guard by an attacker. But nothing came.

Turning back to the path, I ran faster than I'd ever run in my entire life. When I reached the hut, Alexa had already burst through the door without waiting for me to invite her in. So at that point, I was starting to think I wasn't crazy, but I was dealing with a crazy person—or maybe she was being followed. Just in case, I bolted the door shut behind us and drew the blinds closed. When I turned around, she was holding a baby out to me. The little one couldn't have been more than a few weeks old.

"Here, take her. She is called Ariceli." With a mournful sob, she laid the newborn in my arms. This night was becoming more and more bizarre. The sleeping child drew me in while I listened to Alexa rumble in her backpack. She was laying a stack of papers on the kitchen table when I looked over.

"Here's her diaper bag with everything you'll need for a few days. I don't have much time to explain. They're coming, and I have to lead them away from here. I didn't have much of a head start, so I'll have to make this quick. I had adoption papers drafted soon after her birth, listing you as the mother," she said.

"What?" I said, stunned beyond belief. First of all, we were barely even acquaintances. Second, I was thinking, *I'm nineteen and you want me, a complete stranger, to take responsibility for a baby?* Third—WHAT?

"You can keep her safe. She's your own flesh and blood, Aishling."

"What do you mean? How can that be?" Alexa's gaze was torn between the door and the baby. The young woman looked so weary and desperate, as she stood before me crying and pleading.

"I have to go. Please sign these. I have to know that she's going to be okay. Please, Aishling, I'm begging you!"

"But I'm still a teenager. I'm sure there are laws prohibiting this," I offered in my last attempt to keep this conversation sane.

"Generally you have to be at least twenty-five years old to adopt, but I assure you these papers will be legally binding as soon as you sign them, and she will belong to you. I have to go. Please!" she begged again.

I skimmed the papers to make sure I wasn't signing away both kidneys or something. Then, against my better judgment, I reached to sign the papers with my free hand. She left the documents on the table, kissed the baby on the forehead, and ran out of the hut and into the night.

The screen door creaked and banged shut. I rushed to push it open and ran to the pathway in front of the hut. "Wait!" I yelled. "I can help you!" Then I looked down at the sleeping child in my arms.

The jungle undergrowth swished and snapped back into place as the frightened mom cleared a path through the plants. The moon was snatched away by an intrusive cloud and I couldn't see very far ahead. "Wait!" I tried again, but all I heard in reply were the snap of branches on the jungle floor and the animals screeching from the invasion.

When I walked back into the hut, shock and confusion and a dozen more feelings assaulted me. This event was surreal. I peered down at the baby again. In a matter of a few minutes, my entire world had been scrambled. I needed to try to catch up to Alexa; however, there was no way I could help her and protect her child too. *Think, Aishling!* I paced and patted the baby as a myriad of potential solutions rolled across the conveyor belt of my mind.

Cearnaigh! I laid the baby on the couch and rushed to the hawthorn tree; the marking swirled onto my face. From a low-bending limb, I snatched my cloak. The faerie cross stone rested atop a thick root; I knelt to grasp it and opened my eyes. The baby was fast asleep. I pulled my necklace from inside my shirt and pushed the two rocks together. Cearnaigh appeared.

"Aishling, my dear, what seems to be the trouble?" That was the moment Ariceli chose to wake up with a wail. The strange noise startled both Cearnaigh and me. I didn't have much experience with the babies at the orphanage, and I had gotten used to the quiet of the hut. My maternal impulses weren't exactly firing on all cylinders just yet. I was a fighter, not a nurturer. The cloak produced an electric charge that seeped into my skin as I moved to lift the baby. I bounced her a little, but her cries grew more intense.

"Here," I said to Cearnaigh, while laying the babe in his arms. "I need you to guard her; take her away from here if you have to. Her mom's in danger. Diaper bag is on the table. Be back soon."

"But—"

I pulled down the hood and thought of the young mother. I wasn't used to having access to the cloak. My chances of getting Alexa away from whomever or whatever stalked her were better now.

When I landed in the jungle, the angry wind bore down on me. The faerie cross sparked and the blue light illuminated the way at least fifty feet in the distance. An otherworldly roar battered the air, and I crouched down below the canopy, calling my taggert from the hawthorn. Armed, I ran toward the unseen source of the noise. Alexa had to be close. I pulled out the faerie cross so I could see.

Chains rattled to my right and my head snapped that way. I placed the faerie cross light underneath the cloak to douse it. Then I held the taggert level with the ground as I crept forward. A moan tore through the air. Someone must be badly hurt if I could hear the cry with the winds bellowing so. The sound of the clinking chains receded. I moved farther in the direction of the moan and used the faerie stone to see ahead of me. A large swath of jungle had been plowed down by something and I moved up the new trail with my weapon ready.

Then I saw her. It had to be Alexa. I charged toward the scene, ready to take on whatever had harmed her. My anger flared and the cloak sparked with electricity as I looked down at the lifeless body that was contorted at an odd, twisted angle. Blood seeped from deep gashes across her entire body. Something had mauled her, and there was a word or phrase burned onto her face in a language I'd never seen before. I jumped back and turned in a circle with the taggert pointed at the swaying vegetation. I hadn't had time yet to check for a pulse, but I didn't believe there was any way Alexa could still be alive. The winds rumbled through the carved jungle pathway like a thundering mass of tigers. My hair blew behind me, almost yanking me in the direction that might bring safety. I didn't move. I waited on whatever was coming. The creature that had done this was going to pay.

The jungle ferns and trampled foliage were bathed in shimmering sapphire from the faerie cross. At the bend in the path, a monster of a horse blew fire from its nostrils. Defiance cloaked the Dullahan as he sat atop the great beast.

My eyes narrowed and I blew a faerie dart at the fiend; the missile launched at the creature like a bullet. Although he was headless, the Dullahan's yowl—like a circular sawmill blade ripping shreds into wood—reverberated down the pathway. Must have hit my target. I covered my ears as the beast lurched forward. The faerie's cloak billowed around him. The fire from the horse lulled me in some way.

I rolled on top of Alexa's broken body. The cloak surrounded us and I dropped the hood. Instantly, we were in the side garden of Tilarán General Hospital. I reached down and checked her pulse; it was faint. I dragged her to the glass door and peeked in. A nurse was near the desk. With the marking on my face and the cloak on, I couldn't afford to draw attention to myself. I'd have to leave her. I knocked on the door and flew backward in the cloak to hide behind a tree at the back of the garden. The nurse warily pushed open the door and looked around. She saw Alexa and yelled for help. Two other nurses rushed to the door and saw what was happening. One called for a gurney, and a man wearing scrubs pushed the cart out the door. They lifted Alexa onto the cart and disappeared inside the hospital.

Due to the horror back in the jungle, I had not been able to think, only act. Now that the adrenaline had retreated, my emotions were no longer repressed. With anger, then with tears, I thought about the baby and the fact that she might never see her mother again. I could almost feel the pain Alexa must have endured at the hands of that cruel, soulless monster. The tears subsided as once again my fury incapacitated me. The Dullahan and I had a death match coming, even if I had to go to the depths of Uffern to find the beast.

28

Soul Tempest

(Rafe)

The hospital was quiet tonight, which was a good thing. A mighty wind barged through the window of my office, stirring me from my late-night drowsiness and also stirring the paperwork I had laid out all over the desk while I worked on patient charts. Jumping from my chair, I slammed the window shut, grabbed files from the floor, and attempted to straighten the chaos on my desk.

Soon giving up, I dropped the folders I was holding and moved to the window, watching the trees bend and the leaves rustle. There had been no storm in the forecast, but it appeared the meteorologist was wrong.

I placed my hands on the windowsill while I stared at the shades of night and allowed the darkness to creep in. My own personal hell—emptiness. It had been a few days since I'd allowed myself to think of her, but Aishling was never far from my mind.

Without warning, the thick ice around my heart that I'd so meticulously kept frozen, began to crack. I clawed at my chest and growled at the ache—growled at the darkness within and the darkness without. Why was this happening now with such brutal force? I couldn't stop it. Physical torture would have been less painful than this gripping, relentless torment. Roaring, I stood over my desk and swiped everything off into the floor. I tromped down the hall, hoping to escape out the side door that led to the garden.

"Dr. Delacruz!" a nurse called out. I wheeled around, poised to attack. Then I shook my head, pushing the demons back. Relaxing my posture, I approached her. "Are you okay?" she asked.

"I'm fine." *Was a white lie a damnable offense?* "What do you need, Sophia?" I asked, with what I hoped was a normal voice.

"Someone just brought a young lady to the side door and left her. We've got her prepped for surgery, but she's fading. I know Dr. Mendoza is on surgical call tonight, but he's five minutes away. I don't think she'll last that long. It almost looks like an animal ripped her apart, except for the gruesome burn on her face."

"Let's go," I said. I ran toward the operating room, trying to clear my mind of its prior turmoil.

When I completed a fast scrub-down, the nurse tied off my surgical mask. After pushing through the swinging doors, I stood over the operating table. The bright lights amplified the cavernous gashes down the patient's face and neck. I opened her up and tried to repair the internal damage.

A phrase in demonic script was etched onto her face. This was not an animal attack. Demons were in the area. But why? They couldn't be coming for me, could they? If so, why did this poor soul get caught in the middle? The angels had rescued me and threatened Satariel with repercussions if I were harmed.

Every now and then, I glanced at her face and tried to decipher the marking, trying to remember some of the language, but the words were unfamiliar. A sense of dread loomed and I tried to prepare myself for the worst.

Fifteen minutes into the operation, the patient's heart rate plunged. There was internal bleeding. It seemed impossible that I could save her, but I still had to try. I needed answers from her. Who was her attacker? Why her? Who had brought her to the hospital and left her? Maybe if I could track down that person, I could figure out what had provoked the attack. I could find out why the demons were here.

The nurses scrambled as the patient flat lined. I grabbed the defibrillator paddles and attempted to shock the patient's heart back into rhythm. Over and over, I sent the electric pulse through her system, but she wouldn't return. Sweat poured down my face behind the mask.

Sophia gripped my arm. "Let it go, Doctor. You did everything you could. She was too far gone when she arrived."

Throwing the paddles down, I shoved the swinging door into the wall and stormed out into the garden. I looked up to the now-visible stars. The night was calm, so different from a half hour ago. Despair threatened to pull me under. I had lost patients before, and I knew that death was necessary for the new life Diaga offered. But this death seemed more tragic than most I encountered, and I couldn't explain that.

Bent over with my elbows on my knees, I held my head in my hands. Angry and alone, the ache in my chest stabbed me. I ran my hand down my face, swiping at the tears, and looked up. The fantasy seemed so real. Aishling appeared in the garden, strolling toward me—a glowing angel. She wore a blue dress and her hair swung above her waist. Her eyes sent rays of sapphire before her to light the way. Further chiseling away at the ice inside me, she stood in front of me and raised one hand to my cheek. Warmth spread, and the sensation of water dripping off the ice soothed me.

"Aishling." I leaned into her hand and closed my eyes. My soul tempest eased. When I opened my eyes, she was gone. I was so weary of trying to keep her out. Bring on the illusions.

With an eighteen-hour shift behind me, I was ready to crawl into bed. But there was something I had to do first. The entrance to the crude driveway that led to my house was a couple of miles from Tilarán. Dusk licked at the heels of the jungle as my blinker clicked, and I swung left toward my haven. From the turnoff, five miles of rough terrain called for slow speeds and sturdy wheels. Trudging onward, I drove my old army jeep down the road that snaked through the jungle. The drive was usually a great stress reliever for me after a hard day's work at the hospital, but tonight I was in a hurry, so the muddy ruts only served to gouge grooves into my patience.

My house was situated near the Viento Fresco waterfalls, and the creek pouring from the falls curved through the driveway at different intervals. Sometimes I'd stop the jeep in the middle of the creek to just reflect on my day or enjoy the beauty. Tonight I splashed on through. After crossing the creek seven or eight times, I pulled up to my oasis.

The house was not elaborate, but I neither wanted nor needed anything fancy. It was the right place for me—a *casa* on the creek in a peaceful spot. The style was Spanish stucco with exterior walls of forest green. Spanish terracotta clay tiles flowed in waves across the asymmetrical roofline. The windows were all arched and outlined with brick the color of the roof. The house was square in shape and built on thick concrete pillars so the creek could pass underneath it.

My rascally Keeshonds, Eden and Elkan, barked as they raced beside the jeep the last few yards to the house. Throwing my legs over the side, I was attacked with love before my feet even hit the ground. After I gave them the attention they demanded, they followed me to the shed below the house by the creek. In the leftover ash of the fire pit, I traced with a stick the intricate symbol of keruv—the fearsome beast with four different faces and four wings. Then I gathered supplies from the shed and assembled the towering bonfire above the image.

I busied myself, setting up the tall, grated platform above the wood, and placed upon it the necessary herbs: ginger, angelica, damiana, holly, jasmine, anise, and violet.

The stars, so much more astute in the backwoods, stood witness to my guilt as I struck the match and tossed it on the kindling. Remorse washed over me because I knew that this meeting had the potential to spiral out of control. With this particular blend of incense, it would likely draw an unwanted presence in addition to the audience I was appealing to. Flames heated my face. I shivered in remembrance and took a step backward. Eden jumped up with her front paws landing on my hip—breaking the trance.

The incense rode on the breeze, sending an almost melodious odor dancing in my direction. Inhaling the concoction, I could tell it was about time. I stepped back and waited. It wouldn't take long for the watchers to take notice of the evocation, my petition for an audience with one of the Keruvim—an expert in the tongues of the supernatural. A pair of watchers flew down close enough that I could see the disturbance in the atmosphere, an iridescent wave. I closed my eyes and tilted my head to the sky, allowing them to draw the information from my mind.

Searching the stars, I waited for an answer to my request, but my wait was too long. A rumble shook the ground and I growled. It seemed the worst-case scenario was going to unfold. With intensifying strength, I hauled a thick tree trunk toward the hell-hole and with the brute force of a dozen men I charged the fire, using my battering ram's log to scatter the flaming limbs. The platform toppled and the herbs crinkled on their descent to the consuming inferno. Still the earth tremored.

I braced for the wrath of the Sergatim, the hounds of hell that did not like to be disturbed—much less, summoned—even if it was inadvertent. I had hoped to douse the flames before Marax caught a whiff of his favorite scent, as this herb mixture used to be his calling card when he had been among the watchers—before the fall.

The fire exploded; lasso flames whipped out to sting me. Paralyzed, I collapsed to the ground. I knew it was coming, but the effects never ceased to unnerve me. A squadron of the vampire-bat-like creatures crawled from the fire, slinking toward me elbow over elbow, with foaming fangs and fiery eyes. Where in the blazes was Marax? His pets wouldn't kill me, not with the demons lurking within me—the same ones now hissing at the Sergatim to retreat. But their bite would send me into a state of delirium for several days and, that, I could not afford. I was still unable to move my legs to kick at them, and they were almost at my feet.

About that time, Marax, my former partner in crime, rose from what was left of the flames. In demonic chant, he called off the Sergatim, and they backed into the fire, never taking their bleeding, beady eyes from me. Marax lifted his nose to the air and drank in the intoxicating aroma. "Ah, you sent my girls to find me. Jasmine always smells so much sweeter here." Marax had an odd fixation with women who bore the name of his precious herbs.

He turned in a circle with his arms held wide and then stepped toward me, brushing ash off his black shirt. Feeling returned to my limbs; I sat up and rubbed my legs. Marax was the only demon I could ever trust; yet, my trust in him was shaky at best. But I needed him now for information, so I'd have to take the beastly with the bad.

"You rang, Raphael," he hissed, plopping down on the ground next to me. "And I came, but you owe me. I was having quite the time with Damiana from Denmark."

"Nice to see you, too, Marax." Demons could change their appearance whenever they wished, but Marax had always preferred the same look—long, brown hair; six-foot-three; devilish goatee; and designer clothing. "You weren't the intended recipient of my herbal wares, but I'm not sure if the angel will come. Maybe you would offer your translating services?"

"An angel—coming here? Private audience?" he jeered. "Stepping up in the world, are we, Raphael?" He placed his left hand, palm up, toward the blaze and a rod of fire spiraled to his hand. "Not likely," was his one-sided commentary—under his breath, of course. "Anyway, what do I get in return?"

Fatigue threatened my self-control. I had to be careful around Marax, though. "What do you want?"

"Hmm." He grinned, tapping his finger on his lips. Marax eyed my bag of hard-to-come-by herbs and tipped his head toward it.

I groaned. "Do you know how hard it is to find angelica? I compound my own drugs for some of my patients with it." He laughed as I tossed the drawstring pouch at his feet and I watched as he stowed my stash beneath his coat.

Blowing out an exasperated breath, I handed him the mud-soiled paper. He looked over the writing, as I said, "I know the first part translates to 'devil,' but I can't decipher the rest."

Fire burned underneath his skin; I could see it shifting and bending around his neck. He closed his eyes and shook himself, rolling his neck forward and sideways. A coil of smoke snaked from his lips to mingle with the fire before us. Once settled, he lifted the paper again. "Why do you ask?" he inquired, one eyebrow lifted.

"Why do you ask why I'm asking?"

A devilish laugh poured from his lips. "Devil's wife," he blurted. "That's what the script says."

The young woman was obviously human. Devil's wife? Impossible. I stood to pace. "Know of any recent demon activity in this area?"

Marax stroked his chin. "Maybe." I stopped and stared at him. His gaze remained on the fire; the light flickered on his face. Flames slithered from his eyes toward the larger fire. "You call me up here to ask for my protection?"

With my hands locked behind my neck, I resumed my pacing. "Satariel knows he can't get to me. I'm on a probation, of sorts. So why would they come here?"

"All I know is that it has to do with some princess," he disclosed.

"So the one they claimed to be the devil's wife was a princess?" I asked. It didn't seem right.

He was about to speak when a shout trumpeted from the heavens. A meteor devoured the black air, leaving a trail of white light in its wake. It was headed straight for us. The angel I'd asked to speak with plummeted to a spot about ten feet above the earth and hovered there.

The Seraph roared at the demon, then turned furious eyes on me. "Raphael, what is the meaning of this entreaty? Still consorting with the damned, I see."

"Hadriel…"

The mighty wings of the angel stretched to the sky. In slow motion, they lowered, bringing the wrath of the clouds with them. The stars escaped. The clouds attacked. Needle-like icicles, poisonous to the devil's children, fired from the air like bullets into the flesh of the demon. With a howl of agony, Marax bounded into the fire and sunk into the flames.

Prepared for my punishment, I knelt before Hadriel. Yet, when I looked up, the angel was gone.

29

Amor De Mi Corazón

(Aishling)

The Fates had just handed me a baby. Surely they wouldn't kill me off during my episode with the Dullahan, whenever that was, and leave this precious angel without a mother again. I wanted to check on Alexa at the hospital, but I couldn't let them know I had brought her in. There was no way I could answer their questions, but I was so worried about her.

When I landed in front of the hut and pulled down the cloak hood, the loud blast of an instrument carried through the walls, along with the wail of a baby's cry. I rushed through the door to find the newborn laid on the bed and Cearnaigh standing over her. He was blowing through the mouthpiece of a bronze carnyx—a five-foot-tall, ancient Celtic war trumpet with an open boar's head for the bell at the top. It produced such a harsh sound; I covered my ears. "Cearnaigh, stop! You're givin' the babe a fright she may never recover from."

He wheeled toward me, and other than the whimpering infant, the silence was soothing. "Where did that thing come from?" I squawked at him as I went to lift Ariceli in my arms.

"Listen, I was ne'er in the house carin' for the wee ones. My wife did the woman's work," he sighed and looked down at the tearful babe in my arms. "Couldn't get this little one to quit screamin', and I tried everythin'. Figured she might like a li'l music." He threw his hands in the air.

"And that's what you call 'music?'" I chuckled and held the baby to my chest, rubbing her back to calm her.

"My kind o' music," he rumbled and puffed out his chest. "Always got me fired up fer battle." He slammed one fist across his body into his broad shoulder.

"Remind me never to contact you for babysitting again. I'm certainly not the best at mothering, but I know enough not to blow a trumpet in her ears."

"Hmph," he grunted. "Where'd ya take off to? What happened to the babe's mama?"

Ariceli whimpered and I prepared a bottle while I held her. Once I settled down on the couch with her tucked against me, I gave her the bottle. Almost instantly, her cries ceased and her eyelids closed, as she made sweet sucking sounds. I looked up at Cearnaigh and he smiled down at the child. "I'm afraid her mom might not make it. The Dullahan was there. Looks like the creature got to her. She was really messed up when I left her at the hospital door."

"The Dullahan was out there? Blimey!"

"I struck the creature with a faerie dart, but I'm pretty sure it didn't kill it. I saw the beast ride away. Don't think it'll be back anytime soon, though."

"What're ya goin' to do?"

"She wanted me to keep the child—even brought me adoption papers to sign."

"But Aishling, this is not yer purpose. She's not yer responsibility."

"Maybe this is my purpose." My brows wrinkled. "Or at least one of them," I whispered and lay the sleeping infant on the couch." I stood with Cearnaigh by the door. "I'm really beat. Can we discuss this some other time?"

"Right. Take care, then," he said.

I nodded, closed the door of the hut behind him, and locked it. Then I grabbed my weapon, just in case, before sitting down on the sofa. Cradling my new baby, I just stared at her for a solid hour, wondering what in the world I had gotten myself into. I wondered how Alexa knew I was the Siridean. I didn't even know what the prophecy meant, and she seemed to have an inside track.

Watching the *niña* sleep, I wondered how she could have lain there dreaming during all of the preceding commotion and turmoil. She was so beautiful and fragile. Her delicate skin was light olive, and soft jet-black curls graced her crown. Her Cupid's-bow lips were turned up into a sweet smile, and I couldn't help but reach out to touch her perfectly round, rosy cheeks. She grasped my finger in her tiny hand.

The baby stirred and looked up into my eyes; she smiled, and just like that I fell in love. I was taken aback to realize that she in fact had the eyes of my family—intense blue violet—even as a newborn. There was no doubt about it. I would fight to the death to protect her, and I wondered if that was what I was being called upon to do.

"Well, Ariceli, *amor de mi corazón* [love of my heart], what now?"

I surveyed the room to see what I could use to improvise as a crib until I was able to buy some furniture. One side of my bed was pushed all the way against the wall, and there was a small chest of drawers. Taking one out to use as a temporary bassinet, I lined it with pillows and blankets and laid it on the side nearest the wall. I'd never been around many babies until I had come here to the orphanage, so I was concerned about my abilities to be a good mother. I wished that my mom were there to help me. She'd know what to do. Thinking of her made me think of my father, and I cringed, wondering how he would react to this news. I had a strong feeling that I couldn't share this with him, and I made a vow with myself and with Ariceli that I'd do everything possible to hide her from him until I got some answers.

Restless, I stirred at first light, trying to shake off an odd dream. Then I heard something stirring beside me on the bed, and I turned to see the drawer lying there. I peeked over the side and saw the baby. When she saw me, she smiled as if she had been waiting patiently for me to wake up. Maybe this wasn't going to be so bad after all. While giving her a sponge bath and dressing her, I made another mental note to pick up a small tub and baby supplies when I went into town that morning.

After I had my shower and was ready to go, which took twenty minutes longer than usual, I wrapped Ariceli in a thin blanket and slung my case over my shoulder. While we headed to the orphanage, I thought again about the danger surrounding this little one the previous night, and I decided to change her name to something bolder. She would need all the help she could get. The Irish believe there is great meaning and power in a name. I decided she would be called Kaillech, who was the Gaelic goddess known as "the Veiled One," a destroyer and teacher of the arts of war. I would have to train her as she grew to help her fit into the name.

I found Señora Martinez and told her a portion of what had happened last night: how Kaillech had been left on my doorstep. She came around the desk and held out her arms. "May I?"

"Of course." I positioned the baby in her arms and stepped back. She bounced Kaillech in her arms and patted her back.

"I'd like to take care of her if that is allowed," I said.

Her attention shifted from the baby and she looked at me.

"Actually, I'd like to speak with an attorney in town today about adopting her," I clarified, thinking this was the only way to get around this abnormal situation. I couldn't very well tell the señora that I was already Kaillech's mother.

"But Aishling you're so young. The courts will never agree."

"I want to try at least," I replied, shrugging my shoulders.

"You have your whole life ahead of you. Take some time and think this through. Okay?"

"Last night I spent a lot of time thinking about it. I feel attached to her already. I'm going to try to make her mine."

"Very well then. I wish you luck. I'll help you all I can." Señora Martinez gave her consent and told me she would have one of the volunteers cover my normal class time with the children that morning.

I had no infant car seat yet, so I borrowed one that belonged to the orphanage and strapped it into my beat-up VW. Once I had Kaillech settled, we headed down the road to Tilarán, which was about a five-mile drive from the orphanage.

After parking the car by the square, I cradled Kaillech in my arms and wandered into town. People were lounging in the park for it was almost siesta time.

It wouldn't be very long before the market would shut down, so I hurried down the sidewalk two more blocks and entered the courtyard gate into Mercado Central. This was a large, open-air market with stalls lining the perimeter and many rows spanning the central portion. I'd been there many times since coming to Costa Rica. It was a fun place just to explore. There were fresh-produce vendors, flower stalls, handmade Costa Rican leather products, coffee roasting and grinding vendors, arts and crafts vendors and, of course, clothing vendors, which was where I headed first.

A young lady tending the booth with baby clothes helped me pick out several outfits for Kaillech. Then I wandered to the end of the row where a furniture vendor helped me find just the right crib. It was made of rare cocobolo heartwood, handmade in Sarchí, a city in Costa Rica known for its fine artistry in furniture making.

I found all the other baby items I needed. The man handed me a receipt and promised that all the items would be delivered to the orphanage later that afternoon.

People lounged on the stone wall surrounding the cathedral as I exited the market. I decided to take a chance and go down to the hospital, hoping to overhear some news about Alexa. The benches outside Tilarán General were crowded, but I found a spot and settled in between two nursing mothers. I strained to hear bits of conversations; I hoped Alexa's family might be there. Kaillech woke up crying. Searching through her bag, I found her bottle and realized that I still needed to go to the *supermercado* to purchase more baby formula and diapers.

A half hour later, I still had not gathered any news on Kaillech's mother. When I stood to leave, a hearse pulled to the emergency room door on the right side of the building. With a casual stride, I moved toward the door. A gurney was wheeled out that held a covered body. Two young men loaded the body into the hearse and went back inside. Instinctively, I knew it was she and tears stung my eyes. The Dullahan would pay for this—and for so many other crimes. Holding the tears back, I rushed toward the car. The driver had not emerged from the hospital yet. I dawdled by the side of the car that faced away from the emergency room doors. For a second, I debated the risk of getting caught. Then I grabbed the handle, opened the door, and ducked down. Cradling Kaillech in one arm, I reached in and uncovered the face of her mother. I gasped and my throat clogged with emotion. This time I let the tears fall, as I covered her back up and trudged away.

When we arrived back at Vista del Mar, I took Kaillech with me to Señora Martinez's office. She was surprised when I told her the adoption was going through. "Kaillech is welcome in the main house any time you need to be away," she offered.

"Gracias, Señora." I was very grateful knowing that my baby would be well cared for in my absence.

Kaillech was asleep in her seat. I placed it on the couch so I could call Uncle Brádach. There were two phones in the orphanage, one in the main office and one in a small room near the office that was often used for different kinds of meetings. Señora Martinez allowed me to pay for my portion of the phone bill when it came due.

Uncle Brádach picked up after about five rings. "Howya," he said.

It was so comforting to hear his voice. "Well, it's about time you made it to the phone," I said, joking. "Old bones don't move so quickly, huh?"

"Who ya callin' old? It's often a man's mouth broke his nose, ya know. And I'll have ye know, forty-eight is the new thirty-five."

We both laughed, excited to be able to connect over such a long distance.

"Oh Uncle Brádach! I've missed you so much," I sighed. Tears threatened to spill over.

"I know, lass. I've been missin' ya too." It sounded like he got choked up. "Kheelan has become a menace since ye left. The new stable hand got bucked e'en after a month workin' wit' him. He's nursin' a broken leg now for all his efforts. That horse has sure got spirit, just like his owner."

"Oh, you'll have to apologize to him for me. I hope you gave Kheelan a good scolding."

"I don't think there's nary a cure for ornery. I've learned 'for what cannot be cured, patience is best.'"

"You have to be the most patient man I've ever met."

"Any patience I have is hard-earned," he said, laughing.

There was a moment of silence. "So what's troublin' ya?" he asked. "I know my lass, and I know something's wrong. You're stalling."

Uncle Brádach had always preferred straightforwardness, so I plunged into the story and explained everything that had happened since last night, except for the part about the Dullahan being the murderer. For my safety, he would have ordered me home, but I couldn't go yet. For the first time in my life, Brádach Kavanaugh was speechless.

"Uncle Brádach? Hello? Did the phone go dead?"

"Nay, I'm still here," he replied. "I just don't know what to say."

"Well, that's a first."

"Hmmph. Remember what I said about broken noses?"

"Very funny," I conceded. "What do I do? Tell me what to do," I pleaded. "Have ya talked to yer father about this?"

"No! I never know what to say to him, especially about something so important. You know him as well as I do."

"Aye, yes, I s'pose I do. Maybe Anlon would know somethin'," he offered.

"No, you can't involve Patrick's father either. Not until I know more."

"For the love of Samhain, why not?"

"You know why." I moved to the wall to rest my forehead. "Father would never forgive me if I did anything to damage our clan's relationship with the Kavanaughs. I'm already afraid of how he's going to react to this child. I've got to figure this whole thing out before I present the dilemma to him or the rest of the Kavanaughs. So not a word about it for now."

"All right, lass. They'll not be hearin' about it from me."

There was a comfortable silence. I gazed into the face of my child.

"Uncle Brádach, the baby—she looks like me. The woman who brought her to me is Costa Rican, but the baby looks like me," I said with chill bumps tingling up my arm.

"Then she's got to be beautiful. God rest her mother's soul."

"Thanks. I just feel awful that I couldn't do more for Alexa. I tried to save her."

"And, child, that's all we can do is give things our best effort. Ya can't go blamin' yerself for her death. Ya did nothin' wrong."

"I guess so," I replied. "Well, I'd better go for now. I'll try to call when I know something further."

"Ye'd better see to that wee lass, and Aishling, be mindful o' what surrounds ya."

"I will. I love you."

"Love ya too, Ash. Slán."

30
Kaillech And The Angels

(Aishling)

At suppertime I was in the kitchen helping feed the babies, including Kaillech, when my furniture arrived from the market. After giving the men directions to the hut, I returned to the chaos of trying to feed ten babies at one time.

When Kaillech and I returned to the hut for the evening, I opened the door to an overpowering feeling of home. Sitting down in the beautiful new chair, I rocked my baby—my *baby*. That phrase was going to take a lot of getting used to. She was nodding off into her dreams, and I just stared at her with a longing that I couldn't quite express. I'd never known that a child could add such rich dimensions to my heart, and I felt a tear slip down my cheek.

Tired from the long day, I closed my eyes as I rocked her, and a strange sensation crept up on me. It felt as if someone else were in the room near the door right behind Kaillech and me. I reached down and lifted the front of my pants leg to secure my ancient dagger.

With Kaillech in one hand and the dagger in the other, I leapt out of the chair and twisted around to face the door. Nobody was there. I had never been a paranoid person, but I couldn't shake the feeling that someone was still there even though I could clearly see there was no one. This was the same feeling I'd had every birthday when the Phantom Queen showed up. I placed the dagger back in its holder at my ankle, crossed the room, and laid the blowgun beside the bed—just in case.

I laid Kaillech back in the drawer where she had slept the previous night so I could make up her new bed. In the process she awoke crying. I picked her up to soothe her, rocking her back and forth in my arms as I sang an old Irish lullaby. She fell back into her dreams, and I held her as I finished smoothing out her sheets. I kissed her on the cheek, placed her into her crib, and covered her with the sheet. It had been a very long day, so I turned in early.

The next morning I got ready for the day. In case Kaillech was still asleep, I tiptoed into the room, but she was cooing and nibbling on her fist. I lifted her into my arms, and she smiled at me. *She loves me*, I thought with joy.

While I rocked her in my arms, that same sensation came over me again—that someone else was in the room with us. Having laid her back in the crib, I scanned the room, but still no one appeared to be there. In my mind I went to the hawthorn tree and reached out to touch its trunk. "*Ta me i gcruachais*," I petitioned the hawthorn, summoning my weapon. The marking sprawled across the right side of my face while my taggert appeared in my hand. Doing the one thing I *could* do, I spoke to the empty space around me.

"I know someone's there. Did Morrighan send you? Does the Phantom Queen have an assistant, a ghost she sends on errands? Or are you Alorcán scum? Don't be a coward. Show yourself!" I said in the spirit of the fightin' Irish.

In that instant, a being with the appearance of a man materialized before me near the door, and I angled the weapon toward him. Keeping a defensible space between us, I studied this stranger from another world. At first I was frightened by his intense glare and warrior-like stance. He was built like images I'd seen of the great Norse god Thor. I lowered the dart rifle. I couldn't shoot. I couldn't look away.

242

He gave off a vibe of pure exhilaration from being discovered there. His slow smile became infectious, and I was soon smiling back. He was trembling with such excitement that he kept fading in and out of view. I was awestruck by his beauty. He had to be an angel. There was no other explanation that was even plausible. There wasn't a physical light that shone around him, yet there was a definite inner light that was radiating from his very core.

The being had an overpowering presence. He had to be close to seven feet tall. I knew that Patrick was a little over six feet tall, and this being was much taller than he was. He had wavy, unruly blonde hair that fell to his chin, which made him look like a surfer who was high on life. He appeared to be close to my age, although it was hard to tell for sure. His piercing steel blue-gray eyes seemed to look right through me, straight to the heart.

His apparel was also mysterious. He wore a hooded Australian duster made of dark worn leather with large pockets on the front; yet the duster was oversized, almost like a cloak. Such a bulky coat was out of place in Costa Rica, yet his bare feet made him fit right in.

"Thank you for calling me here to your realm. I can't come to you unless you ask for me." He smiled, showing all his exquisite teeth.

"What are you?" I asked.

"Ariceli's guardian angel," he bragged, looking at her with fondness. "I've been with her since the moment of her birth into your world. My name is Micah."

"I'm Aishling, and by the way her name is now Kaillech."

"Oh, I know who you are," he stated as a matter of fact. "Nice marking, by the way. I understand you are some type of Gaelic protector."

"Yes, that's correct. And why are you here, Micah?"

"I led her mother to you because I'd already determined that you were the most worthy member of your family to care for the child. It's my business to know these things. Why the name change for her?" he queried.

"She needed the name of a fighter if she's going to be my daughter." I moved to her crib to caress the cheek of the tiny angel. "And I'm afraid to say she needs that name more than ever now." I looked up to meet his gaze. "Alexa was killed last night."

"What?" He lamented, stepping closer. "Who did this?"

"The better question is, 'What did this?'"

"Okay, what did this?"

After placing my taggert on the couch, I sat down. Micah stood by the chair. "May I?" he asked, pointing to the chair.

"Please," I said, motioning to the seat.

Elbows resting on my knees, I placed my palms together. "The Dullahan, the most feared faerie from Celtic lore, killed her. He was there in the jungle. I saw him."

"Why would this faerie be interested in Alexa?" he asked with his brow pinched.

"No clue." I shook my head. "So you weren't around last night to see the horror?"

"No. Once I led Alexa to you, I stayed with Aric—Kaillech, I mean," he said, shaking his head and smiling. "The new name may take me a few tries to get right."

"It's a great name."

"Yeah, it is," he agreed.

His gray eyes beamed. It was hard not to stare at his eyes. I had seen mine do something similar, but I assumed it was just a faerie thing. "So Alexa is Kaillech's biological mother?" I queried.

"Yes," he answered.

"Who is Kaillech's father?"

"I don't know," he replied. "When Kaillech was born, I was sent to her. For two weeks I followed her and her mother before leading them to you. During those two weeks, I had completed enough research into your family to know she'd be safe with you. I know you've been trained for battle," he said. "Her safety is my primary concern, after all."

"And your research didn't reveal anything about the father?"

"No, I'm sorry. It did not. But I only skimmed the surface. There's a lot of darkness in your family."

"Yeah, I know." Frustrated, I switched gears. "So how does this work? Are you with her every moment of every day?"

"I'm not with her all the time, but angels travel at the speed of light, so I could, for example, be on the other side of the world and sense she was falling out of her highchair and be here before she hit the linoleum." He looked smug.

"I'm impressed," I admitted.

"You should be."

"Well, you're not the angel of humility," I joked. I wondered if I had overstepped with friendly jest too soon.

Micah burst into laughter. "I was joking. But your being impressed only means my Creator made me impressive."

I could tell he and I were going to get along just fine. With his presence more stable now in this realm, he looked like a very muscular, very dangerous man. While we spoke he took both hands and pulled his shiny goldenrod hair into a band, making a short ponytail. One strand escaped the holder and hung near his temple on the right side of his perfect angular face. With his hair pulled back so severely, he looked like a renegade, one I'd be afraid to anger. He turned his mischievous smile on me, and I stopped my gawking as I moved forward to stand by him.

The clock reared its face, reminding me of the time and my duties. *Distracted by an angel—what a way to start the morning!* "She and I had better get up to the orphanage for now. They'll be wondering where we are."

He nodded and then disappeared with a rustle into the wrinkling air pocket.

31

Féth Fíada

(Aishling)

One week later

With the Dullahan on the loose nearby, it was my duty as a faerie slayer to protect the people. What the fiend had done to Alexa was abominable. If there was something that evil in the jungle, I needed to see that all the children were safe. This was the Gaelic night of Litha—a smaller festival, but one where the thin places were still breached—and the rabble-rouser was sure to draw other rebellious faeries to its sordid bash. The Dullahan was a mercenary, but I couldn't comprehend what the beast expected to gain for its troubles.

That evening the breeze was searing. I wouldn't doubt if my cheeks were wind burned by the scorcher of a night. After dropping Kaillech off at the orphanage, I followed the path back toward the hut, and then veered off into the jungle. It worried me to leave her, but if I were successful tonight in my hunt, then I could lay my fears to rest. Besides, I'd never known the Alorcán to storm buildings; they clung to the earth. Kaillech was as safe at the orphanage as I could make her. Plus, I knew Micah would be with her there.

With my taggert in hand and loaded, I roved through the foliage, heading in the direction of the spewing volcano. Almost every night it erupted—a powerful reminder that humans are not in charge. Scads of three-wattled bellbirds drowned out the other jungle sounds with their "bonk" echoes as I wandered into their territory. The laughing falcons snickered at me. Maybe they were right. Maybe this was a joke, me—a rookie faerie slayer—attempting to take down a fearsome pro. Nevertheless, I strode onward, my cloak billowing behind me in the sweltry draft.

Scouring the jungle, I searched for traces of the hellish goons. Night marched in at a slow but steady pace, and the blackish shadows loomed ahead. One foot in front of the other, I wove my way through the vines and muddy offshoots of the waterfall in the distance. While my faerie cross emitted its strange blue light, I looked ahead to see a snake with its head lifted off the ground. It hissed and barreled in for the attack—the aggressive fer-de-lance, a venomous pit viper. I aimed and blew my dart through the tube. It struck the midsection of the coiling viper, and the predator was grounded to a standstill. With its final spasm, the snake ratcheted open its jaws and spat venom from the tips of its fangs to land at my feet several yards away. My head dipped to land on my chest, which expanded in unsteady jolts to draw in air. That had been close. Shaky, I reloaded the blowgun and leapt over the carcass.

Blackness seized the dusk. The faeries loved this exact moment. I pushed on deeper and deeper, more wary now.

Suddenly, a power surge overtook me and I dropped to one knee, bracing with my hands on the ground. I could feel the mark chiseling onto my right cheek; yet, it didn't stop on my forehead as usual. It crept down my left cheekbone as well. That was new. And I could feel the weight of my entire arsenal, hidden beneath the cloak, even though I'd not called the weapons from the tree myself. My head popped up and sapphire light streamed from my eyes.

In my mind's sight, I sped in fast-forward through the rainforest to the natural pool below the waterfall. My virtual self saw Ina with her hands bound to a tree. The symbol for the Siridean—a circle with crossed crystals in the center—was toed into the sand at her feet. A horde of faeries was grouped around her.

"Ina!" I called out, before I remembered I wasn't really there. She looked so small and fragile among the bullies of the Otherworld, who had all chosen to take the appearance of the Dullahan. But somehow I sensed he was not among them. The poor kid would have nightmares for the rest of her life.

It felt a lot like I was in one of those carnival bungee-run inflatables: where the cord is attached to your back, you take off at a sprint, and at the moment of greatest tension, your body is jerked from behind and yanked into the puffy wall. I sped in reverse to reunite with my body. *So that's what it feels like*—transforming into the Searcher. I was beginning to wonder if I'd ever figure out that part of my existence.

The tingle of the mark helped soothe the sting of the earlier windburn while I shifted in the direction of the intruders in a split second. When I landed atop the waterfall and surveyed the scene below, one thought kept repeating in my head—*How am I going to take on that many faeries and rescue Ina?* The brave girl squirmed and scowled at the faerie nearest her, but she was okay for now. Even if I tried to get close to her in the cloak, I wouldn't be able to escape with her—some sort of electrified bubble surrounded her. *Might as well make my presence known.* I sent a cross dart rocketing through the waterfall mist to strike the faerie that towered over Ina. The impact drove the Dullahan look-alike onto its back in the weeds, so she couldn't see its demise. Ina gasped and the other faeries turned to her as another dart impaled its target in the back of the pack. On guard now, the remaining dozen or so brandished their spiked clubs and backed closer to their prisoner.

I dove off the top of the falls and broke the surface of the water, going deep, and curving upward. Opening my eyes as I neared the surface, I saw three of the fiends hunched over on the bank, looking for me. I came up fighting, knocking two of them down with a roundhouse kick as I burst from the pool. The third lifted its club to bring it down on my head like an axe, but I slung Diaga's dust in its open neck, and the monster fell into the water, burning.

I crouched on the ground—ready. Ina was only ten feet away, but I couldn't get to her. Not sure if she could hear me, I yelled anyway, "Ina, I'll get you out. It'll be okay."

A headless imposter stalked in my direction, sword drawn. Rising from the ground, I reached for my weapon. The sword resonated as I unsheathed it. I waited. The faerie charged. A heavy *klunk* reverbed as our claymores collided. I was holding my own, parrying and blocking, until one of the fiends grabbed my waist from behind and lifted me off the ground. My only defense at the time was my legs, and I kicked out, knocking my first attacker off its feet.

The faerie that held me aloft brought both of his arms across my chest and squeezed the air from my lungs. I struggled to reach into the pouch to retrieve the dust. I was able to scoop out a handful and I scattered it in the air to disengage the pack closing in. Three of them went down, as they clutched their necks and disintegrated as in an acid bath. The faerie that held me locked my arms to my chest, while another beast charged from the left and gouged its blade-like talons into my side. My head bowed back and a wail of pain escaped my lips. I could hear Ina screaming and it made me sick that I had failed her. *What kind of faerie slayer am I if I can't defend those I'm sworn to protect?*

Blood seeped from my wound and a woozy feeling bogged down my senses, but I would not give up. With a thunderous shout, I rammed my head into the chest of the one that held me, and wrangled my way to the ground.

A thick fog crept in and engulfed us. I tried to crawl to Ina, but I fell face down in the mud at the edge of the pond. Rolling under the misty blanket, I scooted off into the water to soothe my wounds; my head and back rested on the bank while I faced the waterfall. Before they found me, I needed to get some Diaga's dust into the gashes for the healing to take place. My lids blinked in heavy lumber as I wrestled to remain conscious.

A low bass *awhoo-whoom...awhoo-whoom* tremored in the air, like a tiger gearing up to a roar, only the sound was much fiercer with the rumble of an entire ambush of tigers. At the brink of the falls, the fog swirled. Out of nowhere, a swarm of dragonflies with wolf-sized bodies and the wingspans of pterodactyls torpedoed down from the fog like ballistic missiles, barreling for their headless targets. Bioluminescent stingers of pulsating blue glowed from the tails of the frightening creatures. If this were a mirage, I'd take it. At least the faeries were leaving me alone as they scrambled to flee.

I felt a comforting kinship with the dragonflies. Maybe they would carry Ina to safety. My lifeblood was draining, and I didn't know how much longer I'd last. The dust of Diaga was in my pouch; all I needed to do was reach out and take hold, but I felt I was too weak.

Turning my head to the right, I saw blips of light as the dragonflies winged in and out of the fog in their aerial bombardment—bombers carrying explosive payloads. They clutched the faeries in their claws and vanished into the fog, instantly reentering the air without the faeries they had just held. They swooped and vanished on unseen currents, then blipped back in. It was the féth fíada—it had to be—the magic mist the ancient Tuatha Dé Danann used to cloak themselves from the enemy until they chose to reveal themselves. *Did Morrighan send them?* I wondered as I drifted away.

"Aishling!" someone called. My eyelids allowed in enough light to see the form of a warrior with long hair kneeling beside me, but the scant rays of moon glow were soon doused. I felt the pressure of his lips on mine—just a soft caress, just a second.

My eyes bolted awake and alert, and I surged to my feet, ripping back the cloak and touching my side—healed. Alone. The silence was a sweet sound, but only for a second. Ina! I pitched myself to the spot where she had been fastened earlier. The inescapable bubble she had been shackled in was no longer in place. With her hands bound above her in the thick ropes, she lay with her head twisted to the side, resting on the tree bark. She was breathing. My dagger made a quick slice through the knots, and her hands were freed. She had fainted but would probably awaken soon. I lifted her in my arms and whisked the cloak around us.

Sitting on the edge of Ina's bed, I watched the dust of Diaga swirl above her head like a thought bubble, and then disappear. The dust would put her in a dreamlike state. Hopefully, that would be enough to curb some of her questions. Her tiny disco ball nightlight cast purple and silver sparkles on the ceiling and walls as it revolved. I stared with such love into the face of the wee girl. *What if the dragonflies hadn't come when they did? I could have lost her.* My throat clogged as tears threatened.

Ina's eyelids swung open and she popped up, wrapping her arms around me in a hug. Quick as a whip, she jerked back as if she were afraid she'd hurt me, and then she lifted my shirt on the side, searching for my already-healed wound. *Note to self— ask Cearnaigh how to mend stab holes in a magic cloak.* Ina's face scrunched in confusion. Lifting tiny hands to my cheeks, she examined me, checking for the mark. "Miss Delaney, I…"

"Shh," I crooned, placing a finger on her lips. "You'll wake the others."

"Oh. Right. Sorry." She grinned and looked at her folded hands.

"Heard you were asking for me earlier," I added.

She scratched her head and began again, whispering, "I had a dream…or a nightmare, I guess. I'm not sure. A pretty faerie came into my room and told me you were in trouble, so I followed her out of the orphanage and ran toward your hut. Only, before I knew it, I was in the middle of the jungle, and the faerie had disappeared." She covered her mouth as she yawned. "I know I didn't leave the path, Miss Delaney. Then you came to save me and these really bad monsters showed up. And there were these—Is the right word, big-gantic?—dragonflies…"

I chuckled. "Ina, what a brilliant imagination you have. Time to go back to sleep, dear one. No more monsters," I winked, tickling her belly for a second until she lay down. Pulling the covers up to tuck them under her chin, I kissed her on the forehead and wandered to the nursery.

32

An Angel Whisper

(Aishling)

Moseying toward the hut, I was enjoying the colorful sunset and the exotic scent of the tropical flowers that had begun to invade the path. Kaillech was in the baby sling that held her tight against my belly. She seemed to enjoy being that close to me. We approached the hut, and I stopped in to get her car seat. Then we meandered down the path.

When we arrived on the cliffs, I set her carrier down, placed her inside it, and covered her with a lightweight blanket. It was a warm evening, but I didn't want her to be chilled as dusk approached. Removing the baby sling from around my neck, I took out my fiddle and ran the bow across the strings.

I'd only been playing for a short while when I looked down at the lake and saw Micah flying toward me. At first he startled me, but then I just had to smile. He had such a childlike spirit. He was dipping and soaring on the wind like a bird. When he saw me watching, he showed off a little, twisting and whirling through the air. I had never witnessed anyone enjoying himself more. He looked so carefree and unburdened, and I wondered what that must have felt like. Maybe he could teach me how to lighten up. He landed right beside us on the cliffs and leaned down to kiss Kaillech on the head.

"How was your day?" he asked.

"Great. Busy." I placed my fiddle back in the case and wrapped Kaillech to me in the baby sling.

"How was yours?" I asked, wondering what an angel did all day long.

Micah then sat down in front of me and animatedly gave the details of his fascinating day. When he left us that morning, he had gone to Greece to fly through Vikos Gorge. Then he flew to Lake Como in Italy and sat up on a mountaintop overlooking the lake to watch the sun set. He said that Bellagio was one of his most favorite places on earth.

"I went to Bellagio once," I told him. "It was a present when I graduated from high school. I went with my two best friends and their family. I love it too!"

There was a subject I'd been thinking about all day, but I didn't know how to broach the topic with him other than just blurting it out. "Micah, have you ever heard of Uí Bracile?" I assumed that as an angel he'd heard of every place, even phantom islands.

He looked thoughtful for a moment. "No, I don't believe so. Why do you ask?"

My head drooped as I looked between my knees and swept the rocks on the ground together with my hands. "Um…it's nothing. Never mind," I mumbled. Soon I had a little pile, and I started pitching them off the cliff. It was a minor stress reliever, but it helped.

The next month passed with each day similar to the one when I'd first met Micah. I taught at the orphanage and helped out wherever I was needed. Micah would travel around the world, always knowing the right time to meet us at the hut at day's end. Phone calls and letters from Patrick had become more and more sparse, which at first was a welcome relief with all my added responsibilities with Kaillech. Once I had time to stop and think about it, I wondered if he was breaking his promise to me—the one where he was not supposed to change.

An outsider, if they were able to see Micah, would have viewed us as an ordinary family. Angels and humans were not meant to be part of each other's worlds, but sometimes Micah seemed so *human* that the line between "species" grew fuzzy. It was hard trying to maintain a comfortable distance from him while promoting a friendship or sibling kind of relationship. To me he was like a tall, handsome, adventurous brother, but it was hard to tell how he saw me. Spending so much time with someone was sure to produce emotional ties of one sort or another, and he had no experience with human relationships.

One evening at twilight I stood in front of the screen door, patting Kaillech in the baby sling at my stomach and watching Micah. He was leaning against the awning post and looking at the monkeys jumping and bending the tree limbs in their pursuit of each other. Being near Micah was very hard to describe. I had always heard that angels were tough and scary. He had the potential to be bad-to-the-bone (especially when protecting Kaillech), but he was quirky for an angel. I guess that opposing side of him came from protecting children for so many years; he was fun-loving and innocent.

I smiled to myself while I thought of another unique thing that made Micah who he was. He was a serial hugger. When he would lift me off the ground, he felt solid at times, yet transient and vapor-like on other occasions, like he could disappear from my life in the next second.

There were moments, like that night, when he had a faint glow surrounding him like starlight. The screen door squeaked as I pushed it open and stepped out to the tiny porch of the hut. The scent of orchids made me close my eyes for a moment to simply inhale.

"The monkeys are screeching somethin' fierce tonight," I said as I wrapped my arms around Kaillech in the sling. He looked down with a half-smile. As I stared at Micah, I tried to guess his age. If he were human, I'd have had a hard time putting him in the proper age bracket. Sometimes he appeared about ten years older than I was, but when he became so animated, I would have said he could pass for eighteen.

"What are you thinking about so hard out here?" I asked him. "Your brow is all scrunched up." Kaillech sighed in her sleep and I swung her side to side.

He looked up to the diamond-filled sky. Then he stepped toward me, and I leaned my head backward to look up at him. The closeness was making me a little nervous. Patrick had been the only boy I'd ever been around outside of school, unless you count those few miraculous hours I'd spent with Raphael at the Hogueras Festival almost four years ago. Every time I allowed myself to envision him, a new wave of sadness crushed me, so I tried with full-blown desperation not to think of him.

"I'm thinking about how beautiful you are."

"Oh," I said. Now *my* brow was all scrunched up. "Well, thank you." A mammoth centipede glided across the tiny patch of concrete under the awning, and I examined it with such intensity as if it contained the answer to a crucial research project. *Is an angel hitting on me? Have I been giving off the wrong vibes?*

"Hey, Ash, I didn't mean to make you uncomfortable." He laughed. "I was really just thinking about how much it has meant to me, being here with you and Kaillech over the past month. It feels…right. And you *are* beautiful—motherhood suits you."

Relieved, I looked up and offered him a friendly smile.

"I want to show you something cool. Are you in?"

"Okay?" I squeaked out.

"That sounded like more of a question than an acceptance," he chuckled.

For a second, I gave him my best sisterly evil eye. "Alright, Mr. Angel man, this won't take long will it?"

He perked up. "Less than ten seconds." He held one pointer finger toward me. "Go on, touch it," he said, and I slowly lifted my hand, "if you dare," he joked.

My hand pulled back a fraction, but then I fused my finger to his. A sensation of flying in fast-forward motion among the clouds made my knees buckle, although we never left the ground. Micah reached out to steady Kaillech and me. I shook my head and closed my eyes to stop the whirling in my head. "Well, that was intense," I remarked, gaining my balance and taking a few steps away from him.

"Yeah, you never know what you're going to get into hanging out with me." His words disrupting the silence made my gaze snap back to him. His eyes portrayed the fierce angel side of him. "Are you ready for a little adventure in your life, Aishling?" he challenged me.

"Bring it on! Just not tonight. I'm exhausted, and this little angel needs to stretch out in her bed," I said as I lifted the fabric to check on Kaillech inside the sling.

"Are you always such a party pooper?" he complained.

"No, I'm just a mom now, so no more late-nighters," I said, trying to sound like a grown-up.

There were so many new emotions and adventures I had experienced this past month. It was hard to keep up with each new feeling and sensation.

Most nights, Micah stayed and helped while I gave Kaillech a bath and put her to bed. It was oddly comforting to have a man around the house. Besides the times that I would stay at Uncle Brádach's, I had not had a man at home with me at night since my mom had died and my dad had become so disconnected from me.

"Are you going far away tonight?" I asked, still uncomfortable with the scene from earlier.

"Do you want me to go away?" he asked.

Trying for nonchalant, I replied, "Kaillech and I don't want to upset your normal routine."

"Okay then. I'll hover over the hut in case you need me. I'll *try* not to get too distracted with all the nightlife in the jungle and take off on an adventure."

"Thanks, Micah. No pushing sloths off limbs or swinging with the monkeys. Focus would be good here."

"Yeah, yeah. I'll be good. Angel's honor," he pledged, while crossing both arms across his chest.

I went into the bathroom to get ready for bed while he sat and rocked Kaillech. A sweet giggling sound flowed to me as I opened the door into the main room. I rushed to stand over the chair and peered down at Kaillech, who was cooing and grinning in her dreams.

Micah's face tilted up. "You know what they say?"

"What?" I played along.

"When a baby laughs while sleeping, an angel is whispering in her ear."

Smiling, I asked, "So, what did you whisper, then?"

"Ah, maybe she'll tell you when she starts talking." He winked.

At that, Kaillech giggled again and I leaned down to kiss her cheek.

He put her in her crib and moved toward the door. He smiled and wished me sweet dreams before leaving and closing the door behind him. I locked the door, cut out the lights, and crawled into bed. My eyes moved to the crib, and I could just make out Kaillech's form through the faint glow of the nightlight.

As I drifted into a rare, peaceful night's rest, I heard Micah whisper through the air, "You're extraordinary, you know. The angels guard you especially." Half into my dreams already, I just smiled and let the darkness have its way.

33

Adrenaline Junkie

(Aishling)

Micah was an extreme adrenaline junkie—me not so much. He often overestimated my sense of adventure, like the time he told me we were going fishing, and we ended up swimming with sharks.

Then there was the day he dropped us down right in the middle of a river in a two-person kayak. *There is no good that could possibly come from this*, I thought. He proceeded to tell me that we were waterfall kayaking down the Royal Gorge in Northern California—of all places. Of course he put me in the front seat, not wanting me to miss any of the action. These were two mistakes I didn't care to repeat; besides I had to leave Kaillech at the orphanage during those times. I already didn't get enough time with her. Fortunate for Kaillech and I, Micah had a knack for turning hours into minutes and freezing time somehow. From then on I made Micah clarify in great detail our activities before he dragged me along. He slipped up sometimes though, and surprised me.

Kaillech was taking a nap at the orphanage with the other babies. While I waited for Micah to return from his daily escapades, I wandered down to the cliffs to watch the storm come. To me there had never been anything more exhilarating than witnessing nature change into all its forms—that was until I started hanging out with an angel of course.

Standing on the edge of the cliff, I watched as the dark clouds tumbled toward me. The earthy scent of the promising rain attacked my senses. I could feel the electricity in the air as the lightning started putting on an impressive display in the distance. I would have to move to shelter soon, but for the time being I closed my eyes and lifted my arms, tilting my face to the sky and feeling the power of the approaching storm.

When I opened my eyes a few moments later, as the thunder boomed its piercing shrill across the sky, I found Micah watching me. The wind twisted my hair across my face, and I wondered what he was thinking. I didn't have to wonder for long.

"You're stunning," he said, approaching me. "You look carefree standing there, Ash; you should look that way more often. I wish I could take away some of your burdens." He tucked my flyaway bangs behind my ear.

"Micah, your friendship is enough. Nobody could be around you for long and feel depressed."

"Well, I take that as a great compliment."

"Well, you should."

"I saw that Kaillech was with Esperanza when I stopped in to check on her."

"Yep," I answered.

Raindrops plopped to the earth, here and there, in no apparent rush. "So what's on the agenda, Micah? I told Esperanza I'd come for Kaillech in an hour."

"Well…"

All of a sudden, his mouth slammed shut and a deadly snarl tore from his lips. His wild eyes locked on mine, and I couldn't believe what I was seeing. Was this some new form of adrenaline rush he was trying out on me? If so, I didn't like it. I backed up a few paces and readied to summon a weapon if need be. But his gaze ripped from my eyes to the tree line, while a flaming sword appeared in his hands. A burly man, a little shorter than Micah, stalked toward us, dragging the tip of his sword on the ground. His look was more feral than Micah's if that was even possible. I wanted to shout to the man, "Danger—angel here! You don't want to mess with him!" But I also didn't want to draw attention to myself.

Rain now plummeted from the heavens and lightning thrashed above us. The man gripped his sword in front of him and roared as he charged Micah. Micah stood his ground, appearing unfazed.

I backed behind a tree to monitor the skirmish. Micah didn't know about my powers, and I didn't want to inform him unless he needed me. For now, I watched and waited. Micah's body emitted a golden light that started at his feet and built its way upward through his limbs. When it poured through his hands, the sword lurched forward and sent fire hurdling toward the man. My hand shot to my mouth. The man fell to the ground, burning and twitching. I gasped as the creature arose—this was no man.

Micah skulked forward; he was a soldier first and foremost. He dueled with the creature, their swords clashing. The fire from his sword was hypnotizing, and I shook my head to get a grip on myself. The angel was a sight to behold. With the hilt of his sword he punched the beast in the face and, while it was reeling, he thrust the blade through its chest. A shrieking howl whipped the air and the ground opened up to swallow the dead.

Micah wheeled around, crouched low, searching for more intruders. He lifted his sword to the sky and it vanished from his hand. His face contorted in pain as he flew toward me. He whipped his cloak around us with such force I didn't have time to ask questions. In a millisecond, we landed near the trees beside the orphanage. It was dark, and the storm was howling, blowing sheets of rain sideways. When he unwrapped his cloak from around me, the wind almost tossed me to the ground. I grabbed a tree to steady myself.

He leaned into my ear, but it was still difficult to hear him above the storm. "Go get Kaillech. Tell Señora Martinez that you'll both be gone for a few days." Then he grimaced in pain.

"What? Micah, are you hurt?"

"Just go. Get her. Hurry!"

I took off running toward the building as if my life and Kaillech's depended on it, since I had no idea what was happening.

Finding Kaillech asleep in Esperanza's arms in the nursery, I gathered her things and tossed them into her diaper bag. Esperanza handed her to me, and I went to find Señora Martinez in her office. I explained to her that Kaillech and I had to go away for a couple of days.

With Kaillech nestled in a blanket and clutched to my chest, I dashed through the rain to the guanacaste tree where Micah waited. I had barely made it to his side before he had us inside his cloak, traveling to an unknown destination.

In one moment we were in a raging storm, and in the next moment we were standing in the beautiful sunshine atop a high mountain. Looking around I noticed that we were on a tall island in the middle of an ocean inlet. From pictures I had seen, it looked like a fjord. The sides of the island disappeared sharply into the water below. It would be difficult for anyone to reach this place. If they were to come by boat, it would be almost impossible for them to climb up the sides of the vertical land mass.

Kaillech stirred in my arms and Micah reached out to take my hand as he led us into a forest. There was a sharp rock cliff atop the mountain that could be seen through the trees, and a short time later Micah stopped at the base of it. He opened his mouth and breathed on the rock. A door appeared.

"Angel's breath—not just for making young ladies swoon," he jested, pushing open the arched door while I stood there and forced a laugh. I knew he was trying to downplay the brawl I had witnessed. That was his way to lighten the mood, so I played along.

"Micah, that sounds like a cheesy commercial for breath mints."

"It's important to always be minty fresh," he replied, showing off his pearly whites. He held out his hands for the baby and I laid her in his arms. Leaning down, he nuzzled her nose with his while she cooed at him.

Smiling, I followed him into a wide room that looked like the entryway of a grand basilica except for the fact that there were no windows—stained glass or otherwise—since it was built underground. Down the palatial hallway, we passed through arch after arch, each ornate with its own elaborate glass and stone mosaics. Each appeared to tell a story, part of angelic history throughout the millennia, and I was eager to examine the celestial tales. The third one intrigued me the most, and I stopped to gaze up at it. There were many angels falling toward the earth, their wings useless. The colors were not the vibrant, multicolored hues of the previous mosaics. This one was fierce in its simplistic use of every shade of black imaginable: charcoal, aluminum, smoke, slate, steel, seashell, storm. It was so creative in its monochromatic style that I was moved more by it than the greatest paintings I'd ever studied.

I was drawn into the intense tragedy of the piece. Micah leaned down to whisper, "That was the saddest day in the history of my kind."

"No doubt," I replied in hushed tones, afraid to intrude on the reverence surrounding it.

"Come on." He grabbed my hand and pulled me down the corridor.

Soon the massive square pillars that supported the arches became my focal point. Regardless of the fact that they looked like simple gray concrete, there was nothing simple about them. Upon first glimpse they were rather dull in contrast to the intricately crafted glass artwork that crowned them, but on closer examination they were consuming. Curiosity won out, and I let go of Micah's hand again. I wandered to one of the imposing pillars and traced the ancient engravings with my fingertips. From ceiling to floor, the columns were filled with a language that was unfamiliar to me. It appeared to be a cross between Hebrew and Akkadian, yet I could not make out a single word.

"Micah, what is this?" I circled the pillar, trying to find any similarities between these symbols and the Semitic writings I had studied.

"Trust me, it's a language that would never be offered at your nearby university," he said, smiling.

Kaillech woke up crying, distracting me from my examination. Micah led us to a seating area, and after I had changed her diaper, I rocked her while she drank her bottle. Micah left us for a few minutes, but he had returned by the time I got her back to sleep.

"The suspense is killing me, Micah! Answers, please!"

"We're in New Zealand, at Lake Manapouri in the Doubtful Sound. Very remote, virtually inaccessible, so it's perfect for an angel refuge. Angels come and go from here in a constant stream. It's our home—visible solely to those who are invited into our world."

"Well, I feel very privileged to be here then," I said. "But I don't see any angels other than you," I said, frustrated.

Micah turned then, motioning toward the other side of the room as if to urge someone forward. I should have remembered they wouldn't just appear in front of me. I couldn't see anyone even though I could sense they were there. As I had done with Micah when I first met him, I spoke to the empty room, asking whoever was there to please appear.

The angel materialized, looking like a disheveled—but still strikingly handsome—musician or artist. His hair was almost as long as mine but medium brown in color. He knelt before me, took my hand in his, and bent to kiss the top of it.

The angel released my hand and propped himself against the wall. Kaillech whimpered, so Micah took her from me and bounced her up and down. He babbled to her as he walked a little way down the hall.

The angel crossed his arms and grinned. "I've known you since you were four years old, ever since your parents decided to have you learn the fiddle. I am Maestrino, and I've helped inspire your passion for music all these years. Your loyalty to this art, as well as in other areas of your existence, is admirable."

"So you helped me learn to play?"

"Yes. Do you know how truly gifted you are? You could play solos on a stage anywhere in the world and have sold-out concerts. What holds you back, my dear?"

"You know, I've never thought of playing professionally," I admitted to my teacher. "I guess I've always played because it's my passion—my release from all the overwhelming emotions in my world. When I play I pour all of my struggles, my emotions, my troubles into the instrument."

"Well then, it's indeed a tragedy that such pain had to be involved to produce such beauty," he chimed in. "If you ever change your mind, I'd love to be in the wings coaching you."

"Okay, if I ever decide to go on tour, I'll let you know," I said, smiling back at him. Changing the subject, I asked, "So do you follow me around like Micah does Kaillech?"

"I'm one of ten guardian angels who have been with you throughout the course of your life."

"I required ten angels?"

"The more responsibilities given, the more guidance needed."

Hands on hips, I tried to read into his unspoken message. "You mean since my life is so hazardous, I need more protection?"

"That's part of it," was all he offered.

I tried to put the stare-down on him so the uncomfortable silence would prompt him to open up, but he was much better at it than I was. I gave up.

"Now that we've raised you, so to speak, we come to you only if you're in peril—as in, unconscious. Of course, now that you know about us, you can always just call for us, and we will come."

Lost in thought, I paced the corridor before coming to stand in front of the angel. "So it was you outside the hospital when I was hurt?"

"Yes."

"I thought I was hallucinating."

He inhaled deeply and looked away, as if reliving the memory. "Kheelan was wandering into the mountains, and you were barely hanging on. The snow was so fierce, he couldn't sense his way home. We all came and got you and Kheelan to Blackrock. We couldn't exactly take you into the hospital, so we put you in a place you'd be easily found." He looked at me with a half-smile.

Tears welled in my eyes as I looked into his. "Thank you."

A simple bow of the head was his only reply.

"So you know about the faeries, then, and the importance of my calling?"

"The past several years have been a trial for your angels, as you have taken command of your duty. Every human must fight his or her own battles to an extent. We cannot interfere in the day-to-day choices you make. You have chosen to fight; therefore, you have weighed the risks, and the angels have stepped back to allow for your freedom. What's even more maddening for us? As you near your time of full maturation, we don't even hear you as loudly anymore; you're changing frequencies," he brooded.

"Frequencies? What do you mean?"

"Your angels are entangled within you. It has always been so. Like a radio station that comes in with no static, we have been attuned to you. Over the past several years—static. We get glimpses, pieces of your life. Something bigger shadows you. Something bigger calls you."

I shuddered at his revelation and slunk down onto the bench.

"I'm alone," I whispered.

Maestrino knelt before me and took my hands in his. "No, you're never alone. And you're strong, Aishling." I looked at him and squeezed his hands.

"Are the other angels here now?" I asked.

"No, just me, but the others should be around in the morning."

Before the conversation could resume, Micah broke in. "Well, I'm sure Aishling would like to find a bed for Kaillech and get some rest herself. I'm going to take her to the south wing so she can have one of the balcony rooms."

Maestrino nodded and left us.

34

Hide And Seek

(Aishling)

Micah took me through many corridors and down several flights of stairs. I wondered just how big this place was. The hallways were wide and had magnificent bricked archways with elegant lanterns illuminating the paths.

He pushed open a heavy wooden arched door, and I followed him in. After feeling like I'd been underground for the past hour with no natural light, I marveled at the bright pool of sunshine streaming in through the glass doors that led out to the balcony. Micah had a crib waiting for us; I placed Kaillech there and covered her with the blankets. Needing to be outside, to breathe, I made my way to the doors and stepped out into the crisp air. Micah followed.

"Micah, what was that creature you…disposed of in the jungle? Why are we here?" I asked him before he could even sit on the stone bench beside me. "I mean it's lovely here, and I'm so fascinated by your life and grateful that you want to share this with me, but Kaillech and I don't belong here."

"I can protect you both better here. We may not go back. I'm still trying to decide." He blew out a frustrated breath.

"Are the orphans in danger? I'd never forgive myself if—"

"No, Ash, calm down. The pursuers are not concerned with them. Don't worry. Besides, orphanages are crawling with angels. Trust me."

"Don't worry? You know, I remember Kaillech's mother saying she was being followed the night she brought her to me. She

267

acted like it was some kind of evil presence. What is out there in the jungle, Micah? What is so evil that Kaillech and I had to travel so far away?" I asked.

"I'm wrong to interfere like this. Already I will be disciplined for my actions and involvement thus far. I can be a little impetuous when it comes to something I feel strongly about. Please, Aishling, trust me and your angels to protect you," he said as he reached out to place his hand on my cheek.

I closed my eyes, lost in thought, wishing that my life could have any sense of normalcy. Take this moment, for example. There I was sitting in a fortress on an island in a fjord in New Zealand of all places, being willingly held captive by a group of angels while my adopted daughter—who was forced upon me when I was only nineteen—slept in the next room. Sometimes I longed to escape into another dimension that paralleled the one I inhabited. That life couldn't possibly be as unsettling as this one.

"Micah, I have to know," I pleaded with him. "How do you detect when Kaillech is in danger? I mean, you go away from us during the day. It wouldn't take but a split second for harm to come to her?"

His shoulders tensed while he looked toward the lake. "Maestrino explained it to you somewhat. When I'm sent to guard a baby, in a sense I become a part of them. Since they can't defend themselves and since they don't realize when they're in trouble, I have to feel what they're feeling at any given moment. We call it *sünomoreo*—the entangling. She and I are corded together, bound up in one another. Kaillech is so well cared for and happy that I simply feel joy most of the time. Things get interesting, though, when she starts having a temper tantrum." He smiled to himself as if recalling a particular moment.

This newsflash was so overwhelming, I stood to pace, my hands covering my forehead as a headache started pounding away. "Okay, I guess I can understand that, but how does it relate to what's roaming the jungle that's so terrifying I just braved an electrical storm in order to retreat here with my baby?" I battled, throwing my hands out in surrender and sinking to the bench.

He looked away, tortured, as if this were information he should not reveal. Secrecy was a concept I knew all about, and I respected the confidentiality he was bound to in his position. But at the same time, I had a child to protect now. When she was threatened, I was threatened. So I waited for him to make the decision whether or not to let me in.

Still looking away, he whispered, "Demons."

Surging to my feet, I paced to the stone wall, propping my hands on the cool rocks. I looked out toward the lake, and I could sense Micah standing right behind me.

"Ash, say something," he begged.

"How can you sense demons near her when you're so far away—sometimes all the way on the other side of the world? How?" I asked as I turned back to face him.

"I told you I feel what she feels. Well, the demons spend the majority of their days scorching in the fires of hell. Whereas humans have cooling mechanisms to get rid of excess body heat, the demons do not. Blistering flames consume them, trapping the warmth inside. It's just another punishment they suffer: eternal burning even when they leave the fires for short periods of time. They have no way to thermoregulate, or keep their body temperatures within certain limits. When they're near Kaillech, I feel tremendous heat within myself, almost to the point of becoming dizzy and dysfunctional. At those times, I rush to her to take her away, to save her and myself from the intense pain of the burning."

I placed a hand on his arm and looked through the windowpane to the crib. "They are bringing pain to my child—to you, Micah?"

"I tell you that demons are stalking your child, and that is your response? At the mention of demons, I was afraid you would pass out or something."

"I'm not really surprised by the supernatural anymore, Micah. So, I assume that was a demon you killed earlier?" He nodded. I paced back to the wall. "Didn't look like what I had pictured. At first, I thought it was a man—a doltish half-wit."

"Yeah, the demons can take on any appearance."

"How do we stop them?" I fumed. My fists clenched at my sides.

"We're working on it."

"*Who's* working on it?" I demanded. "I have the power to help."

"The angels are on it. Don't worry."

"What can I do?"

"You could stay here, for one thing."

"That's not possible, Micah. We can't hide forever."

"Why not?"

"I never liked hide-and-seek. I prefer to face a challenge head on and get it over with."

As he was about to respond to that, Kaillech wailed. I gave Micah a look that said I would table the conversation for the moment, but we would pull out the chairs and sit back down later.

When he strolled into the room, I had a blanket laid on the floor and was shaking a rattle above Kaillech. She reached and kicked and blew bubbles. At first Micah stood towering over us. Then he squatted beside Kaillech. And this fierce angel, who only a short time earlier had taken down a demon, was now baby talking to my little angel.

He reached down to lift her into his arms and placed her head on his shoulder. As he rocked her, Kaillech's eyelids fluttered and fell. "Aishling, I promise you that we're going to keep you both safe. You have my word. We're going to rid your life of the demons."

"Thanks, Micah."

He laid her in the crib and covered her up. "I'm going to fly out and get you something to eat. Be back soon."

He returned a few minutes later with boxty (an Irish potato pancake) and vegetables. The moment he appeared, I inhaled one of my favorite scents from my homeland. "Micah, you're my favorite."

"Do you tell everybody that when they make you happy?

"I can't leave anyone out." I snatched the box from his hands and settled at the small table to eat.

"She only likes me for my food." He headed for the door.

I laughed. "Thanks, Micah. You're the best."

"Good night," he whispered, shutting the door.

Later that evening I wrapped a blanket around my shoulders to fend off the cool night air, and I stepped out onto the balcony. The moonlight bounced off the water, and I enjoyed the peace.

Suddenly the scene in front of me changed into a frightful vision. The once tranquil lake transformed into a rolling sea of fire. The smell was putrid, like blazing sulfur. As I backed toward the wall to try to elude the sense of realness of the vision, a being started flying toward me. While he came nearer, I could see that his eyes were molten fire, and I gasped in fear of him. He landed right on the balcony and reached out to me, not as if he meant to harm me but like he wanted me to help him. He kept his distance and was silent, although his body language spoke of extreme peril and he had a look of pleading. For what—I didn't know.

Trying to avoid his fiery eyes, I took in his other features. He was very well built, and I knew he could easily crush me if that was his intention, but somehow he seemed harmless to me even with his eyes spewing fire. He had a cloak covering him from head to bare feet, but he drew his hood back to reveal a kind face. Aside from the demonic eyes, this being was handsome, and I shivered at the instinctive realization that we had met somewhere before. An inner pulley drew me toward him.

I reached out my hand in welcome, but the vision evaporated. Still clinging to the wall, I tried to get my heart to return to its regular rhythm. I once again stared into the moonlit water. Then it hit me, and my feet could hold me no longer. My back inched down the wall until I fell into a clump on the cool stone balcony. I squeezed my eyes shut and shook my head in disbelief.

The being had looked like Raphael.

A teeth-chattering cold roused me, and I trudged to the bed. Even the flannel sheets and mounds of blankets couldn't fend off the chill. I rode the storm-tossed seas of sleep until the sun slanted in through the balcony doors.

It was strange being there at the refuge since the orphanage had become my home. Having grown accustomed to being with all the children, I couldn't get used to the utter quiet in this place. All morning up to noontime—silence. The walls were suffocating me. I wasn't sure where Micah was, but I knew I had to get out of there. It felt too much like being back at the castle with all the years of solitude I had felt. Earlier in the room, Kaillech and I had breakfast—a bottle for her, waffles and bacon for me. Micah was spoiling me.

After we had eaten, I grabbed her diaper bag and my fiddle, and we headed outside to the cliffs beyond the refuge. The sun was warming the air, and as I watched the bottle-nosed dolphins playing in the water below, I felt more content. Kaillech was kicking her legs in the bouncy seat, entertaining herself as I played an upbeat tune on the fiddle. When I had finished the song, I laid the instrument in its case and propped my hands on the ground behind me, lifting my face to the sun.

The sweetest song moved over me like a whisper; it was like a spirit from the heavens, in a language I couldn't determine. It translated to my ears as a song, but when I turned, all I saw was Micah coming toward us with a lineup of angels, and they were simply conversing as they moved. Fascinating! When they approached they fanned out around us in an arc. The sweet song

I was hearing—which seemed to be the language of angels—ceased, and Micah switched over to English.

"I'm sorry I wasn't here this morning, Ash. There was something I needed to take care of. I hope you both had enough to eat."

"Yes. Thank you," I said, while I stared with curiosity at the menacing angels shading Kaillech and me from the sun.

"On my way back, I ran into some friends who are anxious to finally meet you face to face. Since you know about us, I figured there was no harm in just bringing the whole crew. You've already met Maestrino."

I looked to him as he nodded. Then I turned to face the rest. Micah went down the line, naming each angel, and they bowed in turn: Maximilian, Fiorello, Leopoldo, Luciano, Gianpaolo, Salvatore, Renato, Tristano, and Marcellus.

"We are at your service, my lady," Renato said, stepping forward. A chorus of "hear, hear" rose from the bass voices.

"It's a great honor for me to meet all of you. Thank you so much for all you've done throughout my life and for the things we have yet to do together. It's comforting to know I'm not alone."

Tristano moved forward from the line. "We must be on our way, dear one. Godspeed!" he said, and they all turned to leave—all but one.

"This is Marcellus," Micah introduced the angel again.

"Hello," I said. "So have I given you trouble in all my years growing up?"

"On the contrary, beloved. You are a masterpiece of the Creator."

"You angels really know how to sweet-talk a girl."

Smiling, he said, "I'm not going to debate you on that particular subject because I know the truth of it. Anyway, I've been with you through your visions of things to come. I've helped control the revelations of these visions, unraveling them for you in small doses. We've all tried to help you have as normal a life as possible under the circumstances."

"Thank you. I don't know what else to say, but I have about a million questions."

Laughing, he said, "I'll bet you do."

"Marcellus, last night I had another vision." I went on to explain the details. "Who is he—the being in my vision?"

"He's someone who may become a part of your life. How much of your life he consumes will be controlled by you—and him. You will have to make a very difficult decision about him one day, but the angels will not take away your freedom of choice."

"Is he evil?" I asked, not believing the words as I spoke them.

"In an imperfect world, all mortals are easily swayed toward evil, but that too can be controlled."

I blew my bangs out of my eyes in frustration, and haggled, "Yes, but you didn't answer my question."

"The answer is found in the journey, my dear. It's a question you'll have to answer for yourself. I must ask you to excuse me now, Aishling." Following his statement Marcellus left, taking my answers with him.

"Micah, I need to get back to the orphanage. Have you determined that it's safe again?"

"Is anywhere ever safe enough for you and Kaillech?" He sighed as he leaned back to look into the sky. "The angel refuge would be a great place to live. You'd have everything you need here. Won't you consider staying?"

"I can't, Micah. I've given my word to teach at the orphanage this year. They need me and I will not leave them shorthanded."

"What about Kaillech? You'd take her back and put her in harm's way?" he rebuked, looking at me in disbelief.

"Micah, that's not fair. You know I'd lay down my life before I'd let anything happen to her. It's just that I know how the faeries operate, and I'm getting a handle on the demons. If they mean to find someone, they find them. So we're just as safe at the orphanage as we are here. Am I right?"

He knew it was true. His silence droned on for several seconds. I could almost see his brain working overtime, trying to find some way to refute my logic.

"At least we showed those filthy creatures who's in control," I seethed. "Maybe now they'll back down."

"Not likely. It's obvious they want something from us, if they're deranged enough to kidnap or harm an innocent baby. I'll stay closer. Your angels are going to be around more as well, sweeping the jungle, trying to find clues as to the purpose behind the demons' obsession with Kaillech—and with you."

"See then? No need to worry. Can we go now?" I was anxious to get back. I had lesson plans to prepare.

"We'll go back, I guess. I'm not happy about it, just so you know."

"Bad mood noted. *Now* can we go?" I asked and wrapped Kaillech in the baby sling. I stepped up to wrap my arms around Micah's waist.

"Do you need to go back to your room for anything?"

"I have everything right here." With one last look down to the aquamarine water at the base of the island, Micah snapped the cloak about us, and off we flew back to Costa Rica.

35

Flags And Flames

(Aishling)

It was September 15, Costa Rica's Independence Day, and we were taking all the children to watch the parade in town. Before heading to Tilarán, I stopped in the main building to call Uncle Brádach. It had been a couple of weeks since I'd spoken to him, and I was anxious to hear news from home and see if Kheelan had been behaving.

"How's my girl?" he asked before I even said anything.

"How'd you know it was me?" I said, laughing.

"I always know when my child is callin'."

"Yeah, I guess you always have, haven't you?" With the one person in the world I knew would listen and understand, I vented, "Despite everything that he's done, I need to know if my father is okay. It's been so long since we've spoken that I wonder if he still even thinks of me."

"He's one selfish so-and-so, but I know he cares for ya deep down, child. He came o'er just last week to pay Kheelan's board for another year. I asked him if he'd spoken to ya of late, and he said he hadn't but would be talkin' to ya soon, lass. I didn't mention that we'd talked scads o' times since ye've been across the sea, seein' as I didn't want to set him off on a tangent."

"Yeah, that was probably best."

"Ash, I have to tell ya though. Somethin' strange has been happenin' on Delaney land. I didn't want to burden ya with it, but I feel ya need to know. Ye know I've been a close friend of yer butler, Sullie, for goin' on twelve years or so now. He called me yesterday and said that two of yer father's lackeys have gone missin'—yer cousins Powell and Sean Delaney."

"Missing? What do you mean? Poor Aunt Maeve—she must be devastated. Any idea what happened to them?"

"Don't know, but the police have been questionin' yer father. It happened the night before last. Accordin' to Sullie, yer father told them he kept hearin' a horse ridin' across his property all that night, but Sullie said there was no such thing happened. He said yer father had been shakin' in his boots e'er since."

"My father...afraid?" I scoffed, but then the blood seemed to drain from my body when I recalled my own experience from the night I got Kaillech. That night, there had been a horse in the jungle, and it had been the Dullahan's. Could these incidents be connected somehow?

"Yeah, it's a right bit peculiar," Uncle Brádach replied.

The phone went silent for a moment. "I have to go for now. We're taking the orphans to a parade in Tilarán, but would you let me know what's happening and if they find Maeve's boys?"

"Sure thing. Aishling, keep yerself safe. I don't know what I'd do if somethin' happened to ya. Yer too far away from me, and I can't protect ya there."

"All right, you big teddy bear. I'll be careful. I've always said you're all funnel cloud, no touchdown," I said, teasing him.

"Ya know what I always say?"

"Oh no. What is it this time?" I wondered, laughing.

"A silent mouth is musical." I could tell he was smiling.

"I love you. Give Kheelan a kiss for me."

"I love ya, child. Slán."

Disturbed by the news from home, I was having a hard time focusing on the task at hand, which was helping cram sixty or so children onto the overcrowded bus. With the excitement bouncing off the seats and in the aisle, it was hard not to get caught up in the children's enthusiasm, and soon I was transported back to the present, most traces of worry gone.

When we arrived in Tilarán, we found a spot beside the road, settled the children, and waited for the parade to come. The ratio was three children to each adult so we could keep up with all of them. I had Kaillech, Ina, and Adalina with me seated on my mom's old patchwork quilt. People were crowded together as close to the road as possible and as far as the eye could see down both sides.

"*Viva* Costa Rica!" someone yelled, which set off a chain reaction of cheers like a wave of fans at a rugby game. Or should I say a World Cup soccer game? After all, I was in Costa Rica.

Kaillech, content in her bouncy seat, cooed in response, and I peered with adoration at my baby girl. With the police-car sirens signaling the commencement of the parade, we all gazed to the left down the street. Blue, white, and red flags—the colors of Costa Rica—whipped in the air while the procession moved forward. Women and children dressed in traditional Costa Rican garments passed by. As they danced, the girls' dresses flew around them: swirls of cherry red, dandelion, and royal blue.

Everything in Costa Rica was vibrant in color. They even pulled the black, gray, and other dark colors out of the children's crayon boxes, I'd recently learned—the colors were too depressing. As I took in all the vivid shades, I had to admit it did make me happy. The atmosphere was uplifting, and for a little while I forgot everything but the joy of the moment.

A drum cadence beat a lively rhythm as a high school band approached. At the front of the band was a group of about twenty students who were playing glockenspiels. The tinkling bells resonated, and I was amused to watch Kaillech twist toward the sound, locked on in concentration. She craned her neck to watch as the chimes faded in the distance. I made a mental note to try to find her a toy xylophone. Maybe she was going to be a musician like her mom. Her head jerked back to the left as a shiny red fire truck blew its horn and I lifted her into my arms so she could see better. The firemen waved to us from their perches all along the outside of the truck, and the swirling red lights were hypnotic.

The fire truck inched away, and the crowd on the other side of the street became visible again. It was then that I saw him standing in the back of the crowd, diagonal from where I sat. It was impossible. He had the same features as the being in my vision a few nights earlier. But this was no demon. He was smiling at the passing children in the parade. *What a beautiful smile he has!* He was even more ruggedly handsome in person, and I had to wonder, *Could it be Raphael?*

I stared at him towering above the crowd, but Ina spilled her drink on the quilt and I looked down. It was only for a few seconds, yet when I gazed back he was gone. I got to my feet and shifted Kaillech to my hip; I tried to stretch to see over the multitudes, but he was nowhere to be found. If it were not for my duties, I would have plunged through the middle of the parade and gone after him. I settled back down on the quilt, and I comforted myself with the fact that my visions were a shadow of things to come. I would see him again.

We waited until the end of the parade to see the arrival of the flame of independence. While the torchbearer carried it toward the center of the park, we gathered the children together to follow them down one block and across the grass to the pavilion. A loud cheer went up at the ceremonial lighting, and everyone joined in the singing of Costa Rica's national anthem:

> *Noble country, our lives*
> *Are revealed in your flying flag;*
> *For in peace, white and pure, we live tranquil*
> *Beneath the clear limpid blue of your sky.*

In the center of the park, Señora Martinez and a few volunteers were using several of the brick fire pits to grill hamburgers for *cena [dinner]*, and soon most people were stuffed and relaxed, but I was more keyed up than ever. Taking my three charges with me, I set off through the square, searching for the mystery man, only to return disappointed a half hour later.

Night settled in and a huge bonfire was built in the park. Drawn to it I stared into the blaze, thinking about Almeria, Spain, and the Hogueras Festival so many years ago. In that city on that night, I had felt like there was evil all around me. The city and this fire seemed to produce the same feeling in me for the first time since I'd moved here.

Having given up on my search, we wandered back to sit with our group for the fireworks display. All eyes were on the sky as the fireworks, like shooting stars, came twinkling and fluttering down to earth. Kaillech stiffened and cringed into my chest, peeking through the shelter of my long hair at the colorful parade in the sky. When the cannon-boom fireworks exploded, she boomed with them. Maria smiled and offered to watch my other two children so I could comfort Kaillech.

Her cries lessened the farther we escaped into the downtown area. The streets of Tilarán were mostly deserted since everyone was gathered at the square. I was thinking about the Hogueras Festival again when I happened to look down a dark alley between two of the buildings in town and saw tiny specks of fire coming from a bush. Entering the alley a few steps, I thought it must have been from the fireworks. Maybe some stray sparks had landed there. The bush was close to the buildings, and I was afraid they might catch on fire.

I needed to find some help, so I whirled back toward the square. The specks of fire hissed, and I could do nothing but turn back to them. I moved toward them as they called out my name. Then the specks of fire merged, and two sets of fiery eyes glared back at me from the bush.

When I was almost to the end of the alley and within grasp of what awaited me there, a hooded figure came rushing at me from down the sidewalk on my right side. Grabbing Kaillech and me up into the safety of strong arms, our savior delivered us to the side of the cathedral, just a few steps from the safety of the Independence

Day festivities. Maybe this was one of my angels, I thought, but when I turned to thank my rescuer, all I could see was a retreating back with a cloak floating behind the mysterious phantom.

A few seconds later, I was being physically turned toward a fuming Micah. He was holding my arms, checking on Kaillech, and shouting. "What are you doing alone with her near the shadows? There are demons here. I feel them. What if I hadn't been able to get here in time?"

"Actually, Micah, you didn't get here in time." I looked over my shoulder to where the caped stranger had run into the darkness, and Micah's gaze followed mine.

I turned back to him as he demanded, "Tell me *exactly* what happened."

"The details are a little fuzzy. It's like something much stronger than me had control of my mind. I remember eyes like fire sitting in the bush at the end of the alley. That doesn't make any sense...eyes of fire just sitting there." My brow furrowed as I bounced Kaillech and watched Micah pace.

He jerked to a halt. "This is war! They're so low. I've heard rumors of them projecting before, but this is the first time I've seen it in action."

"What do you mean?"

"I didn't feel the heat until just now, Aishling. They were projecting an image of part of themselves to the alley to draw you in. Since they weren't actually there, the heat wasn't present, which kept me away."

"But Micah, someone else was there. Someone saved us. He brought us here, and then he ran that way," I revealed, pointing in the direction he had gone.

"Well, it seems we have a friend. Hmm!" He burst back into action and resumed his pacing. "Okay, no more wandering away from the crowds. Got it? Do you *want* me to babysit you 24/7?"

"No, Micah. I'll be more careful. I promise." He didn't quite look like he believed me.

Later that night, after we laid an exhausted Kaillech in her crib, Micah and I played a couple of rounds of five-card draw. Soon I was yawning, and he took that as his cue to leave.

Before he opened the door, he quizzed me on proper anti-demon behavior. "So tomorrow morning as you and Kaillech make your way to the orphanage, if a small voice calls to you from the jungle, what do you do? A, run. B, run. C, wander into the jungle, or D, run?"

"Micah!" I rolled my eyes. "You can be so condescending sometimes."

"Just answer the question."

"I was being controlled!" My voice notched two degrees above a whisper, and Kaillech stirred. We waited until she was settled again before continuing.

"That's no excuse for being in the deserted streets!" he fired.

"You know, on multiple-choice tests statistics have proven that when in doubt you should choose C." I laughed while his lips formed a grim line; he looked like the fierce angel that he was. I started backing toward the door myself as he advanced. "Calm down, Micah. All right, I concede. A, B, and D, I run."

"That's better," he said as the childlike Micah returned to the room, and he rumpled my hair.

"Micah, why do you keep using the door? What happened to just disappearing?" I giggled.

"It's more polite to use the door. I'm trying to pick up cues of appropriate behavior in your world. I can tell now that my efforts aren't going to be properly appreciated." He growled with a smile. After he had shut the door behind him, I heard his voice through the walls. "Let's see, how does the quote go? 'Women— can't live with them, can't banish them to their own planet.'"

"Hmm, let's see. 'Angels—can't get one of them to close his yapper, but I do have the power to banish him back to his own realm,'" I whispered, knowing he'd hear me. "Guess that makes me more powerful?"

As I headed to the bathroom, I heard his musical laughter.

36

Short Circuit

(Aishling)

A month had passed since I'd last seen the mystery man. I wondered if he had been a figment of my imagination at the parade. Days turned into nights and nights to days as I continued my routine at the orphanage and nurtured Kaillech. Micah tried to entertain both of us each evening, but I was becoming increasingly distracted with each day and frustrated with all the unanswered questions.

Letters from home had been coming in a more regular stream. I'd received a news-filled letter from Patrick the day before, and he had seemed more like his old self. There was also a letter from Claire telling me all about her escapades with Niul. Despite her father's attempts to keep them apart, Claire had been relentless in her pursuit. Several years earlier she had traded in her Barbie persona for a cowgirl one, much to Patrick's surprise and mine. Now she was helping run the stables. She had been mucking out the stalls each night with Niul, and he had been assisting her with the horse training schedules, routines, and exercises. They sounded like a very well-matched pair.

October was drawing to a close, and the heat was still sweltering. My thoughts drifted to the Emerald Isle, and I wondered if the Cooley Mountains behind the castle were snowcapped yet. I could almost feel the frosty air in my thoughts as I placed Kaillech in her crib. Pointing the fan toward her to help circulate the stale air coming through the mesh screens of the windows, I slipped between the refreshing sheets of my bed and hoped for rapid slumber.

The vision I'd had more than a month earlier of the demon-turned-handsome stranger kept me tossing and turning all night. It played through my mind in succession like trains running through someone's backyard, waking me every hour on the hour through the night.

I woke tired from the restlessness. Sunshine was streaming in through the two windows on each side of the door in the hut. Despite the fact that it was still the Costa Rican rainy season, we'd had a full week of sunshine. Already the day was muggy, so I dressed in my white, ruffled Costa Rican-style dress. It was my favorite because it kept me cooler than some of my other clothes. The neckline was wide, but the elastic on the top of the puffy sleeves held it just on the top of my arms. The skirt cinched at the waist and had three tiers that cascaded to my ankles. A bright purple sash tied at the waist completed the look. I dressed Kaillech in her cotton shorts romper with the tiny pink flowers so she could also be comfortable as the day's heat progressed.

When I opened the door of the orphanage, Graciela was waiting with her arms open to receive Kaillech; she would be watching her for me today. Graciela had started as a volunteer two weeks earlier and had formed an immediate bond with Kaillech. She was a grandmother and had recently become a great-grandmother. All the children at the orphanage had fallen in love with Graciela, treating her as their own *abuela,* and she acted not merely as a volunteer but as a surrogate grandparent.

The day had come for the long-awaited field trip to town for the children. They were doing the reverse of what I was doing in Costa Rica. Instead of Spanish immersion, they would be role-playing and doing English immersion. As their teacher and as a language learner myself, I knew how important it was to practice language in real-life scenarios. Several of the merchants in town spoke fluent English, and the plan was to visit each of them in shifts so we wouldn't overwhelm them with too many children at once. There were forty-six in my class who were divided among three volunteers and me for the trip.

Armed with our common English phrases and our picnic lunches, we boarded the creaky bus and headed to Tilarán. The driver pulled into a spot in the center of town near the park, and each group headed to its first "classroom." My group was filled with a dozen children of various ages from four to fifteen years old. Our first stop was La Tienda supermercado. The children filed into the store behind me; the older children helped me watch the younger ones. We went through the store and named different items in English as we went. The children, especially the younger ones, were so proud of themselves when they were able to make a language connection. One by one, each child took his or her drink to the cashier and practiced the exchange in English.

The plant nursery was our next stop. When we finished there, as each carried his or her own plant, the children chattered about the morning's activities as we ambled toward the park. I wondered how Kaillech was doing back at the orphanage as I carried little Carmelita. She was four and had been giving my arms a workout all day as she had a slight leg deformity.

Following our picnic in the park, my group and I headed east toward the library. After we had crossed the intersection, I saw a young boy, about four years of age, running toward the street. A car zoomed in the direction the boy was heading. Before I could do anything, the boy ran into the road and the car struck him, leaving him lying in the road as it fled away.

I was paralyzed, shocked by what had just happened. The child was motionless and bleeding. Regaining my senses, I squinted to get the car's license plate, and then I turned to my older students and told them to watch the younger children on the sidewalk. I rushed into the street to help the injured child. Several onlookers gathered as I leaned over the boy, checking his vital signs. He was breathing, so I didn't perform CPR, but he was not responding to me as I tried to get him to answer, and the gash on his head was oozing blood in a steady stream down his face. Having ripped a piece of cloth from the hem of my skirt, I pressed the makeshift bandage to the boy's head to try to get the bleeding to stop.

"Does anyone know this child?" I asked the onlookers, but everyone shook their heads. Supporting his neck as much as possible, I lifted the child into my arms and sprinted toward the small hospital two blocks down the street, while my group of students ran behind me.

"Please, help me get him there in time," I prayed. A feeling of peace swept over me, like I was enclosed by heavenly arms on every side.

After pushing open the door to the hospital, I looked down a long dingy-white hallway toward the far end, where I could see some nurses and a doctor gathered around the nurses' station. Encumbered by my fiddle case slung over my shoulder and by the weight of the child in my arms, I ran as fast as I could down the long hallway. I could see that the doctor was staring in our direction, and I wondered why he didn't rush to help. Halfway down the corridor, the vision of the man with fiery eyes blinked in and out of my line of sight, like a TV screen short-circuiting. When the vision cleared from my view, I knew that it was him. The doctor who was staring at me was the man from the parade.

My blood raced at the nervousness I felt in approaching this being, and I experienced the opposing thrill and relief of finally meeting him face to face. I still couldn't shake the feeling that we'd met somewhere before—somewhere besides the vision. He was built like a warrior, with a rough-and-tumble scar that rippled in a jagged, diagonal slash the length of his left cheekbone. The perfectly placed dimples in that rugged face were potent in their allure, reminding me of Raphael. I squinted as I stared at him, trying to transform the man I was running toward into the man I'd longed for the last four years.

My memory of Raphael had blurred with the seasons that had come and gone with no word from him. This man had dark hair that was much shorter than Raphael's. And the scar on his face troubled me so much that I wanted to reach out and trace it with my finger. He had a slight mustache and goatee that appeared to be there as an afterthought, like he had rushed to work without having time to shave. Snapping out of my momentary study, I rushed faster. It was impossible! This was not him. It *couldn't* be him. It would be too much of a coincidence.

Drawing closer to him, I gasped for breath and wheezed out, "Are you the doctor?" I stared at this gorgeous young man who was clearly a doctor, since he was wearing a white lab coat, but I wondered if he didn't know English since he was taking so long to answer me.

"*¿Es usted el médico?*" I tried again in Spanish.

"Forgive me for zoning out, but yes, I do speak English. I'm Doctor Delacruz. Please, lay the child on the stretcher here." He motioned me over to one pushed up against the wall. "What happened?" he asked as he examined the boy.

I relayed the events to him that had happened in the street just a few minutes earlier, and he asked more questions. The voice was wrong, deeper than my memory of Raphael's, and his attitude was one of impatience, very unlike Raphael's demeanor. Dr. Delacruz? Raphael had never told me his last name.

The doctor promised to return when he had any news. I relaxed knowing I would get a chance to talk with him again soon. He would have to take the child down the hall for some tests. When he left I sent one of the older students down to the library to explain what had happened and to tell the librarian we would not be able to come that afternoon. The children and I went to the small, shaded courtyard just outside the main entrance to the hospital. Exhausted from the day, the children were happy just to sit for a while and listen while I played my fiddle to entertain them. A few strangers sauntered over to listen too.

After about thirty minutes, Dr. Delacruz found us. Absorbed in the music, at first I didn't notice that he had propped himself up against the side of the building, but when I turned to look, he was watching me. When I had finished the piece, I looked up to see him coming toward me, a look of interest in his russet-brown eyes, and I stood to meet him. There was attraction there. I could see it in the way he moved, and I felt it too. Little Carmelita hobbled to my side as soon as I laid down my fiddle, appearing wary of the tall handsome doctor.

He stood so close to me, looking down with such a serious expression, that it was like he could read what was going on in my heart. The copper flecks in his irises sidetracked me; I stared when I should have looked away. I much preferred this look to the eyes of molten fire in my vision. When I gazed into his forceful eyes, there were, once again, images of lions stalking me, and I backed up a few steps. It couldn't be. I was having delusions.

As I regained my composure, I found my voice. "How is the child?" I asked.

"He has regained consciousness. We did a CAT scan, and it showed he suffered a mild concussion. Otherwise he'll be fine. Our standard procedure in such cases is to keep the patient overnight for observation. Are you related to the boy?"

"No, when he got hit by the car there seemed to be no one around who knew him, so we brought him here," I said, looking at my students. The doctor's gaze took in my blood-splattered dress, and I peered at the ruined fabric. "The boy lost so much blood," I added. "Did he have to have a transfusion?"

He shook his head, "No, it was just a surface cut. Head wounds bleed worse than others, that's all."

"Forgive me for not introducing myself before. I'm Aishling Delaney." I extended my hand toward him. If this were, by some miracle, Raphael, he would remember my name, wouldn't he? But as he took my hand, he didn't show any signs of recognition.

Carmelita moved from my side and pulled on his lab coat. As I listened she thanked the good doctor for helping the boy and informed him that I was her teacher. She had come a long way with her English for one so young. After a short time, she lost her momentary bravery in the presence of the tall stranger and reached for me to pick her up again.

"So you are in Costa Rica to teach English?" His eyes lit up.

"I teach at the Vista del Mar Orphanage. These are some of my students."

I asked the doctor to send the hospital bill to me at the orphanage, and I told him I'd stop by to check on the boy the next day. Then I turned and motioned for the children to join me so we could head home.

I started to reach down to pick up my fiddle case, which was very difficult with Carmelita still in my arms, but the doctor rushed to grab it for me. He was standing much closer to me now as he placed the strap across my shoulder, and I noticed again the beard stubble against the tanned skin of his face. I imagined that in a town this small, he was one of very few doctors, so he was probably overworked, and I wondered about the last time he'd been able to sleep. That could have explained his slow response when we'd first come in earlier, I thought, giving him a break.

Unaccustomed to such attention, I was caught off guard by his intense stare. Old feelings stirred within me that I had experienced only with one other person on one special night many moons ago, and I looked away before he was able to see how affected I was. I couldn't be affected by him—or by anyone for that matter. It was not in the cards for me, and it was much too dangerous.

Placing myself on guard, I thanked him again for helping the boy, and I started to lead the children from the room.

"Miss Delaney," he blurted, and I turned back to him.

"Are there any children at the orphanage who might need me to come and do a check-up? Things have been kind of slow this week, and I like to help out where I can."

From his unshaven face and tired eyes, I couldn't imagine that he was having a very slow week, but I wasn't about to turn down free help for the children—or the chance to see him again. "Sure, that would be great. Thank you."

"I can come by the day after tomorrow."

He wore the oddest expression. Fear that maybe he appeared a tad overeager? Maybe he did recognize me and didn't want to speak up for whatever reason? *Why am I analyzing him?*

"Well, we'll see you then," I replied and turned around.

While the children and I went back toward the bus, I couldn't stop thinking of the attractive doctor who seemed very nice too—a total package for some lucky girl. What was his connection, though, to the demon from my vision? Surely they couldn't be the same, but the resemblance was too striking to dismiss. He offered to make a house call at the orphanage. *How kind and thoughtful,* I reflected. And he would be coming by the orphanage in a couple of days. *I should make myself scarce while he's there. But*—I wrestled with myself—*maybe we can be friends.* Even in my crazy world, I was allowed friends, right? Micah was my friend, and nothing bad had happened to him, but he *was* an angel. I could leave it to fate. After all I was trained well, and I could defend him if it came to that, I thought, satisfied. Just knowing that I'd found the stranger and that he really existed made my steps a little lighter. And the fact that he reminded me so much of Raphael—well, that was an added bonus.

37

Mortal Angel

(Rafe)

heard the sound of another falling heart, but this time it was my own. The sound in the heart is usually the same when it happens even though it unfolds on the surface in different ways: a look, a catch in breath, a sigh, laughter. But everything in my years of medical training told me I should be dead right now. My heart rhythm was interrupted. I heard it. I felt it. The closer she came to me, the clearer I heard her own rhythm, and mine had become in sync with the tune. It was a phenomenon I couldn't explain, nor would I ever try to. The thawing of that heart chamber happened so instantaneously; I grasped my chest at the beautiful pain.

It was terrifying, yet so beautiful in the same instant. I was standing at one end of the long hallway at Tilarán General Hospital at the nurses' station. The door at the far end of the hall opened, and although I'm generally too focused to look up from the charts I'm studying before checking on the next patient, my gaze was pulled toward the door like there was no other option.

It couldn't have lasted more than thirty seconds, yet it seemed as if my whole existence from the beginning of time flashed before my eyes, and in that instant I was unshackled, liberated. There she was, running straight into my heart, holding an injured child. She was flanked by a dozen or so children of various ages and by an army of angels.

Being an angel myself—or a former angel, I should say—I was always able to see the hosts that guard individuals every day; that was until I became mortal. Recently, though, I had begun to see the angels again, and it was a sweet miracle, a gift from the Father. Most people have one or sometimes two angels. It was hard for me to believe what I was witnessing here, and even though I vaguely heard the nurses calling my name, I could not take my eyes off of this majesty. In the thousands of years I had traveled back and forth to earth, I'd never heard of or witnessed such a display of holiness, except for one time in Ireland in a minefield. As I examined the scene more closely, I saw angels also accompanying the children. Of course the nurses had no idea that I was stunned; they couldn't see into the unseen realm.

Since becoming mortal I had tried to be on my best behavior, but maybe I had committed an unintentional wrong. Were the angels coming to take me away to Sheol to bind me until judgment? Yet at the same time that I saw the angels, I also felt the presence of three, maybe four demons lurking nearby. For a moment all I could think about was how to protect all my patients and these children from the fight that was surely coming.

But my fears were quickly cast aside when I sensed the outnumbered demons retreating. I guess the evil thugs had shown up to see if their work had paid off. Whatever the case, the demons somehow got to that little boy. I don't know how, but I needed to search for the answer.

Ten angels surrounded the young woman leading the group that was running toward me. My first thought was, *Who is she to deserve such a display of power?* Then, as I stared, her beauty overwhelmed me, and it was a beauty that frightened me, for it was she, the girl who'd awakened my soul so many years ago. I'd finally given up hope of ever making her part of my life. But there she came. Like a rockslide shifting the side of a mountain, Aishling came barreling down on me, shaking the earth around me and altering my life into a new formation.

Was she a demon in disguise sent to torment me, another phantom to shake my resolve, to make me waver over my decision to be back among the angels? Satariel often masquerades as an angel of light.

No, she couldn't be a demon, I sensed with great relief. Other supernatural creatures hear thoughts, but the abilities of angels and demons are more fine-tuned. They hear the motives and the desires of the heart. They know what the heart is capable of, and I could sense her pure thoughts as she ran toward me. This was definitely the mortal angel I'd met on the streets of Almeria and jumped fires with at midnight so long ago. The one who I joined in a dream wander more than two years ago. It was unbelievable that she had crashed into my world again. Yet there she was, no longer a young girl, and I was even more devastated by the tempting siren she had become.

Even with the angelic hosts gathered around this young lady with all of their magnificence, I could not take my eyes off of her. She was pulse-spike beautiful and looked so much like a seraph herself that I shifted my eyes to search her neck for the mark of the angel.

Finding no such insignia, I returned my attention to that refuge that so long ago had lit the dark corners of my soul. Immersed in the flood of her gaze, my memory of her eyes had not faded: still blue as ice caverns and sapphires and as intense as either. Her hair was longer—a flowing, black river pooling right above her waist. Her face and arms were a slight pink tone, just sun-kissed. Breathtaking! She also had a long, narrow pack slung across her body and hanging off her back, reminding me of a warrior princess with an arrow pouch sticking up from behind, ready for battle. As she drew closer, I could see that her white dress was splattered with blood from the injured child she was holding. I knew I should run to her to help with the boy, but I was riveted, absorbed in her, and I could not move or look away. She spoke first.

"Are you the doctor?" she asked me in English. *She doesn't recognize me*, I thought dejectedly.

I couldn't get my mind in gear to form a coherent thought. She also spoke in that melodic Irish accent that I was unaccustomed to hearing in this part of the world. Once again I was fascinated. *Focus, Raphael!* She had to ask me again in Spanish before I realized that she thought I had not understood English, which was funny since angels understand all languages.

"Forgive me for zoning out…but yes, I do speak English. I'm Doctor Delacruz." I withheld my first name, hoping she'd figure out that it was me.

After I'd checked the patient, I visited the courtyard. I knew it was a crazy plan, but I had dreamed of this moment for so long, and I had to see if she had remembered me at all, even the tiniest recognition. It seemed at one point, there was a flicker of knowledge in her eyes, but as soon as the flicker flamed the connection was lost.

This feeling was so new to me. Even though I was mortal now, I'd only been living through an angel's viewpoint of life. I was a gifted doctor; how could I not be, since I was created as the angel of healing? But I had been so focused on the job I was there to do, on my penance, that I'd barely experienced being human since I'd left the demons.

Sure, compassion for the sick and the dying came naturally to me, but other human emotions had eluded me—until now. She was back in my life. Somehow we had been brought together. Coincidence? I didn't think so. But this time our coming together in this world might have a hope of becoming something more. When we had first met, I was a mess, shackled by my own demons. Every day, however, I came closer to being released from the bondage that has had me chained for so long. This woman was constantly moving me toward freedom. Maybe now I could have a fighting chance with the angel who had haunted my dreams these fourteen years.

38

Forbidden Wish

(Aishling)

It was overcast as I drove around Lake Arenal toward town. I looked toward the volcano in the distance, and a heavy cloud cover obscured even its usual looming presence. Soon I was pulling up in front of Tilarán General Hospital, and I was anxious to check on the young boy we had rushed there the day before. Even though I didn't want to admit it, I was also hoping to run into the handsome doctor—a wish I shouldn't have been wishing but one I couldn't control nonetheless.

The nurses showed me to the boy's room and I knocked gently, not wanting to wake him if he was sleeping. Hearing no answer I pushed open the door. There was a woman sitting in a chair right beside the bed. She looked so weary, as if she had been holding vigil throughout the night.

"Hello," I whispered.

She looked up startled, tears streaking down her ruddy face.

"I'm sorry to bother you."

"No, no, come in," she insisted, trying to recover her smile. "You must be the one who brought him to the hospital. You saved him! Thank you!" She cried as she wrapped me in a warm hug, and soon she had me sitting in her place beside her son.

"I was just in the right place at the right time. I was glad to help. How is he?" I asked her.

"He woke up a few times last night, and he knew that I was here. Even though he didn't speak to me, I knew he was aware it was me. The doctor said he will have to stay here for a few more days, but he should fully recover."

"Still, I'm sure the waiting is hard," I said to her.

"Sí. I feel kind of helpless, you know?"

We both looked toward the boy as he stirred. I watched as she brushed the hair back from his forehead, and he opened his eyes. The silent exchange between mother and son made me ache inside for my own mother. When she had been there to soothe me, there was no greater comfort and security in the world, and my heart bled that I was unable to help her now in her place of torment. The moment I was witnessing left me feeling so void. I had to get out of there.

"Well, I have to be going," I decided. I stood and moved toward the door. "But I wanted to stop by and make sure he's all right," I said, with my hand on the door handle.

"Miss Delaney?" I guessed the nurses had mentioned my name to her.

"Yes," I said.

"I'll never be able to repay you for everything you've done. I know of your willingness to pay for his expenses. My family has little money. I've never known such compassion. I'll never be able to thank you enough."

I moved back toward the lady and hugged her again. "Seeing how much you love him and care for him is all the thanks I'll ever need. Just promise me that you'll never take him for granted."

"I promise."

Nodding, I moved back toward the door. "Good-bye."

"God bless you, angel," she cried. I escaped to the hall, the ache dulling a little the farther I moved away from the room.

At the nurses' station, I inquired where I might find Dr. Delacruz. "Down the hall, last door on the left," the nurse said.

An odd tingle climbed my back: excitement accompanied by fear. I had thought of him often the night before when I'd arrived back at the hut. He reminded me so much of Raphael. Then again, every man I'd seen since my trip to Spain seemed to take on his form. But what were the odds of the same man being in the same place as I was all the way across the world almost four years later? And a doctor? He hadn't said anything about being a doctor or even aspiring to be one that night on the beach.

Standing in front of the open door, I looked in to see him absorbed in his paperwork. I examined him, trying again to draw out the memory; suddenly I saw it, and it triggered my encounter with him to the forefront of my mind like the rapid shot of a bow. As he worked he chewed on a guitar pick. I had known only one other person who did that. Moving closer to the door, I studied him, confirming the truth.

The doctor was the man I'd met at Hogueras, the man who had disappeared on me. He was four years older, more sure of himself, and ruggedly attractive. The scar that now lined the left side of his face only added to his mystique. It had to be him.

Softly, I knocked and stood in the doorway. He looked up with a scowl at first, being interrupted. However, his gaze softened when he saw me, and a look passed across his face—almost a look of desire and passion that I didn't understand. *He* had left me by myself that night. *He* was the one who forgot to come and see me off the next morning. And I'm fairly certain he was the one who had left me the confusing letter and flowers at college almost a year after we'd met.

"Raphael?" I asked.

A slow smile built across his face. "You can call me Rafe. Most people do now."

Standing, he came around his desk and propped himself up on the other side, facing me. "Hello, Aishling. I've been hoping you'd remember."

Taking a tiny step forward, I asked, "But why didn't you say something yesterday?"

Shrugging, he answered, "I wanted to see if you recognized me."

Getting straight to the point, I plunged ahead. "I waited for you in front of the hotel that next morning. You didn't come. I thought we were becoming friends." I looked down.

Rushing toward me he latched on to both of my arms, willing me to meet his gaze. He looked as if there was so much he wanted to say, but every time he started to speak, I could almost see him backtracking in his mind.

"Aishling, I'm so sorry. I tried to get there, honestly I did. You have to believe me."

"What was so important?" I challenged. It was as if four long years seemed to drain away, leaving me standing alone on that sidewalk in Almeria, hurt all over again.

Letting go of me, he sat back down on the desk. A beautiful arch formed between his eyebrows, smoothed, and formed again. I watched as he ran his hand down his face, and finally he spoke. "I was attacked on the edge of the city and captured that night."

"Attacked!" I gasped. I rushed to him, leaving proper protocol in my tracks as I lifted his chin with my trembling hand. "The scar?"

"Yeah, it's a constant reminder. I'd rather not talk about the details."

Letting go, I moved to sit down in one of the chairs facing him. I needed a moment to rewrite the history I'd inserted in my mind as fact. This new information had the potential to change everything. A young girl's fantasy of the dashing stranger had now become a young woman's forbidden desire. The thing was that I was older now too, more responsible and more sure of my inherited duty. Thoughts of Patrick interfered with my renewed joy at seeing Rafe again.

"Rafe, I'm so sorry. I'd like to know what happened to you that night, but I won't push you. Maybe in time you'll feel comfortable telling me. You seem to be doing well now."

"Yeah, being a doctor here in the jungle isn't very glamorous, but it's the life I've chosen for myself."

"Well, I think it's very admirable." I smiled at him and then I looked to the floor. "Rafe, I know you're busy," I blurted out as I stood from the chair and backed toward the door. "I should go." As I turned around, he caught my hand, and I turned back.

"Aishling, I hope we can be friends."

The look he gave me this time was one of fire—not spewing, crackling fire as in the vision but desire building, threatening to consume me. The smoky browns and yellows of his gaze assaulted me, starving me of oxygen. I felt the air back up in my lungs. When I exhaled, the back draft from the fire exploded, and I felt as if I were standing in a room with flames crawling the walls and ceilings. My body seemed to float toward him, yet I had not taken one step. There was a door behind me. I knew that if I backed toward it, I would be safe. I could escape.

But the flames whispered to me, and I was obsessed by him. His eyes held me there in the fire with him. This was insane. It almost felt like one of my visions, where I was controlled by it until it was finished with me. But this was very different. This was a decision I had to make right now. The choice was easy; I'd already decided there was something about him that was so dangerous that I should walk away, but there was something that was so appealing I couldn't resist.

I strolled through the flames to meet him, and the room was calm again.

I took a moment to compose myself and consider. I replied, "If that's what you want."

"More than anything," he rushed to say.

"Okay then. I'll see you tomorrow at the orphanage?"

"Looking forward to it."

My hand was on the doorknob, and I could feel his gaze on my back. Looking over my shoulder, I told him what I'd wanted to tell him for years. "You know, Rafe, I probably shouldn't admit this, but every year on the last night of Hogueras, I've thought of you and what a good time we had."

"Me too, Aishling. It was a special night—well, before I had to leave anyway."

"Since we met, every year on December twenty-first, I've tried to recreate that feeling. I've found myself at the lake near my home, running into the frigid water, making wishes that never came true." Already having revealed too much, I turned away, embarrassed.

Feeling his hand on my shoulder, I closed my eyes. "What was your wish, Aishling? Tell me, please," he begged.

"Rafe, I have to go." I couldn't exit the room fast enough. His phone rang, and he turned toward the sound.

"I'll see you tomorrow," I heard him say as I made my way down the hall.

39

Saint Status

(Rafe)

I replayed the scenes from the day before so many times in my head during the long night. Her warmth, her vulnerability, and her beauty were still etched in my mind. As I came around the main building of the orphanage toward the sound of the children in the backyard, I could hear Aishling was finishing her class under the gazebo. Many of the children were already running off to play. She saw me at the same time I spotted her, and her face lit up like daybreak again—that same smile I had held close in my memory bank all these years. Aishling seemed as excited to see me as I was to see her; a surge of relief washed over me.

"Well, Doc, *buenos días* [good day]. You did make it. Great timing too. We've just finished class."

"Buenos días to you as well, señorita."

"Come on, I'll show you to the child who's sick. I have to warn you about something. By the way, little Ina has the flu."

"Oh, don't worry, I'm very immune by now to all such things."

"That's not what the warning was for. My warning is that she'll undoubtedly draw you in like she has the rest of us. You must like children, doing what you do, especially in this area of the world," she said. We passed through two generic hallways.

"Yeah, I love children. I enjoy watching the world through their pure and uncomplicated eyes." What I couldn't say to her was that I very much enjoyed the heart language of children. Often I would go to the park just to be around their purity. Some times they would be lying on the grass staring up at the sky, and I could hear their innocent hearts communicating with the Father. On those occasions, I would be at utter peace.

"Well, you've come to the right place then."

We entered the girls' dormitory and Aishling led me down a long hallway to a room near the back of the building. She knocked on the door, peeked in first, and then opened the door for me. Stepping into the room, she turned to the young woman tending to the girl.

"How is she today?" Aishling asked.

"Her fever is down a little bit."

Aishling turned to introduce me. "Maria, this is Dr. Delacruz from the hospital. He has offered to help us when any of the children are sick."

Maria looked at me with admiration. "Well, God bless you, Doctor. Thank you so much for coming."

"Are you kidding? I live for this." They had no idea just how much, I thought. Moving to the bedside, I knelt down by the girl.

"Now, little one, how are you feeling today?" I asked in Spanish.

I was surprised when she answered in English. "It hurts much, Doctor, but if you kiss me on the head like *madre* did I'll feel better. *Mi madre* had magic kisses."

Her faith gripped my heart. I hurt for the child who had lost her mother.

"Well then, let's see if I do too." When I bent to kiss her on the forehead, I could feel that she was burning up with fever. After taking the thermometer from my bag, I placed it under her arm.

While we waited on it to register her temperature, Ina tried to say my name, but she couldn't pronounce it. "How 'bout you just call me Dr. Rafe?"

"Okay," she said, coughing.

"Ina, where did you learn to speak English so well?"

"From Señorita Delaney. She's an excellent teacher," she said, beaming a smile up at Aishling, just short of total awe. Aishling

304

returned the smile and moved over to brush back the fever-induced wet hair from Ina's brow.

"She's just a very attentive student," Aishling offered.

"Well, I'd say you both are right," I replied. Ina closed her eyes, and I thought she was drifting off to sleep.

A moment later she opened them halfway. With a groggy slur, she asked, "Dr. Rafe, did you see any butterflies in the yard today? I love pretty butterflies."

"No, I don't believe I did, but I promise I'll look for some on my way out."

"'Kay," she said, and she closed her eyes again.

When I looked at the thermometer, it was not as high as I had first suspected, but it was still bad enough at 102.3. I took out a different antibiotic than had been prescribed for her by the clinic doctors, and handed the bottle to Maria.

"Ina is to take three doses a day. If her fever doesn't come down, put her in a tub with lukewarm water and call me immediately no matter the time."

"Thank you so much for coming, Doctor," Maria said.

"Any time."

Turning back to Ina, I told her to get some sleep, and I promised to look for butterflies and see her again tomorrow. After leaving the room, Aishling took me to the dining hall during lunch, where I watched in amazement as three women tried to keep the room from utter chaos. These brave souls were refereeing squabbles from older children in the midst of feeding about twenty other children who were too young to feed themselves.

"Is it always like this, Aishling?"

"It's generally not this bad. I assist with the feeding when our volunteers don't show up."

"Well, I'd better go so you can help." I turned to leave even though I desperately didn't want to go yet. A miracle happened; the door swung open and two volunteers arrived to save the day.

Aishling was able to play tour guide. We went to the courtyard. From there, she showed me the rest of the buildings on the property: the boys' dormitory, the gymnasium, the washroom, and the dairy. The orphanage kept the dairy running in order to feed the children, of course, but also to generate revenue for the upkeep of the property. The tour was coming to a close, yet I felt no compulsion to leave. Aishling made the decision for me.

"So have you had enough for one day, or would you like to hike a bit more? I was going to head down to the cliffs. If you have time, you could walk with me."

She nibbled on her bottom lip. *Does she think I'll refuse her?* Maybe I was being rewarded for good behavior. If that were my gift—a few more minutes with Aishling—I'd gladly take it.

"My shift at the hospital doesn't start until later tonight, so I'd love to accompany you."

"Great! This way." She headed toward a wide path that led to the north, away from the orphanage. She and I enjoyed a companionable silence while the forest creatures carried on their own conversation around us. She stopped on the path, reached down to pick a yellow tropical flower, and turned to look at me.

"So how long have you been in Costa Rica?" I asked her.

"About six months. I love it here," she said with a serene gleam.

She had been there for that long without my knowledge of it? I cursed myself for having buried my connection to her under layers of ice. I had wasted half a year that I could have been with her.

"Must be quite a change from Ireland," I said.

"Yes, but in a good way."

A gargantuan tarantula darted out across the path, and she didn't jump. I guessed she was accustomed to the furry creatures by then. She merely stepped over it.

"I don't remember asking you this when we met before, but what county in Ireland does your clan hail from?"

"Louth County. I'm from Blackrock. I grew up there, lived in the same house all my life until I went away to college in Dublin. I'm in my senior year at the university."

"So how did you end up in Costa Rica working at an orphanage?"

A smile stretched across her heart-shaped face as we continued down the path. "My major is Spanish, so I had to choose a Spanish-speaking country to live in for a year for my language and culture immersion. I love working with these little angels."

She was probably unaware that she was surrounded all the time by the largest group of angels I'd ever seen with one person, and she had no idea she was standing by a one-time angel with a demon pinned down inside. I knew I shouldn't have been there with her, but I was so intrigued by her and the rekindled emotions, I couldn't leave. She was my one temptation, the one thing that kept popping up in my life to challenge my allegiances. I hoped Vitale didn't show up to ruin our reunion.

We strolled down the path through a small area of jungle vegetation, far enough away that we could no longer see the orphanage or hear the children's laughter. We had to be getting close to the lake; I could feel the famous winds gusting off it. Near to the cliffs overlooking Lake Arenal was a small hut that couldn't have contained more than one room; she explained it was her home for the time that she was at the orphanage. She stopped there for a moment so she could put away her book bag and fiddle. I saw her slip something into her back pocket before she made her way back to the door and shut it.

"The area around this place reminds me of my own land about six or seven miles from here. It's very peaceful," I said.

"There's nothing like it. I'm close enough to the orphanage that I can walk to work, but far enough away that I can have privacy when I need it."

We rounded another curve in the path, and then the jungle gave way to a rocky landscape with patches of grass every so often. There were native plants with tropical flowers scattered along the cliffs. About twenty yards ahead, the land dropped off and we were standing on the edge of the cliff. The view straight across the lake was of the giant windmills that provided much-needed electricity to the surrounding areas. Far away in the distance, on the extreme opposite end of the lake and to the left of where we were standing, was the great Volcano Arenal, which lit up the sky most nights with a spectacular display like fireworks—but of course was much more deadly.

Aishling motioned for me to follow her farther to the left as she pushed away the limbs of some nearby banana trees and a grouping of tree ferns. We stepped out near the ledge and sat on the ground facing the lake. It felt like we were in our own little world there.

"Well, Rafe, have you always lived in Tilarán? If I remember correctly, you aren't from Spain."

How to explain myself? With desperation I wanted her to know me and not be frightened, but I also knew I would never be able to explain in the way I wanted. I opted for the next best answer. "I've lived in many different places, nowhere long enough to call home. My most recent move was from Texas to here." She smiled, so I guess that answer satisfied her for now.

"Tell me about your family," I said.

She looked away with an almost sad expression. Focusing on her heart, I tried to understand her reaction. She recovered so quickly, though, that I couldn't read her hesitation.

"My father is in politics in Ireland. My mother died before I turned seven. I'm an only child. That pretty much sums up my family."

Okay, I knew there was a lot more to this story, but I wouldn't pry yet.

"You look young for a doctor," she said, examining me. "If you don't mind my asking, how old are you?"

"I'm twenty-three. And how old are you?"

"I'm nineteen, about to turn twenty."

"Whoa! You're in your senior year of college at nineteen? You must be a super brain."

"No, I'm just a product of private school and private tutors. Look at you, though, twenty-three and already a doctor. That's impressive," she said, looking at me with admiration.

"Well, I just passed the boards about a year ago. Now I'm doing my residency in internal medicine here at the hospital in Tilarán. Part of my required hours are spent on medical mission tours to different locations, mostly in Africa and Honduras."

"Oh, I've always wanted to go on a mission trip," she revealed. "Do you have to be a doctor or nurse in order to go?"

"No. There's always so much that needs to be done that doesn't require a specialized degree. As a matter of fact, we have a trip planned to Honduras next month. You should come with us."

I watched as she bit her lip and looked down toward the water. "Who else is going?" she asked.

"So far my assistant Miguel has committed to going and a nurse from the hospital named Sophia. I have a good friend in the United States named David who has gone with me on several trips before who might come with us. He's still trying to work out a scheduling conflict."

"Hmm...well, I'll think about it. Thanks for inviting me."

"No problem."

Together we turned to look at the lake, content just to be silent for a time. The windmill blades revolved at breakneck speeds, and Aishling stared at them unblinking. I tilted my head to watch her. The wind whipped her hair back and forth; at times it blocked her face and other times left it bare. I ached to touch her.

She reached into her pocket and pulled out an envelope. I instantly recognized the calligraphy on the outside. Sweat formed on my brow, and I looked away, wondering how I was going to explain the letter I'd left for her in Ireland. I never dreamed she would keep it. Squinting, I looked toward the sky as if some revelation would appear in my mind.

"Rafe?" she pleaded, unfolding the letter and grasping it firmly as it crinkled in the wind. "Rafe, I have to know. Were you there? I can't explain it, but I felt you there at my college a year after we had met. I found this letter." She handed it to me, and I stared at the words I had penned as she continued. "Somehow I felt that it belonged to me along with the flowers, and that somehow you had found me in Ireland. Do you deny it?"

After a brief pause, I answered, "No." Yet I still couldn't face her.

"I don't understand. You came all that way. You found me. Why didn't you meet me there in the garden? I've read the letter so many times, and it always leaves me confused. I knew it was meant for me, but I need some help decoding it."

Reaching out, I grasped her hand, so tiny in mine, and I looked her in the eyes. "Aishling...I...can't," I evaded, aching to tell her everything but unable to do so. Taking her hand from mine, she looked toward the volcano. "I'm sorry," I said, wanting to take her in my arms and whisk her away from there just as I'd written in the letter.

"I guess it's for the best anyway," she said. Turning to face me, a hint of a smile graced her lips. "We can be friends." She shrugged her shoulders as she stood. I could see now that the letter had caused her pain. Vitale was right; I should have left her alone.

"Friends," I conceded. *For now.*

"I'd better get back to the orphanage. They need me to help with the dinner prep work today," she said and started bolting away.

Jumping to my feet, I brushed the dust from my pants and rushed after her. I was a mess. I could feel the fire in my eyes, and I hoped she didn't turn around to look at me just then. We moved in silence while I calmed down. When I felt in control, I said, "Well, I'll be back tomorrow to check on Ina. The new antibiotics I gave her should already be taking effect. I'm predicting that by the time I arrive you'll probably be having to chase her, since she'll be feeling so much better."

"I hope so. It makes me worry like a parent when any of the children are not themselves for whatever reason."

"You have an extraordinary heart." I knew this firsthand since I had an angel's view of it.

She shook her head as she looked to the ground and then back at me. "Anybody who came to work here would feel the same way."

Three giggling girls saw us emerging from the jungle-laden path, and they ran up to grab hold of Aishling around the waist. Leaving her with them, I promised to come by again the next day.

I thought about the last thing she had said, and I had to disagree in part. It took a special soul to leave their home thousands of miles away and come to a place like this, working with orphans and living in a hut in the jungle. She seemed unaware of her saint status, and that was another thing that made her exquisitely beautiful. *Well, I'd better get to work,* I thought. There was Aishling's heart to try to capture and there were butterflies to catch.

40

Ina And The Butterflies

(Aishling)

The next day I had just finished feeding Kaillech and the other babies their lunch when I saw Rafe advance through the orphanage cafeteria—eyes on me. I thought about the letter. Apparently the years we'd spent apart had not strengthened his feelings for me, but instead had quite the opposite effect. Because if he felt this irrational, unexplainable connection to me that I felt with him, he'd fight this invisible foe to be with me—wouldn't he?

I shoved my disappointment aside and thought of Kaillech. I told myself it was for her protection that as few people as possible knew she was my adopted daughter. As I looked at Rafe, though, I somehow knew that the fact that I was nineteen and had a child already would not bother him under the circumstances. Still I wrestled within myself. If he knew, I would be relinquishing another part of myself that had to be kept private. By holding myself back from him and keeping this on a friendship level where it had to remain, there would be no hurt feelings when I left for Ireland in May. I could return to Patrick and fulfill the marriage alliance as I was bound by honor to do. If I told Rafe about Kaillech and let him into our world, he would begin to matter too much, and I couldn't allow it. So to him, Kaillech would just be another face in the crowd.

"Hello," he said, approaching me. Today, instead of his hospital attire, he wore a fitted rust-colored T-shirt and acid-washed black jeans. His hair was damp, and his bangs had blown across his forehead in a disheveled but alluring way. Glancing around I could see the teenage girls and the female volunteers gazing at his perfectly chiseled features and whispering among themselves. I tried not to let him faze me, but I was struggling. He had shaved the beard stubble away, which made his dimples more pronounced. Mulling over the contrast, I thought I kind of liked it better the other way. He looked more rugged. *Okay, stop noticing the little things*, I scolded myself.

"Hi. You were right," I said, smiling.

"Really. About what?"

"Ina's fever broke last night, and she's had a normal reading for the past two or three hours. Thanks for helping her. She's been trying to jump out of bed all morning, and she's been driving Maria insane asking when you'll come by. Looks like you made quite an impression on our Ina."

"Well, Ina made quite an impression on me too. Do you think she could come outside with us for a little while? I think some fresh air would do her good."

"You're the doc. If anybody could answer that question, it would be you."

"In that case, let's go get her."

When I opened the door and Ina saw Rafe, she jumped out of bed. Her nightgown floated around her ankles as she rushed to wrap her arms around his long legs.

"I have a surprise for you, little Ina," he said with adoration. He brushed her hair back so he could see her eyes. She reached for him, and he gathered her up in his arms.

An ecstatic smile danced onto her face. "*¿Qué es* [What is it]?" she asked.

With the tenor of his laughter, my traitorous heart stirred.

"Now, if I told you it wouldn't be a surprise. You'll have to wait until we get outside, but we can't stay out there for too long. We have to get you all better, you know."

"But Dr. Rafe, I feel all better now. Kiss me on the head again and you'll see," she said, leaning over so her forehead was near his lips.

314

Lovingly he leaned in and pressed his lips to her skin. "Yeah, you're almost better, but we still can't stay out long." He laughed as she groaned.

Carrying her around to the yard, Rafe had her close her eyes as we approached a large canopy tent. It was big enough for adults to stand up in and had see-through mesh sides. I wondered what on earth he had done, and I found myself as curious as Ina; she shook with excitement. After setting her down by the front flap of the tent, he had her open her eyes and step through.

The beautiful sight that unfolded was like heaven on earth, a child's marvel at the complexity yet simplicity of creation. We peered in through the mesh to watch her while hundreds of swarming butterflies surrounded her. Green, red, yellow, blue, small, fat, thin—you name it. If it was a butterfly, it was represented in her tent of wonder. Ina turned to us through the rainbow of colors surrounding her, and with her mouth open in shock she danced as the butterflies swirled around her. Next to Kaillech I'd never seen anything more lovely. Ina skipped, spun, and swiveled to the beat of flapping wings and was almost lost in the flurry of color.

Her laughter was contagious, and Rafe and I soon joined her inside the tent. We locked hands with her, formed a circle, and turned clockwise like a wheel. As we lifted our faces upward, it was like looking through a kaleidoscope. Dizzy after minutes of whirling, we all dropped to the ground, laughing as we went down. A small scarlet butterfly with black spots landed on Ina's nose, and I laughed until I thought my sides were going to split as I watched her eyes cross in concentration, trying to watch the butterfly up close.

In all my life, I couldn't remember a more relaxing, enjoyable time—or a better birthday. I had not told anyone, preferring to keep my big day a secret. I knew that my friends at the orphanage would make a big deal about it, and I just wanted to be low-key this year. I knew they couldn't afford a party and presents. They had a hard enough time doing something special for the children on their birthdays. It was also nice to have a break from the annual Kavanaugh birthday extravaganza, even though I appreciated their efforts very much.

After about an hour of play, Dr. Rafe decided we'd better get the patient back into bed. He loaded Ina onto his back and carried her to her room. I followed.

Before he left her, Ina asked if he would return the next day, and he assured her he would. Rafe and I walked side by side down the long hallway into the yard.

"That was a really beautiful thing you did for her."

"She kind of got to me," he said, grinning.

"As she does with everyone," I said. We approached his jeep.

With my hands in the back pockets of my walking shorts, I was about to say good-bye—which I didn't want to do but knew I should do—when he spoke up.

"Will you have dinner with me tonight?" he asked, looking so unsure of himself.

I looked down, trying to decide; I was tormented. A simple invitation for dinner shouldn't have distressed me, but I knew where it might lead, and I couldn't let this go anywhere. Again the confusion over the letter flashed in my mind. As if he could read my thoughts, he rearranged the question to make it a little easier to answer.

"As friends, I'd like to hang out with you, get to know you better. There's a place in La Fortuna that has a great view of the volcano at night, and they have the most amazing *casado* plate. What do you say?"

"Sounds like fun," I said, showing more enthusiasm.

"Pick you up around seven o'clock?"

"I'll be ready."

"I've got to run to the hospital and look in on some of my patients, but I should be able to get away by then. If I'm going to be late, I'll call the orphanage."

"Okay. See you later." I watched as he jumped up into the jeep and took off down the hill.

About five o'clock that evening, when I had finished giving Kaillech her bath, I jumped in the shower. The cool spray helped to ease the tension I felt and relieve some of my anxiety. Even though this was not a date, I found myself wanting to look my best for Rafe. I moved to the chest of drawers and sifted through what clothes I had brought with me.

In my mind I thanked Claire for her excellent sense of style and the gifts of all her hand-me-downs. By the time she had worn something two or three times, she was already bored with it and ready for the next shopping spree. Not wanting to be wasteful, yet enjoying cute feminine clothes, I was always happy to take her done-withs. When I spent the money I'd made working for Uncle Brádach in the stables on clothes, I'd been content to search through all the mounds of used clothes in heaps on the floor at what we called "The Dig Store" in Iniskeen Village back home.

I settled on a white sundress with large tropical, blueberry-colored flowers that Claire had always told me brought out the color of my eyes, and I dug under the bed until I found my white sandals. Washed clean, my hair was shining black, and the soft curls bounced above my waist. My bangs, as usual, formed a veil over my right eye, but I didn't want to wear my hair up. Looking in the mirror, I was satisfied with my appearance, and the literal butterflies from the afternoon seemed to flutter in my stomach as I watched the clock. My electric nerves spiked and volleyed, and my short-lived smooth hair billowed around me. It seemed to get worse the older I got. I tried to focus on being calm to make it back down. It was starting to become obvious that something was happening to my body, but I had no one to confide in.

I was reaching in the crib to tickle Kaillech when I heard someone whistle behind me. *Speak of the angel and he shows up.* Twisting my head I saw Micah enter, eyeing me up and down—and, I might add, for an angel his perusal was almost inappropriate—almost.

"Did we have a date that I forgot, sweetheart?" He circled around me, still watching, and he reached into the crib to scoop up a giggling Kaillech.

"No." I said, flustered.

"You're a knockout!" He embarrassed me by whistling again. Kaillech cooed at him while my cheeks burned. "So what's the special occasion then?"

"Well, if you must know, it's my birthday, and a friend is taking me out to dinner. But the friend doesn't know about the birthday part. I just thought it would be nice to go do a little incognito celebrating."

"Your birthday? How'd I miss that?" His head drooped and his forehead wrinkled.

"Zipped lips, Micah! Nobody here knows about my birthday, so you're in a special club—the *private* birthday club. Private, meaning you and I are the only members. No leaving any messages for Maria or the others to find. Got it?"

As he took in the gifts and flowers strewn about the room, he said, "I guess your Irish friends didn't get the low-key memo?"

"No, but I anticipated the birthday circus, and I called and told the florist that I'd tip extra if whatever was being sent to me today was brought discreetly to the hut."

"Oh, you're a sly one," he said, grinning. "Why are you so birthday shy? The people here adore you. I think they'd be hurt if they knew they missed it, just like I'm shocked and appalled that I was kept out of the loop," he said, poking out his bottom lip in a hideous pout.

"I adore birthday parties. But they don't have the money for that."

"Always the noble one," he said, shaking his head.

"No, just practical."

He swung Kaillech up into his arms and asked the one question I'd been hoping he'd avoid. "So which friend has the honor of escorting you out on your birthday unaware?" He gave me a conspiratorial smirk. "Maria? Esperanza?"

"No. You don't know this friend."

"Hmm, and I thought I knew all your friends. Am I going to have to hide in the bushes to discover the identity of this friend?"

"No! You most certainly will not!" I fussed.

"So it must be a guy," he said, rubbing noses with Kaillech. He moved to the rocker to bounce her on his knee.

"Just a friend, Micah. Like you are my friend," I said as an afterthought.

"Yes, but I'm a friend who can't take out his second-best girl on her birthday."

"I'll let you take me somewhere on Saturday to make up for it. Okay? Somewhere Micah-style," I said, wincing already at the negative implications of that.

"Somewhere like heli-skiing in the Swiss Alps?" His smile was about to split his face.

"Ah, man! You sure know how to make a girl feel guilty." Against my better judgment, I said, "The Swiss Alps, it is. Yippee!" I said the words in a facetious tone, but Micah, of course, was totally oblivious to my sarcasm.

"You're going to love it!"

"I'll take your word for it. By the way who exactly will be flying the helicopter?" I asked, afraid of his answer.

"Oh, probably Maestrino. He's been wanting to learn," he said excitedly.

"You want to take me up in a helicopter with a pilot who's never flown before?"

"Calm down, Ash. You'll be with two angels. You'll have nothing to fear."

Giving him my evil eye, I turned him around and pushed him toward the door. "We'll have this great fun you speak of on Saturday. But for now I need you to head on to your exciting nocturnal life. I've got to get out of here."

"If this friend touches you, he's a dead man," Micah assured, turning back to me.

"Micah, get out!" I shoved him farther toward the door.

"I'm going. Can't even tease the girl," he said to himself as he exited.

Laughing, I put Kaillech in the playpen for a second so I could look at my hair again. After running the brush through it for about the fiftieth time, I decided I'd better hit the trail so I wouldn't be late. The hair had decided to lie down for the moment.

41

Fate Sealed With A Kiss

(Aishling)

I t was time. In the orphanage nursery I handed Kaillech to Esperanza. Smoothing down my dress as I went, I hurried into the front room and arrived just as Rafe stepped through the front door. Dressed in khaki pants and a white polo shirt that set off his native tan skin, I stared in spite of myself. He stopped short, clutched a handful of his shirt, and exhaled loudly. After a moment had passed, I wondered what he was thinking as he smiled at me.

"You look...uh...amazing," he stammered. "Very nearly stopped my heart."

Trying to keep the mood light, I said, "You don't look half bad either, Doc. Are you takin' me to dinner already, or shall we go eat with all the chaos in the cafeteria?"

"Uh, I think we should eat as far away from that mayhem as possible."

He opened the door to the jeep for me and helped me in. A shockwave passed between us at the touch of our hands, and my eyes fluttered to his. He was still holding my hand. I had to break his hypnotic gaze. I was becoming involved. *Not a good idea.*

My life was already like an intricately crafted labyrinth with no apparent way of escape. The easy path, a door, was missing somewhere. It was like trying to decipher Egyptian hieroglyphics without the Rosetta Stone. With Rafe, it seemed as if he were running in a parallel maze to mine, both of us able to hear the other one on the other side of the ever-enclosing walls but no way to break through to reach out. I was the first to look away and to drop my hand, and I didn't look back to notice his expression.

Rafe had put the top back on the jeep for the evening, and I was very grateful as we had about fifteen miles ahead of us, with some paved and some dirt roads. We talked about the children at the orphanage, especially Ina and the fun we'd had earlier in the day, as we drove toward the volcano. The last rays of light were disappearing into the jungle as we rode over the high, somewhat terrifying bridge spanning the Rio Arenal Gorge. He stopped the jeep in the middle of the bridge. To the left we could see the La Fortuna waterfall crashing down the mountain. The water rushing beneath the bridge churned with a wild spirit.

"And some people say there's no artist behind this beauty." He shook his head.

"I know," I agreed. "It's magnificent. I could sit at the base of it all day long."

He put the jeep back into gear, and we rolled on toward our destination, a few more miles up the road. He pulled into an empty space near the old Spanish-style stucco church building and came around to open my door.

"It's such a nice evening, I thought we'd walk for a bit, if that's okay with you," he asked.

"That'd be great. I've only been to La Fortuna once, and I didn't have time that day to see much of the town."

We strolled through the park, passing between the rows of vendors set up underneath strings of bare bulb lights, reminding me of the lights strung above the Christmas tree farm back home. I rushed ahead, eager to investigate the unusual goods that were sure to be present in a town sitting at the foot of an active volcano. Stopping in front of the first booth, I had already looked through the smallest stack of the souvenir photo collections of the volcano when Rafe stepped up.

"There are some amazing shots in here!" I knew instinctively that it was he who was standing behind me, even though there were hundreds of people in the park, and I had not turned around. When I looked up at him we shared a smile and he linked his fingers with mine, tugging me to the next booth.

"It's like a carnival here. Is it always so festive?" I asked.

"That's one thing I love about La Fortuna. On any given night, the town is as alive and vibrant as the fiery mountain."

We passed booths with T-shirts bearing pictures of toucans, monkeys, and frogs. There was an artisan from Sarchí selling the famous *carretas* (hand-painted oxcarts) that have made the village well known. The vendor had every size one could imagine, from miniature up to full-size, with a multitude of colors and designs. As with everything in Costa Rica, including the houses people lived in, the carts were painted in bright colors. Some had geometric starburst patterns while others had tiny intricate pictures of the Costa Rican landscape decorating them, and I was quite enthralled by them all.

The only thing that tore my gaze from the carretas was a loud shout that went up from the crowd. We turned toward the noise and saw a mob of people dashing through the park. The ones in front waved enormous flags followed by smaller flags rippling behind. "*Viva,* Costa Rica!" someone yelled. During the ensuing cheer of the crowd, Rafe turned to the nearest vendor to find out what all the commotion was about.

"Costa Rica won the international soccer championship tonight against Venezuela," he informed us.

"Oh! No wonder they're celebrating," I said. It was hard not to get caught up in their enthusiasm. While we dodged people, trying not to get mobbed by the running fans, I was drawn to one of the last booths in the row. The vendor had rocks of all kinds that had been discovered in the area. Some had been found in Lake Arenal, some in the lush jungles that skirted the volcano, and some in the nearby river, the vendor explained. There were rocks of red cinder, others of glassy black onyx, stones of pale green and darker green. Out of all the brilliant colors shining from the rickety plywood booth, however, it was the evocative stones of the faerie cross that called to me.

From my studies of these stones in the past, I knew that Costa Rica was one of the rare places to find them. But I was surprised to find them in this exact area. Usually the stone on the chain that forever graced my neck was worn underneath my clothes, but I pulled it out now to feel the texture as I stared at the unique formations of the ones before me. The vendor turned to help another customer, and Raphael noticed my stone. He lifted it between his fingers to examine it.

"What's the story behind your necklace?" he asked.

I couldn't explain to him the exact reason for my stone, so I settled. "It's called a faerie cross, and it's supposed to protect the wearer from harm. The stone has been handed down in my family. It belonged to my great-grandmother, Morrighan, dating back to the sixteenth century."

"Wow! So this rock has seen a lot of wars come and go."

"You have no idea," I grinned.

He looked back toward the vendor and turned loose of the stone. As it fell to my chest, I looked up at him in wonder. Before he let go, his fingertips had brushed the dingy-brown crystals, and they had glowed sapphire blue. He had not seen it, but I had. Studying him now as he conversed with the seller of stones, I wondered again exactly who—or what—he was. Comparing the sinister being from my vision with the friendly doctor standing before me, I was in the midst of a dilemma, trying to force myself to reconcile the differences. He looked like a regular human, but I knew all too well how supernatural beings walked among us every day undetected; I was one of them. As in the vision I'd had of him, I could tell he wouldn't harm me, but why had he been in the form of evil in my revelation then?

As I stared he turned and smiled. "You ready to eat?"

"I'm starving."

"Well, in that case, let's get some food in you."

Tiki torches lit the path to the entrance of the Rancho La Cascada restaurant. The waiter seated us at a window near the patio facing the volcano and left to get our drinks. The lava spewing down the side of the triangular mountain was dramatic to watch. This was the most intriguing night out I'd ever had—aside from the thrill of the hunt. Of course there had not been many nights out for me of this type, so maybe this wasn't a fair comparison.

"What's on your mind?" Rafe asked.

Smoothing my brow, I smiled at him. "Just wondering how these people live here with such calmness. Don't they know that at any minute that thing could awaken with violence and overtake them without warning?"

"They have scientists who live nearby and continually study the readouts of the volcano's activity. I guess they feel as if they would have sufficient warning."

"I hope that's the case," I said.

Like many buildings in the country, this restaurant was open-air, and a gentle wind carrying small particles of ash wafted through, tickling my nose. Lost in thought, I stared up into the fascinating ceiling of the restaurant. It was a thatched, hut-like structure composed of three tiers of bamboo pipes that supported the massive roof. I wished I'd brought my camera, for the ceiling alone would have made an interesting picture. The crowd milling around in front of the restaurant was getting heavier as the soccer fans spread out from the park. By the time we got our meal, the restaurant was packed with cheering fans ready to celebrate with loud music and good food.

"I think I may have picked the wrong night to come here," Rafe apologized.

"No, it's fine. I like their energy." Tasting a fried plantain, I exhaled a pleasant sigh. "I'm not going to tell Maria, because I think it would hurt her feelings, but this is by far the best plantain I've ever had."

"I'm glad you're enjoying it."

"I needed this. Thanks for bringing me. I've never gotten out much. I guess I just haven't had the opportunity."

"But I thought you said your father was in politics back in Ireland. I would assume you've traveled the world." He looked at me, expecting an answer, while I mulled it over.

"My father had to be away a lot on business, and I attended a private academy, so I couldn't go with him. Besides I had tutors and fiddle lessons, and I had to practice every day. I always felt like I'd traveled the world with my horse, Kheelan, though. He and I would ride up through the mountains, and I'd pretend I was heading to faraway places. When I was about twelve, I found myself in trouble the day I'd wished myself to Jamaica." I laughed and propped my face on my hands, remembering. "Kheelan and I were on the trail a couple of miles from home when it started to snow. It barreled in with such speed and heaviness, I was struggling to see the path, and then it just got so cold I almost fell off."

Leaning forward in his seat to rest his arms on the table, he asked, "What happened?"

"My friend Patrick, on his horse Torin, came and found us. I had remembered that not far from where I was, I had brought a tarp and some rope one day to build a makeshift fort. When Patrick came riding in to rescue me, I was curled up in a ball underneath the tarp. It seems as if he has been rescuing me all my life." Smiling at the memories—some fond, some not so fond—I looked up, and my smile faded at Rafe's tense expression.

"What is it?" I asked. It was like his face was frozen in that position, and I wondered what I'd said to make him look like I'd just slapped him.

"Nothing. Just caught up in the story is all." He took a giant gulp of water.

I could tell there was more, like he wanted to ask something, but maybe he was trying to find the right words. He dug into his food as I stared at him.

"So…is Patrick your boyfriend?" he asked, averting his eyes.

"He's been my best friend all my life," I admitted, hoping that would be enough information for now. And then I added, to balance the conversation, "Do you have a girlfriend?"

Smiling as if my question pleased him, he shook his head as he answered, "No." He was staring at me again. The lava flow in the distance reflected in his pupils, and I looked away, trying to shake the image of his molten eyes from my vision. I shredded my paper napkin and started to wring my hands when Rafe reached over and placed his hand on top of mine.

"Are you okay, Aishling?"

Lifting my head, I focused again on his eyes, trying to block out the memory, not believing there could possibly be any evil in this man; his eyes of chestnut returned. "I'm fine. Sorry about that. Just thought I saw something, but it was nothing. The meal was delicious. Thanks again."

"Thank you for the pleasure of your fascinating company," he responded with a full smile that made his eyes sparkle. His masculine beauty was devastating, but his attentive focus on me, and my charged response to him, were potentially catastrophic to my future.

"I guess I should be getting back to the orphanage. There are still lesson plans to work on for tomorrow. A teacher's work is never done."

Rafe tossed down some bills to cover the meal and tip, and then jumped up to pull out my chair.

A few minutes later we left the restaurant, and he grabbed my hand, leading me over to the volcano observation point across the street.

"Can you spare just a few more minutes?" he urged. "I have something for you." His strong hand felt so good in mine.

"There's more? I'm already feeling spoiled," I bantered, unable to resist him. "Okay, a few more minutes."

We stood behind a fence and gazed at the red mountain with the intense heat scorching the air, and the touch of his hand in mine searing my flesh. *I could so easily fall for him again.* Dropping his hand, I stepped away, trying to put distance between us.

"Aishling," he said to draw my attention back to him. "Happy birthday!" When I turned, he was holding out a bracelet I had seen earlier at one of the booths. There were about ten small faerie cross stones linked together to form the unusual piece of jewelry. I didn't know how he had bought it without my noticing, but it was very thoughtful of him.

"Here," he said, as he placed the bracelet on my left arm. "I thought it would go well with your necklace. Now you have faerie crosses from Ireland and Costa Rica."

"It's beautiful. You shouldn't have."

"Think of it as a thank you gift for keeping me company tonight. I get tired of eating supper alone."

"Well, in that case, you're welcome," I giggled. "By the way how'd you know it was my birthday?"

"A man is entitled to a few secrets." He winked.

When Rafe dropped me in front of the orphanage later, I was thinking of the beautiful evening we had shared. He came around to open my door and help me climb out of the jeep. Still holding hands, he led me to the front of the orphanage. "Can I see you to your hut?" he requested. "It's so dark out." Concern was evident on his face.

Before this progressed to anything it shouldn't, I stacked the stones of my wall again and placed things back in the friendship realm where they would have to stay. Dropping his hand, I backed a few steps away from him. "I'll be fine. I've got to go in and check on a few things before I go to the hut. I had a lot of fun. Dinner was perfect, and the bracelet was very thoughtful."

"My pleasure."

"Are you coming by tomorrow to check on Juan Carlos?" I rambled. Embarrassed and mentally kicking myself, I ran my hand up my arm and looked toward the side yard. There was too much silence. I looked back at him.

Smiling again, as if he held some other secret he wasn't willing to share, he said, "Yeah, I'll be around in the morning to check on the little mischief-maker. He'll be terrorizing the girls again by the end of the week."

"Yeah, he's full of pluck. Keeps class interesting."

There was another moment of silence; neither of us seemed to want to be the first to leave. We seemed joined somehow, like life had not begun until we had discovered that the other existed.

"Well, good night," I voiced, taking another step backwards. Some heavy emotion rode his expression and he thrust a hand through his hair. He turned around as if heading to get into the jeep and I watched him rake his hand through his hair again. He stopped, turned, and came to stand in front of me.

He reached out to clasp my hands in his. Time was running out. No more thinking it through—I had to make a choice. My breath seemed to leave me and my heart rumbled as I looked up into his eyes. My scattered brain flew on autopilot since I wasn't giving it any instructions, and I moved into his arms. He leaned down and gently brushed his lips with mine. His slight beard felt so masculine against my skin. He pulled back and my lids fluttered open. He seemed to search my heart, my soul. Longing filled his expression and his lips met mine once more. The kiss changed as Rafe wrapped his arms around me. When our lips met, I saw things, some of which I'd never before seen in reality. I saw a million twinkling stars that were so close I could reach out and touch them. Colorful meteors burst across the sky. I saw mighty streams and meadows filled with sunflowers. From atop the highest peaks, I saw sunsets and the Northern Lights.

Then, as he brought me even closer, a warmth spread throughout my entire body. Flames of intense fire exploded in the background—not totally unpleasant, but again, odd for a kiss. It felt like I was in the same fiery scene I'd experienced in his office that day. If I didn't break the connection soon, I knew, I'd be pulled down into some fiery pit. He pulled away first, raining kisses across my cheek, and the fires extinguished as I opened my eyes. I looked up again through the haze and saw fireflies, hundreds of them, descending from the heavens, but instead of just green lights flashing, there were reds, yellows, and oranges.

My emotions were on overload. I had never felt so much in one moment. I had never felt so much—ever. He embraced me, leaning his head on top of mine, and we stood just like that for a long time with the geckos chirping a chorus.

He pulled away and placed a simple kiss on the tip of my nose. "Good night, Aishling," he said, and I backed away.

"Night," I responded. I hurried up the steps and disappeared behind the door. From the shadows of the unlit front room of the orphanage, I peeked through the curtain to find him still standing where I'd left him. My evening with Rafe had been so special. With my limited experience, I still had a hard time knowing how to act around guys. Patrick was the only one I'd ever been allowed to hang around with and then date when we were old enough, more like old-fashioned courtship. Over the past couple of months, I had developed my odd friendship with Micah. Now *this*.

A minute, maybe two passed before Rafe turned and whistled on his way to the driver's side of the jeep.

Blinking, I jarred myself away from the intensity of the encounter and was glad to be in the darkness of the empty room. Ashamed of myself, I shook my head to try to clear the image. I wrapped both arms across my chest, trying to calm down. I couldn't let this happen. I couldn't fall in love with him. Marcellus had said that how deeply I became involved with Rafe was up to me. Well then, I needed to apologize for letting things get out of hand and I had to tell Rafe that our relationship couldn't be that way.

Setting my resolve, I went to gather my sleeping baby and trudged back out the front door. I stopped for a few seconds in the exact place I had stood earlier when I had been so happy. But once again I turned away from these new and exciting feelings and any future other than the one that had been chosen for me. Stirring the stagnant darkness, I put one foot in front of the other. Step, breathe, step, breathe until I made it to the hut. But I was not alone anymore. I looked down at Kaillech as I closed the door behind us.

"We're going to be fine, just you and me," I reassured her.

Midnight came and went. No visit from Morrighan.

42

Crosscurrent Drifting

(Aishling)

That fateful October day at the hospital when I first saw Rafe again began a string of peaceful, happy days. Despite my attempts at remaining disconnected from Rafe, I craved what I knew was going to sever my heart in the end.

Sometimes when I looked at him, my cheeks flamed as I remembered how it felt to be held by him. I could still feel the conflicting emotions raging within me—his lips against mine, the comforting strength of his arms around me.

One night recently, Rafe and I were in a dangerous place—sitting on a moonlit bench outside the orphanage, overlooking the lake. His arm lazed on the back of the seat. The silence was nice, comfortable; too bad I had to break it.

"Rafe, there's something," I hesitated, "we need to talk about."

"What is it, Aishling?" He moved his arm from behind my shoulders and shifted to grab my hand.

I thought of Patrick and knew this was the right thing to do; although, it was not what I wanted. "It's just...we agreed to be friends. And the kiss..."

"But, Aishling, it's taken us so long to get to this place, to find each other. Don't you think we should give *us* a chance?"

I sighed and turned toward him. He grabbed both my hands and caressed them with his thumbs. "Rafe, this bond that we have is special; I don't deny that. But you keep things from me, and I have my own secrets. What about the letter, Rafe?"

He stood and lifted his face to the moon. "I wish I could tell you everything, Aishling. But I'm afraid you'd run. At least, this way, I have a chance that you'll remain my friend." He looked at me with a defeated half-smile.

Why can't we just be honest with each other? I moved to stand beside him, and I reached out to link my fingers with his. "I'm not running anywhere," I promised. "Friends?"

He nodded in agreement.

It was truly a miracle that up to that point I'd been able to keep Micah unaware of Rafe, given all the time I had been spending with him. Not that I needed his approval or anything. I just had this feeling—you know, the little twinge in your stomach that tells you it would be better for all parties involved if you kept certain things concealed. Well, I'd been struggling with that little twinge in my own gut for several weeks. Of course I could never tell Rafe about Micah anyway for obvious reasons. And Micah tended to lean a lot to the overprotective side, so I didn't want him making more of my friendship with Rafe than it really was. Micah knew I'd gone out with a guy on my birthday, and aside from some teasing later that night, he had let the subject die, treating it as an isolated event.

Since Rafe was very busy with his work at the hospital, I didn't see him every day. But he came to the orphanage when he could to check on the sick children, and he would search until he found me either at the hut or in the middle of teaching. He tried to persuade me to go with him on the mission trip to Honduras, but I put off answering because I didn't want to leave Kaillech. I procrastinated until the final day came to reserve my airline ticket. When Rafe stopped by the orphanage to ask me that morning, I agreed to go.

Kaillech fell asleep early, and I didn't know where Micah was. I tried to imagine at times what he was doing. I stared at the ceiling as I attempted to fabricate his day. Most likely, he was off swimming in the springs of the deep or flying on a shooting star. I could imagine it with clarity, and I smiled to myself.

After finishing my lesson plans, I decided to curl up in bed and read a little. The suspense thriller, accompanied by the low lamplight beside the bed, gave the small room an eerie feel. I looked around, wishing that Micah were there and checking to make sure my taggert was loaded and close by.

I turned the page and delved back into the story. The main character was riding a horse. Strange, but my imagination took flight as the sound of the horse's unrelenting gallop echoed like it were right outside my hut. I placed the book in my lap, straining to hear any odd noises coming from outside. *It's just because Kaillech and I are here alone*, I thought, dismissing my fear, thinking it must have been the volcano rumbling more than usual.

I picked the book back up and tried to read, but the sound amplified by degrees, and the hoof beats grew louder. I jumped to my feet and ran to the crib; Kaillech smiled in her sleep. An oppressive weight bogged down the air; I coughed and gasped as if there was no air to breathe. Kaillech seemed undisturbed by the crushing heaviness I was feeling.

It was then that I looked toward the door and saw a bright light shining around the fringes of the blinds that covered the windows. Electricity boiled in my blood, and the hair resting near my waist floated around me more than usual.

After I had tiptoed to the window and lifted one of the blind slats, I couldn't determine anything about the rider. Whoever was out there held a massive, ancient-looking lantern that had such a powerful fire in it, a black, smoky veil surrounded them. The overbearing force in the room slowed down my supernatural senses, and I found myself crawling inch by inch to the hawthorn tree.

With a last-chance effort, I stretched my arm out and made contact with a tree root. I felt the cloak brush against my shoulders and arms. My taggert and dart belt appeared in my right hand while the marking tingled, etching the powerful tree onto my face. I stood up and had just attached my belt with the supply of darts around my waist when the main door swung open and banged into the wall. I tried to move toward Kaillech so we could escape in the cloak, but a powerful wind swept in, knocking me off my feet. The flimsy screen door—the only barrier left—creaked back and forth on its hinges until the powerful gusts ripped it from the hut.

The lantern light blinded me, and I lifted my arm to shield my eyes. I crawled toward the light and pulled myself up using the doorframe. Balancing myself, with my back to the wall, I aimed my weapon at the rider's midsection. As the smoke from the lantern wafted, I could see through the haze to the rider. Fear gripped me as the Dullahan towered over me. This time his presence was no vision that was just going to dissipate any second.

He was a ghastly sight, with severed bones sticking up where his neck should have been. Ripped arteries draped from his collar down the front of his charcoal-gray cloak, turning it crimson from all the oozing blood. There was something hanging beside him on the horse, which I assumed was his head. I wondered briefly why he had covered it, but the thought left as soon as it had come; I tried to focus.

The more I concentrated on the training that had prepared me for this moment and what needed to be done, my fear became anger, and my anger took on a slightly mad form. The visions he had starred in over the past several years came to mind in flashbulb memories. As the winds whirled around me, my body began to change somehow. It felt like a leaden substance surged through my veins, and the weight of it helped me withstand the winds. Crazed by his looming presence in my life, I advanced toward the gruesome faerie with little regard for self-preservation but with enhanced maternal instincts, ready to fight to the death for my child. She was so helpless, lying asleep in the crib a few feet away.

"What do you want?" I spat at him with as much venom as I could produce. The dart gun was loaded, and I was ready to block the faerie's path to my daughter.

The headless beast leapt to the ground and stalked toward me beside the horse. They moved forward as a unit. The shrouded figure lifted his arm, and I could see his skinless, bony finger point past me—to Kaillech.

"No!" I yelled at the wicked faerie. "Micah, help," I whispered, and then shouted, "You'll never get to her! Do you hear me? You can't have her!"

The stallion moved toward me; his eyes of molten fire hypnotized me, and his nostrils flared a stream of red-orange fire. *The eyes are so red,* I thought, mesmerized. *Burning fire, orange, red, peaceful, fire.* I couldn't think of anything but the flames reaching out to me. It was so hot. A power I'd never known before controlled me now, and I could do nothing but listen to the bellowing cry coming from deep within the monster. Sitting down on the ground under his trance, I dropped the dart gun and waited for him to come.

Somewhere between my standing and sitting, his cry became music, the soft tune of the music box my mother had given me. I stared into the horse's burning eyes, relishing the happiness I felt at hearing the sound that had always brought me peace.

Just as the Dullahan was about to overtake me, I was lifted into the air. Everything was a blur. I felt drugged, and then all was darkness.

Still hypnotized by the eyes of fire and the soothing music, I stared at a vaguely familiar wall, and someone started to shake me. As if in a tunnel, I heard muted sounds of a baby crying, as well as someone calling my name over and over. "Aishling, Aishling, Aishling!"

Regaining control of my thoughts, I realized that Micah held both Kaillech and me on his lap, and he squeezed us in his strong arms as he muttered to himself.

"He has my music box," I mumbled. I was terrified that the creature from my nightmares had been so close to me when I'd slept on the patio the day my box was stolen.

"What are you talking about, Ash?"

"Micah?" I focused on his face only five or six inches from mine.

"Ash!" He hugged us fiercely again before pulling back to examine me. Kaillech was still crying, so I took her from his other arm and held her to me, soothing her with her favorite Irish lullaby.

"I was almost too late—again," he berated himself. "I could have lost you both."

"Micah, stop," I whispered. "You came. You saved us, Micah," I replied as I lifted his chin to force him to look at me. "Thank you."

"What was that thing, Ash? It's obviously not a demon. There wasn't the kind of heat signature I sense when a demon is lurking."

"That *thing* back there happens to be the most dreaded and feared of all the Otherworld. Even the Alorcán fear it. It's considered a rogue mongrel—half demon, half faerie, existing outside the laws containing and condemning the most lawless creatures. The Alorcán and the demons created it. They call it the Dullahan. But they can't control it. It lives in an untouchable realm of its own in the Otherworld."

I proceeded to explain to him many more of the Irish legends surrounding the creature, chronicles I'd heard over the years from Uncle Brádach that had been passed down through many generations. Each time I remembered the stories, a shiver rocked me.

"Ash, you're shaking," Micah said, tightening his grip.

"The horse hypnotized me," I fumed. "Next time I come up against it, I'll be prepared," I ranted.

"Next time? Do you honestly think I'm going to allow there to be a next time?" Micah boomed, infuriated.

"Micah, I live in the seen world and the unseen world. That's just the way things are. I can't hide from it. I've always had immortal guards and mortal guards—well, until I came to Costa Rica. Like I said before, given enough time the Dullahan would find me even here at this refuge if it were that intent on finding me. The thing is…when I asked the faerie what it wanted, it pointed to her," I said, squeezing Kaillech.

Lifting me to set me on the bench, Micah got up to pace. "Why her?" he grumbled, with pain-filled eyes.

"I don't know. It doesn't make sense to me either."

Still pacing, he said, "So this Dullahan creature only comes at night?"

"Yes. According to legend, it has to wait for the cover of night. But it's not bound as most other faeries are. Most can only cross over between worlds on the nights of the four Gaelic festivals. But the Dullahan occupies its own dimension and can cross over any night the beast chooses. He doesn't even have to wait for fire like the demons do."

"Okay then. No more night trips for me. I stay where you two are," he decided.

"Well, under the circumstances, I agree with you."

He knelt before me; his hand caressed the side of my face. Just as quickly, though, he cleared his throat and backed away from me.

"I'll see you to your room."

My room at the angel refuge was getting a lot of use. I believe Micah liked it that way. He was happy as he bounced Kaillech up and down on our trek down the hall. I was about to make him very unhappy, so I figured I might as well get it over with. He opened the door to my room and placed her in the crib before moving to open the balcony doors, allowing in the salty sea air. I crawled into bed and yawned, so exhausted from the earlier ordeal.

He was headed toward the crib when I detoured him. "Well, I'm leaving in a week for Honduras for a mission trip. I committed today actually."

Waves crashed below as Micah came crashing down on me. I had never heard an angel growl before, but I witnessed it now. Kaillech's whimper shifted to full-throttle wailing, and he touched her, putting her to sleep before getting in my face. He was so angry, he was drifting in and out of view again.

"No, Ash. I forbid it." His face was mere inches from mine. If he'd had veins, they would have been popping by then with the way he was looking at me. His potent angel breath stirring the air was too much for my system, and I became dizzy.

Shaking my head to clear it, I retaliated, "Listen here, angel! I have the right to do what I think is best, and I feel like I'm needed on this mission." I sat up higher, and he moved to sit on the edge of the bed beside me. I knew Cearnaigh had been right. I needed a serious distraction from my upcoming death match. The mission trip would be nonstop work according to Rafe—just what the doctor ordered, the pill I needed to lessen the symptoms of my fear of what lay ahead, not for myself but for my mom if I failed.

"What about Kaillech?" he asked, interrupting my thoughts.

"You think I'm a bad mother because I'm going away for two weeks?" Maybe I was. I started to second-guess myself. "I thought you'd be supportive. It's a mission trip—you know, angel-approved."

He ran his hands through his shaggy blonde hair. "What about your safety, Ash? Don't you ever think about what Kaillech would do without you if something happened?"

"I can't live in a bunker, Micah. Something could happen to me even here, you know that. We've already ridden this horse—numerous times."

He leaned forward, and I fell backward. The bed creaked as he captured my hands above my head. I could feel his angry breath on my chin.

"Yeah, well my seat atop this particular horse is causing rub burns."

We were both breathing heavily, swallowing the anger like bitter morsels, neither willing to compromise. He was staring at my lips. *What is going on here?*

"Back off, angel!" I warned him, blowing my bangs out of my eyes. "You're not acting very angelic at the moment."

I could see the instant when he regained a portion of control. He released my arms and bolted for the door. His back was to me as he said some of the most hurtful words I'd ever heard, especially from an angel: "Maybe you weren't the right one to care for Kaillech after all!" Then he slammed the door, and all was silent, even the waves.

I trudged to the crib to pick my baby up. Micah was wrong. She was mine, and I was the only one in my family who would care for her the way she deserved, the way she needed. Holding her helped to calm my voracious fury at him. *He has no right to say such things!* I closed the balcony doors and grabbed some blankets off the bed. Then I turned out the lights and moved to sit in the rocker, wrapping us both in the warm fleece. Cradling Kaillech to me, I hummed a song that was unfamiliar to me. It bothered me that I couldn't place the tune, but it was so calming.

The door never opened, but I felt Micah's presence, and I stiffened my spine against any more slander. I was almost asleep when I heard him.

"Ash, I'm so sorry. I was wrong."

He looked more like an angel now than he ever had. He was glowing white in the darkness, and the look on his face was one of self-loathing and revulsion.

"Don't torture yourself, Micah. We all say stupid things sometimes."

"So you forgive me?" he asked, kneeling at my feet.

"Of course, ya big brute." I smiled sleepily.

"Just one request, Ash."

"You can ask, and I will consider," I answered, a bit on edge. I didn't want to fight with him again.

"Will you let me keep Kaillech here at the angel refuge while you're gone? You could tell everyone she's staying with family, which is true. I'm the only dad she knows."

"Is that why you were so angry—because you thought I was going to leave her undefended? I guess I should have made it plain that I expected she'd be with you while I was away. You're the most logical choice to keep her safe."

He ran a hand through his hair and smiled. "Should've known you'd be an angel about this."

He moved the blanket to kiss Kaillech on the cheek. "Micah," I said as he met my gaze, "thank you—for everything."

His smile and his glow were both intense as he stood. He stopped beside the chair and reached out to stroke my hair before he faded from view.

By mid-November I was almost prepared for my newest adventure. I'll admit I was a little apprehensive about going away with Rafe, but I was comforted by the fact that his friends would be on the trip as well. I'd have to dig deep into my reserve of self-control; the main reservoir had already run dry. There were other factors to consider as well—the troubling visions and the multitude of questions surrounding Rafe. Since I had somewhat come to know him, I kept waiting for the demon to appear, but it hadn't shown up. Not yet at least.

Patrick had seemed a little suspicious during our last phone call. Maybe my stomach knots were just guilt for having feelings for anyone besides him. He had questioned me more than usual about what I had been doing in my spare time. I assured him that between milking cows, doing laundry for all the kids along with my own laundry, coming up with lesson plans, and teaching at the orphanage, there wasn't much "spare" time. Still I always wanted to be honest, especially to the man I would one day marry.

He told me he would be out of the country for a couple of weeks on government business, which couldn't have been timed more perfectly. Since he wouldn't be in contact with me anyway,

I didn't feel it was necessary to mention my trip to Honduras. I didn't want to add more worry to his already overloaded plate. He told me he missed me. I missed Patrick too—in the same way I missed Claire. There were few childhood memories that didn't involve my two best friends. I knew he wanted more, and I was going to have to gain a backbone and either say "yes" to Patrick or "no" to him—and my father.

By the end of the phone conversation, I felt like I had an angel sitting on each shoulder—one really good angel shaking his head at me as if in disgust and a second one who was a little more lenient, giving me the thumbs-up as if to say, "At least you're attempting to be good."

Did it count that I was trying with every breath to defuse the feelings that kept threatening to ignite every time I was with Rafe? I was beginning to wonder if I had any control over that particular detonator.

43

Quantum Entanglement

(Rafe)

It was November 17, the day we were leaving for Honduras. We were in the airport terminal in Liberia, Costa Rica, looking for my friend David, who had flown in from the States. He and I shared the same vision, which was the eradication of common diseases in Third World countries—diseases that could be controlled with medication and education. He'd been on many such trips with me in the past couple of years.

"Rafe!" I heard someone call from the door of the gift shop.

I looked up to see him wading through the people. "David," I called out, swerving through the travelers to bear-hug my colleague and friend. Everyone else caught up to us.

Shaking hands with each in turn, I introduced the group to him. "David, you remember my assistant Miguel."

"Miguel, *mucho gusto*," he said, laughing. "Been dreaming of snakes lately?"

"Ah, David, don't joke, man. I could ask you a similar question about spiders, you know."

"Good to be back with you, Miguel." They slapped each other on the shoulders good-naturedly and then turned back to the ladies as I continued the introductions.

"This is Sophia, a nurse at the hospital in Tilarán. And this is Aishling," I said, putting an arm rather possessively around her shoulders. "Aishling's teaching English at the orphanage right outside Tilarán."

"Pleasure to meet you, ladies," he said. I watched him gaze at Aishling with interest, and I didn't like the look. I was hoping maybe he was just curious about her since he had never heard me speak of any women, not as far as being in a relationship.

The Toncontin International Airport in Tegucigalpa, Honduras, was known to be one of the most dangerous in the world for landings. Aishling was a captive audience as David explained to her the peril involved. Due to mountains surrounding the airport, the pilot was forced to execute a severe U-turn.

As we braced for the landing, we had an opportunity to look down on the city that would be our home for the next two weeks. It was hard to believe that there was extreme poverty skirting its borders. The skyline looked a lot like the larger cities I had visited around the world. Our pilot, apparently a pro, landed without a problem.

We found our way to the baggage claim area and retrieved our suitcases and supplies. Aishling stopped to make a call back to the orphanage to check on one of the babies I noticed she was particularly attached to, while I filled out the paperwork for the van rental. After all of the bags and supplies were loaded, I drove us through the city of Tegucigalpa. I had reserved the front seat for Aishling. I moved her quickly to that spot and closed the door before anyone else had a chance to get there.

We were going to work in Comayaguela, across the mighty Choluteca River from the bigger capital city. After we crossed the river, we headed up the mountain. I sensed Aishling's heart inflating to include all of these people in its vast caverns as she took in the shantytowns that housed the people we'd be assisting. The shelters were nothing more than improvised dwellings that looked like they were leaning together; one neighbor's east wall became the other's west wall. A roof of loose metal from one house helped secure the roof on the next. I could tell by

Aishling's expression that she had never seen anything like it. It was miles and miles of scrap metal, like a giant junkyard. These makeshift homes looked as if one major gust of wind would make them topple like dominoes. These were the people who needed us.

We made it to the top of El Picacho, a rugged mountain overlooking the city of Comayaguela, and drove into the small village where the medical mission building was located. I pulled the van through the high fence there, and five armed guards greeted us.

"Why all the security, Rafe?" Aishling asked.

"The people here are desperate. They've broken in before to steal the medical supplies."

Before we unloaded the van, I grabbed Aishling's elbow to lead her forward into the building, my eyes sweeping the area for any potential danger. Then David, Miguel, and I handed medical supplies to the Honduran workers who kept the mission going year-round. The guards kept a watchful eye.

I introduced the crew to the local physician, Dr. Teyo Castanada, and his assistants, Natalia and Madalena. Then I took everyone on a tour of the facilities. Behind the medical mission building there was a fenced-in area with high walls and barbed wire at the top like at a prison. It was a safe space for the neighborhood children to come and play. There was an armed guard on duty there at all times.

After the tour, we loaded back into the van to drive to the town where we would be staying. Farther into the mountains, about fifteen slow, rugged miles from the mission, we entered the charming town of Santa Lucía. Cozy shops lined the cobblestone streets that looped through the main part of town. The mountains enclosed the tiny oasis on every side and native tropical flowers spilled out from hanging planters on the lampposts down Main Street.

I headed north of town. About a half mile out, the street became a dirt road, and we followed it for another mile. On the right side, a sign read, "US Peace Corps Training Facility." I turned the van in and stopped at the gate. Once we were all signed in, the arm of the gate lifted, and I followed a road around to a cluster of about ten small houses. Stopping in front of the last house, I announced, "Home sweet home." Inside there was one bathroom, a small kitchen, a living room, and a couple of bedrooms with two twin beds in each. There were not enough beds for everyone, so I had already volunteered to take the couch.

Once we had our things put away, we loaded into the van and drove back to Santa Lucía. "There's a great little café up here: La Casa del Jaguar. It's really good. Hope that's okay with everyone."

"Sounds like a fun place," Sophia said. "I've never seen an actual jaguar. Does the restaurant have a mascot?"

"Nope. Sorry. But if you sit there long enough at night, I'm sure you'd see one stalk by."

Sophia and David were seated in the front row of the van, chatting nonstop for most of the trip. This was a good sign. Maybe his interest in Aishling was not too personal.

We ate supper on the fern-surrounded back patio with frogs bellowing and geckos screeching from the small pond behind us. Due to the high elevation, this area was known to have a spring-like climate year-round. It was very pleasant just to sit in the cool of the evening, sharing stories from our day and learning about each other. It was important for everyone to know the team they would be supporting.

Things were busy at the medical mission the next day; one entire family was diagnosed with a bacterial disease—leptospirosis. Sophia taught Aishling the basics of nursing so she could assist us with the patients. As I worked I watched Aishling float through-out the room doing whatever was needed in the moment: cleaning vomit from the floors, checking temperatures, and placing wet washcloths on fever-ridden foreheads and necks.

I was multitasking, still watching her, when a child began crying a few beds down from where she was mopping. He kept repeating, "*Quiero a mi madre.*" He wanted his mother, but she was so weak she didn't even wake to his pleading voice. He was a boy of about three years of age named Emanuel. I watched Aishling rush to him and lift him into her arms as she sat on his bed. She sang a Gaelic lullaby as she cradled him. He looked up into her eyes knowing that she wasn't his mother, but he seemed to settle for her as a substitute.

Her heart was unfathomable, I thought as I watched her with the child. She was in a league of her own in the heart department. How was I ever going to make her mine? Did I even have the right to try? Demons had never been able to coexist with angels. That was how I saw her—as an angel, as pure as any I'd ever known. Even through my self-degradation, I couldn't stop myself though. I moved to her, placing my hand on the small of her back, feeling her soft hair. I didn't even startle her this time, as if my touch were the most natural thing in the world.

"Everything okay here?"

"Yeah," she said, brushing the boy's wet bangs away from his forehead. She combed her fingers through his hair, soothing him until his eyes once again drifted shut.

In my mind I pictured her holding our child, and my emotions were so intensified in that moment. *Too much, Raphael! You have to stop*, I begged the demons inside, for they were tormenting me.

Aishling looked up when the child had fully drifted back to sleep, and she smiled at me. I wondered if she could tell the degree of my feelings for her. Our years apart had only increased my affection.

I would forevermore be in love with Aishling Delaney.

I didn't know what in the world I was going to do about that fact other than stay the course I had been on these few years. I knew I would pursue her beyond earth and back if it meant that I could be with her—that she could be mine in the end— regardless of the command to leave her alone. But I didn't want to scare her off with my exuberance by asking too much of her too soon.

When I turned and started down the hall, three things happened all in the same instant. First, I felt like I was having a heart attack, and I fell to my knees in agony. The pain was excruciating, and I completed my fall to the floor. Second, I could hear the pronounced clang of a metal tray striking the ground and its contents pinging off the floor. Aishling had been carrying one of the small trays with doctors' tools on it. Through blurred vision I turned my head sideways and saw her lying on the floor too, appearing unconscious and surrounded by her angels. I reached out my hand toward her, but I couldn't move my body. The nurses scrambled around us both. I couldn't make my eyes stay open.

Third, *it* happened. I had never been sent to guard a human being and to maintain guardianship throughout the span of their life, so I had never felt this, but I knew exactly what it was— sünomoreo, the entangling. I heard the incantation—the beautiful words of angels, which sounded like the most triumphant song—repeating the vow, binding me to Aishling for the remainder of her life. I didn't hesitate.

"I will," I said.

This opened up a new world for me. No more sneaking around, wondering if I was going to be banished from her presence. I had to guard her now; it was my duty. With my heartbeat restored to me, I could feel the entangling coursing through my system. I could feel her emotions, her fears, her joys as they combined with my own. It was a fiery, agonizing pleasure.

"You will what?" Dr. Castanada asked, in a concerned tone, as he bent over me.

I sat up so quickly, the doctor was knocked off-balance into the wall. "I'm sorry," I said, helping him up and rushing to Aishling's side.

I didn't care who witnessed it. I leaned over her and cradled her head, kissing her on the forehead. Her eyes popped open, and she looked up at me.

"Rafe," she sighed, as she tried to sit up. I helped her to a sitting position on the floor, and she rubbed the back of her head.

"You left me for a minute or two." I rubbed her back as she scratched at the point of her heart. Did she know what had just happened? As much entanglement as she had in her system, it probably didn't faze her as much as it did me. I was seeing three of her and everyone else in the room, and my pulse had skyrocketed; yet I remained at her side.

Scientists call it *quantum entanglement.* It's the idea that two objects are linked together so one can no longer be described apart from the other even though they may be separated by time or distance. In an angel-human sünomoreo, they become so entangled you can separate them as far apart as you physically can, but still a change in one will be simultaneously produced in the other. Sünomoreo. That was how the angels guarded people. They became physically and emotionally entangled with the individuals.

Aishling and I had been somewhat connected in the past, but now we were fully joined. I could feel what she was feeling just like her angels could.

"I'm okay," she said as she got to her feet. Her angels motioned me toward the hallway.

"Are you sure?" I asked. I felt her heartbeat inside mine, a little extra skip that was invigorating, and I felt her chest rise and fall, supplementing my own oxygen. It took a beat or two for me to become accustomed to the extra power within me. There was such a spirited force circulating through her veins. I knew I would have to save the exploration until later.

"I'll be fine. I should get back to work." She smiled and moved to tend a patient. David and Sophia rushed into the room.

"What happened?" Sophia asked. "Are you two okay?" She turned to David, "It could be a virus or a stomach bug." Then she turned back to Aishling and me. "Maybe you both should go lie down for a while."

"I'm fine," Aishling and I said at the same time. She giggled and I smiled.

44

Comrades In Comayaguela

(Rafe)

I could not stop smiling, even with the dread of the impending confrontation. But I didn't see how they could reverse the süno-moreo. Moving to the end of the hallway, I entered the office the mission allowed me to use while there. Closing the door I faced eleven bloodthirsty angels.

"How did you accomplish this, Raphael?" Vitale yelled in a livid tone.

"I don't know for sure. We were already connected somehow and this just...happened."

Maximilian shoved me up against the wall, his words seething. "Try getting to her in that restrictive human body, Raphael!"

"And without a cloak," Maestrino scoffed.

Maximilian threw me aside and moved into the angel circle underneath the bare lightbulb. They argued among themselves as if I weren't in the room.

"Because of our essence, we don't transfer any emotion, power, or negativity to Aishling. But this half-breed demon can send her his damaging filth at any time since he's trapped in this body," said Leopoldo to the others before turning to address me. "Will she feel the demons? They will not enter her mind and warp her. I'll—"

"I won't allow it!" I yelled. "I will never harm her! Don't you understand? I love her."

Silence fell as the mighty angels fanned out and formed a semicircle around me.

"I say we kill him since he threatens her," said Tristano. "We have the right to do so."

"Just hold on a minute." Vitale moved in front of me. "Raphael has been given a second chance. Now, we don't know how this unprecedented sünomoreo has taken place, but there will be no harming my charge today. He's done nothing wrong."

Fiorello moved in to stand before Vitale. "There've been a whole lot of unprecedented happenings since our former commander here decided to play renegade, and now he dares to impose on our mission."

"I say we untangle the entangling," said Salvatore. "I'll do it. I'll enjoy pulling out each and every strand from the demon," he sneered.

Marcellus paced behind the others with his arms folded behind his back. "There will not be an undoing. The sünomoreo is already engaged. We are all so bound up in her, it would kill her if we attempted to unbind the strands in him."

"Unfortunately he's right," Maximilian replied, more steady now. He turned to look at me and the others joined him. "And we can't kill him, because that would kill her too, I presume."

"So now we also have to guard him in order to keep her safe," Luciano bristled, sending a cold shaft of angel breath swirling through the room.

Gianpaolo stepped forward, lifting me off the ground by my neck. He growled in my face and squeezed, cutting off my air supply.

"Control yourself, friend." Tristano grabbed his arm, and I fell to the floor, choking. "You just did it to her too."

Five of the angels had already vanished to check on her before I even dropped to the ground.

When I could breathe, I got to my knees and bent my head, crossing my arms over my chest as I made a vow: "As Heaven is my witness, if the day should come when I harm my own heart, Aishling Delaney, I will remove myself to the pits of hell and remain there for all eternity."

"Oath captured," Fiorello said, holding a great book in his hands. As he slapped it shut, the book disappeared. "I guess that will have to do for now. Of course, should that day come, we would have to rip out the entangling bonds from you first. We won't let her feel the effects of your trip to the fires."

With the weight of the vow I stumbled and used the wall to regain my footing. Gianpaolo shoved himself through the group and was once again in my face. "There's got to be a way to undo this, and I *will* find it," he said with loathing.

The five angels reappeared. "She's fine," they said in creepy unison.

Everyone looked relieved. Renato remained in the corner where he had been standing for a while, lost in a trance. When he prowled toward the center of the room, everyone moved back to welcome him into their circle.

"Raphael did not initiate the sünomoreo. Aishling did."

Arguments and murmurings broke out in the tiny office among the angels while I stood speechless by my desk. I didn't even hear what they were saying to each other. I was so confused, trying to make things fit in my own mind.

I could hold it in no longer. "But Aishling's not an angel. How...?"

"No, she's not. And that's all you need to know, demon!" Gianpaolo, the enforcer of the group, hissed at me before he vanished. The rest followed him beyond the air.

Only Vitale remained.

"How did Aishling engage me in the entangling ritual, Vitale, if she's not an angel?"

"I don't know. The Malakim are hiding something about her, and you know as well as I do that they don't associate with other angels. We'll never be able to find out what's going on. I'm actually surprised they had this conversation in front of us."

"I love her. I have to try to find out."

"Raphael, I can't keep bailing you out. I don't know what's at play here, but there have to be other forces involved. Do you feel the demons still?"

"Sometimes," I said, running my hand through my hair. "That's what I fear with this, and I don't understand how it happened either. I can't allow her to feel the scorching, the lust for everything, the hopelessness. I can't! Help me, Vitale."

"Aishling's coming, Rafe. We'll have to discuss this later," he said before his aerial exit.

On the other side of the door, I felt her heart beating fast. I wanted to jerk open the barrier, pull her into my arms, and never release her. I leaned my forehead on the door, waiting for her to knock. A strange power thrummed under her skin, and I could feel the electricity. Her angels had to know the secret she held. I wished I had some inkling of what she was. For a moment I felt like I had taken flight. It reminded me of all my cloud-riding days: the joy, the exhilaration. My lips tingled as if I were feeling her kiss. Did she want me to kiss her again?

My head popped up off the door, and I stared at the wood barrier, wondering what to do. This longing was going to snap me in two. I pulled open the door as she had her knuckles in the air to knock.

"Hi," she said, putting her arm back down. "I—I thought I should check on you…after what happened, I mean. They told me you had passed out too."

She gasped for air and I remembered I had been holding my breath. Exhaling, I gave her what she needed.

She coughed. "I'm sorry," she said. "My body has been reacting very oddly over the past hour."

This was going to take some getting used to. I needed to be more vigilant with my reactions and emotions so I wouldn't hurt her. "No problem, Aishling. Come in and let me have a look." She hopped up on the desk and stuck out her tongue.

Taking a tongue depressor from the jar, I held it in her mouth and shined the light down her nice, pink throat. Then I checked her neck. I didn't have to check her pulse to know it was soaring, but she didn't know that I knew, so I had to complete the formality.

"Everything seems fine," I assured. She jumped down, and we stood facing each other. Neither of us spoke, and it seemed that she was reluctant to head for the door.

"Well, Madalena needs me," she insisted.

"I'll walk you." I followed her out, shutting the door behind us.

Relief workers passed us in the hallway and we nodded to them. I tried to play it cool when I spoke to her. "I'm glad you came. It's nice for me—having you here."

She started laughing.

"What's funny?" I asked.

"Oh, it just reminded me of my Uncle Brádach back in Ireland. All my life he has quoted old Irish proverbs, and they come to my mind often. What you said made me think of the one that goes, 'There was never a scabby sheep in a flock that didn't like to have a comrade.'" She laughed again.

"It sounds like this uncle of yours is a character."

"Yeah, Uncle Brádach is the best. He's like a father to me."

We moved to either side of the kitchen door to make way for one of the volunteers who pushed a food cart out.

"I'd better get to the operating room, but I just have to say that you're amazing, Aishling. I'm so proud of how you handled yourself in there today."

"Yeah, I'm a great help with all the passing out and everything," she said, animatedly putting her arm to her forehead in a mock faint.

I grabbed her arm to bring it down, and we both laughed.

Later that afternoon, I went back to the room where Aishling had been working and overheard her and Miguel discussing the weather. A tropical storm in the Caribbean was gaining strength, and its status had been upgraded. Hurricane Sebastien was now expected to make landfall on the northern coast of Nicaragua within the next forty-eight hours. The projections by the National Hurricane Center in Miami were showing that the worst of the storm would pass far north of where we were located, so none of us were too worried.

Things at the mission had calmed down by that point, so I gathered my team. As we headed to the van, I was filled with cheer.

"You guys up for an adventure?" I asked the group.

"Sure," Aishling chimed.

"You all go on ahead. I'd like to go to the park in Santa Lucía and then have a nice quiet dinner," Miguel replied.

"Yeah, Sophia and I have already made plans for the evening. Sorry, Rafe," David apologized.

"Well, Aishling, it looks like it's just you and me," I said, maybe with a bit too much excitement. But if I was reading her smile correctly, she was just as excited that it would only be the two of us. My heart jackhammered. It alarmed me at first, but then I knew—it was her heart in me. She was nervous, yet I felt more peace than ever before. Maybe she was expecting that kiss. My smile was so broad, bordering on goofy, that I took a few seconds to work it off by the driver's side door before opening it and hopping up into my seat.

45

Moonlight And Madness

(Rafe)

After we dropped the others off in Santa Lucía, Aishling and I headed to La Tigra National Park, which wasn't too far from where we were staying. We had the van windows down, enjoying the peaceful breeze, and Aishling was humming an African American spiritual—"Come Down Angels," which I, of course, found especially endearing.

We pulled up to the parking area at La Tigra, and I heard Aishling sigh. What a complete pleasure this was going to be in my continuing study of her! It felt kind of like we were on a date even though I knew that wasn't the case. I had just gotten lucky that nobody else wanted to come.

There were several trails that led in various directions, meandering away from the visitors' center. Recalling Aishling's reaction to the waterfall near the volcano, I took a gamble and headed on the path that would take us to the lake and the falls. As we started up the trail, I reached out to hold her hand. She grasped mine with no hesitation.

I asked her what appeared to be a very basic question, but it was one that had become very vital to my existence: "How much longer will you be in Costa Rica?"

"At least until next May."

So I had some more time.

We came upon the lake then and stopped to drink from our water bottles.

"This place is incredible!" she remarked. "It reminds me of home. On Delaney property there's a lake similar to this with the Cooley Mountains rising up behind it—like these mountains here only with far fewer trees."

"Do you have a waterfall on your land back home?" I asked, hoping to show her something she didn't see every day.

"No, none at all." She smiled at me.

I held out my hand to her again and led her back to the path. Enjoying the sounds of nature, we strolled in silence for a while. The jungle was full of life. Swirls of purple, gold, and scarlet winged by as tropical birds whistled past us, chased by monkeys diving from tree to tree. La Tigra was considered a *cloud forest* because on most days there were low-level clouds forming a canopy through the trees. The abundant moisture nourished the mossy forest and ferns grew everywhere.

"It's eerily peaceful here," she said as we waded through the damp vegetation.

The path meandered underneath an overhanging rock cliff, and Aishling stopped to touch the jagged granite. "I wonder what these marks mean. The message is broken here," she examined. She used her finger to trace along the stone.

I moved in closer to try to see what she was looking at, but all I saw were a couple of cracks. "Marks, Aishling?"

"Yeah, right here. Looks like ogham," she added, pointing to an area where the rock was smooth.

"I don't see anything there," I maintained.

"You...I...um," she stammered, looking embarrassed. "Maybe it's just the way the light is casting shadows through the trees." She moved on down the path as if she couldn't get away fast enough.

The churning water pounded the rocks up ahead and I tugged on Aishling's hand to pull her forward. We jogged through the remaining barrier of the forest to stand at the foot of a waterfall that had to be at least a thousand feet tall. Tilting our heads skyward, we watched the water rush over the top of the moss-covered hillside. She let go of my hand and moved to sit at the base of the falls near the pool. Yes, I sighed, although not audibly. I went to join her.

"So are your parents still living?" she asked.

"I guess you could consider me something like a foster child, currently without any family to speak of," I offered.

"Obviously your upbringing didn't make you bitter, like life often does to people in your situation. You turned it into something very positive. Does it make you sad though, not having a place to call home?" She caught me off guard again with her insight.

I took a moment before replying. "You know, I think I've been searching for home all my life. My path has taken lots of twists and turns because of it."

"I know what you mean," she said. "I've always felt the same way. I used to talk to Uncle Brádach about it a lot. He had the home I'd always wanted to grow up in. You know what he would always tell me?"

I just shook my head with a smile on my face, waiting for her fascinating reply.

"Another of his ancient proverbs, of course. He would say to me, 'Asher, girl, you just keep on walkin', 'cause the longest road out is the shortest road home. Keep walkin'.' Over the years what he said to me started to make more sense—that life is a quest for meaning, and when I truly discover my purpose here, it won't be long before I find home." She stopped then and stared at the pool.

Her words hit me like the impact of a barreling meteor. Through all my struggles and wrong decisions, was I being offered grace here? Was I also being allowed a chance to find home—to find an earthly refuge in her? Surely our entangling meant something, if only a partial pardon for me so I could protect her as I was now bound to do.

"Aishling, you speak of this uncle of yours like he is a father figure."

"Umm, no. It's just that my father has always been a very busy man," she evaded.

I knew her well enough now, I thought, to know that she would never say a harsh word about anyone no matter how they treated her. She was defending her father with grace. I could feel it. But I didn't press the matter. My plan was to meet him before too long anyway, and then I could make my own enhanced assessment of the situation. While I deliberated, she continued with her answer.

"Uncle Brádach and I aren't related. He is of the clan Kavanaugh, and they live on the other side of the river from me. He runs the Kavanaugh Stables, and is in charge of all of the horse breeding and training. My horse Kheelan is boarded there."

"Sounds like a beautiful place and a beautiful people."

"The Kavanaughs are like family to me, and I to them. Uncle Brádach practically raised Patrick, Claire, and me as his own. Patrick and Claire are fraternal twins, a year older than me. Their father is the leader of the Kavanaugh clan and the owner of Kavanaugh Farms. Uncle Brádach is his brother."

I needed to find out more about this Patrick fellow, but how could I proceed without giving too much away? I watched Aishling smile at the toucans chasing each other in front of the falls. Then she hugged her knees up to her chest, resting her chin on them, and looked down at the water spilling over the rocks.

"So I'm sure these friends of yours are missing you about now." I delved into risky territory.

"Yeah, I guess so," she acknowledged.

This was killing me. I pleaded with her in my mind, *Please don't make me ask another question.*

As if in answer to my unspoken thought, she said, "They called me last week to tell me they're coming to Costa Rica for Christmas holiday, and they want me to play tour guide for them while they're near Tilarán. I can hardly wait!"

That was *not* the answer I wanted to hear. I couldn't have her dwelling on this Patrick, especially while she was with me. She must have read my mind, for it was she who changed the subject.

Shifting to face me with a playful look on her face, she said, "Okay, Rafe, since you think you've got me figured out, let's move on to you. I've thought about the question you asked me in Spain, the one about spending the day with one of God's angels. Well, I thought of one myself, so I'll ask you kind of a similar question."

"All right. I'm kind of intrigued. What is it?" I laughed.

Animatedly she turned to me, seeming to enjoy our discovery of each other. "So if you could be any other thing in creation besides a human, what would it be and why? A flower? A tree? An animal? There's no limit. Pick something. Anything!"

Several moments passed between us, she waiting for an answer, and I unable to look away from her. Breaking the hold she had me in, I looked to the ground and found a leaf that I shredded vein by vein. Finally I looked to the sky as dusk settled into the scene below the forest clouds, and then I gazed back at her. I knew she had been trying for a laid-back response, but I couldn't stop myself.

"I'd be the moon, Aishling. That way I'd always be with you in the darkness so you'd never have to be afraid of the shadows."

I heard and felt her quick intake of air as my fierce emotion for her poured into her system. I moved closer to her and placed my hand on her cheek. The urge to kiss her was so strong, and she was looking at me with expectation. I might have gone through with it had it not been for the overwhelming sadness I experienced with her in the instant I viewed her heart. Not to mention that the guilt monster was diving and surfacing through her like a dolphin. My head dropped to hers, and I planted a kiss on the tip of her perfect nose. *What holds you back, Aishling?* On one hand I finally felt like a man with this insatiable need for her, but more intense than that emotion was my desire to battle with whatever was stealing her joy.

Maneuvering through the forest at dusk, the fog surrounded us like a dream. I didn't want our time together to end, but they say all good things must. I hoped that wasn't foreshadowing.

By the time we made it back to the house at the Peace Corps facility, it was around nine o'clock. Miguel, Sophia, and David were playing cards at the small table in the kitchen. They had the television going in the background, keeping an eye on the hurricane. In the time that Aishling and I had been gone, the storm had strengthened even more to a category 3 hurricane with sustained winds of 115 miles per hour. With the track of the storm still uncertain, the National Hurricane Center had placed our area under a hurricane watch.

I sat down on the couch to keep an eye on the weather. The door to the house was open, with the screen door in place to keep out mosquitoes and other pests. Not wanting to interrupt the card game already in progress, Aishling retrieved her fiddle from the bedroom and went out on the porch to play.

I could feel the storm coming. There was a certain charged feel to the air. As Aishling played, the beautiful notes wafted into the house like a gentle breeze, but I could feel the winds building in me, and I closed my eyes to feel them pushing me to the ground. Like the coming storm, the pressure of opposing forces was weighing on my soul. How could I have been overtaken in this unrelenting whirlwind? I felt that deep down she wanted to give me more of herself, but something was holding her back. It was as if she and I were separated on two parallel islands with a monster squall churning the ocean between us, and our lives were never meant to converge. I could picture her in the distance, standing on the shore. Through the raging storm, she smiled at me, offering hope, promising peace—but still out of reach. I felt an uncontrollable compulsion to burst through the tempest and save her, but I realized I would need to know what I was fighting against first. The funnel cloud was still revolving in the sky, refusing to drop down and reveal itself. I opened my eyes to a mass of swirling colors on the weather station radar, and the colorful nightmare was marching our way.

That night Aishling consumed my every thought. We fought through the whirlwind, trying to get to each other. Frightened by my own emotions, which were much stronger than the upcoming storm, I bolted upright off the couch, almost knocking the lamp off the end table. Dazed, I sat back down on the edge to get my bearings. The clock read 4:36 a.m.

Feeling my way down the hallway in the dark, I went to check on Aishling. The door to her bedroom was ajar and a soft light beckoned. I told myself I would just peek in, but when I looked in moonlight poured through the window, caressing her face, lighting my path to her. Her beauty propelled me forward. She looked like a glowing angel illuminated by the moonlight.

For the few minutes that I stared at her, she tossed from side to side. Her anxiety and stress escalated within me while I watched helplessly, unable to relieve her suffering. What unglued me were her silent tears; she bit her lips to hold in her grief. I had to try to help her. Her pain ripped through me. I must have been transferring my sinister dreams to her.

Kneeling beside the bed, I whispered, "Aishling…. Aishling." I touched her arm, hoping I wouldn't wake Sophia sleeping in the next bed. Aishling sat up, surprised to find me there.

"Why are you crying?" I pleaded.

"Oh, Rafe. It was just a bad dream." She reached for a tissue from the nightstand and wiped her eyes. "I'm okay now. I didn't wake you, did I?" she asked, ashamed to be caught in a weak moment.

"No, I was just heading to the restroom."

Another tear sat atop her eyelid, almost sparkling. As her head drooped to her chest, the tear fell, and I reached up to capture it with my thumb. Her face felt like smooth silk, and I couldn't seem to make my hand obey my mental command to pull away, especially when she leaned into my touch. The box springs squeaked as Sophia flipped over on the side facing us. Aishling pulled away as Sophia mumbled something with her eyes closed.

"Well, I guess I'll get back to bed. Only dream good dreams, you hear?" I commanded with a smile.

"Yes, sir!" she said as she gave me a mock salute, and I returned the gesture.

The next morning, not long after I had awakened and gone to the kitchen to make some breakfast, Aishling appeared. Her hair was still damp and hanging down to perfectly frame her face.

"Good morning," she yawned. "Is everyone else still sleeping?"

"Miguel went for a walk, but David and Sophia are still asleep. I make a mean stack of pancakes. Would you like some?" I offered.

"Sounds great. Thanks." She sat down on one of the barstools and leaned her elbows on the counter. "Did you sleep well?"

How was I supposed to answer that one? I could hardly tell her that I might have had two hours' sleep at best. I'd spent most of the night thinking of her. Being awake was much better than being asleep. I wasn't afraid every moment that when I woke up, she'd be gone—that this all would have been an illusion. It was hard to think of her with only a wall between us in the house without wanting to go to her, just to hold her as she slept. Maybe then I could sleep through the night.

"Not very well," I answered truthfully. "How about you?"

"Aside from the nightmare, when my head hit the pillow I was gone."

So she had gone right to sleep. What did that mean for me? That just meant I would have to be very patient, and I would have to work a little harder to make her think of me.

After breakfast we headed to the mission. Our objective had been decided for us already due to the approaching storm. Hurricane Sebastien was forecast to slam into the coast of Nicaragua mid-morning, along the Miskito Coast south of Puerto Cabezas as a Category 4 hurricane. The storm was projected to travel toward the northwest on a path that would bring it barreling down on us within the next twenty-four hours.

We worked with local agencies throughout the morning to warn people to move to nearby shelters; we went to each house in the shantytown that covered the hill above the river.

For the remainder of the afternoon, Miguel, Sophia, David, and I saw patients in the clinic; Aishling assisted some neighborhood volunteers in boarding up the windows of the clinic and putting supplies inside in preparation for the approaching storm.

Around suppertime we headed back to Santa Lucía where we would ride out the storm in the shelter at the Peace Corp facility. The hurricane was still hours away from our location, so we stopped at the café to eat supper when we arrived in the village. Then we headed back to the house to gather our things.

46

The Uffern Ultimatum

(Aishling)

Rafe was still over at the Peace Corps facility. The rest of us had finished boarding up the house and we still had a while before we'd have to move to the bunker. Thinking about being underground all night, I already felt suffocated. I had to get away and breathe. And think. I was still so troubled about what had happened the previous day. It made no sense to me how I could have clearly seen pieces of some ancient language carved in that rock at La Tigra, and Rafe had seen nothing. And I missed Kaillech. I hoped she was adjusting okay without me. As usual, my thoughts kept fleeing to the refuge of Rafe. I wanted him to be my moon, my stars—my hope. It felt like together we should be able to fend off the Delaney curse—with his power and mine combined. But was I brave enough to try?

I was sitting by the creek, playing my fiddle and watching the storm clouds assemble, when a young boy about four years of age ran by on the other side of the stream. I could tell he was upset even before he started speaking.

"My mama! She's hurt at the lake! Help me!" he said in Spanish. I jumped up and shoved my case under a high rock ledge; I hoped the overhang would protect it from the worst of the coming rain. Then I took off after him. This was a terrible thing to happen, especially with the storm coming so soon upon us. I knew the others would be worried about me, but there was no time to do anything but react, so I ran.

"*Niño!*" I called out to him, but he kept running, so I followed him farther and farther into the jungle. The sprinkling rain, bouncing off leaves and rocks, played a soft melody as it fell. It was hard to keep up with the child. I came upon a trail and ran in the direction of a small footprint I saw in the mud, but soon the prints stopped and there was no way for me to know if he had gone left or right. "*Niño!*" I yelled again, as the rain trickled down my cheeks, but he didn't answer.

Up ahead a smooth stone of good size rose up like a bench for a weary traveler. As I drew closer, I could see marks on it similar to those I had observed the day before. They appeared as ancient rune carvings that the Gaels had etched in the trees and the rocks. This couldn't be mere coincidence.

I moved closer to study the archaic communication form of my Irish forefathers. It had been a while since I had translated any ogham. I had seen it, of course, on stones and parchments at the exhibit for the Book of Kells at the Trinity College Library, but I had not practiced reading it for years. The Gaels had used it as a secret language, a way for them to communicate with each other to keep their plans a mystery to outsiders. I stopped and ran my finger through the grooves in the symbols, searching through my memory to analyze them. My body grew cold and my limbs felt numb as I read the words:

"Soon, we will come for you, Siridean,
on the night of the Ten Colds Moon.
Beware of the beast who hunts you now."

What is that supposed to mean? I looked through the surrounding jungle and the ever-increasing veil of rain. Before I had even read the script on the stone, I had felt like I was being watched. *Where are you, kid?* Thunder roared around me, and I jumped. When I looked back at the rock, the etchings were gone. I settled myself, pushing my wet bangs out of my eyes as anger took over.

Continuing on my journey, I decided to go left; the rain sifted through the trees, running down my face to obscure my vision. I rounded a bend in the path and saw the boy sitting on a mossy log; his bottom lip was tucked in his mouth and his sobs were heart-rending.

"I can help, but you need to stay with me. Let's go find her," I said to him. He rushed over to wrap his arms around me, and then he grabbed my hand and tugged me down the path. The wind and rain progressively increased as we ran.

"*Madre!*" he shouted over and over. His tiny, round face became soaked with tears and rain.

I wasn't sure how long we ran, but he stopped when we came to the shore of a small lake. To my left, a rocky creek poured down the sloping hillside, feeding the lake; to the right, a small river borrowed from the lake. A rusty rowboat with one broken oar lay nestled in the wet sand. With the high winds, the waves rose in swells and the boat would soon be set adrift.

The young boy pointed to a light shining on the other side of the lake. "*Madre!*" he yelled, and his face transformed with a sweet smile.

He jumped into the boat and looked to me, as if he were expecting me to follow. I got in and began the complicated task of moving us through the waves and direct winds with one oar. It was a very slow process, and by the time we reached the center of the lake, I had to stop to rest. As soon as I removed the oar from the water, we swiftly drifted backward. I looked behind me, and when I turned back around the boy had grown up. My eyes bulged, and I gasped in shock. A man wearing a black pinstriped suit smirked at me.

"Who are you? Where's the boy?" I exploded. A knowledge trail left crumbs for me in my jumbled brain, and I followed the seeds of discovery to the villain. *Stupid faerie tricked me!* With a sudden jolt the boat was lifted at least a foot from the surface, and it revolved in a perfect circle. I leaned over the side to peer into the murky waters, but I couldn't see anything. Horrified,

I scooted backward off the wooden seat and moved as far away from the faerie as I could in the small space. I clung to the sides of the boat, and my heart thundered while I heard a haunting Gaelic song—*Skellig Island*—rise from the depths below.

I peeked over the side again and saw dozens of webbed hands holding the boat up. Moving my gaze below the seaweed-covered arms, I stared into ancient, water-wrinkled faces similar to men but they had wide mouths and teeth like a Goliath Tigerfish.

"*Murchadha!*" I mouthed to myself in fear. The sea battlers were there to avenge something. Maybe something my father had done. I had no clue. There was no way I could fight all of them. Where was Morrighan when I needed her? I knew one thing: they wouldn't take me without some resistance.

"Aishling Delaney, we meet again," the faerie mocked, drawing my attention back to him. "Except this time ya didn't bring those pesky dragonflies."

"What are ya talking about? Who are you?"

The faerie gasped in shock. "Ya mean ya don't recognize me? Well, ya must not know your Who's Who among faeries." He winked and I snarled. "The name's Tarlach. Ring a bell?"

Inwardly I flinched, but outwardly I was composed. Not wanting to further inflate the Alorcán leader's ego, I withheld what I really knew and on impulse blurted, "Not at all."

"Hmph," he grunted, "Well, I'm the one who can stop this horrid curse on yer family."

My shock got the better of me with his statement, and I inhaled in a quick burst.

He sneered and continued. "Yer precarious situation makes me recall the pathetic Delaney family motto. Let's see. How does it go again? Oh, right: 'pressed down, yet still lifted up.'" Another round of maniacal cackling echoed all around me as the faerie moved closer.

Closing my eyes, I reached out to the hawthorn, repeated the enchantment, and summoned my sword. The marking scorched violently this time onto my face, one brushstroke at a time, taking much longer than usual. I opened my eyes and saw the reason why. My hand rested on my knee, palm up, preparing for my weapon. His hand hovered over mine, and some form of purplish electricity sparked between the two as if he were pushing my weapon back to its realm. He looked up with an easy, wicked grin that I so wanted to smack off his face.

"I've eons more experience than ye, Siridean. Nice try, though."

The scorching on my face stopped, and I reached up with my left hand to feel it. The electric sparks had subsided, and he linked his fingers with mine in an intimate way that made me want to gag. When I was this angry, my thick Irish accent came out, and I could feel it rising now along with my ire.

"Don't ya lay one hand on me, Tarlach, ya soulless, devilish faerie!" I dared him with as much defiance as I could muster. I revolted against his touch, tried to shake him off me, but he was stronger.

"Aishling, lass, ye hurt me feelings slanderin' me in such a way. And I came in relative peace," he parried and smirked at his minions. "I happen to be nothin' like Satariel and his hellions. I've much more pizzazz—Irish panache, I suppose."

Confused, I quickly ran through the timelines in my mind. "But Samhain has already been. How did you…"

"How did we find a thin place in the off-season? Well, let's just say that I made a very lucrative deal wit' the devil and be done wit' it."

"You disgust me!" I spat in his face, which was now so close to mine. I wasn't about to give him flattery, even if it meant getting kicked in the teeth.

He had my body locked to his before I could form another insult. He grabbed my hair and yanked my head back until my body bowed away from his in an arc. I had to strain to look into his hate-filled eyes.

"Ye'd hate for anythin' to happen to that doctor *chara* [friend] of yers now, wouldn't ya?"

My horror-stricken face must have been amusing to him. His hyena-like laugh echoed off the waters and bounced back in my face; the odor of his dead breath mingled with the sound. "Ye and the doc are quite taken wit' each other, I've been observin'."

"What could the leader of the mighty Alorcán want with me? I don't have the pow'r to give ya anythin', so I don't know why you're here botherin' me," I sassed, trying to draw his thoughts away from Rafe.

"Aye, but ya don't know the full extent of it yet. Ye have great pow'rs and much more control o'er others' destinies than ye realize. If ye live long enough, ye'll know what I'm talkin' about. Yer bein' a smart bit ornery for one so at a momentary disadvantage."

He laughed again, and the other monsters joined him, slapping the water and making all kind of racket. The wind kicked and my hair twisted across my face; then it retreated behind me, leaving my face exposed. Tarlach's groomed hair didn't seem bothered at all by the whirling wind or the spray of the water carried on the air.

He jerked my head up by my hair until I was inches from his face. His eyes were tiny slits. "I *want*...my music box," he scolded, like I had stolen it from him. His putrid breath made me turn away. I quickly filled my lungs with fresh air again before he shook me and forced my face back toward his. The lake waves were tall enough now to lap into the boat. The pounding rain streamed down my face and nearly blinded me.

"I don't have *my* music box anymore," I wrangled. "Someone stole it from me before I came to Costa Rica."

He glared at me as if he were gauging the honesty in my eyes. Then he pushed me back down on the seat and lifted his eyes to the ferocious, army-green clouds that marched in right above the tallest trees, thick and ready for shock-and-awe battle. I was baffled. I thought Tarlach had helped create the Dullahan. Why didn't he just have the headless faerie deliver the music box to him? You'd think he could call the creature to himself. Maybe this was good news for me. At least I'd only have one dragon to slay to retrieve what was mine.

"Whether it's still in yer possession or not, I want it returned to me. I'll be back on Beltaine, Miss Delaney. And when I see ya again, ye'd better have that box. I don't care what angel or faerie ye have to summon to get it. Just get it—or we take Raphael down to Uffern." A wicked smirk tore across his lips. Deep anguish rocked my very soul, while panic and guilt took up residence in my already battered heart.

I quickly brushed those feelings aside; anger built in me like the gathering storm clouds. Across my dead body would be the only way they'd ever get to Rafe and take him down to Irish hell, and even then I had a sixth sense that death wouldn't keep me from him.

The rains battered us with violence, and lightning rippled across the sky. The faerie dove overboard, with a dolphin-like tail forming just before he hit the water. The boat dropped with a heavy thud and wobbled in the giant waves. I grabbed the sides to hold on as I sank down to lie on the floorboard. As I reeled from this encounter, the evil faerie leaned over the side and kissed me on the cheek as if he were my lover instead of my loathsome enemy. My world went black again.

41

Derecho

(Rafe)

After I got everything set up at the bunker and spoke with the director there, I returned to the house and packed my bag in the den while I chatted with Miguel. Aishling was not in the front room with the others, so I knocked on her bedroom door. There was no answer. I pushed open the door and noticed her packed bag on her bed.

"Have any of you seen Aishling? I asked the group as I came back into the den. "The rain's started. We'll need to move to the shelter soon."

"She said she was going to the creek to watch the storm come," Sophia said, shrugging her shoulders.

"What's the latest on the weather?" I asked David, who had been glued to the television, getting the latest forecasts.

"The eye won't be passing over us for a couple more hours, but the outer bands of the storm are moving in. There's about to be some nasty wind and rain."

"Well, I'd better go get Aishling. Be right back," I said, heading out the door.

The creek's soothing ripple welcomed me, while the sky's aggression objected to my intrusion. Tumbling gray and charcoal clouds forced their dominance, and the friendly skies scrambled to retreat. The sprinkling rain progressed toward a steadier downpour, and I was surprised I had yet to see Aishling coming back toward the house.

I ran the rest of the way and topped the small hill that hid the creek from view. I looked toward the rock where Aishling always sat to play her music. She wasn't there.

"Aishling!" I called out. I was not the type to panic, but I could feel that something was not right about this situation. Maybe she had wandered away from the creek and gotten lost. I knew time was running out. The storm was strengthening.

I turned around to start back to the house to get some help when I saw it. The sight of Aishling's fiddle case tucked under the rock ledge brought on a full-scale panic. She was never without that case.

Retrieving it, I rushed back to the house, burst through the screen door, placed her case on the couch, and ran for my medic's backpack. I had already filled it with all the essentials in case we needed it at the bunker.

"Aishling wasn't at the creek," I told the group, as I tried to remain calm, "but I found her case there. She knows about the hurricane. She wouldn't have just wandered away, not with a storm of this magnitude coming." I paced to the screen door and leaned my hands on the doorframe. The storm would be unleashed soon. "Something's wrong here. I've got to find her," I said, grief and fear taking over my mind. Slinging the pack onto my shoulders, I headed for the door.

"Wait!" Miguel said. "I'm coming with you."

"No, Miguel. I can't let you do that. I don't know what I'm getting myself into, so I'll probably have to find another shelter for the night. We can't both be wandering around in the jungle in the morning. There are too many people who are going to need help. We've got long-range walkie-talkies. Mine's in the backpack. Keep yours handy. I'll check in with you in an hour."

"All right, but I don't like this," Miguel grumbled. "If you don't radio back in an hour, I'm heading on a tracking expedition. Take care, man. I'll be praying for you both."

I nodded before pushing open the door and running full speed back down the path.

I started at the creek and followed it, heaving my way through the large leaves of banana plants and palms for about twenty feet before stumbling upon a trail. It was then that I felt her fear—bone-deep, teeth-clenching terror. The beasts inside me roared to life. I shoved at the limbs and plowed through the brush. Her fear turned to anger and pushed against the demons inside me, helping me to think more clearly.

My search was hindered under the jungle canopy and the stormy skies at dusk. Not to mention that shortly into my journey, the rain charged onto the scene in a violent torrent.

About thirty water-deluged minutes later, I came across a slash of vibrant red sticking out of the slick mud. I dug it out with my hands and held it up. It was the paisley scarf Aishling had been wearing in her hair. Relieved that I was going in the right direction, but also concerned, I picked up the pace.

As I confronted the storm head-on, the *derecho* winds pushed against me, making it nearly impossible to run. I had to be heading directly into the squall line because the winds were straight-line. Suddenly the gales brought me to my knees, and I landed in the mud, catching myself with my hands; the rocks and exposed tree roots cut into my flesh.

The rain pounded me, and the limbs of the jungle undergrowth struck me with such force my arms and lips bled. I squinted at the sky through the rain pouring down my face. The jungle canopy was twisting, with a funnel cloud churning over it.

"Aishling, where are you?" I shouted as the rain pummeled me.

I pulled myself up, using the same tree limbs that were bludgeoning me, and continued down the rough trail that had been blazed by the local villagers. Whatever had brought her in this direction, I was sure that Aishling would have stuck to the path.

What if she'd been taken? I thought with despair and regret for having insisted she come along on the trip. I'd never forgive myself if any harm came to her. She was my earthly reason for getting up each morning and doing what I did.

With great resolve I pressed on. I had been running for close to an hour when I came upon an abandoned shelter built into a banyan tree with a base the size and length of a large pickup truck on big knobby tires. The knotted roots ran from the limbs to the ground. Someone had painstakingly carved out an area inside the massive trunk to make a room, which was about ten feet in diameter and seven feet in height; there were walls built from wood, stone, and straw for insulation. The door was made of jagged wood pieces tied together with rope, and the only objects in the tiny hut were a worn hammock that stretched from one thick root to another on the right and a fire pit with a stack of wood on the left. The tree dweller must have moved to a shelter in time for the storm. I took a moment to radio back to Miguel about my progress, and then I raced back into the storm, making a mental note of this location in case I needed to return there for the night.

One minute I was running, and the next I was on the ground, so tired. I couldn't go on. While I lay there with my cheek in the mud, images of Aishling floated around me. Sleep was comforting. She was serenity. A large limb fell on me in my tumultuous dream and I yelled. I tried to push myself up. *Aishling!* I needed to get to Aishling. Why could I not open my eyes? The demons inside shocked me, and the electricity jerked my chest off the ground over and over until my eyes opened.

From my position all I could see was water, as if I were swimming under the surface at the moment. I pushed the limb off me and jumped up, breaking into as much of a jog as I could, competing with the wind. What if I didn't get to her in time?

Soon the path led to a cliff that overlooked a small lake. I tried to shield my eyes with my arm so I could see through the driving rain, but the pervading darkness along with the ransacking storm didn't allow me to see very far into the distance. After taking the flashlight out of my pack, I shined it through the foreboding cyclone. There appeared to be a small boat drifting on the water, and I could see a blue light shining inside it, but I couldn't tell if there was a person in it. Using the trees to brace me, I made my way down the hill so I could get a better look.

"Aishling!" I yelled, but my voice sounded like a whisper against the brutal thundering of the wind. I was able to make it to the shore of the lake. Fortunately the straight-line winds pushed the small fishing boat toward me. Impatient for the rusty metal craft to reach me, I waded out into the water. Soon, the boat bumped my hand, and I pulled it to shore, far enough up the beach area that it wouldn't immediately be pulled back out into the choppy water.

As soon as possible, I jumped into the boat.

"Aishling!"

I looked at her face, spellbound by the exotic marking. The blue tree taking up half her face and sprawling across her forehead had a faint glow. What appeared to be diamonds intermittently twinkled. I'd never seen a faerie before, but I was fairly certain I was looking at one now. Her skin had an iridescent sheen, and I reached out to trace my finger across her lilac-tinted eyelids.

Leaning down, I checked her pulse. She was alive. I said a quick prayer of thanksgiving as I checked her vitals. She was unconscious but breathing, and she appeared upon first examination to have nothing broken. I knew in my gut that she was going to make it, and my faith strengthened. Through her soaked shirt, I could see a sapphire light pulsating like a heartbeat, and I pulled the chain out from beneath her clothing around her neckline. As I held the faerie cross in my hand, I looked to her face again, wondering anew at her secrets. I was also confused that her angels were not with her. After all, she was out cold. Or was she?

Then it hit me. This had to be the work of demons or lower-realm faeries. They had touched her the same way I had on the beach at the Hogueras Festival, and she had experienced *katheudo*, a deep sleep that leaves one incapacitated for a time but not in a comalike state. Her angels thought she was merely taking a nap. That was why I had just passed out on top of the hill: because she had, and we were connected.

Gathering her in my arms, I stumbled back the way I'd come, up the hill, again using the trees to brace us when the gusts became too strong. I was thankful that the shelter I'd found was not far from the lake. In the blackness of the night, the shining stone was a comfort, even though the beam only cut through a few feet of blinding rain at a time. Inch by inch, we made our way toward the tree.

As we rounded a curve in the path, I didn't think I'd ever been happier to see a tree. That old banyan, with its limbs and roots spreading out like a twisting giant squid, loomed in the distance. Lightning bolts crackled and spread, making the tree appear like some scary monster from a sci-fi movie, giving an almost lifelike quality to it.

The reverse trip seemed to take twice as long from the lake back to the shelter. When I kicked the makeshift door open, the stone illuminated the dark places. I laid Aishling in the hammock and then turned back to secure the door. The howling of the wind didn't diminish much in the safety of the well-rooted tree, but at least I could hear myself think.

Setting my pack aside, I radioed back to Miguel. The reception was staticky at best, but we were able to communicate well enough that he knew we were momentarily safe.

I rechecked Aishling's vitals, covered her with the small blanket I had rolled up in my pack, and kissed her forehead. For a while I stared at the intricate detail on her cheek and forehead; then I inhaled sharply as I watched the leaves and the limbs evaporate into the trunk, and the trunk sink into the ground until nothing was left but her flawless pink skin. I rubbed my eyes, brushed my hands briskly through my hair, and I paced. This answered some questions for me, but then again, it opened up a thousand more.

48

Beyond the Reaches of Time

(Rafe)

Seeing that she would come around in her own time, I shone my flashlight toward the ceiling on the opposite side of the room and noticed there was an exhaust flue in the side of the hut above the fire pit. Wind whistled through it and water seeped in around the edges, but it would serve its purpose that night. I searched through my backpack to find matches and soon had a warm fire crackling.

I was sitting by the blaze, bandaging my wounds, when Aishling stirred.

"Tarlach, ye'll never take him!" she screamed. She thrashed and threw well-executed punches into the air. Before I could catch her she had flipped the hammock and was lying facedown in the dirt. Pushing herself up off the ground, she turned to face me. She ran into my arms and snuggled into me. We sought comfort from each other amid all the tragedy that was happening around us.

I held her head against my chest and stroked her hair. "It's all right. Everything's going to be okay," I reassured her. We stayed just like that, holding on to each other, comforting each other, and for the longest interval, we hovered beyond the reaches of time.

After a while she pulled away, looking embarrassed that she had sought refuge in my arms. Giving her the time she needed, I returned to the fire, sitting on the log I'd vacated. I was about to resume bandaging my arm when she knelt beside me and took over the task. She rolled the gauze around my upper right arm and secured it with small metal clips.

"There," she said, patting my hand. She stared at the obvious mess the trees and branches had made of my face, and she reached out to brush her fingertips across a patch of drying blood on my lower lip. I reveled in her touch and my pulse quickened while hers kicked in to pound with mine.

"Rafe, I'm so sorry," she said as a tear escaped down her cheek. She rummaged through the backpack until she found a washcloth and jumped to her feet, sticking the rag near the loose chimney to wet it. Then she returned to my side and gently washed the blood from my face.

I was so overcome with emotion, for the sweet manner that accompanied every action in her life, that I had to clear my throat to swallow the lump forming there.

She soothed my cuts while we sat by the fire. I watched the shadows fall on the side of her face where the tree had been earlier, while the other cheek was warmed by the fire's glow.

"Does this remind you of anything?" she asked.

"What do you mean?"

"You and me—sitting by the fire—soaking wet." She grinned shyly, as if she thought I might have possibly forgotten that wonderful night or the few days preceding it.

"Hogueras," I reflected. I thought about all that had transpired since that last night on the beach, the almost four years I'd had to live without her. I looked away into the fire. "The best night of my life," I revealed. I heard her intake of breath, and I held mine as I waited for her to say something.

"Mine too, Rafe," she admitted. I looked down to see her fidgeting.

Resuming her attention to my scrapes, she pulled some antibacterial ointment from my pack and quickly applied the balm and bandages to cuts on my right hand and left index finger.

Then she stood and changed the subject. "I saw you had a *guanábana* in your backpack. Care to share?"

I mulled over the question playfully. "Hmm.... I guess not, seeing as there's a raging storm out there and all. I'd hate for you to get lost searching for a banana," I joked. She swatted my arm and then moved to plunder the backpack while I laughed heartily.

"There are some other snacks down in there too." I watched as she dug into the pack and came back to the fire. Sitting Indian style beside me, she produced the prickly, tangy fruit and two granola bars. Famished, we devoured the bars.

Removing my knife from the holder on my belt, I chopped the fruit open and handed her a slice. She surprised me when she began spitting seeds toward the fire. Soon a contest arose, and we stood up so we could project the black seeds farther across the fire.

"I won that one!" she declared. She grabbed my arm and pulled playfully.

"I beg to differ, Miss Delaney. Mine went at least a millimeter past yours."

"Doc, you need to get your eyes checked." She pouted, hands on her hips.

I was enjoying her laughter and this time of freedom where she could let loose a little. There were no expectations here. The storm was holding us hostage, so what better way to pass the time than a bit of creative fun?

"Okay, last one," she giggled with a mischievous gleam in her eye. "This one's going to be serious. We need to move to the other side of the fire so we can have a fresh playing field."

"All right, and we need to pick different-colored seeds so we'll know which is which."

"Loser has to dance around the fire for five minutes," she decided.

"Sounds fair," I concurred, confident that I would win this battle. "Ready?"

"Ready."

We both leaned back and then arched forward at the same time, releasing the seeds at great velocity. Then we rushed to the other side of the fire to see who would be proclaimed the winner and who would have to dance.

"Ha! I won!" I jumped up in the air and grabbed her up, whirling her around. As I set her back on her feet, I went to move the log I had been using as my seat so it wouldn't get in her way. "All right, Aishling, it's time for you to pay up." I held my hand toward the path around the fire, motioning for her to begin.

"You're serious?" she asked.

"Oh, very serious," I assured, trying to hold back the laughter.

"I can't dance around the fire without my fiddle."

"Improvise," I said. "You were the one who came up with the bet. Remember?" She wasn't going to get out of this.

"Oh, all right! But no laughing," she fussed.

"I'm not sure I can comply with that request, but I'll try."

"Whatever!"

Shrugging her shoulders, she took off. Instantly I knew that I wasn't prepared for this moment, just like so many others with Aishling that had taken me by surprise. It was such a graceful, artistic dance, like when I had watched her during her rehearsal at her college. She was doing this from memory, eyes closed. Her arms were in the air as if she were playing the fiddle, and she hummed a fetching tune as she whirled around the fire like a lively ballerina. I was not laughing. I yearned more than ever to hold her.

Caught up in the beauty of her rhythmic motion, I almost missed it. One of the larger logs in the fire pit fizzled. As it cracked in two, part of it landed in the path where she was dancing. I rushed forward to keep her from tripping. She gasped and opened her eyes as I grabbed her, and then everything went still and quiet. It was the most serene peace I'd experienced in the longest time.

As I held her, a slow smile built from my lips and made its way around to hers because of the way I was holding her. It was as if we had been dancing the most elegant waltz and had gotten to the end—the part where the man dips the woman down toward the floor, his face close to hers. The scene was too unbelievable for words. After a blurred amount of time had passed, I brought her up to complete the impromptu dance.

Her hands shook as she backed away from me. Turning around, she moved a small log on the opposite side of the fire to sit down. There was an electric silence filling the room, charging the space between us; she stared into the flames, and I stared at her. I needed to know what had happened to her earlier—why she had ended up at the lake. But she seemed reluctant to fill in the gaps.

I was about to ask, but she spoke up, explaining about the child and her rush to try to help. When she got to the part about standing at the lakeshore, her eyes scrunched up, and a look of sorrow engulfed her. "I don't remember what happened next, Rafe. I was there looking out across the water, and the next thing I knew, I was here in this place with you."

What did those demons or faeries want with her? I wondered if the demons were trying to get to me through her. It would be the perfect way to ultimately destroy me. That was a certainty. Because if anything happened to her, I wouldn't stop hunting them until they were all dead—or I was.

She put her head in her hands, then stood to pace around the fire. "Why can't I remember? Something happened at the lake."

"When you woke up, you mentioned the name Tarlach. Who is that?"

I could tell she was trying to concentrate on the name as she explained, "He's a figure from Irish legends, the leader of the Alorcán faeries." Wrapping her arms across her, she rested each hand on the opposite shoulder as she paced and thought. On her twentieth revolution around the fire, she stopped. Her hands dropped to her sides and her eyes widened. I knew she had the answer to what had happened.

Her mournful eyes lifted from the fire to my face, a look of terror distorting her usually tranquil features, and I felt a sick dread filtering throughout my body. "Rafe, I should go back to Ireland tomorrow. I can't...." She shook her head, and her eyes looked as if she'd been weeping for days, red-rimmed and puffy.

There were words she couldn't make herself say. If they were more damaging words about leaving, then I was glad she didn't continue. "You don't mean it, Aishling!" Desperation took hold in my heart. I had to stir it up, keep it from settling there. "What about the people here who need us? What about the orphans, Aishling? What about *me*?" Once I got on a roll, I couldn't stop that last word.

"I don't know what to say, Rafe. I don't know what I *can* say."

"What happened at the lake? What aren't you telling me?" Grabbing her elbows, I forced her to look up. "Tell me, Aishling. Please!" I begged.

She shook her head at first, as if she were bound to keep the mystery from outsiders like me. But then she did speak, and the riddle remained as confusing as ever. "A decision was made. Now I have to follow through. Isn't that what you called it once, Rafe—a follow-through?" Tears obscured her pupils, and she bit her lip.

I was so frustrated; the demons within me were roused, roiling and tossing. I had worked so hard to fight them, but my self-control slipped, and my anger and pride gave them all the breeding ground they needed to resurface. I could feel the fire in my eyes before I ever saw it reflected back to me in hers. She tried to step away, but I held her with a firm grasp.

A look of shock overcame her. "Rafe!" she screamed, but the sound was distant. I grabbed her to me, and my mouth descended on hers in a rush of adrenaline and power. With the intense pressure of our lips joining, I could feel the cuts that she had soothed just moments ago reopen, and blood gushed forth. My thoughts were in turmoil. I was so hungry for her that I wanted to take and take, but there was a side of this demon in me that knew better. This felt so good—holding her, savoring her.

Even as frightened as she was when she had seen my fiery eyes, it seemed as if it didn't matter to her. She clung to me too, tasting the blood from my lip, entwining her fingers in my hair. This was madness. As I started to lower her to the floor, she twisted away. I didn't know how she did it, but she got away, and that part of me that was good was actually relieved. She stood by the door, wiping the blood from her mouth with the back of her hand. I ground my feet into the dirt, refusing to harm her any further. I took deep breaths, trying to calm down. Closing my eyes, I sent the demons back to hell.

49

Bad Blood

(Aishling)

My own eyes ignited, and the flames spread down to my heels. It was an electric burn, and I felt things I shouldn't have been feeling. Lust warred within me—attacking my better judgment—causing me to cling when I should have pulled away. A beast inside of him thrashed. It stabbed at me, and I didn't know what was happening. I pulled away from the kiss, opening my eyes to watch him through my own crackling wildfire. The predator in him stared back. I pushed against the flames in my system; at the same time I used my enhanced abilities to escape him. I landed by the door, wiping the blood from my mouth.

Something almost savage seemed to awaken within me. My instincts—and something more—had me running to the hawthorn, but my love for this man had me bucking against my own strength. In my head, my hand surged toward the tree trunk, but in my heart I threw myself to the ground and dueled with my own body to keep it away from the weapons. Somehow I knew that this other part of me would not stop until he was dead, but I would not harm him.

This was not the magical kiss we had shared before. This was a joining built by two opposing forces that were never meant to be. It was a monumental mistake. I saw it. I saw why we could never be together. In the flash of a millisecond I received a new vision where there was more than one demon-like creature crawling through a hot, barren wasteland, searching for hope. The vision left me empty.

And the kiss. It invaded my body. I felt…weird. His saliva—something in him was wrong. No, it was the blood from his lip. It had to be. I tasted it, mixed in with all the other intoxicating flavors that made me want to return to him even now, even when my mind screamed no. And the fire. I had seen his eyes flame—red, yellow, orange, just like in the vision at the angels' refuge. That same fire had burned through my body just now, and my eyes had flamed. Yet, his eyes were normal as I looked at him now.

Confused and afraid, I rushed to the door. I yanked it open, and a wall of wind and water knocked me to the ground. Rafe rushed over, pushing against the door with all his strength to get it closed again. I scrambled behind the hammock, backing up into the wall.

"Stay away, Rafe. Don't come any closer," I ordered as he advanced. My warning must have broken through to him, if only a tiny bit, because he paused. "I don't know what came over either of us, but I'm begging you, if you value your life at all you will never do that again. I would not harm you, but others would, and I can't bear it. Do you understand?"

He grabbed his head and bent over, roaring. He surged upright and scowled at me. I took a step backward to grab the wall, but a growl tore from my lips as well. My body felt like it was burning, and I locked both my arms around my head and squeezed. The pain was unbearable.

It was apparent that he chose to ignore my threat because he started toward me like a warrior rushing the front line. The only thing that stopped him was my piercing cry of pain. The kiss. The joining of our lips. The blood from his lip was in me, and something else inside me rioted against its power. There was a terrible ache in my stomach, and I doubled over on the ground, my arms clutching my abdomen. He was already dealing with enough. I didn't want him to know that I knew something was amiss with him and his toxic blood, so I closed my eyes and tried to breathe through the waves of pain.

He rushed to my side and started to kneel when he grabbed his own stomach and fell the rest of the way to the ground. "Aishling!" He winced.

"Rafe?" I tried to lean toward him, but the movement sent a spear-like sensation rocketing through me, sharp and barbed.

He pulled himself up and leaned his back to the wall. "What happened, Aishling? What can I do? Where are you hurt?"

"My stomach. It appears you have the same problem. We must have eaten something that didn't agree with us," I replied through shallow breaths. I knew it was the blood, but I didn't want him to hurt too.

After a while, he stumbled to his feet and grabbed his backpack, returning to sit on the ground beside me. He handed me two different capsules and a bottle of water. "I need you to sit up, Aishling. Swallow these and the nausea will soon go away."

I did as he instructed. He leaned his head against the wall and closed his eyes. "Rafe, you don't look so good. Are you going to take some of the medicine?"

"I will after I get you settled in the hammock," he spoke through clenched teeth. He looked like he was in as much or more pain than I was.

"Rafe, I'll be fine—really."

He struggled to his feet and lifted me from the ground. His eyes closed for a moment while he steadied himself. Then he gently laid me in the hammock and covered me with the blanket. I conked out as he ambled toward the fire.

50

Love And A Lie

(Rafe)

The drug took effect quickly in Aishling's system. Grabbing my lumpy backpack, I tossed it down by the fire and lay down to use it as a pillow as her drugs coursed through my bloodstream. Disoriented, some time later, I woke to a jarring wind, rattling the tree limbs together. I jumped up to check on Aishling—still resting.

I smoothed the hair back from her brow and whispered, "I'm so sorry. More than you'll ever know." I had given Aishling a pill for nausea that sedated her and also a psychotropic drug—a hallucinogen often prescribed for psychedelic therapy. It was non-addictive, so I felt safe in administering it to her.

I had to keep her from remembering what I'd almost done to her without doing another memory swipe. (The first time was when she had died in my arms as a child and I had put her back together.) She would never trust me again if she was able to recall the look of the demons in my eyes or the power of their sensual nature fueled by my own longing. But there seemed to be something in the air that night, as if my strings for a time were in the hands of a diabolical puppeteer. Even so, our entangling had caused her to feel the flames. I had hurt her, and I would never forgive myself.

The heavy feeling in my chest was making me sick. I shouldn't rush to always have her near me; it was too risky. I pulled a log up beside the hammock and sat for hours just watching her breathe while the storm ravaged the world outside and rain poured in under the crude door. A tiny creek flowed from there to the back of the hut, escaping through a hole dug just for that purpose.

Rubbing my eyes, I fought the drugs' effects and watched her until the early morning, singing her dream song to her. A couple of hours before dawn, the hallucinations began, and in her restlessness she tossed herself right out of the hammock again. I had just placed her back in bed and turned to sit on the log when she flipped out onto the floor again. At that rate she would be black and blue by morning and would be wondering what I'd done to her in her sleep.

Crawling into the hammock, I lay on top of the covers and held her to me. Bound up as she was in my arms, it didn't take long for her to give up the fight. She cried in periodic outbursts and screamed several times before being swallowed up in unconsciousness for a while longer. Then the cycle would repeat. The drug caused the demons within to drive me insane. I wanted to lash out at anything and everything. But my oath broke through the madness and brought some clarity. I latched onto her and tried to lie as still as possible while the demons pitched and contorted, screeching inside my head.

A faint light was pouring in through the cracks in the door when her eyelids fluttered open. Her wet hair from the night before had dried, leaving loose, trailing waves down the length of her back. She had smudges of dirt on her left cheek and chin from her time wrestling with the floor. I reached out to try to brush them away, and she jerked back.

"It's okay, Aishling. Just trying to wipe the dirt off your face. You had some pretty explosive nightmares last night—kept tossing out of the hammock. I had to hold you to keep you from harming yourself," I said, testing the murky waters of her memory.

She looked embarrassed. "That must have been a sight to see," she joked, yawning and stretching her arms out in front of her.

She tried to sit up, so I threw my legs over the side, bracing the hammock with my feet on the ground. Rubbing her head, she said, groggily, "My head is splitting. What happened to me?" She must have seen the dried blood on my lip, for she squeezed her eyes shut, and I was afraid that she was drawing the sequence of events from her mind. But soon my soul was set at ease.

"Oh! I remember. Rafe, I'm so sorry about everything. There was this little boy who lost his mom...." She recounted the story to me again that she didn't remember explaining last night. So far the drug had worked.

"When I found you last night, you were in a boat drifting on a lake. I brought you back here through the storm. You were unconscious all night. I've been so worried."

"Really? All night? But I...."

Her entire face was incandescent, and I was sure she was probably recalling the kiss. *Please, let her believe it was a dream!* She looked away.

"Well, everything seems okay now except I have this slight ache in my stomach." She grimaced and held her arm across her midsection.

I had just committed the most despicable sin of treachery: I lied to the one I love.

51

Atmospheric Disturbances

(Rafe)

By daylight the worst of the storm had passed over us. It was still raining, but we'd have to make a run for it. We needed to get back to Comayaguela and see what we could do to help at the mission.

"Do you feel well enough to run?" I asked Aishling.

"I'm fine. I've caused enough of a delay in our departure this morning. Again, Rafe, I'm so sorry. I hope that little boy is okay—the one who was looking for his mother yesterday."

"I'm sure the boy is fine, Aishling. The kids who grow up in the jungle are taught to find their way around, to survive. Please don't beat yourself up about last night. I enjoyed taking care of you."

She looked away, embarrassed. Opening the door, she said, "Well, I'm ready when you are."

We set off at a sprint, but our progress was slow. We kept slipping in the mud and having to detour off the beaten path. Broken limbs and uprooted trees created a wild maze.

The aroma of the deluged world was pungent with so many competing scents. There were pieces of smashed fruit littering the ground and flowers that were squeezed or crushed, making their odors more potent.

An hour later we had found our way back to the house. Aishling jumped in the shower first while I explained to the others why she'd gone M.I.A, and then I took my turn in the shower.

The drive to Comayaguela was long and tedious with downed trees and workers clearing the road of debris. The village was in chaos. People chased the van, beat on our windows, and begged us to help them. I knew that if I stopped the vehicle, we would be mobbed, and the van would probably be stolen in someone's attempt to abandon this madness. Looking over at Aishling and seeing the anguish in her eyes, I almost turned the van around to get her away from this danger.

As we neared the medical mission building, I noticed that there were many more armed guards than usual and a police barricade holding people back. The guards came toward the van and moved the people back from us so we could get through the gates.

Inside the building we joined a meeting in progress. A policeman was giving the grave news. Much of Tegucigalpa was underwater, but Comayaguela had the most significant destruction. The Choluteca River was swollen, and its course was being altered each hour, taking out small villages downstream. Due to the catastrophic flooding, most bridges that led from Comayaguela to Tegucigalpa had been swept away.

The worst news was yet to come. On the hill above the river, where we had spent so much time the day before in the shantytowns, the fallout from Hurricane Sebastien had triggered massive landslides, and the majority of the dwellings on the hill had slid off into the river. I heard Aishling gasp with despair. While we listened to the horrifying news, I placed a comforting hand on her shoulder.

Efforts between governmental and nongovernmental organizations were being coordinated. The people waiting outside would be allowed to come into the mission in a controlled manner to get food, water, and medical assistance. Right away we found ourselves in a whirlwind of activity. A wave of patients poured through the door—some barely standing, others being carried in, and some unconscious on makeshift stretchers.

Aishling knew how to check vitals now, so she helped us with triage and prioritized the patients. As Dr. Castanada, Miguel, and I worked on the more critical cases, Aishling and the other nurses cleaned and bandaged wounds. There were so many, it seemed impossible. Many died on the way to the mission or as soon as they were brought through the doors. Death and hopelessness were everywhere.

I knew I didn't have time, but I had to go to the yard for just a minute to breathe. The agony of the task at hand was taking a toll on me.

Near the front door, I saw Aishling kneeling on the floor to my right. There was blood all around her and on her clothes as she held a dying child—another victim of the demons. I saw the distant look in the child's eyes, and I saw the angels hovering, waiting to carrying her away at any moment. Through her tears, Aishling hummed one of her favorite tunes as she tried to console the little girl. The child's eyes were open and intent on her as she offered the girl a promise that everything was going to be okay.

"Sleep now, child," she crooned in the child's language. "Where you're going there's no more pain. Do you see the butterflies yet? The beautiful sunrise? Ride on the rainbow and catch a star. There's such beauty in *paraíso*. You'll love it, precious one. Sleep now." The child went limp in her arms and a sob tore through Aishling. I knelt by her to try to offer comfort, but she wouldn't allow it.

With gentle care, she laid the girl on the floor and stood, grabbing my arm. "There are so many others. We have to go, Rafe. We have to save some. We have to go!" Seeing her determination gave me a new resolve.

I had surgeries lined up back to back, so I tried to work as thoroughly yet as swiftly as possible. The small surgical room at the mission was not well equipped, but we worked with what we had available. Following a grueling surgery, I took a break on the front lawn and stared up at the shifting colors of sunset. The steady stream of patients dwindled as the Creator painted the sky the colors of impending nightfall. Some of my stress departed, and I thanked Him for the moment of solitude. There were about thirty patients still waiting to be seen and three surgeries still to be performed. We worked nonstop into the night.

As tired as I felt and as hard as that last surgery was to perform, I kept pushing myself. I had to do my part. Flashbacks of Aishling holding that dying child in her arms motivated me, and I just couldn't let her down. I saw her for about five minutes around suppertime, when she brought me some food between surgeries. Her spirits were up, and it was good to see her smile.

Around eleven that night, I finished my last surgery for the day. There was a less serious operation scheduled for the morning, but our group would be able to go back to the house now and get a little rest.

When I found them, David and Aishling were taking inventory of the remaining food supply.

"Hey, Rafe," Aishling said wearily.

"Hey, yourself," I returned. I moved to her side.

I would have held her in my arms; it looked as if she needed to be held, but then David spoke, stopping me in my tracks. "Rafe, if we have the same numbers coming through for food and medicine each day, there will only be enough to last for about three more days. With a disaster of this magnitude, these people will need food supplies for at least a month."

We went to Dr. Castanada to tell him about our findings. He told us that governments from other nations were responding to the disaster and would be pouring in aid to help with the deficit. He didn't know if their response would come soon enough to keep the people from starving and to help with their medicinal needs. Aishling was tuned in to what the doctor was saying. She listened and looked away, listened and looked away again. Finally she asked Dr. Castanada if one of the government workers who had been there at the mission had a phone. She said she needed to make an urgent call to the Irish government. I remembered then that she had said her father was in politics, but I suspected he had much more power than she had revealed.

She followed the doctor outside to a vehicle that held a satellite phone. After explaining the situation, she was allowed to make her call. I stood at a distance in the darkness, hidden in the shadows of the wraparound porch, as I strained to hear. I knew I was eavesdropping, but I couldn't help myself.

"This is Aishling Delaney, code eight five eight alpha. I need to speak with the president of the Executive Council." There was a pause.

Exhaling, she fired, "Tiarnan Delaney is my father, and it is a matter of urgency that I speak with him immediately!" She spoke with authority, her Irish Gaelic accent rounding out her words.

A short time later, her request was apparently granted, and I listened to this very passionate one-sided conversation with a great passion of my own.

"Father, please don't start with me!" she said. "I can't take it right now. Have you been watching the news and heard of the great disaster in Honduras today?" There was a short pause before she went on.

"I'm in Honduras trying to help the people here. I came with a group from Costa Rica on a medical mission trip earlier in the week."

She spoke in a rush, almost like she was afraid he would hang up if she didn't get everything in fast.

"I know I didn't tell you—"

"Yes, I should have, but—"

"Yes, I understand the risk, but—"

"Father, this goes beyond you or me. There are thousands of people here that will go hungry in a few days if the Irish government doesn't step in to help.... Yes, other governments are sending aid, but the red tape is causing delays. The people need food and supplies *now!*"

Exhausted by the conversation, she seemed to lose her seemingly eternal patience. "Are you going to help or do I need to call Anlon...? I'm in Comayaguela.... Fine then! I'll see you the day after tomorrow. Goodbye, Father."

I watched as she handed the phone back to the government worker, and then she sat down on a rock on the other side of the vehicle, slumped over with her face in her hands. She looked defeated. It seemed that she needed a private moment, so I moved back into the building, digesting this new information I'd gathered. Her father wasn't just in politics; he had to be a powerful government official. He also was disapproving of his daughter's being on a mission trip, and she had not asked permission or told him where she was going. I knew that Aishling felt that coming on this mission trip was the right thing to do; she would do the right thing regardless of any roadblocks. That was one of the many things that attracted me to her. Aishling would never ask for such a favor for herself, but like she had told him, this wasn't about her. Every day I was falling harder for her.

Aishling came back into the mission building a short time after I had. She had impressively wiped all signs of strain off her face in that short time, and she came in to inform Dr. Castanada about her phone call. She assured him that the Irish government would be there in two days to bring food and supplies. He thanked her profusely, without any questions.

By the time we arrived back at the Peace Corps facility, it was midnight. The house we were staying in had sustained some roof damage, but it had been patched while we were gone during the day. Everyone headed to get some rest.

"Aishling, can I talk to you for a minute?" I asked, stopping her at the front door.

She paused before turning around, but in answer to my question, she moved to sit beside me on the couch.

"Are you okay?"

In a very Aishling manner, she refocused my question toward me. "Are *you* okay, Rafe? You had an impossible day. I can't even imagine the stress you were under. All those surgeries...."

"I'm fine," I said as I reached out to hold her hand between both of mine. I could see that her struggles still raged within her, and I tried to read her heart. Her mom, her love for her father, his stubbornness, Kavanaughs, faerie cross, Delaneys, the Challenger, war, Patrick—always Patrick. *What does all of this mean?*

I couldn't read thoughts. I could only see desires of the heart—people or objects a person was devoted to. But I wished desperately that I could read her mind so I could piece these things together. Aishling had unparalleled caverns in her heart that included thousands of people. I was in there too, but unfortunately I was overshadowed by the aforementioned list. This had to stop. It was driving me insane. I made a pact with myself right then and a silent promise to her that I would no longer search her heart. It was unfair for me to have this advantage over her. If I were going to have any chance to earn her love, I had to start acting normal—mortal. That didn't mean I wasn't going to search other hearts, though, like her father's when he arrived in a couple of days—and this Patrick's when he visited in December. After all, demons do have limits to their self-restraint.

"You seem troubled, Aishling. I want to help," I offered, but she looked away.

"I'm okay, Rafe. It's late, and you need your rest so you can be sharp for surgery in the morning. I'm going to hit the shower before I turn in. Good night," she said. She took her hand from mine and stood up.

Patience, Rafe. Patience, I told myself.

"Good night then, Aishling. Sweet dreams." I watched her walk away.

Before she closed the door, she looked back and gifted me with her angelic smile. "You too, Rafe," she responded, and I did dream sweet dreams—of her.

52

Storm Front

(Rafe)

efore dawn, the phone awakened me. Dr. Castanada needed all of our help at the mission. There was a severe outbreak of dengue fever transmitted by mosquitoes. The mission was clogged with hundreds of people who suffered from the acute illness. There's no treatment for it; all we could do was focus on relieving the symptoms, with fever being the one we needed to monitor the most. The Peace Corps was focusing on the mosquito problem.

By the time we arrived, cots had been brought in from the Peace Corps facility and set up in the fenced-in yard, for there was no room left to hold everyone inside the building. Mosquito nets were linked together to form a huge canopy around the lawn. The less severe patients were in the yard along with the volunteers taking care of them. I watched Aishling for a moment as she moved from patient to patient. She had taken to nursing with surprising speed and moved with competence, checking temperatures, massaging muscles that were contorting with pain, and bringing blankets to those who were chilled. I worried about her contracting the illness. We all had worn long sleeves and pants and had practically bathed in mosquito repellant, but these predators were relentless.

I was finishing with one patient that afternoon when word came that the officials from the Irish government were there to deliver the crucial supplies they'd promised. When I entered the waiting room, there seemed to be nowhere to find a path through the back-to-back people. I finally made it through to the kitchen area, and I could see Aishling through the open door with a man who must have been her father. He was a little shorter than I was, about six foot two, and had impeccably styled black hair parted on one side and swept back formally to reveal a regal forehead and scowl. Even in this heat and desolation, he wore a three-piece suit, a tie, and shiny black shoes. I could also see that Aishling was trying to help one of the children at the same time that her father was yelling at her.

The kitchen door was clogged with a steady stream of people carrying supplies or food to the people in the yard. I had to find a way to get to her. Aishling pulled her father away from the anxious child toward the left corner of the yard near the building. There was a small utility room on that end with a door that led to the outside. Nobody was there at the moment.

I was halfway through the door when two fierce-looking angels grabbed my arms. Knowing these two personally, as they were members of my former squadron, I knew I wasn't going anywhere. Now, if I had still been immortal, these two would have been in for a fairly even match. After all, I had trained them and knew their weaknesses. Vitale must have been watching me and knew I was about to overstep my bounds. Their intervention wasn't just about my involvement with Aishling. I sensed that my current confinement had more to do with her father. Something about him begged for deeper investigation, but before I could take a closer look, my focus became entangled in her again.

Even though I couldn't get to her, I witnessed the whole scene and heard almost every word. Her father had grabbed her by the arm and was pulling her toward the entrance gate of the mission, while his security personnel fanned out surrounding them. Aishling dug her heels into the ground, and her father jerked backward a few steps. He turned and glared at her with incredulous eyes—a gaze that demonstrated his power and his lack of concern for his daughter's wishes, daring her to defy him.

"Aishling, I demand that ye leave with me right now!" the imperious Delaney commanded.

"No, Father! I have to stay here and help. I refuse to believe you could be so numb to all of this. These people need us. Stay and help—please!" Aishling begged.

"Ye know I cannot stay here. I only came to retrieve ya. Ye've interrupted very important business with all of this, Aishling. Don't ya realize there's a war goin' on back at home and that my people need me?"

"Do you think Mom would approve of what you're doing right now? Use your position for good, Father, not for selfish gain or clan pride."

"Ye've got yer head buried in the skawly bog, Aishling. Wake up to yer responsibility!" he fired back.

"So it's true—you've reassembled the IRA to fight this war of yours?" she asked, looking mortified.

"What if I have? Ye mind yer own business, young lady, and I'll mind mine. I'm tryin' to keep us both out of a coffin."

"If you wouldn't provoke the MacEgans, they wouldn't come after you. The way I see it, you're the instigator here, not Zhawn MacEgan!" she accused.

I watched the tension build in him as he took the back of his hand and smacked her across the face. I fought against the angels holding me, but given my limited human strength, they easily held me back. Aishling held her hand across her right eye and cheek. I knew that her face was stinging because I felt the hit too, but Aishling held her emotions in check. Her eyes watered, but she quickly fought back the tears. She didn't acknowledge his outburst.

He didn't apologize as his rant blazed on. "Ye know that ye put our entire clan at risk by staying here? Do ya not care about our survival?" He was despicable, playing on what he considered to be Aishling's weakness—her loyalty and compassion for others, particularly her clan. In reality, this was her greatest strength.

She didn't even hesitate as her heart expanded to include all the people involved in the devastation here in this place. Okay,

I know. I'd start the whole not-peeking-at-her-heart thing over again after this confrontation was settled.

"I'm sorry, Father. But there are so many more important things right now than clan wars and alliances," she said to him, and I tried to decode the encrypted message. I felt from her that this was a very weighted answer filled with so many unknown arenas on which I could only speculate. As I watched this scene unfold, I stood there immobilized, deep in thought, wondering what all the secrecy was about.

"How dare ye speak to me this way!" he accused. "I've done nothin' but provide security for you and the best of everythin'. How dare ya!"

Aishling looked at him then, resigned, and said, "I don't care about the castle or the position or the money. All I ever wanted was your love, don't you see? It seems like you used to love me before Mom died, but now you just feel lost to me, and I don't even know you anymore. I haven't recognized you for a long time." She paused, looking over her shoulder toward the sick little girl. "If you'll excuse me, I have to get back to work. Good-bye, Father."

With moistened eyes and an unsteady stride, she turned away from him. Knowing Aishling, I was sure it wasn't the physical abuse that had brought her to tears but the man's calloused soul. Her heart splintered, and it hurt like tiny needles in my chest.

"Ye ungrateful child!" he shouted toward her back as she left him standing there angry and baffled. He must have been unaccustomed to anyone refusing him. I wondered if she'd ever stood up to him before. "Aishling! Ya don't understand the world we live in. Ye've got your head buried in the mire!"

To her credit she did not counterattack. She just kept walking. With my enhanced hearing, I heard her whisper when she was about halfway back to the child, "You don't know me at all."

He yelled at her, but she moved back to the sick child. She wet a washcloth and covered the child's forehead. She ignored her father and sang to the child as she rocked her in her arms.

Standing in the doorway, watching this abuse occur and not being able to retaliate, was unbearable. I shook with an inconsolable fury. The guards gripped my arms tightly. If I got loose, I'd throttle the Irishman. How could he treat his own daughter that way? Could he not see how perfect she was? What an immeasurable gift he was just throwing away! I felt like I'd just been punched in the gut, so I couldn't even imagine how this was affecting Aishling. I had to go to her. The angels needed to let me go so I could go to her.

When her father was tucked in his helicopter and in the air, the angels released me. I started out the door, but one of the angels again grabbed my arm.

"Let her be, Raphael! She needs to settle down for a while. She's embarrassed about the ruckus."

I jerked my arm away and started out the door. "You'll not do her any good running out there half cocked," he warned again. Without acknowledging his advice, I turned back to run up the steps and disappear into the building.

With loathing, I watched the chopper fade from view. I knew that Aishling would never leave the people here unless everything was under control, so I went to find the other doctors, and we set up a schedule for shifts.

Our group now comprised one whole shift, so the five of us loaded into the van and headed back to Santa Lucía. The townspeople pitched in to help clean debris from the streets, but the damage was minor in this area. We ate supper at the same café as our first night there. Everyone was tired, to say the least, but we were in relatively good spirits. It appeared Aishling had been schooled in the art of diplomacy and was perfecting that art all throughout supper. Anyone who had not witnessed the scene unfold with her father that afternoon never would have guessed that she was in terrible pain. I kept waiting for her façade to crack, but she remained flawless.

The night was not going as I'd planned. I had hoped to confront her with the knowledge that I'd overheard part of her conversation with her father; I'd planned to prove to her that I could be trusted with her secrets. However, as we finished with our meal and roved down the cobblestone path in front of the café, Aishling said she was going to make a call back to the orphanage to let them know she was okay. Then she and Sophia were going to some of the shops there on the main street for some "girl time." I was exasperated.

Miguel, David, and I wandered toward the park, where a group was gathered listening to a band. I didn't hear the music. I couldn't take my mind off of Aishling. We had agreed to meet back at the van in an hour, so I didn't have too much longer. David and Miguel went to get some ice cream, and I stayed in the park thinking of her. She was certainly an enigma. I'd never known a more mysterious creature. Part of the puzzle was that she wasn't intentionally trying to be mysterious. She wasn't trying to prove anything to me, her family, or anyone else.

We had about fifteen minutes left before we were to meet, so I headed back toward the shops, hoping to see her a few minutes early. I was going past the supermercado when I felt an other-worldly grief overtake my soul. For a moment, I couldn't move. *Aishling!* Sure I had flown faster, as an angel, but I had never run faster than this. I saw Miguel sitting on a bench in front of a clothing store. A split second was all I needed to hand him the keys and convey to him that Aishling and I would walk back. Then, running at full speed, I took off toward the church building at the end of town. I could feel her heart beating out of her chest, out of mine. I didn't even go in the building. I knew she was in the garden.

At the entrance, I heard weeping—not crying as if someone were sad but gut-wrenching sobs. Running through the garden archway, I saw her on the ground, her back to the stone wall. Her knees were tucked into her body, and her forehead was resting on her folded arms.

She was so involved in her private pain that she didn't even hear me approach. Her anguish stirred the demons inside, making me want to seek out her father and destroy him.

"Aishling," I whispered. In a movement so quick it was supernatural, I watched the faerie girl go from being curled in a ball on the ground to standing in a defensive martial arts stance. So she had been trained to fight. That was good. It made me feel better, knowing that as small as she was, predators might not get to her so easily if she were ever challenged. But it also added another dimension to my study of her, leaving me mystified yet again. It was amazing that such a tiny thing could possess such potential power.

53

Lost Searcher

(Aishling)

There were so many circumstances I had no control over, and my thoughts about them all were making me physically ill. Yes, my tears were due in part to my father and our broken relationship. They were also for my mother—the fact that she was lost out there in a distant realm, and I didn't know what the Searcher in me was searching for in order to free her. Concentration, meditation—nothing had loosed the faerie cross in my mind that would reveal this snippet of information. Then there was Patrick. Father was pushing the marriage now more than ever because of the political ramifications. He needed the Kavanaughs on his side in this war of his.

But what I had the least control over was this immersing need for Rafe. As I thought of him, I looked up and he was there. I wasn't surprised. Somehow I knew he would always find me regardless of the barriers. Shaking my head, I tried to remember where I was. I looked down, unaware that I had even surged to my feet. Slowly I unclenched my fists and dropped my arms.

Driven by emotions so raw and bleeding, I rushed the line of contention in the way of the Irish, nothing held back. I leapt into his waiting arms. The look of fire, of predators, was back in his eyes, but I didn't care. "*Tá mo chroí istigh ionat*! [My heart is within you!]" I confessed before I crushed my lips to his. A growl tore from within him, and for a moment I thought he might lose control—that this might be the end for me. I could feel his nails digging into my back, and it took all my strength to pull my face from his.

"Rafe? Look at me." I crooned. His fingers eased from my back, and he placed my feet on the ground. I watched as he tried to regain control. "My heart beats within you, and I feel yours in me," I revealed as I held on to his arms and closed my eyes.

After a brief moment, I heard him whisper, "My heart is within you too." I looked up. The fire was gone. With passion he affirmed, "You know...you *know* that you've always had my heart. I love you so much!"

My eyes squeezed shut for a moment. Then I stared at his chest before lifting my gaze to his. "I love you, too, Rafe."

His smile was so beautiful as he grabbed me up in a hug and swung me around, laughing.

"I'm the happiest person alive," he beamed.

Leaning my cheek on his chest, I sank into the warmth of his embrace, and said, "I remember the kiss on the night of the storm, in the tree. I remember, Rafe! I know what you are. And I don't care."

He lifted my chin, and I looked up to see tears in his eyes. He trailed kisses from my eyebrow down to my chin. I leaned up to kiss the scar, the cause of our separation for so long. As so many emotions overwhelmed me, my legs gave way, and Rafe caught me. Cradling me in his arms, he carried me to a nearby bench in the garden and held me in his lap.

"Are you okay, love?" he asked, looking down at me with concern on his face.

"Aye," I reassured.

A cool breeze winged through the garden. When I shivered he wrapped me tighter in his arms. Strangely, with the immense danger I was in at this moment, I had never felt more secure. With his free hand, he caressed my face; my eyes closed and a sigh escaped my lips. Reality soon intruded. With regret, I advised, "We'd better get back. It's late and they'll be wondering where we are."

"It's okay. Miguel has the keys to the van. I told him that when I found you we'd walk back. So we're in no hurry."

"I'm sorry you had to see me like this," I said, moving to sit on the bench beside him. He put his arm around me and drew me as close to him as possible.

"Aishling, I came to find you this afternoon, and I heard the argument with your father. You have every right to be upset. Can you explain to me why he treats you this way? I don't mean to pry. I just need to understand."

"Yes, I suppose you do," I agreed, taking a moment to look out at the darkening mountains. "My mom died of some kind of rare blood disorder before I turned seven. My father won't talk to me about it. He's had me tested, and it appears that I didn't inherit that from her. What I did get from her, though, was her love for people. Oh Rafe, you would have really liked her! She was an amazing woman, and everyone loved her. Even those who were natural enemies of my father couldn't help but love her. I think they only pretended to tolerate him for her sake."

Burrowing into his chest, I continued, "There are so many myths in Ireland concerning its politics that sometimes reality and legend get mixed. My father is a member of the Irish parliament, as are most of the clan leaders, but my father also has an assumed power handed down to him from centuries of folk legends. It's very hard to explain. Before my mom died, there had been peace among the clans for several centuries. But after her death my father became consumed by hatred. He barely noticed me anymore. As his pain from the loss of my mom increased, the hostility among the clans in our province escalated. It was like he was starting his own war to soothe his pain. At first I thought he wanted to die, and I was afraid I would lose both my parents." I stopped, shaking my head to will away the bad memories. "Anyway he tends to take his power to extremes."

Rafe squeezed my shoulder in support, and then he stood to face me. I could tell there was something he wanted to say or ask, but he was having trouble voicing it. Finally he spoke. "What did your father mean when he said you're putting the whole clan at risk by being here?"

I'd been afraid he had heard that part—the one question I didn't want to answer. I stood, facing away from him. "It's just more Irish legend and assumed power stuff. It doesn't matter."

"Aishling," he entreated, turning me to face him. "Whatever involves you matters to me." He wrapped his arms around me, holding my head to his chest. A chorus of tree frogs croaked, as we stood in the encroaching darkness. I was able to tune out all the chatter as I closed my eyes and listened to his heartbeat—steady, just like the man who held me.

In the next second, I was falling.

"Rafe!" I called out, but he wasn't there.

The blue flying helix wrapped me in its core; it was like being caught up in a vortex that lifted me from the ground. But instead of wind, this was the swarm of dragonflies that saved me in the jungle. I gasped and wrapped my arms around my body. Squeezing my eyes shut, I tried to wish myself back to Rafe's arms, back to safety. When I lifted my lids, a tranquil feeling warmed me, stilling my fear. The dust of Diaga swirled within the whirlwind, and I breathed in its strange power. Every so often, hulking wings softly grazed me, merging to form the effect of helicopter blades.

Dropping my gaze to the ground, I was startled to find a massive faerie, watching me with adoring eyes. He was about Micah's height and had the build of a soldier. His raven hair fell to his shoulders. The cloak he wore was the reverse of mine—black on the outside with blue scrollwork inside. He seemed familiar somehow, and I cocked my head to return his intense perusal.

In his right hand he wielded a Gaelic claymore very similar to my own. He tensed and then dropped his weapon; the metal rang out on its descent to the earth. The faerie stepped forward and lifted his hands to the sky. The dragonfly swarm flew higher with the lift of his hands, and in the process, lifted me higher in the night sky.

I could sense the anger he tried to shield from me, as he turned toward some threat below and roared. Two of the dragonflies broke ranks and barreled into the woods.

There were other emotions he allowed to slip through that slammed into me, feelings that caressed me in my flying shackles, the powerful dragonflies. For a minute I let his affection wash over me. His love fed me, offering beautiful memories from what seemed like a thousand years. This being knew me. I saw myself in his dreams, and I was the most desirable woman in all the realms. He loved me with a fierce, all-consuming love.

Then Rafe seemed to push away the competing thoughts. I needed him. The power that Rafe and I shared began to shove against the feelings of the strange faerie now pacing the bottom rung of the helix.

A howl of pain coiled around me, squeezing me. I couldn't breathe. For a brief instant, the faerie let me into his eyes. I saw myself in a hundred poses. Only me. I didn't know how to help him. I needed to go. Suddenly I left his mind, and I was back in the spin, breathless, hurt—because a strong part of me wanted to stay with him. I belonged here. I felt it.

"You will join us soon, my queen." He bowed, his now blank eyes never leaving mine.

A boom of eerie laughter crept from the shadows, and the helix disbanded, dropping me about twelve feet into the waiting arms of the faerie; he cradled me possessively in his arms. Wings of Egyptian blue and navy formed a barricade between the intruder and me. A menacing buzz rippled down the length of the dragonfly brigade.

"Well, if it ain't two of the most esteemed members of the formidable Tuatha Dé Danann," an unidentified voice boomed to the assembled group. The man paced in shadows, and I strained to see his face. "Yer lookin' particularly magical, Miss Delaney." He paced closer to the dragonflies, but the only impression of him that I could form was that I would not want to meet him in the moors. "Kaél MacEgan, me boy," he said to the faerie holding me, "I see ye brought yer self-righteous dragonflies to the party." He snarled, spitting toward the winged creatures that appeared to be shielding me.

"MacEgan!" my mind shouted. I looked at the faerie in a new light.

A unified hiss rumbled low, while the dragonflies faced the threat. From the side, I studied the dragonfly floating right in front of the faerie and me. Its sapphire eyes covered the entire upper half almost like a motorcycle helmet, stretching across the cheeks to the ears and all along the forehead. The nose and mouth appeared like a wolf's snout, and the creature growled, revealing sharp fangs. The blue wings were expanded to about eight feet from tip to tip, looking like crinkly fabric.

While the troops from the ends of each side of the line converged on our mystery guest, I turned to look up into the face of my family's ancient rival as he cradled me high in his arms. For many centuries, the MacEgans and the Delaneys had been at war—over what, I wasn't even sure anymore. I didn't believe I knew this particular MacEgan, but I was certain that being with him would constitute treason against the Delaneys, and they didn't take betrayal lightly. This Káel person was focused only on me now, and I on him as I tried to figure it all out, as I tried to piece together why I was with them and why this one seemed so compelling to me.

"Aishling!" his voice faltered as he said my name. Strong emotion rode his eyes. "It's almost time."

"Time? Time for what? Why am I here?" I screamed. There was a ruckus happening in the background, but I barely heard it. Flashes of flapping wings drew my attention upward, away from his searching gaze. The large winged creatures chased away the enemy until there was silence. A whooshing sound increased in volume as it approached us, and I looked back to see that the larger beasts had transformed into the smaller batlike dragonflies from my vision so many years ago, and they swarmed around

Káel and me. Together their beating wings composed the song of my music box.

I was not staying here one minute more. I left the vision feeling weak, having forced myself out of that world. I had never been able to exert my will in a vision before, but I'd just learned another skill I was capable of. My eyelids fluttered open to see the man I'd fully given my heart to: Rafe.

They say that vision is the power to perceive what will be. I had come to the conclusion that my supernatural perception was distorted. What did my future hold? I was holding him now. And that was the opposite of my so-called destiny. Of course I knew there was a monster to slay within him. Vision produces clarity of thought and inspires action. I was not so naïve as to think it was simply going to disappear.

54

Uninvited

(Aishling)

Three days later, Sophia, David, and I left Honduras. Rafe and Miguel were staying for another week to try to keep the storm-related disease outbreaks from getting worse. It was the most difficult good-bye of my life. By the time Rafe would arrive back in Costa Rica, I would already be facing my fate in Ireland, and the odds were not good that I would ever return.

"Welcome home," Micah said without his usual humor as I came through the door of the hut. "You're early. We weren't expecting you back for another couple of hours."

"Yeah, well, we caught an earlier flight," I mentioned, looking toward the crib where Kaillech bounced and babbled. Her eyes widened when she saw me. She must have thought I'd left her forever. I rushed to my daughter, swung her up in the air and brought her to my chest to squeeze. She clung to me with her head on my shoulder while I talked with Micah and rubbed her back, and then she reached up to pat my face. It was such a sweet moment that my mind tried to block any future trips away from her, but I knew there was one more—one I'd have to take alone. The Ten Colds Moon loomed.

"I'm so exhausted," I mumbled, slumping down on the couch. Micah and I sat and talked for about an hour as we passed Kaillech back and forth. He was engrossed in my recollection of the events of my trip. He seemed different, more reserved, like he had grown up more in the two weeks I'd been gone.

Looking to the window, I noticed that the last traces of daylight were rapidly fading. "Well, I'd better run back to the car for my bags before it gets too dark. I'll just be a minute. Can you grab the little pixie for me?"

"Of course," he sang, snatching her up. She smiled, revealing a tooth that had emerged on the bottom row of her mouth and another that was beginning to break through.

"Look at those teeth!" I drawled, pulling down her lip as Micah held her. Her grin spread as she showed them off for me.

"Yep. That's my girl." He kissed her on the cheek, and she giggled.

Watching them together was heartwarming. Micah was great with Kaillech. He was so involved with tickling my daughter, I'm not sure he heard me say, "Be right back."

In the short time I was gone, Micah transformed the room into a colorful party atmosphere. When I opened the door, he yelled, "Surprise!" Kaillech squealed, with a trace of chocolate icing on her cheek, more icing down her arm, and a wad of cake being pulverized in her tiny fist.

Taking everything in at once, I burst into a fit of laughter. He had built a giant web of orange, blue, and purple streamers, and he was trying to get untangled from the center of the web without bringing the whole contraption down. While he worked, he had placed Kaillech in her highchair too close to the cake, and she had taken full advantage of the occasion. The harder I laughed, the bigger mess Kaillech made. Rushing to the sink, I grabbed a towel to wet it, and I started cleaning her while Micah sank to the floor under the streamer web and crawled to the kitchen.

"Well, that didn't exactly work out like I'd planned," he said, coming up from behind. He put his hands on my waist and leaned over me to laugh at Kaillech while I continued to de-frost her. He was making me uncomfortable, so I decided to remove Kaillech from the chair and bathe her. I had gotten off most of the cake already, but this diversion tactic would put a more familiar distance between Micah and me.

I was on the floor beside the tub, floating a rubber duck toward Kaillech when Micah came to stand in the doorway. He had removed his leather duster, which was a rarity. Granted, the ceilings in the hut were only seven feet high (the tiny bathroom doorframe was six feet), but because of that fact, Micah looked even more massive in the small space. He was so tall; he had to lean over, his arms raised above him resting on top of the doorframe.

His chin-length hair, the color of golden wheat fields, was pulled back again into a ponytail, and a generous lock had escaped the band on either side of his face. With his signature angel-gone-rogue grin, he showed off his perfect teeth. He had on a snug white T-shirt tucked into a stylish pair of jeans. Right now he looked more man than angel, and he was gazing at me in such an affectionate way, I wanted to run out the door and take on the jaguars rather than face him. Yeah, he was nice-looking, but he was a brother figure to me, and brothers didn't stare at their sisters this way.

I started to reach up to grab a towel to wrap Kaillech in when he entered the tiny room. "Let me get that for you," he said. As I picked Kaillech up and placed her in the towel he was holding, his arm brushed mine, and I looked up. The trance that he held me in spoke of a longing I'd never really sensed from him before. I was so confused. He knew he didn't belong here on earth, so why pursue a human? Or was his peculiar behavior since I'd returned just because he'd missed his best friend? I didn't know what was going on in that glorious head of his, but I knew I was going to have to put a stop to whatever was forming in there.

"Excuse me," I said, trying to get past him. But there was no escape; I was pinned in.

While a bundled Kaillech snuggled closer into his chest to get warm, an unsettling silence passed between us before I spoke again. "What's wrong?"

"Something about you has changed, and I'm trying to put my finger on it." He seemed to be examining me like I might shape-shift into a faerie in the next moment.

"Well, I can assure you I'm just the same old Aishling." Shooing him toward the den, I realized that the initial signs of claustrophobia or something equally disturbing were settling in, and I needed some space. As he cleared the door, I rushed around him toward the table. Cutting a piece of cake, I gave myself a few moments to settle my jangled nerves before turning back to him.

"The cake is delicious. Thanks for the party, Micah. It was very thoughtful of you."

He shrugged it off as he towel-dried Kaillech's hair, and then he slipped her pajamas over her head. "I missed you," he confessed, and then he kissed Kaillech's cheek and put her in the crib. "I'm thinking that mission trips are overrated." He moved to take my hand and pulled me to the couch.

"And this coming from an angel! You of all people—I mean you of all beings should be promoting mission work."

He still had not let go of my hand. Kaillech had pulled herself up and was staring at us through the bars of the crib like a mini felon, which made me smile, dropping my anxiety level a few bars on the apprehension meter. I turned my attention back to Micah.

"There are plenty of people to do His work elsewhere. You are needed here," he said. "That's why your trip here was orchestrated, so you could minister to the orphans and protect Kaillech."

Dropping my head in thought, I was surprised when Micah tilted my chin toward him. "And I need you here," he stated, placing his massive hand on my cheek as he stared at my lips.

Uh, oh...big time! I was so caught up in my own drama; I didn't read the signs. I didn't stop to consider what our time together might mean to a being unfamiliar with human relationships.

Pushing against his chest, I tried to gain some leverage, but there was no quick fix for this situation. His strength could hold me unyieldingly to this spot for the duration of my life if that were his goal, but my weakness and the resulting tears were the keys that broke open the lock of his meekness. He let go. Burying my face in my hands, I tried not to cry. I tried to pretend that I was invisible. How could an angel even think this way? I pondered. Micah was supposed to be different. He was a guardian angel. I wasn't supposed to feel so exposed, so vulnerable, so open to attack with him. Not him! I wasn't supposed to have to build a wall of defense against this angel who I'd come to depend on—not only as Kaillech's guardian but also as my own.

"What's going on with you, Micah?" I reprimanded him.

"Well, that's not the reaction I was hoping for," he grumbled, rubbing his hand down his face before leaning forward to rest his elbows on his knees. He rubbed his hands together. His head was dropped, and I could tell he was hurt, but I was hurt too and I didn't know how to help him. I just wanted things to return to normal, but I didn't see how they could. For a moment I thought about uninviting him to the earth realm. He'd still be nearby if Kaillech needed him, but we wouldn't have to see him every day.

"Micah, I need to be alone right now, and I think we both need a few days apart to bring some perspective back to our relationship." I remained seated while he lumbered to the door.

"Ash, you know I'm crazy about you. I don't think anything could ever change that fact. If you need me to stay away a few days, I'll be out of sight, but I won't be gone. If you need me, all you have to do is say my name, and I'll be here." With that said, he ducked through the opening and closed the door behind him.

A couple of days after the "incident," I called Micah's name. I was beside myself with worry over Kaillech. I couldn't get her to eat, make her happy, nor seem to get her to stop crying. In other words I needed help. She wanted Micah. As much as I was not ready to face him yet, I called out for him for Kaillech's sake.

"Hey," he said, appearing by the door. "What's up?" He tried to act as if this was a normal day in our joined-at-the-hip lives, but

I could tell he was still bleeding. As I was about to answer, Kaillech cried, and he moved to lift her from the crib.

"I don't know what's wrong with her other than the teething. Her temperature is slightly elevated, but I read somewhere that babies often run fevers when they're teething."

As I explained what little I knew, Micah carried Kaillech with him toward the refrigerator, rocking her up and down as he went. The crying intensified. He grabbed some ice cubes from the freezer, placed them in a glass that was sitting on the counter, and then filled the glass with water. After a moment, he turned Kaillech around, stuck his index finger in the frigid water, and then stuck his finger in her mouth. As the coolness soothed her aching gums, she relaxed while she chewed. He rescued his finger, thrust it into the water again, and before he could bring it back to her mouth, Kaillech had captured it and brought it the rest of the way. She was making the cutest sucking sounds.

"You might want to buy her a couple of teething rings so you have one in the freezer getting cold while she chews on one," he advised.

"I'm so inexperienced."

"You're a great mother, Ash. I'm just here to fill in the gaps in your education."

"Thanks, Micah. I don't know what we'd do without you. I mean it," I said, wanting to convey my gratefulness but also hoping to repair some of the damage from a few days ago.

"About the other night, Ash, I—"

"You don't have to do this, Micah," I interrupted. "Let's just let it go. Okay?"

"What if I don't want to let it go?" He moved toward me, but Kaillech was between us this time, so I felt somewhat safer. His whole body reeked of emotion on a broad spectrum from frustration to fear to guilt, even to anger. His eyes bore down on me, and his expression made it seem as if he could read me, and he didn't like the competition he saw in the inside edition. I was glad he couldn't really see what was going on within me, because then I would be forced to admit that while I did love Micah, it was the love of a brother, one I would have loved to grow up with.

And Patrick—it was evident we had shared a case of young love that obviously didn't endure the torment of growing pains.

My love for someone else was so much more—someone I was connected to in a way I'd never been connected to anyone. Although I believe there are many people in our lives who draw out strong feelings, there is only one who can expose the soul of another—and that someone for me was Rafe.

It confused me even further when Micah backed down. I watched the intense emotion drain from his features, and my bantering friend returned. "Okay, fine, I'll leave it alone—for now, a *ghrá* [love]." With a potent wink, he handed Kaillech back to me and disappeared.

55

Blood Book

(Aishling)

Over the next few days, when Micah came by the hut, I noticed that a cynical attitude had emerged. He was withdrawn, and I knew that the one thing that would cause this change in my friend was rejection. I tried to lighten the mood when we were together, but he didn't seem to want peace. He was moody and gruff, with a look to rival any brawler looking for a fight.

One evening, out of the blue, we both spouted off questions at the same time.

"What is *wrong* with you?" I ranted.

"Who's Rafe?" he accused.

He looked away.

"You've been spying on me?" I spat. How else would he know Rafe's name? I certainly hadn't mentioned it. So many responses came to my mind to answer the question he had posed, but I refused each one.

"Yes. Yes, I have. I care about you, Ash."

After a moment I relented, "Rafe's the doctor who led the medical mission trip to Honduras, and he's a good friend of mine."

Without answering my own question, he jerked open the door, slammed the screen against the outside wall, and tromped off into the jungle. As I watched him, I wondered how an angel could have such lack of control in regard to his emotions. His behavior since I'd returned from Honduras had been so erratic.

I wished so much to have the old Micah back, but I didn't know if that could ever be.

A few days later, on Saturday, I planned to take Kaillech to the park in town for a little while. She was starting to sit up a bit, and I thought she might enjoy being out in the sunshine. I would have to leave her late the next night, and I had been nauseated for days worrying about her, questioning her future. Would Micah raise her at the angel refuge? Should I take her to Ireland with me and choose one of my relatives to raise her? Micah's research was not exhaustive; I had a lot of bad relatives, but I also had some who were good. I even had a fleeting thought that I might actually accomplish my goal of slaying the indomitable beast so I could return to her. She cooed and I swiveled toward the crib, lifting her into a morning hug. Holding her head to my chest, I savored the moment, allowing her to yank my hair as she giggled. I settled her on my hip and I wiped tears away.

Soon, I was putting her things in the car when a private messenger service vehicle pulled up. The man who stepped out of the driver's side could have been a bouncer. He moved toward me with a package and clipboard in hand and some sort of pouch slung over his shoulder. My college portrait was attached to his paper. He looked from it to me. "Aishling Delaney?"

"Yes?"

The pouch hanging on his shoulder held a small electronic machine that he pointed toward me. "It's a fingerprint recognition device. Put your index finger inside, please."

I obeyed this very over-the-top request, and after a few seconds a beep sounded. He pulled the machine away from me and looked at the monitor.

"Sign here," he said, handing me a pen. I guess I passed the test. He handed me the package and turned to leave.

Seeing the return address, I knew what was inside. It was the ancient *Chronicle of Íosa* manuscript from the Kavanaughs' library vault, which I had requested from Uncle Brádach. There were only three of these books in existence, so I knew it was very valuable, but I would do anything to help my mom. While in Honduras I'd had a vision, and in it I was holding this book. It was a key, and I had to figure out what it unlocked.

Uncle Brádach had tried to talk me out of it. "Legend says the book is dangerous," he had said. "That's why it's in the vault. Nobody's opened it for centuries." But when I had explained about my mom being lost and how the book could help release her, he had reluctantly agreed to send it.

"Thank you, Uncle Brádach," I said out loud, putting the package in my backpack. I'd have to wait until I got to the park to explore its contents since it was almost time to feed Kaillech again, so we headed off to Tilarán.

Costa Rica is one of the sunniest places on earth, and that day was the epitome of glorious weather. After a sweltering night, a front had pushed the worst of the heat out, replacing it with a tad of natural air conditioning. I lifted my face to the breeze and inhaled as I stepped out of the car at the park.

Throughout every day I was constantly telling Kaillech how much I love her, and I told her again now as we made our way into the park. I didn't want her to have to grow up guessing and wondering if there was love there or not, like I had.

After spreading a blanket on the ground underneath an old sandbox tree, I laid some of her toys out and played with her. She was so beautiful. Her hair was getting a little longer and was naturally curly and black like mine, but hers had a different texture. I grieved for her buried mother. And I grieved for her father, that for whatever reason, he was unable to see her grow and witness her childlike sweetness and angelic laughter.

I carried Kaillech around the park, stopping from time to time to peek at other babies. After a while we made our way over to the swing set. I put her in my lap, and we swung for a while.

Every time we'd reach the pinnacle in the air, she'd laugh that carefree laugh of childhood, and my heart would soar. As we played I vowed that I would do everything within my power to ensure that she never had to feel any fear or loneliness, that she could live her life with joy, and that it would be filled with many people who loved her.

Under the tree we ate our lunch and talked to passersby. By the time our meal was over, I could tell that Kaillech was about to drift off to her dreamworld, so I laid her in her seat and loaded everything back into the car. Since I had parked at the end of the lot between some trees, we were alone.

I was putting her dusty sandals on the floorboard beside my backpack when I remembered the package. With the windows rolled down and a light breeze drifting through, Kaillech napped while I climbed into the front seat and opened the book flat on my lap. It was so old and musty, I could almost smell the battles and the years that had passed since the Gaels had transcribed it. The manuscript was bound at each corner with worn leather strips run through rough holes in the yellowed parchment. As I turned the first crinkly page, I could hear the waiting secrets that had been bound up for centuries. A rush of images flashed before me along with Gaelic phrases being whispered in the distance. While my mind whirled, I tried to focus on one of the images, but it rushed past, not wishing to be disturbed. This was no ordinary book. The pages were smeared with blood, making a large majority of the text impossible to read.

An otherworldly wind, which sounded and felt like breath, was filled with electric crackles and Diaga dust as it coursed through the passenger window, leaving the surrounding trees unaffected. The pages of the book flipped swiftly and my hair whipped through the other window, straight as a windswept flag. One of the dragonflies I was beginning to recognize as my own landed on the window ledge. Its head tilted sideways as it peered at me with intelligent eyes. I squeezed my lids shut. This part of the vision was the detail I had hoped to avoid. Yet, as I opened my eyes, I knew the dragonfly waited. The wind still tore through the car, but the pages ceased their turning. The two pages holding the midpoint of the chronicle were obscured by dried blood. In my mind, I reached out to the hawthorn tree and retrieved my bag of dust as I felt the tree etching and tingling onto my face. The leather pouch appeared in my right hand. I held up my left hand and the bat-sized dragonfly soared to land there, its furry legs tickling my hand.

Working now on instinct alone, I grasped the dragonfly by the tail. Its wings vibrated so fast, they were barely visible. A hum winged to my ear and a pleasant vibe stole my senses. With my free hand, I reached into the bag to grasp a handful of dust. I held the dragonfly over the book, its wings strumming a beat. Lifting my other hand high in the air, I sprinkled the dust of Diaga down through the holey wing structure. The page glowed and the blood lifted from the book to float in the air. The dragonfly tugged on my hand and I let go. The creature flew through the air to capture the life drops before it soared out the window and disappeared.

On the left hand side of the page, a paragraph was handwritten in the old script. There were a few words I was able to decipher: *Lubog*—a hole covered with water, *Abhainn*—river, *Geasar*—geyser, and *Uaimh*—cave. The diagram on the right had been in my vision. I recognized the ogham symbols for the four elements as well as the names of the twelve winds.

I reached out to touch fire, and I was slammed into darkness.

My mother called to me from the shadows. I ran toward the sound of her voice, among the woody heather thickets, toward the hill beyond the moors. As soon as I reached her, she grabbed my hand, and we ran through the bramble. Flaming arrows screamed past our heads, illuminating the blackness and setting the scrubby woodland afire. Soon loosed from the twisting briars, we escaped up the hill and crouched down behind a large boulder as a second round of arrows raced and plummeted overhead. The years melted away as I stared at her. She was strong, very different from the last year of her life on earth, when the blood disorder had sapped her vitality. What I couldn't understand was why we were both drenched.

I looked around, trying to gain a sense of our location. The bushes were burning out, and all was becoming dark again. Suddenly a light flared in the distance. My attention travelled down the hill about a half mile to the west. The key that I had needed fit into the lock, and the door was opened. The backdrop of the ruins of Mellifont Abbey was vivid in the blaze of the Dullahan's lantern. I would always recognize that tall square-towered gatehouse as the place where we'd had our last family picnic before Mom had died. Considering the fact that I was wet and we were apparently at River Mattock, the last piece fit into place, and I was able to burst through the mental door. I knew where the Dullahan's lair was. I knew what I had to do, and I was fairly certain that I would die in the process.

The shouts were coming closer, but I couldn't resist smiling. I had missed Mom so much, and she was holding my hand now. The last thing I heard before the vision evaporated was "*Maraígí roimh a sealsa í* [Kill her before her time]!" I awakened with a gasp to the blinding light of a Costa Rican noon.

I turned to see Kaillech still in her peaceful dream world as I departed my turbulent dream otherworld. I knew I'd have to leave her soon, and the mere thought of that clutched my heart in a vise grip. I didn't want to think about it anymore, not that day. Facing the front I wiped the sweat from my neck with a towel, slammed the book shut, cranked the car, and headed home.

Later that evening, while Kaillech slept, I sat down to write a very difficult letter—a farewell to Rafe.

56

The Soul's Lantern

(Aishling)

I felt my sins stacking up, but time was running out; I had no alternative. If I had not deceived Micah, he would have followed me and joined the battle, and what if something happened to him? This battle was supernatural; angels could die too. He would have left Kaillech with one of his comrades at the refuge, but she needed *him* to protect her throughout her life, not some random angel. There had been times in the past when I had almost confessed all to Micah: my fate as the Siridean, my true lineage of Maolán faerie, my love for Rafe, and my impending marriage to Patrick. It always boiled down to one question: what good will it accomplish for him to have this knowledge? I couldn't think of a reason. He knew I had some powers as a protector; he just didn't know the full extent of it.

Beginning today I was officially on my winter break from school. I had planned to stay in Costa Rica over Christmas, but then Cearnaigh had delivered the grave news—the date of the Ten Colds Moon. Now I found myself charging toward Delaney Castle in my cloak on the morn that would later give way to a sick, sinister moon.

I had left Micah and Kaillech fewer than two minutes ago, and now I stood in my bedroom in Ireland. It was early morning in Costa Rica, but it was a little after the noon hour in faerie country. Micah had questioned me, of course, especially when I could hardly let go of my baby to walk out the door, but I had told him that something had come up in Ireland and I had to go home. It was too dangerous there for Kaillech with all the clan wars, so he didn't hesitate when I asked him to watch her at the angel refuge over Christmas break for me.

After living in a hut in the jungle for most of the year, being back in my lavish bedroom was surreal. I didn't belong in the castle. Taking a brief moment to look around, I opened the door. Hopefully my father was home. I needed a moment to tell him good-bye in a roundabout way.

Christmas trees with multi-colored lights adorned the hallways in my wing, the staff's way of honoring me even though they weren't expecting me for Christmas. They knew I preferred the bright colors as opposed to the white lights in the rest of the castle. When I pushed open the door to the kitchen, pumpkin spice and nutmeg assaulted my senses. Sullie's back was to me as he prepared my father's coffee tray. He turned.

"Lady Aishling? We weren't expecting you. What a lovely surprise!"

"Hey, Sullie," I said, trying hard to smile.

"Are you here for Christmas break?" he asked with a hopeful expression.

"Yeah," I answered.

"Are you hungry?"

"Not really." I twisted my clan crest ring and looked out the window to the frosty moors. "Is my father here?"

"Yes, my lady, but I have yet to see him this morning. I was heading to his room to carry his breakfast. Shall I tell him you wish to speak with him?"

"Please. Thanks, Sullie."

He nodded and toted the tray out of the room. Sitting on a stool by the kitchen island, I picked at a blueberry muffin and watched the horses galloping in the field. I couldn't wait to see Kheelan. He would lift my spirits.

Midway through my muffin, the door swung open and Sullie rushed in huffing, in a tizzy. "Lady Aishling," he said between breaths.

I jumped off the stool, clutching his arm. "What is it?"

"It's Master Delaney...I cannot wake him. I called to him from the door, as he has commanded me to do, but there was no answer. I heard an odd mumbling. He said something about the moon."

I burst through the kitchen door and raced down the corridor, Sullie lagging far behind. As I approached my father's room, I heard an unfamiliar voice, but none of the other servants would have been in the room. Sullie was the only one allowed.

For a few seconds, I listened. The strange voice was creepy, as if it were coming through a vacuum. Then I froze. *That voice.* Immobilized, I stood, staring at the door. All these years I had struggled to block the memory, but now it exploded through the wall of reflection, filling me with grief once more.

I was six years old, and my mom lay unconscious on a hospital bed in a room of the castle. The blood disorder was stealing her life. She couldn't talk to me. She never opened her eyes. Needles were jabbed into her skin and tubes covered her pretty face. Machines surrounded her so closely; I couldn't even hold her hand anymore. I could only guard her from a distance.

Dad moved in behind me and placed his reassuring hands on my shoulders. I hadn't even heard him come into the room. He lifted me into his arms and held my head to his chest, and we both kept watch until she left this world for one far greater.

His grief ripped into me. I stood back as he slung equipment away from her. The beeping monsters crashed into the walls and shattered. He jerked the tubes from her body and held her—lifeless. I rushed into the hallway and ran to the garden. I couldn't breathe. I couldn't cry. Falling to my knees, I tried to feel—anything. I prayed for a long while.

She wasn't really gone. A lightness swept through me. I made a plan. I'd go back to the room, and when I got there, she'd be fine. The castle door was heavy, but I shoved through and sprinted back down the hallway. At the intersection of the corridors, I stopped to catch my breath. Looking to the right, three doors down, I saw a faint light spilling from mom's room, and I heard a voice other than my father's. I tiptoed closer.

"No!" my father's harsh voice boomed. "Ye're wrong."

"Your daughter *is* the reason for your wife's death. Just because you don't believe me, doesn't make it less true," the eerie voice taunted. "I can bring her back, you know."

"Get away from me, ya fiend! Don't touch 'er!"

I walked closer. A spigot of tears gushed down my face. Who was that bully, coming in here right as my mom died, and making my dad so angry? *He thinks I killed my mom?* Through the crack in the door, I saw my dad, but I could see no one else, even though I heard that menacing voice.

"Time will tell. When you learn what your daughter is capable of, you'll come find me. You'll understand. Until then…"

The door creaked as I shoved it open. I was not going to stand out there one more minute, listening to this abuse. My father gasped and looked around. Where had the stranger gone? Then my father turned to me with suspicion in his eyes. He had never looked at me that way before.

Shaking myself away from that awful flashback, I knocked, and the sounds of the stranger from my past vanished. "Father," I called out and knocked again. No answer.

I pushed open the door and stepped into the dark room, flipping the switch to turn on the bedside lamps. Sullie came in behind me. Quickly, I ran to the closet and then the bathroom, searching for the intruder. Nobody was there. *How can that be?* As I walked toward the bed, I massaged my forehead, willing the intensifying headache to crawl back under its rock and stay there.

Never had I seen my father so pale and peaked. Sweat glistened on his handsome face, less rigid in his sleep. His head rolled from side to side while eerie mutterings escaped his lips.

"Leave us, please, Sullie," I stated.

"Yes, my lady. I'll be in the kitchen if you need me." He bowed, then shut the door as he exited.

I sat on the edge of the bed and grasped my father's hand. "Wake up, Father," I begged.

His head twisted in rapid succession as he spoke a stream of disconnected thoughts. "They're comin'…it's here…Aishling… no…Aishling…"

"I'm here, Father. Open your eyes."

He was scaring me. This was too similar to the nightmares I'd been having. Grabbing his shoulders, I shook him. "Father!" I shouted.

"The moon rises…blood…" He trailed off from there with mindless babbling. It seemed that an otherworldly presence had him in its grip.

Closing my eyes, I approached the hawthorn and scanned its gnarling branches. Hanging on a thorn was my pouch, the keeper of the dust of Diaga. I snatched it down from the tree, and the thorn—the size of a railroad spike—broke off and bounced on the ground. Nothing like this had ever happened to me at the tree. I lifted the sharp barb and stowed it in the pouch with the dust. The marking felt cool on my face this time. I needed to come up with a plan so father wouldn't see what I was forced to hide.

Opening my eyes, I looked down to see the pouch in my hand. Father was still speaking gibberish. I moved to the door and peeked into the hallway. Empty. Cearnaigh had trained me in measuring dosages, so I pinched the right amount from the pouch and blew it through the air. It snaked, coiled, and flickered on its journey to the target. My dad breathed it in and his back arched off the bed. With a lengthy intake of breath, he sat up. I dashed down the back hallway as I heard him call for Sullie.

Until the marking faded, I stayed in my room. Then I wandered back to his bedroom.

Outside the door to the master suite, Sullie's voice carried. "Yes, Master Delaney, Aishling is home. She was here a moment ago."

I knocked. "May I come in?"

"Enter," my father consented. The butler cleared the remains of father's breakfast while I moved toward the bed. Turning to Sullie, he said, "That will be all I require." Sullie nodded and carried the tray out, closing the door behind him.

My father and I stared at one another. "Pull up that chair," he nodded toward his reading cove. "I need to speak wit' ya."

I did as he asked. Facing him was difficult, especially in this weakened state. The commander, I was accustomed to. This was new territory and I sat on edge, waiting for his bark. The word-battle he had waged on me in Honduras pierced me with its dagger even then, and I cringed recalling it.

"Everythin' has gone well in Costa Rica?"

"Yes, sir," I answered, wringing my hands. "Are you well, Father?"

"Nothin' to concern yerself wit'."

He sat motionless while the nightstand clock ticked one minute, then two.

"Have ye been to see Patrick?" he chided, breaking the silence.

"That's my next stop, but I wished to see you first."

"Is somethin' wrong then?"

My head drooped before I could stop it. I jerked my head to the right, my gaze landing right where I needed it the most—on mom's face. Several years after she died, my father had ordered all her pictures be taken down. It just dawned on me that now she was everywhere I had turned in the castle.

I lifted my eyes to his troubled ones, and said, "Mother is with us again."

"She never left."

My lips parted as I downed a sharp gulp of air. I squeezed my eyes shut. My father had no tolerance for tears.

I prayed that I wasn't too late to save mom. What if I did accomplish this impossible task and Dad and Mom were united for a moment? Would it change the way he saw me? Would he change?

"Aishling?"

When I felt my control strengthen, I looked up.

He didn't look away as he spoke these shocking words, "I'm sorry 'bout everythin' that happened in Honduras. And I'm sorry for takin' the strap to ya a while back."

My brows drew together in pain. *Did my father just apologize to me?* Confusion over his behavior swirled through my mind, but I was open to see another side of him.

No matter how much darkness envelops a heart, the light will refuse to extinguish. Even if there was only a speck of oil left in his soul's lantern, my father in that moment fought to rouse the dormant stream of fuel that remained.

Maybe we could have a relationship after all. That is, if I defeated the Dullahan tonight, along with the forces of hell. *No problem*, my sarcastic side threw in.

Overwhelmed by emotions I had hidden in regard to my father, my spirit screamed for escape. I reached out to embrace him and he pulled me in, running his hand down my hair. "You need to know how much...I love you. I'm sorry," I stammered. "I...I...need to go." Breaking free, I bolted from the room, grabbed my coat, and ran out the front door of the castle.

I sprinted through the side courtyard, stopped amid a small grove of trees, and fell to my knees. Leaning over to prop up with my hands, I sucked in air and exhaled, frost from my breath combined with tears, obscuring my vision. After a time, I sat back on my heels and swiped the back of my hand under my eyes. I was sure to be a mess. Maybe Uncle Brádach wouldn't notice. *Yeah, right.*

57

Rise of the ten Colds Moon

(Aishling)

While crossing the stone bridge to Kavanaugh Stables, I felt some of the tension leave my body, leeching out into the river to be swept downstream. A haunting wind whistled around me and the bare trees click-clacked. I picked up the pace, pulling my coat more snugly around me. Strings of big-bulb Christmas lights in orange, blue, red, and green were festively strung around the perimeter of the stables.

I shoved open the barn door and stepped into the smell of home—horses, hay, and leather. A singer crooned "White Christmas" over the loudspeakers and Uncle Brádach's magical voice blended in with the tune. It was so soothing to my ears, bringing back such happy memories. He stood at the makeshift counter writing in his training books, and I snuck up behind him, placing my hands over his eyes. This was an old game of ours, and I could hear his swift intake of breath. He knew I was home.

"Aishling?" he sputtered, twisting around. You have never heard the likes of the whoopin' and hollerin' that ensued as he grabbed me up and swung me in the air.

Claire stepped out of the office. "What's going on out here?" she fussed.

A shrill squeal erupted from her mouth as she came running to embrace me. She grabbed the walkie-talkie off her belt and spoke into it, "Patrick, you're needed in the stables *now!*" *Leave it to Claire to make a big deal out of my arrival.*

I was catching Claire and Uncle Brádach up on the latest news when I heard Patrick yelling from the corridor to the south. He couldn't see us as he stomped the length of those stalls. "What's so blatherin' important?"

The three of us looked at each other, trying not to laugh, as he rounded the corner. When Patrick saw me, he stopped in his tracks. Then he rushed forward to lift me into the air.

Running his fingers through my hair, he breathed one word. "Asher."

Uh oh!

"I'd say the lass has been missed," Uncle Brádach chimed in.

"You could say that." Patrick seemed to come to himself, remembering that we were not alone. With a sheepish grin he placed my feet on the ground. But he didn't let go; his arm wrapped around to pull me against his side.

"We're all excited that you're here, Ash, but we didn't think you were coming home over Christmas," Claire grilled me, "since we'll be coming to Costa Rica for holiday in a few weeks."

"Excuse us a minute," Patrick announced, taking my hand and leading me toward the office. "Asher and I need to talk." I looked back at them with my eyebrows raised. My arrival back in Ireland had caused all sorts of weird reactions.

Once we were in the office, Patrick shut the door, sat me on top of the desk, and moved in to grab my arms. "I've missed you," he said with passion. "You're even more stunning. Confident. You're all grown up, Asher."

"I've missed you too, Patrick," I reciprocated with a smile. Thoughts of Rafe cascaded in my mind like snowflakes, picture after picture on each one. I knew I shouldn't be thinking about him just then, but I couldn't help it. We were connected, probably through our combined powers.

I looked away from Patrick's serious gaze to a bookshelf that held training books and knickknacks, and I zeroed in on a picture of Patrick and me. It was my sixth birthday—right before mom got sick—with the Kavanaughs, the Delaneys, and a few classmates in attendance. Mom thought we should do things up right and have a bona fide royal party. All the parents dressed as kings and queens, and the kids as princesses and princes. The castle had never been so lavishly decorated. My emerald and diamond tiara matched my sleeveless emerald dress that trailed to the floor with a frilly tiered skirt. Patrick wore an Irish tartan kilt of green plaid, a black military jacket with service patches, a tartan beret, and a sheath around his waist with his sword.

Patrick noticed what I was staring at; he went to lift the picture and bring it to me. "I've not thought about that night in ages," I told him, as I held the picture closer and examined it. Mom was laughing in the background, as wee Patrick kissed me on the cheek.

He grinned, looking down at the picture. "I remember everybody giving us those 'Oh, they are so cute' stares."

"'Cause we were," I laughed.

"I was mad because you kept ignoring me," he admitted. "You, in your tiara and gown, were more interested in riding the dragon's—I mean, Sullie's—back and slaying the wicked faeries."

I tugged on his shirt. "And you kept trying to steal kisses from me."

"I've always been a smart fella." He winked and moved in closer. "But not the best thief. How 'bout you grant me a kiss, my princess?"

I searched his forest-green eyes. I didn't want to hurt Patrick. With a sudden jolt, I felt Rafe's heartbeat inside me veer quite a bit off-beat, and I clutched at my chest. Gnawing pain seared me, and I lay back on the desktop. I could feel the heat, and I turned sideways on the desk so Patrick couldn't see the fire I knew was in my eyes. Everything within me wanted to lash out at my best friend, which made no sense. I wanted to scream, but I knew I had to hold it in. Rafe must have come back early. He was hurting.

He had found the letter.

When I felt the heat no more, my eyes popped open, and I worried, but then I remembered the time it would take him to get here, and I calmed down, knowing that even if he did come, he would be too late. The battle would be over, and he would be safe. If by chance he were to come here, nobody knew I would be fifty or so miles north when the Ten Colds Moon rose.

"Asher, what's wrong?" Patrick was so worried. He lifted me from the desk and cradled me in his arms in the desk chair. "Your skin is so clammy. Are you ill, *a ghrá?*"

I sat up on his lap, trying to be stronger than I felt. "Must be a healthy dose of jetlag. I'll be fine. Why did you want to see me in private?" I asked, afraid—really afraid—of what he might say.

He looked at the opposite wall trancelike, but then said, "It can wait. Claire will be fiery irate with me if I keep you any longer."

I hopped down and gripped the doorknob.

"Are you sure you're okay?" he asked.

"I'm fine, Patrick," I fibbed.

"All right then. Later."

I smiled at him and went to join the rest of my family.

"While you two were in there doing whatever it was you were doing, I came up with a plan." Claire beamed. "You look a little flush, Ash," she said, smiling like she had just caught us kissing or something.

"And your plan is..." I asked, changing the subject and already knowing what she was going to suggest, as I had seen it in my vision.

"Belated birthday party! Yay!" She clapped, jumping up and down. "I've got so many preparations to make. Ash, you need to come to the house at—" She looked down at her watch, "Three o'clock. That should give us enough time to get ready. What do you say?"

"Sounds perfect," I responded, not wishing to dampen her spirits. Who knew? The Fates might smile on me tonight, and I could even make it to my party fashionably late.

Patrick backed away. "Yeah, I've got some things I need to take care of too. I'll see you later, Asher." Then he turned and jogged away.

"Okay," I replied to his retreating back as Claire took off running as well.

"Be at the castle at three o'clock, Ash."

"Okay," I repeated.

"So, what's got that boy all in a dither?" Uncle Brádach asked.

"You know...I don't know." Shaking my head, I routed toward Kheelan's stall as Uncle Brádach followed.

"Haven't seen Patrick look so shaken since the day so many years ago when ya fell in the river and he jumped in to save ye. Five years old ye were, if I remember right. It took ye several more years to learn to swim like a mermaid."

Laughing, I recalled the vague memory. "Patrick has done his fair share of saving me over the years."

"And ye yer fair share o' savin' him."

I looked over at Uncle Brádach, feeling uncomfortable. He had always picked up on our behaviors and failures as if he had a telescope that peered into our brains. I wondered how much he knew about Patrick and what had caused the rift between us.

Kheelan heard my voice and began kicking the stall door and grunting. As I approached the door, he neighed.

"Stop your barkin'!" I said with love, opening the stall door. If horses could hug, Kheelan hugged me, moving to brush up against me, waiting for me to throw my arms around him, which I did. "That's my boy." I petted him for a moment and then grabbed a brush and stroked his hair just because I knew he loved it so.

Uncle Brádach moved into the stall, leaning up against the rails. "So why are ya really here, *iníon* [daughter]?"

He had an uncanny ability to read people. I brushed Kheelan's hair in silence while I thought of what to say. I would not insult Uncle Brádach's intelligence by pretending it was just because of Christmas break. "There's something I have to do." I kept brushing.

"I see," he mumbled, taking off his hat and running his hand through his hair. "And would this *something* be related to the *Chronicle of Íosa?*"

I stopped brushing Kheelan to face him. "Yes...in a way."

"I can help, Aishling," Uncle Brádach insisted, moving beside me.

I looked up into his wise eyes. I so loved this man. "No, Uncle Brádach. I'm afraid you can't." Turning back to Kheelan, I moved the brush through his mane.

"Has the change started in ya then?"

I wheeled around.

"What?" he asked. "Ya didn't think I could put two and two together to come up wit' yer transformation into Morrighan's granddaughter, a Maolán? I've seen it comin' for years, lass. Ya can't change what ye are or who ye are."

"Does Patrick suspect?" I asked.

"No, and I don't believe ya should be tellin' him until ya have to."

"What does all this mean? Can I be a faerie and marry a human?".

"The Challenger was human, and he married Morrighan."

"True," I agreed, one arm holding my stomach while I stared at my feet.

"So has Morrighan given ya somethin' to do then?"

"No," I confided, looking him straight in the eyes. "The Moerae have."

The discussion ended. Uncle Brádach knew he couldn't challenge the Fates. I just wished I could have ebbed his tears. He thought of himself as my dad, and he felt that he failed me now, not being able to stop what was happening to me. I tried to reassure him, telling him I had been trained for what I had to do. It didn't help his feelings much.

At three o'clock, I headed into Kavanaugh Castle. Halfway up the stairs, I looked back across the field and then to the sky.

I couldn't see the moon yet, but I could feel it rising. The sensation was unnerving.

Before I could even reach Claire's bedroom, she darted into the hallway, yanked me inside, and shut the door.

"Now, I have taken the liberty of choosing these dozen or so dresses for you to choose from for the party tonight, but if you don't like any of them, I'm sure we can find you something else."

I chanced a trip into her out-of-this-world closet and sifted through the dresses she had chosen. Among them was the dress from my vision; I had known it would be there. *Might as well play my part.*

I pulled it out. "This one will do great. Thanks, Claire."

She grabbed my chin and turned my face side to side. "Makeup looks great. Maybe a little more blush and lipstick," she said, letting go. "Have a seat in my office and allow me to put some curls in that gorgeous hair." I sat down in front of her wide mirror in the bathroom. "Patrick's been acting so weird ever since you showed up today."

"How so?"

"Sullen, moody, ordering me around."

I laughed out loud. "Sounds like typical Patrick to me."

She got quiet for a minute, which was unusual for her. "If you ask me, I think he's going to propose tonight."

I froze, horrified. *Not now!* I mean I knew I needed to marry Patrick to break the curse, but since we wouldn't be eloping today, his timing couldn't have been worse. "What makes you say that?" I asked in an opposite tone from a normal bride-to-be. Claire stared at me for a moment with her right brow raised in question. Quickly I rearranged my features, giving her an over-exuberant smile.

"I just have a feeling. He is my twin, you know."

I had decided a while back that when Patrick ever did propose, I would not drag him into a marriage without telling him about the curse. My people needed saving, but I wouldn't do it

451

dishonestly. Patrick would have a choice. My shoulders slumped as I thought of Rafe—the one I wanted to marry. What a mess!

Claire finished curling my hair, and I slipped on the floor-length, medieval gown made of black velvet. It was beautiful with its puffy sleeves and black ribbons, and it fit just right. In three or four hours' time, I would hate to see what it looked like after I had dragged it through the Dullahan's lair.

Claire looked me over to admire her handiwork. "Your eyes need to be more dramatic to match the dress." After lining my eyes with charcoal-black liner and sweeping my lashes with mascara, she declared me a finished masterpiece.

"You are perfect. Okay, now I've got to get ready. It's four-twenty. Be back here before seven."

"I'll do my best."

The corridor was silent as I passed by Patrick's room. The door was ajar, and I saw him staring out the window. Fortunate for me, their bedrooms faced away from the stables. "Goodbye, Patrick," I whispered before dashing down the steps and sprinting for the stables.

I had hoped to trump the vision and change out of the dress before heading out, but I was late. Uncle Brádach was chatting with a stable hand on the far end from Kheelan's stall and down a different corridor. He wouldn't see me leave. I was glad. I didn't think I could face him just then.

When I approached the stall, I noticed that my saddle was already on Kheelan. Uncle Brádach knew I was leaving. With a weak smile, I swung up into the saddle and fastened my black cape around me. Then Kheelan and I fled through the barn door, running west by the river. It felt so good to ride again. When I hit the open moors, I flipped my hood over my face and entered my destination in my mind: Mellifont Abbey.

58

Spun By The Fates

(Rafe)

My flight landed in San José very early on Sunday morning. After the drive back to Tilarán, I was able to grab a handful of Z's before my half shift at the hospital. I couldn't wait to see Aishling. It would be a surprise to her, for she wasn't expecting me back until tomorrow.

I'd already planned a picnic for one day this week. I wanted to bring her to my house, hoping that she'd love the land as much as I did. There were some waterfalls about a mile from my house that I wanted to show her. We'd have lunch there. I had sensed some extreme sadness within her over the past few days, and I needed to understand why my chest was aching. I hoped she trusted me enough now to tell me her secrets—and I planned on telling her mine. She needed to know the truth about our past—her death and resurrection. Somehow it felt wrong to keep it from her.

Following my shift, I took off to the orphanage.

"Aishling," I called out as I knocked on the partially open door of the hut. Again I knocked, but there was no answer. I pushed open the door and stepped in. Love slammed into me, being there among her belongings. I could feel her presence so strongly, and her sweet scent lingered in the air, a hint of tropical sunshine mixed with summer rain.

I was turning to leave when I saw an envelope on the kitchen table. When I moved closer, I could see my name on the outside. This was not good. A sense of dread clawed at me. I grabbed the note and sat down on the couch, needing some support as I tore into the envelope and unbound her words to me.

Rafe,

The legends surround me, flying on my flanks. I can't go anywhere now other than where they lead me. A story is powerful, especially when spun by the Fates.

You once said, in your letter, that you had been forced to withhold your feelings. You would have given me a choice to run away with you even if to another realm or a faraway universe. The ironic thing is I understand. It is I who now wishes I could give you the choice to follow me to a strange new world, but it's mine and mine only for the conquering.

Going to Honduras was the most selfish thing I have ever done. I realized that fact too late. I just needed to be near you once more before I had to go away. Please forgive me, a r n mo chro [secret of my heart], for making that choice

454

then and for leaving you now. There is no other way. If life were fair, I'd follow you into forever, but life wields a double-edged sword, so I fear I must say good-bye.

In my heart I feel you even now, and I don't understand how that can be, but I know it will comfort me in the place I must go. By the time you read this, my fate will already be sealed. Whether I win or lose the battle I fight today, I still cannot return to you. The Fates command me. I would say that they can't control how my heart will always feel you with me, but the Fates demand what they demand, so I'm sure they will take that from me as well. What I will leave with you in this moment is what I can give you: the words I love you, Rafe beyond the compass!

T mo chro istigh ionat [My heart is within you],
Aishling

The note fell from my hands to the floor. A violent roar climbed its way out of my body, along with the fire that threatened to consume me. On my feet, I kicked the recliner into the cabinets and tossed the kitchen table all the way across the room into the far wall, hearing the splintering of its fibers as it shattered into tiny fragments. I felt like a demon. Every posture, every animalistic quality I'd ever absorbed came rushing back to me like a long-lost friend. Running through the jungle toward the volcano, I contemplated jumping in to rejoin the demons.

Vitale had other plans. He blocked my path, and my claws emerged to cut him through. Withdrawing his sword, he prepared to fight me. Good. I needed a fight. The demons inside that I had worked so hard to restrain came back full force. Their power felt good as they twisted and churned. My demonic instincts took over, and I attacked him in the air as he flew upward to defend himself.

"Raphael, I don't want to do this to you, but if I don't, Aishling's angels will come here to destroy you."

Aishling. Aishling. I thrashed side to side and tried to calm the demons down. *Aishling.* I roared at them. Fire spat from my eyes. In my confusion, Vitale bound me, and I dropped to my knees.

"Raphael, get a grip on yourself. You're hurting her."

That's all he needed to say. I couldn't believe I had let myself lose control. Bound up in his powerful cords, I fell sideways and fought the demons back down, rolling over plants and into trees, pummeling myself to win back my self-restraint. Jerking and bashing, I finally sent them back to that prison I had created within me. All was still.

I sat up, propping my bound arms on my bent knees. "I'm sorry, Vitale. That must have been an ugly sight." I could feel blood dripping down my forehead, and I could taste it on my tongue. After all the intense violence of the past few minutes, I broke down crying. Vitale unbound me and sat down on the ground beside me, wrapping an arm around my shoulders.

"Vitale...."

"No, Raphael."

"What if she dies, Vitale? Will I die too?"

"Yes, I suppose so."

"You, my angel, are going to let me die?"

"I can't do this, Raphael. I can't let you go, but I can't let you stay. You're a hard case, you know."

"So, does this mean you're taking me there?" I asked, hopeful.

"Come on," he groaned, wrapping the cloak around us.

59

Diabolical Masquerade

(Aishling)

It was four thirty in the afternoon when Kheelan and I burst onto the scene at Mellifont Abbey. A morbid power emanated from the Ten Colds Moon and Kheelan reared on his hind legs. The mammoth moon was dramatic as it began to rise, spilling its blood-tinted light across the moor and seeping into the River Mattock. The light flowed toward me, as if it were trying to touch me, but I didn't want to feel the caress of the wicked beams. I turned Kheelan, and we ran to the safety of the ruins of the chapel, escaping the bloodthirsty moon if only for a moment.

Leaping down from his back, I tied Kheelan up outside the ruins and entered the Holy Place feeling secure inside its four walls. The moon was coming for me; as there was no roof on the ancient stone structure, I wouldn't be able to hide for long. I closed my eyes and pictured what the sanctuary would have looked like in its time and opened my imaginary eyes to see the stained glass and the lantern light radiating out to the wooden pews. Compelled down the aisle, I knelt at the foot of the cross, or where I imagined it to be, and dropped my head in prayer. I had never prayed with more conviction or weariness of soul and mind. When I tilted my head to the sky, I sat in a pool of light. The Ten Colds Moon had found its target.

The brilliance of the moon was no match for my ten angels, who surrounded me now. There had never been a more beautiful sight. Maximilian reached down to lift me in his arms, and his healing touch soothed and strengthened my spirit.

459

"Aishling, you don't have to do this," he pleaded.

"I do, Maximilian." As I spoke, he set me down but kept ahold of my hands.

"We're here to help," promised Tristano.

"I'm ready to take out some demons. You just point the way, Lady Aishling," said Gianpaolo. He was such a tough-looking angel. I was glad he was on my side.

"It goes against everything in our natures to let you cross into that realm, Aishling, where we cannot follow," Marcellus grumbled.

"I'm going."

"We know, but we don't like it," Salvatore countered.

"Why can't you go there? I thought angels could go everywhere."

"Angels cannot go where the light does not reveal itself," the quiet Fiorello explained.

I was about to ask another question when I was shoved to the middle of their circle. Everyone was quiet, and I heard nothing more than the wind bristling the trees and winging its way down the aisles of the hollowed structure. Peering underneath the throng of wings, I saw a stream of Diaga dust creeping through the air toward the angels, diffusing as it tried to wrap around them.

"Do what I tell you this once, and back up to the wall!" I yelled.

The angels flew backward, and I held up my faerie cross stone to rein the power in to it. As it soaked up the dust, the great Morrighan floated up the stairs of the old church and entered through the doorway followed by a squadron of Maolán faeries.

Spying the hovering angels, Morrighan blurted, "Well, what do we have here?"

At the same time, one of the angels commented, "This ought to be interesting."

I was caught in the middle of two very distinct battalions of supernatural soldiers. It would be a battle like the world had never

460

known. Stepping forward, I bowed before Morrighan. "Maimeó, these are my angels. They're here to fight the demons." They stepped forward, staring at the faeries, and the faeries stared back.

"Very well then," she clipped. "The Alorcán as well as the demons are almost here. We should go to the river. We don't want them to presume we are hiding." Motioning toward the angels, she asked me, "They know how to kill demons, but do they know how to take down a vile faerie?"

Remembering the bag I'd retrieved from the fishing cabin below the castle, I ran to Kheelan, brought the heavy sack in, and laid it at the angels' feet. Leopoldo lifted the bag brimming with faerie cross rocks and opened it. I explained what the rocks were.

"To kill a faerie, you must thrust the rock into the jugular, crystals facing toward the neck. It works kind of like acid on the faeries of the dark underworld. They will disintegrate. Oh, and if any of you gets scratched by one of them, let us know, and we can rub some dust into the wound. Trust me, you don't want to let it go unattended. I've seen the results." It felt good to be giving instruction to my angels, who had helped me all my life.

Maximilian smiled, "Ah, but we brought our own supply of healing balm."

"We brought as many troops as we could, Aishling," divulged Morrighan. "The majority of the Maolán are trying to hold back the gates of hell. We can't have all those demons keeping you from your mission. You must find the cave, and you must destroy the beast, Siridean. Godspeed."

"Let's go!" she commanded her troops.

My angels followed me down the front steps of the chapel ruins. I swung up onto Kheelan, setting my mind for the attack.

"We will sense you when you emerge from the underworld. And we'll be there," vowed Maestrino.

"You can do this, Aishling. Keep the faith." Maximilian hugged me as I sat atop Kheelan.

Whipping the reins, I nodded to my protectors as Kheelan and I bounded toward the river. I passed by the faeries and angels that were standing ready and headed north, going upstream. On the opposite side of the river, to the south, the Alorcán and demons were making their presence known. Rattling chains and galloping horses came like a bad nightmare. The fiery eyes of the demons meshed with the blood moon. It would be a diabolical masquerade.

Soon I was in the forest, following the path that had been carved out beside the churning waters, and I could hear the clash of the war behind me. I tried to tune it out. Gasping, I felt my heart stir within me: Rafe was here. I couldn't let him stop me from my purpose. As much as I wanted to run to him, I pushed Kheelan harder to stay on this path. Holding my faerie cross up, I shined the bright-blue light toward the opposite bank, looking for the cave entrance.

Black snowflakes crept down from the sky. I was in search mode; power surged through me, and my cobalt-blue eyes shone through the black veil of the parallel realm. My long raven hair rose and floated around me of its own electric will. Stupid, blatherin' curse!

The spiky shrubs of the forest bit into my legs while we attempted to outrun the Fates and the black snow that trailed us. The storm shook her angry fist in my face. I pushed Kheelan harder through the thundersnow. Lightning spread like giant tentacles, stretching and whipping the furious sky. It illuminated the wispy fairy flax that gave the illusion we were riding the waves of a furious ocean. The static-charged snow soaked me through, crackling and sparking as it shocked me over and over on its journey to the earth. The wind chill was almost more than I could bear. I could feel the frostbite nibbling at my feet and hands. It was not even five o'clock yet, but the massive horde of dark ice crystals captured the essence of midnight.

There was only one being that had the power to bring the daggerlike snow with it, and the beast was swiftly catching up.

Turning west, I headed in the opposite direction from the wicked storm front, up into the hills. The snow retreated for a moment, and I could see ahead of me. Kheelan had never run with such fury, like he knew that my life depended on his speed now, as he dodged trees and jumped fallen limbs.

Pulling the hood of my cloak up farther to protect my face as much as possible, I looked behind me into the daunting massacre laid out in the storm's wake. The forest was pillaged. Trees were being uprooted and pitched like matchsticks thrown from a box. In the midst of the turmoil, as if he were stirring the chaos as he rode, the Dullahan advanced toward us, his bulky head in his sidesaddle. I must have been getting close to the cave: the one the creature didn't want me to find.

I readied my taggert, aimed, and shot, but some sort of force field knocked the dart off course. Drawing my claymore from its sheath, I prepared for the showdown.

Trying to escape my doom, I pushed Kheelan harder. The face of a dark angel with a scar running the length of his cheekbone flashed in my thoughts, giving me enough bittersweet pleasure in this moment of impending tragedy to keep me fighting. As if I could cut a deal with my relentless pursuer, I begged him in my mind, *Just please, before you deliver my death sentence, please let me say goodbye to the man I love.*

Demons And Dragonflies

(Aishling)

I made a sharp cut to the right on a different trail that led back down to the river. The pouring of water over rocks was somehow peaceful in this instant. Kheelan chased the trail again as I held up the stone to light up the river. A suctioning sound echoed across the water, coming from beside a huge boulder. I jumped from Kheelan's back and leaned in for a brief hug. "Goodbye, old friend," I voiced, turning away from him. There was no room for emotion now—just like Cearnaigh had taught me—only the coldness of the warrior princess.

The long dress and cape weighed me down, as I waded through the rapids, but I kept going. Galloping not too far away now, the Dullahan was catching up. My blue light lit the blowhole, and I could hear the water coming from some place deep to shoot up to the surface and then retreat again to unknown depths. This had to be it. The hole was about three feet wide.

The Dullahan stalked up the river, splashing water as he stomped toward me. I didn't hesitate. I jumped into the underwater cave.

The faerie cross lit the stone walls as the water pushed me along. Sometimes the chamber narrowed so much that I was forced to go below the stream for unnatural amounts of time. It was a good thing I had some supernatural ability in the breath-holding department. Eventually the tunnel opened to an extensive underground cavern network, and the river shallowed, running off into eight different tunnels. The water was ankle deep there, and tiny, round pebbles could be seen down the lengths of the babbling brooks. I washed up on a small island in the middle of the river that held one towering acacia tree in full bloom, with flowers of crimson and bark of purest white. Some smaller cedar trees surrounded the whistling thorn. The grass below the tree was a vibrant green, and the way the blades swayed in unison, it appeared to breathe.

"This is the phantom island Uí Bracile?" Disbelief tinged my voice. "It's not even twenty feet across."

The tune from my music box winged its magic throughout the tunnels, and the sound washed over me. Standing on the island, I looked across the way. To the right, there was a spacious room of earth and rock and a fire blazing from an open pit.

I couldn't use my cloak to get me to this realm, but now that I was there, I could get to Mom quicker. As I pulled the hood up, I saw the Dullahan rise from the waters. It was a sight that would cause nightmares for years to come, if I lived, I was certain. Waves gathered around him, building taller and taller, before crashing down to leave a dry path for the creature to prowl on. He appeared dry as he stalked toward me. The melody of his sword crescendoed as he unsheathed it. I quickly enclosed my head in the cloth and thought of Mom. The cloak soon settled me down in a makeshift prison. I didn't know where this was in relation to where I had just been, but I knew we needed to make this quick. I pulled back my hood and saw her. Relief, memories, and love all slammed into me. With tears burning, I rushed to my mother, who was standing by the wall.

"Aishling!" she cried out, holding me, kissing my cheeks and weeping. "Oh, my baby." She held me at arm's length to look at me.

"Mom," I cried, touching her face.

"But how did you get here, Aishling?" Suddenly alert, she rushed to the metal bars of her dungeon-like cell to look out. "Is the beast here?"

"Yes, but the cloak can get us to an exit point. We just can't cross over the realm boundary in it. It only works within one realm at a time." I moved to stand beside her, and I smiled through the tears, as I grasped her hands. "I can't believe I'm here with you, Mom. I didn't think I'd make it past the creature. How are you still alive? Has the mongrel harmed you?"

She reached up to wipe my tears. "I've only been in this cell for about a week. The rest of the time, I've just wandered in the realm. The beast had left me alone until recently, but he has not harmed me."

"I don't understand."

"Neither do I. You don't even know how ecstatic I am at this moment. Overjoyed. But we have to get out of here. I can't let the Dullahan capture you too."

Building in intensity, the sound of flapping wings thundered down the tunnel, and I peered out to see the flying helix from my vision. In reality, they weren't in their batlike form, though; these were the massive dragonflies. Had they come to help me? How were they able to cross over into this realm?

"Aishling, what are those things?" Mom asked.

"Not sure, Mom, but I believe they are our friends."

I wrapped her in the cloak with me and thought of a hole leading out of the realm. We came to a halt in front of a thin place, hidden by a roaring waterfall that blasted over the mountain above us, blocking the exit. The dragonflies showed up right as we landed.

The only way out was to jump into the waterfall and pray it wasn't too far to the bottom. I guessed we could jump, and as soon as we had cleared the realm boundary, the cloak could work midway down.

A second before I pulled the cloak shut around us, Rafe's heart hammered in my chest, and I threw off the hood. *How was he able to follow me to this realm?* I had to get to him. What if the Dullahan killed him?

"What is it, Aishling?"

"There's something else I have to do, Mom. Stay here. I promise I can handle this. Don't jump unless you have to. I'll be right back."

"But—"

"Trust me, Mom."

Pulling the cloak back around me, I thought of the chamber. Violence rocked my body; my eyes flamed in the flight. When I got there, sounds of screeching metal reverberated through the tunnels. The dragonflies swirled around me, trying to keep me from joining the fray, so I did what I had done the day at the beach when they'd pestered me. Taking my right arm, I wound it behind me and swung it underhanded until it stretched above me. The dragonflies scattered, soaring above me in their peculiar swirling formation.

Across the chamber, on the river island, Rafe was engaged in a duel with the beast, but it appeared to be an even match. Rafe's eyes fired and a violent growl erupted from deep within him; I felt his anger and I growled with him. He had struggled so hard to contain the demons that possessed him; I hated to see him lose control of himself. He shouldn't have come.

"Rafe!" I yelled, but he didn't respond. I took off running at inhuman speed, sloshing through the creeks. On the fly I brought up my taggert and shot a faerie cross dart between the Dullahan's shoulder blades. The creature bowed backward, jerking and twisting side to side. Rafe took that moment to thrust his sword through the beast's chest, but it only served to further anger the faerie. The Dullahan wrenched the sword out of its body and tossed it into the wall. Rafe staggered among the sparse trees on the island and tried to find another weapon. The beast stalked toward him, scratching his claws down the tree trunks, in his pursuit.

The wild faerie knocked Rafe to the ground and knelt over him, throwing punches. I started to revisit the hawthorn and bring all my weapons. Something had to work on this creature. But I rolled on the ground and ached from the beating Rafe was taking; my broken jaw hammered me with agony.

Pivoting my head to the cave ceiling, I watched the odd cadence of the pterodactyl-sized dragonflies. Instinct ruling my actions, I staggered to my feet and stretched my arms to the sky, palms up. The mammoth insects ceased their symmetrical formation and hovered, tilting their eyes toward me. I dragged my arms into my body, forming fists with my hands. Then I pitched my hands sideways toward the battle. A mass of flapping wings rained down from the sky—kamikazes plowing through the air to obliterate the foe. The wind from their assault threw me to the ground, and I settled on my hands and knees to see what I had done. "Rafe," I yelled above the din. The noise was stifling.

Distracted, the Dullahan vaulted to its feet in one of the shallow brooks that split off from the river and faced the oncoming horde. The headless faerie stretched its arms wide, extending to each creek bank, and tilted its arms forward inch by inch until the monsters' claws clasped straight in front of him with a snap. The front line of diving dragonflies was diverted to the right and left of the faerie, crashing into the ground with ear-splitting howls of pain. I wrapped my arms over my head to cover my ears, but the sounds of death plowed through. Part of me felt splintered—unwhole. I had to stop the others. Stumbling to my feet, I wound my arm to the sky, sending the remaining dragonflies hurdling for safety.

Rafe was on his feet now, bounding toward the Dullahan as the beast turned. He overpowered the faerie, landing atop it in the rapids; water surged to tower in the air as the brawlers submerged. On the rocky banks, I rushed upstream to stand at the edge of the battle. The faerie's upper body ascended above the water, its arms rigid as it held Rafe below the stream. "No!" I yelled. "Let him go!" A split second later, I felt the effects of his drowning. I pitched to my knees and gasped for breath; water gurgled in my lungs.

With my last ounce of awareness, I yanked the flap of my pouch upward, and I grasped the maximum dosage of the dust of Diaga—for the kill—and without hesitation, sent it snaking through the air.

When the powder engaged with its target, the beast released Rafe, and he emerged from the waters, sputtering and coughing;

I vomited water and dragged in air. The faerie curled into itself, immobile. Rafe pulled himself up the embankment, rocks clacking, as he fell beside me. "Rafe!" I caressed his bloody face. His eyelids were heavy, but he forced them open. The veins on his cheeks and neck were pronounced as if the creature had drained life from him. I wrenched open the pouch and pinched a small amount of Diaga's dust. I rubbed it into his jaw, and soon mine was healed. Smoothing traces of the dust into his skin, I watched as his normal color returned.

A tale from the *Chronicle of Íosa* spoke of a battle between the Dullahan and the Warlord of Dál Riata. In the legend, the warlord wounded the faerie so adeptly that the Dullahan's pain leaked from his ravaged body, pinning the warlord to the ground long enough for the faerie to finish him off. I recalled the narrative as a wave of power sent me flying through the air to land on my back and Rafe bound to the ground, roaring. The Dullahan knelt in the creek while spasms and flames wracked his form. I prayed this story had a better ending.

The beast was still dealing with its trauma as Rafe stood. "Don't go," I begged. He touched my cheek, then twisted and prowled toward the creature. The faerie legend jumped to its feet and rounded on Rafe, even through its obvious torture.

I didn't see how Rafe could win this battle. "No!" I screamed, but the two fighters continued their advance toward each other.

Rafe couldn't last much longer against the monster. I grabbed the leather bag off the ground. If I had enough dust left, I could stall them. When I opened the flap and stuck my hand in, the hawthorn spike sliced my finger. "Ouch," I grimaced, pulling my hand out to examine the blood. Then it hit me. The thorn. I was running out of ammunition against the indomitable beast. This was to be my final strike against the enemy before I snatched Rafe and disappeared in the cloak.

I grabbed the stocky thorn and flew toward the Dullahan. Landing on the creature's back, I stabbed the blood-soaked shaft into its spine and twisted. His arms reached back, flicking me off as he would a tiny pest. Flat on my back, I gasped for breath and growled; my eyes flamed. For a moment, the creature stood over me. Then it tumbled into the water, body jerking as if electrocuted. I watched the life seep from the beast until its movements were no more.

Rafe roared and stalked toward the downed beast. "Rafe, calm down!" I screamed at him; my heart pounded offbeat and I felt like I was losing myself. My eyes fired along with his, and a powerful brand of adrenaline coursed through my body. In the next second, he had me wrapped in his arms as a predatory rumble reverberated in his chest. He locked me in a fiery kiss. Our intense connection and the events of the day made me woozy. Then everything went dark.

Groggy, I sat up in the creek, shivering. I rubbed my head and looked around. The Dullahan lay prone in the creek a few yards away. Rafe clomped down the tunnel, roaring and bending over, trying to get the demons under control. I sat on the edge of the water, holding my head and rocking back and forth to calm the barrage of sensations. The competing sounds brawling inside me made my skull quake.

Tucking my legs into my chest, I dropped my forehead on my knees and wrapped my arms around my legs. I breathed in. The rocks crackled around me and I was lifted from the ground, cradled in Rafe's arms. His face was so bloody and torn, I couldn't hold back the tears. "Rafe, why did you come?" I wiped my face with the back of my hand.

"I love you, Aishling! We face things together, not apart. Leaving the way you did…well, I just can't handle it. Please, don't ever do that to us again," he lamented, choking back a sob as his eyes flamed and extinguished.

I held on to him for support, and my head dropped as I tried to think of a way not to kill us both. Neither of us could take much more of my strange life. With our bodies connected the way they were, we were being ripped to shreds and left to bleed out by everything the Fates shot at us. There had to be another way to break the curse. Maybe if I killed Tarlach, the Alorcán would disband, and the threat to my clan would neutralize. I couldn't hurt us both any more than I already had. What would Patrick do when I didn't show up?

"Aishling, we need to get out of here, but this conversation is not over."

"I know, Rafe," I agreed, placing my palm on his scarred cheek. He leaned into my hand and closed his eyes, breathing in deeply. Then he set me on my feet.

I looked to where the Dullahan lay, the creek rerouting around the creature's form. Rafe and I together had wounded the unwoundable beast. None of the legends actually told how to kill the wild faerie, but he sure looked dead to me. "I killed the devil," I whispered.

"What did you just say?" Rafe walked up beside me.

My eyes were locked on the defeated beast. "The Celts call it the 'devil.'"

I felt Rafe's breathing shallow and his heart pump faster. I turned toward him and saw him mouth the words, "devil's wife." There were questions in his eyes as he stared at the creature. Then he shook his head and closed his eyes.

"Rafe?"

"I'm okay. Let's go," he evaded.

More secrets!

The defending dragonflies flew on guard around us. Rafe looked to them and back at me. I just shrugged my shoulders as if to say I didn't understand either.

The strains of my music box still wafted through the air. I loved the song, but I wondered how the creature could stand to have it running nonstop. Why had the Dullahan wanted it so badly? I guessed I'd never know. "Rafe, I need to get my music box."

He placed me on my feet, put his arms around me, and I whisked the cloak around us.

Once I had the music box in my satchel and turned off, we landed at the exit point. "Mom, Rafe. Rafe, Mom," I said, introducing them.

Rafe did a double take. "You came after your Mom? I didn't know. Why didn't you say so?"

"I just couldn't, Rafe. I'm sorry."

He moved forward, taking my mom's hand in his. "I've heard a lot about you, ma'am. You have an incredible daughter," he said, letting go of her hand and placing an arm around my shoulders.

"Nice to meet you, Rafe." Mom turned and gave me a knowing smile. She could see how wrapped up we were in each other. "Any man who would brave the Dullahan's lair to come after my daughter is a winner to me," she said, grinning broadly. "Now let's get out of this creepy place."

61

No Mercy

(Aishling)

The three of us appeared in the old church ruins and took a moment to breathe. I tilted my face to the sky, recalling the eerie snow from less than an hour ago; the Ten Colds Moon looked a little less ominous now. Sounds of battle—roaring, the screeches of agony of the retribution dust in action, the tromping of devils, flames of the demons igniting the air, and the thunder of the war angels—assailed the night beyond the church walls.

"It feels so strange to be back in the earth realm," Mom said. She and I held each other while Rafe went to scout out the mayhem. "But I feel the thin places getting weaker. It's almost time for me to go. Thank you for coming for me, *a pheata*," she said, holding my face with both hands and kissing the tip of my nose.

"I love you so much, Mom."

"I love you more." She smiled through her tears.

"Look after your father, Aishling. He needs you."

"I'll do my best." Mom faded and reappeared. "I need to summon Cearnaigh for you. I'm not sure if he came to the battle."

Touching the hawthorn, I started to summon the faerie cross when Rafe came running down the aisle. "Go! Out the back. Now!" he yelled. We exited through the rear of the church building, and Rafe caught up with us. We ran toward the river but south, away from the thick of the battle. Several of my angels broke away from the war to join us, and the dragonflies whirled above my head, sounding like a million cicadas chirping and clicking.

Tarlach and a large brigade of Alorcán appeared out of the air. We skidded to a stop on the banks of the river. The leader of the underworld scum and I had a stare-off. The loathing was mutual.

"You have my music box," he stormed. *How could he possibly know that?* This was my opportunity to take him out, my chance to overthrow the curse. I looked up to the sky; the dragonflies were so thick, the moon was almost obliterated. Since they were there, I wondered if I could use them to take away the Alorcán leader. They seemed to want to please me.

The leader stalked toward us. "Mom," I whispered, "when we start shooting, you run for the scrubby forest over there and hide in the bushes. I'll be there for you as soon as I can get away."

I lifted my taggert and shot darts at the leader while the angels and Rafe fought the demonic soldiers with their swords. In the next moment, capes flew, and beings vanished so sporadically it was hard to keep up with who was where, as everyone reappeared in different locations. Tarlach transformed into a skyscraper dragon breathing fire. I grabbed Rafe inside the cloak and flew to the other side of the river as a stream of blaze projected toward us. Maximilian appeared beside us. We had just landed when the creature stomped through the river, firing again. This time we landed behind the dragon. I attempted to throw Diaga's dust on its tail, but it swished out of the way just in time.

Other faeries converged on us, and Rafe, Maximilian, and I stood back to back, sizing up the situation. "Now," I said, and we battled forward, slicing through beasts and dodging fire. Using Diaga's dust, I took out three faeries at one time, watching as they disintegrated, burning to the ground.

Tarlach was closing in. I clapped my hands, and the dragonflies surrounded me. As I pivoted my arm behind me and swung it upward to the moon, my winged allies followed the arch my arm made. They moved in a clockwise fashion straight up into the sky and swiveled in on themselves, gaining momentum. It was similar to watching the swinging ship at a carnival when it reaches the pinnacle and it looks like it's going to turn upside down, losing all its passengers. Everyone looked to the sky, even the fire-breathing dragon.

"*Ná déan trócaire ar bith air* [No mercy]!" I yelled as I brought my hand back down, slamming it to the ground. The dragonflies shot downward like kamikazes into the earth, carrying the dragon with them. Everyone was speechless.

With their leader gone, the Alorcán scrambled to regroup. In the resulting confusion, I ran for the bushes while Rafe and the angels stayed behind to fight, giving me the time I needed to say good-bye. My mother called to me from the shadows, and I ran toward the sound of her voice among the woody heather thickets, toward the hill beyond the moors.

As soon as I reached her, she grabbed my hand, and we ran through the bramble as flaming arrows screamed past our heads, illuminating the blackness and setting the scrubby woodland afire. Soon loosed from the twisting briars, we escaped up the hill and crouched down behind a large boulder as a second round of arrows raced and plummeted overhead.

I looked down the hill, as I had done in my vision, but the Dullahan was not there. Shouts from our pursuers came closer, but I still couldn't resist smiling. I had missed Mom so much, and she was holding my hand now. I had saved her, and she was going to be fine back in the Otherworld. I called the faerie cross from the hawthorn, placed that stone against my own, and summoned Cearnaigh. He appeared after a few seconds, towering above us as another batch of flaming arrows lit the sky. His eyes grew wide as I yanked him down behind the boulder.

"Skawlin' Samhain! What have ya gotten yerself into?"

"Good to see you too, Cearnaigh." I laughed.

"Evenin', Mrs. Delaney," he said to my mom. "I'm guessin' ya need a lift back to the Otherworld. I knew me girl could fetch ya." He hugged me, kissing the top of my head.

"Mom, this is my mentor, Cearnaigh. He turned me into a warrior."

"Well, I'm not sure how I feel about that, but after what I've witnessed today, I'd say she has benefited from your instruction."

"Cearnaigh, could you give us a minute?" I asked.

He peeked over the boulder. "I'd say a minute's all ye've got, dear one." Cearnaigh turned away as Mom and I said our good-byes.

Mom held me in her arms, combing her fingers through my hair. "Aishling, I've decided to have Cearnaigh take me to Mag Mell. That way I can come to visit you more often."

"Are you sure, Mom? You'd be in a strange place and not with your family."

"I can live with that, especially after being in a cave for the past year. Anything's better than that—which makes me think, I can honestly say that I never want to hear the sound of that music box ever again." She laughed. I sat up, and she lifted my chin. "So I'll see you soon. I love you."

"I love you more," I said. We embraced, and neither of us wanted to pull away. Shouts drifted up to our hiding spot. Cearnaigh pulled mom from me, wrapped her in his cloak, and they disappeared.

Our parting this time was not as tragic. She was safe, and I'd get to see her in a few months when the thin places opened again.

The faeries were getting closer, not far from me now. "*Maraígí roimh a sealsa í!*" I heard one of them say as I pulled the hood over my face and fled back to Rafe. This "it's almost time" crap was driving me insane. I didn't know what they meant, nor did I care.

Landing beside the river, I moved into Rafe's waiting arms. Smoke rose from the earth, and all was quiet. Waking from its sluggish, shadow-dark dream, the snow, now pure and white, fell in a wistful cadence. Kheelan trotted across the moor to join me. "Hey, boy," I said, rushing to hug his neck. "I'm so thankful you're okay."

I turned back to Rafe, and grimaced, "Rafe, those scrapes on your neck look bad. Where else did he injure you? Sit down; let me take a closer look at those. We can't let them fester."

"I'm fine."

Placing my hands on my hips, I raised my eyebrow at him and gave him my best you'd-better-listen-to-me look. He tried to hide a smile, while he lowered himself to the snow-packed earth. I didn't miss his groan when he finally made it to the ground and eased back to lie down. I knelt beside him and took out my pouch. "This will heal you. Just be still." I rubbed the dust into the gashes on his neck and watched them close and then disappear. He sighed and I smiled.

I unzipped his jacket. "Uh...I don't know any other way to do this. Gonna have to lift up your shirt."

He bolted upright and grabbed my hands. "Umm, if you don't mind, I-I'll get those." He looked embarrassed.

"O-kay," I relented. I explained the procedure to him, and he lifted his shirt just enough to be able to rub some dust into a spot on his abdomen. He winced and clenched his teeth as the healing powder took effect. That wound must have been much deeper; usually, the dust didn't cause pain. Sweat formed on his brow and I reached up to wipe it away. He held my hand to his face. His eyes opened and the set of his jaw relaxed. "Better?" I asked.

"Much," he affirmed.

We both stood and brushed the snow off our clothes. Rafe placed a hand on my back. "So what now?" he asked. "Can we go somewhere and be alone for a while? We need to talk." His hair was growing out again, and his long bangs swept down across his face. I stepped forward to brush them aside so I could see his brown eyes. He was such a noble and handsome man, and he had fought so hard beside me today. I couldn't let him go.

My watch read 7:15 p.m. Claire was going to kill me. I couldn't believe it had only been three hours since I had left the castle. It seemed like it had been a week.

"Rafe, I have to get back home for a little while. My best friends are throwing me a birthday party, and I'm late. They don't understand this part of me. And I'm afraid your arrival with me would start another clan war, and I don't have time to explain that right now."

Opening my satchel, I ripped a slip of paper from my notebook and scribbled an address for him. "This is my family's condo in Dublin. We can talk there and decide what we're going to do after you hear all the facts. It's time I come clean. You truly may choose to run in the opposite direction after I tell you everything."

"Don't count on it," he wrangled.

"Have Vitale take you, and I'll meet you there in a few hours. Okay?"

He grabbed me around the waist and pulled me to his chest. "Do you have to go?" His lips moved from my cheek to my ear, and I felt weightless.

Play-shoving him, I said, "You make me forget my troubles. You're awesome at it, as a matter of fact." I stood on tiptoe to brush my lips with his and tilted my head to look him in the eyes. "Thanks for coming tonight, Rafe. You were my moon so I didn't have to be afraid of the shadows." I winked, remembering his words to me that day at the waterfall. "I love you." Moving out of his embrace, I swung up on Kheelan.

"Any time. And woman," he said, grabbing my leg as I looked down at him, "I'll give you to the stroke of midnight, and then I'm coming for you. I love you too." It was a threat and a promise. I reached down and grabbed the back of his head, bringing him in for a dream-worthy kiss. Then I kicked Kheelan into gear and we took off across the moor under the light of the Ten Colds Moon.

62

Fighting Fate

(Aishling)

Slipping into the castle undetected was not going to be an easy task with so many guests. After taking Kheelan back to his stall, and rubbing Diaga's dust into the frostbite on my feet and hands, I ducked into the bathroom at the stable to assess the rest of the damage. It was as bad as I'd thought except for the fact that my tears had washed away all traces of makeup, including the claw-mark eyeliner. I picked as many briars out of my hair as possible and finger-combed my wet locks. The drenched, black dress clung to my body and was covered in mud and grime. I was freezing. Maybe I could slip upstairs and change without being caught. But my plan went horribly awry.

I went around back, thinking to slip in through the fancy living room, the one that was never used. When I entered, however, the lights sprang to life, and the crowd yelled, "Surprise!" In my prior distress, I had forgotten that this was supposed to be a surprise party, and that I was supposed to act surprised. My arm lifted to block the blaring lights, and the celebratory noise of the partygoers quickly died down once they took in my haggard appearance.

"Hi, everyone," I squeaked out. "Thanks for coming to my party." Standing in front of the crowd were the shocked twins. Claire looked me up and down with both hands covering her mouth as if I'd committed some heinous crime, and Patrick was beyond angry. He stormed out of the room.

Uncle Brádach, appearing very dapper in his black tuxedo, rushed to hug me despite my sogginess. "Ah, lass, ya had me frightened. All's well, it seems."

"Yes."

Claire grabbed my hand and pulled me toward the stairs. She cued the band, and they rushed to begin a rock number. Turning to the guests, she spouted, "We'll be right back. Enjoy yourselves while we're gone to get the birthday girl into some party clothes."

We rushed down the hallway. "What happened to you?" she blurted. "We were just about to send everyone away and get the police involved."

"I'm sorry. I lost track of time." She turned to give me the Claire glare. Uncomfortable, I walked ahead of her and into her room.

She ran to her closet to retrieve another dress while I jumped in the shower. My hair could have used a longer scrubbing, but five minutes was all I had. While I blow-dried it, she stared at me in the mirror like I was an alien. As I switched off the dryer, she was ready. "Where were you?"

"I can't say."

"Fine then! You know how people talk about you, Ash. They think you rush to the thin places every time we have a festival. They think you're crazy. Do you want that kind of reputation?"

I'd had enough of the accusations. "What if I *am* out there, but I'm risking my life to protect those same people? What would they say then?"

She thought for a moment as she brushed my hair. "Are you protecting us?"

I had said too much. "Maybe," I muttered. I stood to pull the blood-red ball gown over my head. "I'm sure your parents are questioning the merger. I don't blame them, you know."

"And Patrick? How is he supposed to deal with all of this, Aishling?"

Shaking my head, I looked at the floor. "I don't know, Claire. I'll talk to him if he'll let me."

"I worry about you. You're my best friend and you're like a sister to me, but you're also the absolute most mysterious creature I've ever heard of. Patrick has his hands full just trying to stay a mile behind you." She finished curling my hair and laid the iron down on the counter. "He can't compete with this secret life of yours."

"Are you quite finished?" I asked, meeting her gaze in the mirror. "I believe I have guests who want to stare at me and make sure I haven't transformed into some ghastly beast." Smiling, I tried to lighten the mood. She laughed, and we locked arms, maneuvering down the stairs together.

"You're beautiful," she said. "Even standing there looking like a hot mess when you first appeared at the party, you were like an ethereal goddess. I wish I could pull that off."

"We might need to have your eyes checked, Claire. But thank you," I said.

For the next several hours, I mingled with the guests and tried to repair some of the damage I'd caused the Kavanaughs. Patrick never rejoined the party, and I had a feeling I knew where he was. Many of the guests had begun to leave a few at a time, so I took the opportunity to head to the roof of the castle, stopping to grab a blanket from Claire's room to wrap around me. Patrick could usually be found on the roof when he was brooding, and this was definitely a brood-worthy moment.

High heels were my enemy, and I fought with them as I crossed the length of the roof to the far end, where I found him sitting on the ramparts. As I approached he looked up at the stars and the not-to-be-missed moon. It mocked me even now. I sat down beside him and looked up to the sky as well.

"You don't trust me to help you," he began before I could get settled in my seat. "How can we build a future on that, Asher?"

I knew his male pride had taken a beating. What was I to do? "I'm sorry, Patrick."

He exploded from the wall, pacing, running his hands through his hair. "I've lost you to the wilds of the moor. What's so attractive about that savage land?"

"I didn't ask for this, you know," I argued.

This time he got up in my face, putting a hand on the wall on either side of me. "You can't keep fighting faeries and live, Asher!"

"I know," I whispered. He resumed his pacing.

"We used to faerie hunt when we were younger. It was exciting and dangerous, and we were stupid to do it. But we grew up, Asher, and you never left it. Why are you doing this to me—to us?"

"Patrick, I know you're going to find this hard to believe, but I have no choice."

He dropped down at my feet and pleaded. "Leave that life behind and marry me, Asher."

Seeing as he hadn't produced a ring yet, I felt like he was simply trying to spare my life in the only way he knew how. This was not a romantic request. If I became Lady Kavanaugh, I knew I would give up my freedom to him. He knew he could control me then. I loved him as my best friend, but he was a clan leader's son first and foremost; he had been taught to control.

"It's not that simple, Patrick."

"Explain."

"What I tell you now goes no farther than this rooftop. Agreed?"

After a prolonged hesitation, he nodded. "Agreed."

Moving to the rampart at the front of the castle, I leaned forward, basking in the moonlight. Now that the Dullahan was gone, it didn't seem as menacing. Patrick came up beside me, placing his hand over mine. I turned to face him, biting my lip. Debating with myself, I thought, *Just blurt it out.* "I'm a faerie slayer, Patrick, chosen by the Moerae. I am the Gael Siridean."

He twisted around to plop down on the wall and rubbed his hands up and down his face. Then he rubbed his hands down his pants. After a while he ran his hands through his hair. Silence had never been so energetic. He stood up and grabbed my arms. "What am I supposed to do with that—let you go off and die? I'm supposed to be your protector, your betrothed. But it seems you're the one protecting *me*."

"So this boils down to male pride?"

"Call it whatever you'd like, Asher," he thundered and turned his back to me.

I grabbed his arm and pulled him around. "You think I'm able to do all this alone?"

He towered over me, blocking the moon, as he grabbed my arms. "What do you mean? There are others like you out there fighting? Who are you with when you ride off into the night? Who?" He yelled and shook me.

I dropped my head, and whispered, "It's not what you think." He let go and stormed away.

"I'm leaving, Patrick." The tempest ceased for an instant as he stopped, but he didn't turn back around. "I'm going to finish out the school year in Costa Rica. I guess I'll see you in a few weeks…if you still want to come."

He marched away without another word.

I didn't cry. I was numb. I had experienced too much tonight to feel the emotions of this moment—battle shock, reuniting with my mom, fulfilling the prophecy, etc. Tumbling in a vortex of sensations, I needed to go to the one person who could calm the storm. I needed Uncle Brádach.

Uncle Brádach was still there waiting for me when I came down the stairs. "Ya want to walk me down to me house?"

"Sure," I said, linking my arm through his. It was getting close to midnight, and I needed to get to Dublin before Rafe made good on his promise. I sure didn't need him showing up after everything else that had happened.

We meandered down the paved sidewalk to Uncle Brádach's house by the stables. It was the homiest place I'd ever known.

"Nice party," he said. "And ye made quite an entrance, I'd dare say." He chuckled robustly.

"Yeah, that could've gone better."

"So ya did what ya came to do?"

"Yes, and then some," I answered.

"That's my girl."

"I'm leaving, Uncle Brádach. I'm going back to Costa Rica for the rest of my break. Patrick needs a chance to calm down, and I have some issues to work out myself."

"Figured as much. And ye've that little one to see to."

"I miss Kaillech so much."

"I expect so. Don't mean to pry, but did ya work things out with Patrick?"

"Not really. He understands in a way, but I'm not sure it's something he can get used to."

"And how do you feel about that?" he asked. We entered his kitchen and sat at the barstools where we'd had so many chats over the years.

"How I feel right now is…very confused. Things are so complicated."

"Ye'll figure it out. Ye always have."

I trusted Uncle Brádach like no other person in my life. "I rescued my mom tonight from the Dullahan. I killed the faerie."

He reached out to take my hand as he clutched his chest with the other. His head was bowed, and I could see his lips moving as he prayed. Raising my hand to his lips, he kissed my knuckles and let go. "Mercy, child! Why didn't ya say so when ya headed out?"

"I knew you wouldn't let me go."

"Ye would've been thinkin' right, then."

The clock above his stove read 11:50 p.m. "I'll have to tell you all about it some other time. For now, though, I have another appointment to keep." He wrapped me in his arms; his embrace was so needed after such a tempestuous night.

"An appointment at midnight?"

"Don't ask." I laughed. "I love you, Uncle Brádach." I reached up to kiss him on the cheek, and then I backed to the door.

"Love ye, lass. Come back and visit as oft as ya can."

"I will. I promise."

63

Mirage

(Aishling)

When I appeared in my condo in Dublin, Rafe and Vitale were there. Rafe was trying to pry the cloak away from him. I laughed and both of them turned to look at me.

"I thought I was seeing a mirage." He swung me up in the air, so happy.

Addressing the angel, he said, "Your services are no longer needed, Vitale. Aishling has a cloak."

Vitale looked exasperated as he disappeared into the air.

Rafe cradled me in his arms and sat down on the couch in the den. He had started a fire earlier, and the flickering flames gave a nice glow to the dark room. Gently he placed his bandaged hands on my cheeks and kissed me; it was like a sweet melody, and I sighed as he stopped. Kissing Rafe was my new favorite pastime.

"We'll get back to that in a minute." He winked and placed one arm around my back, holding my hand with the other. "Now, tell me what you've been up to this evening."

I told him about my grand entrance at the party, the fight with my friends (well, parts of the fight anyway), and my conversation with Uncle Brádach.

"Patrick isn't happy with this life you're made to lead and understandably so. My eyes were opened tonight. I had no idea what you were capable of. Your skills are impressive."

"Thank you."

"He's in love with you, isn't he?"

I looked to the ceiling; I had known this conversation would eventually come. "Patrick loves me, but I think Patrick only *thinks* he's *in* love with me when in reality he isn't. Patrick's just in love with the *ideal* of us," I rambled.

Rafe's eyes flickered with amusement. "Interesting way to put it, my dream song."

"I'm your dream song, huh? Well, I like the sound of that."

He laughed and latched his fingers with mine. "I can't blame him for loving you. Who wouldn't? You're smart and gorgeous and exciting and caring and passionate about all the important things. The list could go on and on."

"You know, I could say the same about you, my dream maker."

"So, you think I'm what dreams are made of?" He bantered, one eyebrow lifting.

"In your dreams!" I spouted.

A tickle fight ensued. "Mercy!" I yelled, laughing uncontrollably. He and I both needed this moment after the past couple of days. Finally he stopped, and I lay my head back on the arm of the couch to catch my breath.

He leaned down to kiss me again and then sat me up. "This is amazing. You're amazing," he said, his face so close to mine. "I could get used to this arrangement. But we'd better say good night. You must be exhausted."

On cue I yawned, covering my mouth with my hand. "I guess you're right."

We both stood and stretched.

"So, where do we go from here?" he asked.

"Back to Costa Rica of course." I smiled.

"Okay, I get it—another conversation for another time. I'll be right down the hall if you need me," he assured. Groaning, he reached for me and kissed me long and hard. With his head resting on top of mine, he whispered, "I love you, Aishling Delaney."

"And I love you, Raphael Delacruz."

"Don't let the faeries in tonight," he teased.

Giggling, I moved into the bedroom. "See you in the morning."

I shut the door and smiled. The room was dark, aside from the city lights invading the dormer where I had not yet drawn the curtains. The four-poster bed awaited me, and I was about to dive under the covers when a movement outside the window caught my attention. A flurry of wings beat against the panes. With caution, I crept toward the frenzied thumps.

The evening had taken a toll on my body and my spirit, but my senses were heightened—alert. I closed my eyes and the hawthorn welcomed me while I grabbed my cloak, taggert, and dust pouch. Back inside the room, the marking on my face glimmered off the bedroom walls in waves of indigo. I loaded the taggert and advanced. Banging against the arched sash window was one of the bat-sized dragonflies. I knew this could be a trick, but the poor little guy was going to kill himself if I didn't figure out what it wanted.

I unlatched the glass sashes and pushed; they swung out from the center like French doors. The dragonfly dove into the room, circled the perimeter, and flew toward me. Another one flew in through the open window and barreled straight for the first one. The second winged creature widened its jaws to reveal sharp fangs. When it approached the first one, it latched onto one of its wings. The razor fangs sliced into the base of the wing, and it wafted to the floor. The cruel dragonfly darted out the window while the injured one crashed to the floor.

"No!" I cried out. I dropped to my knees to scoop the twitching insect into my hands. Then I stood and placed it gently on the bed. The dust pouch hung from a belt loop on my jeans, and I reached in to pinch a tiny amount between my thumb and forefinger.

The dragonfly twisted away and fluttered its remaining wings as I tried to approach the open wound. "Hold still, little fella. I won't hurt you." I stroked its long tail-like abdomen, hoping to settle the creature. It looked up at me with intelligent eyes, and for a few seconds, I backed away. *Just fix the wing. Stop being a wimp.* After what I'd just been through, this seemed like an odd thing to back away from. The dragonfly lay still and watched me as I brought the dust up to the gash and rubbed it in. A tiny screech of sorts escaped the insect's mouth, as a new wing grew outward. When the healing was complete, the dragonfly glanced once more into my eyes and flew through the window.

On the edge of the bed, I sat and rubbed my hands over my eyes, and then focused on the gauzy wing resting on the rug.

"A sacrifice fulfilled," a still, small voice whispered.

I looked all around the room—no one was there. I rushed to the window and grabbed the sill, leaning out to glimpse any possible threats in the air. Nothing out of the ordinary. I peered down at the animated cityscape.

Sacrifice? A dragonfly gnawing off the wing of his comrade is a sacrifice? Why? What purpose was there in this dogfight? If the first one was threatened, why didn't it just fly away? Why risk coming to me if it knew it might not survive?

My head pounded as I recalled the first time I'd ever used the dragonfly wings. I pressed my thumbs to my forehead and rubbed.

The *Chronicle of Íosa*. It was still tucked away in my backpack— one of those rare pieces nobody would ever believe was hiding in plain sight. Wrenching myself away from the window, I flew to my pack and retrieved the weathered book. I knelt on the floor and solemnly lifted the sacrificial gift, holding it above the manuscript. The wait was not long. The breathing winds stormed through the window, and the pages flipped so violently, I was sure the book would be carried away. However, the turning stopped on the last page, and the winds inhaled. The page was blank. I grasped a handful of the dust of Diaga and sprinkled it down through the wings. Only one Gaelic phrase appeared: "It's time."

The broken wing manacled itself around my wrist. The mighty winds exhaled and revolved around me. Somehow I knew my world would never be the same.

Glossary

Alorcán—Corrupt faeries that work alongside demons to destroy mankind.

Amonati—Decidedly malevolent angels in the process of turning dark.

Demon—A servant of Satariel (the Evil one) that roams the earth to steal souls.

Diaga—The transcendent One. In Gaelic, "The Divine." Also, known as the Branch.

Gaelic (Gael)—The Celtic people of Ireland, including their culture, language, etc.

Hell—In the afterlife, it is known as a place of torment where Satariel and the fallen angels reside.

Hurling—An ancient Gaelic field game (still played today), where a wooden stick (hurley) is used to knock a sliotar (ball) between the opponents' goalposts.

Keruvim—Another name for Cherubim, angels that have four faces and four wings. They are guardians of Paradise.

Mag Mell—Island in the Otherworld where the war faeries and Delaney's live at death.

Malakim—Aishling's guardian angels—a highly secretive group, like the CIA.

Maolán—Warring faeries that protect humankind. Ruled by The Challenger and Morrighan in the Otherworld.

Moerae—The Gaelic term for the three Fates.

Murchadha—Creatures of the deep, known as the "Sea Battlers." They are avengers for the Alorcán.

Otherworld—A parallel universe where the dead spend the afterlife. The good inhabit a group of islands; the bad occupy the lower realms of darkness.

Parallel Realm (Dimension)—A universe that resides outside our own, where the laws of time and space are different from what we know as reality. Some believe that these dimensions can be all around us, yet unseen and unfelt.

Sergatim—Demon pets that use flames as lassos to strike and sting their prey—temporarily paralyzing them—so they can crawl from the fire and attack.

Siridean—A Searcher, one entrusted with the task of finding and destroying evil faeries.

Sünomoreo—Greek word meaning "joined together; entangled."

Thin Place—A portal where one can cross between dimensions or worlds.

Uffern—Irish word for "hell."

Watchers—Angels that soar above the earth, watching both man and creatures.

Characters

> ## The Delaney's

♣ **Aishling (ASH-ling) Morrighan Delaney:** Delaney clan princess
Aishling (Dream, vision, inspiration)
Morrighan (The Great Queen, Irish goddess of war, but never took part in battle. Later tales have her as queen of the faeries.)
Delaney (Descendent of The Challenger)

♣ **Kaillech (KEE-lek) Alastrina Delaney:** Aishling's daughter
Kaillech (The Celtic goddess known as the Veiled One, teacher of the arts of war; a destroyer)
Alastrina (Defender of mankind)
Delaney (Descendent of The Challenger)

♣ **Marcus Keallach Delaney:** High King of Ireland, also known as The Challenger; rules from the Otherworld. Aishling's Great Great Great…Grandfather
Marcus (Defense or "of the sea")
Keallach (War, Strife)
Delaney (The Challenger)

♣ **Morrighan Delaney:** High Queen of Ireland
Morrighan (The Great Queen, Irish goddess of war, but never took part in battle. Later tales have her as queen of the fairies.)

Delaney (Descendent of The Challenger)

- ♣ **Tiarnan Cormac Delaney:** Aishling's Father, Leader in Irish Parliament, Delaney Clan Leader
  Tiarnan (Pronounced TEER-nawn; Lord, superior, chief)
  Cormac (From old Irish corbmac "son of the charioteer." Cormac Mac Airt was probably the most famous of the ancient kings of Ireland).
  Delaney (Descendent of The Challenger)

- ♣ **Farran Alanna Delaney:** Aishling's Mother
  Farran (The land)
  Alanna (Attractive, fair, peaceful)
  Delaney (Descendent of The Challenger)

- ♣ **Kheelan:** Aishling's Black Connemara Stallion
  Kheelan (Irish/Celtic name meaning "warrior.")

Honorary Delaney Members:

- ♣ **Brógán:** Aishling's main bodyguard
- ♣ **Cearnaigh O'Brallaghan:** Maolán faerie of liberation and justice, guardian of the realm gateways, servant to the Gaelic Council of Seacht, and blood bearer for the crown. Aishling's mentor.

The Kavanaugh's

- ♣ **Patrick Devlyn Kavanaugh:** Aishling's childhood friend, also her fiancé through a marriage alliance established by their fathers. Kavanaugh clan prince. Hurling champion. Works in Irish Senate.
  Patrick (noble)
  Devlyn (Brave, fierce)
  Kavanaugh (Benevolent, merciful)

♣ **Claire Jilleen Kavanaugh:** Patrick's twin sister and Aishling's best friend; Kavanaugh clan princess.
Claire (Clear, bright)
Jilleen (Youthful)
Kavanaugh (Benevolent, merciful)

♣ **Anlon Kildare Kavanaugh:** Patrick's father, Leader in Irish Parliament, Kavanaugh Clan Leader. Owner of Kavanaugh Farm's Connemara Pony Breeding and Stables
Anlon (Great champion)
Kildare (An Irish county)
Kavanaugh (Benevolent, merciful)

♣ **Rionach Shay Kavanaugh:** Patrick's mother
Rionach (Like a queen, regal)
Shay (God's gracious gift)
Kavanaugh (Benevolent, merciful)

♣ **Brádach Énán Kavanaugh:** Patrick and Claire's uncle, Anlon's brother. Like a father to Aishling. Manager of Kavanaugh Farm's Connemara Pony Breeding and Stables
Brádach (Broad shoulders)
Énán (Irish saint)
Kavanaugh (Benevolent, merciful)

♣ **Torin:** Patrick's Black Shadow Connemara Stallion
Torin (Chieftain)

♣ **Hagan:** Claire's White Connemara
Hagan (Youthful)

The MacEgan's

♣ **Kaél Maghnus MacEgan: To Be Revealed in Book 2**

Kael (Strength and compassion; the open hand of God)
Maghnus (Great)
MacEgan (Fiery)

♣ **Zhawn MacEgan:** Leader of Clan MacEgan. Enemy of Tiarnan Delaney.

Angels

Dr. Raphael Delacruz: Former Angel of Healing, Former Commander of the Elite Fighters of Heaven's Army, Demon, Human.
Raphael (God has healed)
Delacruz (Dweller near a cross)

Micah: Riley's guardian angel.
Micah (who is like God, angel of the divine plan)

Aishling's Guardian Angels:

Maestrino: Angel of music

Fiorello: Angel of intervention; keeper of the oath book

Leopoldo: Angel of peace

Luciano: Angel of fate

Gianpaolo: Angel of power; fight first, apologize later

Marcellus: Angel of vision interpretation

Salvatore: Angel of miracles

Renato: Angel of wisdom and logic

Maximilian: Angel of prayer – Radiates comfort to those afraid, hurt or grieving. Assists in the development of the human heart.

Tristano: Angel of justice

Raphael's angel:

Vitale: Oversees good behavior of other angels.

Demons & Faeries

Banshee: In Irish mythology, a faerie that wailed when someone was about to die.

Dullahan: In Irish mythology, a faerie that was headless that rode on its fiery horse and delivered death sentences.

Marax: Rafe's demon friend

Satariel: Leader of the fallen angels and demons

Tarlach (Instigator): Leader of the evil Alorcán faeries

Zakai: Member of the Amonati

Here's a sneak peek at

Shadowlord:

Legend of the Dragonfly

The gripping second book in the Faerie Cross series

Prologue

(Kaél MacEgan)

It was the hour of Ótta on the night of the Ten Colds Moon. It would be months before Aishling was fully transformed and I could come for her, but as the Ten Colds Moon only occurred every ten years, I couldn't waste this opportunity. I would not wait another decade for her preparation. I needed her. The disentangling would take place tonight.

Standing outside the circle on the Hill of Tara—where the High King of Ireland and his descendants were able to cross over between worlds on the nights of the peculiar moons—I awaited the arrival of the High King's great, great...granddaughter. The outer rim was as far as I could go to be near her for now. The dragonflies soared around the perimeter as well, readying to pay homage to their master, the queen of the formidable Tuatha dé Danann.

After the Great War when the evil angels fell, the Master created the Shachath (Destroyers). They were sent to earth to keep the demons from annihilating the human race. They were part angel-like beings and part human. Aishling and I were slightly different from the others, since we also had Gaelic blood mixed with faerie. We were to lead the Tuatha dé, the Celtic sect of the Shachath, and destroy both evil faeries and demons.

Angels guide until the Searchers are prepared for the revealing of what they truly are. Aishling's guardian angels had been preparing her for this moment, the time when they would cut the cords entwining themselves to her and unleash my queen to her destiny.

The moon spotlighted Lia Fáil, the stone of destiny in the center of the circle. It was there that her ten angels laid her now. They placed her in a katheudo state so she wouldn't feel the conflicting emotions and pain that came with the disentangling. Angels entangle themselves with the babies they are sent to guard through life since babies can't call out to them when they are in trouble. They have to feel what the infant is feeling at all times. This is where the entangling, or sünomoreo, comes into play. Since Aishling had ten angels since birth, they were connected tightly within her like large arteries looping through her system. Her angels leaned over her now, working like surgeons to unbind her.

There was also a demon intertwined within her, but that was an error that was about to be eliminated.

About the Author

Joy Stephens earned her master's degree in education and is currently working toward an MFA in creative writing. Originally from the mountains of northern Georgia, she and her husband currently reside in Tennessee. You can learn more about *Siridean*, her first novel, at www.faeriecross.com or www.siridean.com.

www.ingramcontent.com/pod-product-compliance
Lightning Source LLC
Chambersburg PA
CBHW030752260626
47169CB00001B/9